SAN

It was a time of excitement and adventure in America's most turbulent territories . . . a time of new frontiers and new fortunes . . . a time when men and women were driven to carve their destinies from the limitless promises of a wilderness waiting to be conquered.

It was here that Luke Danby, a city-bred boy turned tough lawman, vowed to exact revenge on Domingo Piedra for leading a raid against his wagon train and kidnapping his mother years before. It was here that his plan turned to dust when he met and fell passionately in love with Domingo's exquisitely beautiful and willful daughter Catalina. And it was here that the impossible love of Luke and Catalina overcame all odds to fulfill their challenging destiny and greatest dreams—together. . . .

Ⓞ

PASSION RIDES THE PAST

☐ **SAN ANTONIO by Sara Orwig.** In America's turbulent old West, Luke Danby, a tough lawman, vowed to exact revenge upon the vicious bandit who had raided a wagon train years ago and murdered his mother. But his plans turned to dust when Luke met his enemy's beautiful daughter Catalina . . .
(401558—$4.50)

☐ **THE GATHERING OF THE WINDS by June Lund Shiplett.** Texas in the 1830s where three passionately determined women sought love's fiery fulfillment—Teffin Dante, who was helplessly drawn to the forbidden man, Blythe Kolter, who lost her innocence in the arms of a lover she could neither resist nor trust, and Catalina de Leon, who could not stop her body from responding to the man she wanted to hate. Three women . . . three burning paths of desire. . . .
(157117—$4.50)

☐ **GREEN DRAGON, WHITE TIGER by Annette Motley.** From her barren Asian homeland to the opulent splendor of the seventh century Tang Court, lovely, indomitable Black Jade pursues passion and power with two generations of emperors, and finds her ultimate glory on the Dragon Throne.
(400615—$4.50)

☐ **TO LOVE A ROGUE by Valerie Sherwood.** Raile Cameron, a renegade gun-runner, lovingly rescues the sensuous and charming Lorraine London from indentured servitude in Revolutionary America. Lorraine fights his wild and teasing embraces, as they sail the stormy Caribbean seas, until finally she surrenders to fiery passion.
(400518—$4.50)

☐ **WINDS OF BETRAYAL by June Lund Shiplett.** She was caught between two passionate men—and her own wild desire. Beautiful Lizette Kolter deeply loves her husband Bain Kolter, but the strong and virile free-booter, Sancho de Cordoba, seeks revenge on Bain by making her his prisoner of love. She was one man's lawful wife, but another's lawless desire.
(150376—$3.95)

☐ **HIGHLAND SUNSET by Joan Wolf.** She surrendered to the power of his passion . . . and her own undeniable desire. When beautiful, dark-haired Vanessa Maclan met Edward Romney, Earl of Linton, she told herself she should hate this strong and handsome English lord. But it was not hate but hunger that this man of so much power and passion woke within the Highland beauty.
(400488—$3.95)

SAN ANTONIO

SARA ORWIG

AN ONYX BOOK

NEW AMERICAN LIBRARY

PUBLISHED BY
PENGUIN BOOKS CANADA LIMITED

Special thanks go to:
Jacqueline Cantor, Margaret, Joe, and Caral, Matt
Orwig, Mary, June, and Kay, the Daughters of the
Republic of Texas, and the Texas History Research
Library at the Alamo.

PUBLISHER'S NOTE

This book is a work of fiction. Names, characters, places and incidents either are the product of the author's imagination or are used fictitiously, and any resemblance to actual persons, living or dead, events, or locales is entirely coincidental.

NAL BOOKS ARE AVAILABLE AT QUANTITY DISCOUNTS
WHEN USED TO PROMOTE PRODUCTS OR SERVICES.
FOR INFORMATION PLEASE WRITE TO PREMIUM MARKETING DIVISION,
NEW AMERICAN LIBRARY, 1633 BROADWAY,
NEW YORK, NEW YORK 10019

ONYX TRADEMARK REG. U.S. PAT OFF AND FOREIGN COUNTRIES
REGISTERED TRADEMARK — MARCA REGISTRADA
HECHO EN WINNIPEG, CANADA

SIGNET, SIGNET CLASSIC, MENTOR, ONYX, PLUME, MERIDIAN and NAL BOOKS are published in Canada by Penguin Books Canada Limited, 2801 John Street, Markham, Ontario, Canada L3R 1B4
First Printing, February, 1989

2   3   4   5   6   7   8   9
PRINTED IN CANADA
COVER PRINTED IN U.S.A.

1

February 1846
Near Raton Pass, New Mexico Territory

A BLUE SKY BRIGHT WITH SUNSHINE AND FLUFFY white clouds belied the turmoil of the scene below, on the flat land that spread for miles before reaching the distant Sangre de Cristo Mountains. A brown trail cut across the land, a thin gash in the sparse cactus, winding unbroken except for a spiral of dust rising in the air.

A wagon train was in a small circle, wheels locked together to keep the animals inside the enclosure and to provide a bulwark of defense against the attackers.

Gunshots and human cries sounded in the open space. Beneath a wagon, a sixteen-year-old boy lay on his stomach, his green eyes round as he watched the fighting. In the wagon above him his mother, Harriet Danby, was huddled along with one of the other women.

Lucius Townsend Danby looked incongruous in his elegant eastern clothing, his lanky frame encased by a white silk shirt, black trousers and coat, and a beaver hat that lay in the dust beside him. Orange flames roared and crackled as the wagon next to him burned—their wagon. With a fleeting regret he realized that his father's law books were burning.

Lucius wrestled with new emotions. For the first time in his life, he felt that he might die a violent death. The terror was accompanied by another, unique experience; for the first time in his life, he questioned his father's teachings.

Elmer Danby, a lawyer who had been a lay preacher

in his early days, had instilled in Lucius a love of books. Lucius had never held a gun in his life. Born in Boston, raised by his soft-spoken mother and gentle father, he wished now he had learned the basics of firearms. All his life he had been told to read, to broaden his mind, because he would grow up and become a lawyer. Now he realized that such a philosophy might prove to be fatal.

Choking on the thick dust, Lucius shifted his weight. While guns blasted, terror made him grow numb. They had only four wagons; there had been nine men counting himself, seven women, and six children.

Lucius twisted to look over his shoulder, taking a swift tally: six men dead, two women, and two children killed. Only four children were left and two of them were babies. One of the women, Alice Stein, could use firearms and she fought alongside the men, but they were still far outnumbered.

Lucius scooted forward, inching along on the hard, dry ground so he could see the attackers instead of merely the milling hooves and legs of their horses. His mother had been terrified of Indians: an ironic note, because the attackers were white men. Lucius had heard one of the men call the assailants Comancheros, another had said they were filthy renegades. Whatever they were, there were at least ten of them, and he knew they were closing in for the kill.

Lucius glanced over his shoulder at the last man who had fallen. Dr. Jordan had planned to go West with his wife, his son, and his baby girl. Now he lay sprawled in the dirt, his arms outstretched, the fallen rifle lying across his chest.

Lucius scrambled over to him, yanking up the rifle and turning to aim beneath the wagon. He jerked the trigger and heard a click, but no shot fired. Frustrated, filled with rage and fear, he ran to one of the men who was firing at the attackers.

"Tell me how to load this."

"Get the powder and rod, boy!" Sean Raines

snapped. Lucius scrambled to do as he said, then came racing back to the protection of the wagon wheel as Sean fired again. He watched Sean reload, studying every movement, following it himself as he shouldered the weapon and yanked the trigger. The shot deafened him and the butt of the rifle slammed into his shoulder and knocked him backward to the ground. Sean sprawled beside him, blood pouring from his chest and throat.

Lucius's hands shook as he reloaded and flopped down, inadvertently yanking the trigger again. As the gun fired, the shot ricocheted off a pan hanging on the side of the wagon and Lucius swore. He heard a cry and turned to see another of the men running toward an attacker whose horse had jumped the barrier and the man rode inside their tiny circle. Abe Waters, from Boston, fired and missed.

The man wheeled his horse, rode down on Abe, swung his rifle, sending Abe sprawling in the dirt, then shot him. When Abe's wife, Georgia, jumped screaming from the wagon, the man snatched her up in his arms. And then it was over.

The gunshots stopped. The thud of horses' hooves on the ground and the deep-voiced calls of the triumphant attackers were the only sounds except for the crackle of flames from the burning wagons. Then the screams began as women were yanked from the wagons.

The powder was gone, and Lucius ran to a slain man to take his powder horn when a rider loomed in front of him and pointed a rifle at his heart.

For an instant Lucius thought his life was over. Then the man yanked the rifle from Lucius's hands and motioned to him.

"Get over there!" he ordered, jerking his head toward the huddled group of captives.

Lucius knew his mother still hid in the wagon, and horror gripped him. The depth of fear for his mother made his head swim. He heard his own voice as if from a distance as he yelled in protest and began to run. He saw the butt of the rifle only seconds before it smashed against his temple.

When he regained consciousness, dirt filled his mouth. Dazed, he shook his head, trying to focus on what was happening. Then he saw his mother caught between two men, struggling with them while two more danced with glee. The familiar black metal box lay open on the ground, and their one thousand dollars in gold was scattered in the dust while the men tossed coins in the air.

Lucius lurched to his feet, yanking a pistol from the holster of a rider who was busy watching the women.

"Let her go!" he shouted. The men turned to stare at him, then one of them laughed bitterly.

"If it isn't Sir Galahad hisself. Look at the green dandy!"

"Please, leave him alone!" his mother pleaded. "I'll do whatever you want."

"No!" Lucius shouted while the men laughed. Enraged, he fired the gun. A puff of dust kicked up yards away from any of the men, and taunts followed as Lucius tried to aim, firing first too high, then too low, until his shots were gone. Their raucous laughter added to his humiliation.

"Ever fired one of those things before, sonny?"

Frustrated, Lucius threw the pistol at one of the men. The rider ducked, and the man in command wheeled his horse closer. A rope in his hand snaked out as the loop dropped over Lucius. It was yanked tight instantly, pinning Lucius's arms to his side. The rider backed his horse, keeping the rope taut. He looked down with cold brown eyes, his thick black mustache drooping over full lips. His body was hard muscled and broad shouldered, his skin burnished the color of teak. A pale scar ran across his cheeks and nose.

"Kill him, Domingo," one of the men called. A woman screamed and Domingo looked over his shoulder. "Tie her up," he ordered. "Put them with the children in a wagon. But don't hurt them!"

Domingo wheeled his horse around while Lucius wiggled his arms free. Again the rope was yanked tight. "Hold the woman for me," Domingo said, pointing to Hattie. "I want her for myself."

Lucius had never hated a man before, but he felt the emotion burn hotly in him now. The bellow that tore from his throat seemed to come from somewhere else, a primitive sound of rage that rang in his ears.

Dimly he heard his mother scream, saw her struggling with two men who held her, and then the rope bit into his flesh and he was yanked off his feet. He hit the ground, the breath knocked from his lungs as he twisted and clutched at the rope. For an instant he looked up at the dark-haired Domingo.

"You better kill me," Lucius said, "If I live, I'll kill you for this."

"You dumb gringo. I'll gladly oblige." He spurred his horse and whipped around, urging it to a gallop. The rope bit into Lucius's flesh as he was pulled behind the horse. Rocks and cactus tore at him. His body bounced and dust made him gag as the pain engulfed him.

Lucius tried to turn his face so his arms protected him, but in seconds cactus tore his arms and he rolled, the rope twisting, his body tumbling wildly after the horse. He saw the big cactus looming ahead, the horse veering at the last second, causing Lucius to slam full force against it. He felt as if his face were being ripped away. He heard a scream without realizing it was his own voice.

Wishing he would die, he drifted in and out of consciousness. Then he stirred, and suddenly the ground was gone. He tried to open his eyes and look, but all he could see through one eye was a slit. The world was a blur of red. He was falling in space as the horse plunged down an embankment ahead of him.

Lucius hit the ground with all his weight on his

shoulder and arm. Pain exploded like a ball of fire, and merciful oblivion engulfed him.

Domingo Esquillo Leon de Piedra looked over his shoulder at the body bouncing behind him. He reined in his horse as one of his men caught up with him. Juan stared at the body on the ground.

"I think he's dead."

"Cut him loose."

Juan dismounted and pulled out a knife to make one sweeping slash, cutting the rope. He strode over to the figure in the dust, knelt down and placed his hand against Lucius's bloody throat.

"He's alive, boss."

"Mount up. I'll finish him."

Domingo drew his pistol and cocked it. As his horse pranced, he yanked up the reins, raising the pistol to squeeze the trigger. The shot echoed in the silence, then Domingo spurred his horse to head back to the wagons.

He could hear one of the women screaming before he reined and climbed down, but his attention was on the silent, golden-haired woman who stood beside a wagon. Staring straight ahead, she stood with her hands tied behind her. Domingo's dark eyes swept over her as he strode to her. Her blue eyes met his, but he didn't think she actually saw him. She seemed to stare through him, to some unseen point beyond him. Tears streamed steadily from her eyes, but there was no sound, no grimace from weeping. She was a beautiful woman with silky yellow hair and wide blue eyes. Her son had borne little resemblance to her.

"Get her in the wagon!" he called to one of his men. "Let's move out!"

Soon they were underway, on the trail to Santa Fe and a place where they could sell the women and children. The captives were tied together, huddled in a wagon stripped of its cover. Turning in his saddle, Domingo looked at them without feeling the usual surge of satisfaction. He stared thoughtfully at the woman. He had learned her first name from one of the women. Harriet. Hattie.

The next night they rode into Rayado, a town on the trail. As they meandered down the dusty road that was the main street, a crowd began to gather to look at the captives. Domingo had sold people many times before, and it was easy in towns where there was not yet a lawman or where there were soldiers anxious to get captives back from Comancheros or Apaches to try to reunite them with their families.

They drove to the back of one of the saloons, and as they pulled the women and children from the wagon, offers were made. A man leaned against a post at the corner of the saloon, and watched as the women climbed down. In a short time he sauntered up to Domingo, who was in charge.

"How about that one?" he asked, pointing at Hattie. "What do you want for her?"

Hattie heard the words, but she had been numb since she had watched the one called Domingo gallop away dragging Lucius behind his horse. She hurt in a manner she hadn't dreamed possible. Deep down she had known for a long time that her husband was probably no longer alive. He wouldn't have gone months without a letter, but she hadn't ever given up hope until she lost Lucius. All hope had died with him. She listened to the two men and realized she was going to be the wager in a game of poker. She glanced fleetingly at the lean gambler dressed in elegant clothing, his silver eyes startling. She almost hoped he won her in a game. She wanted away from Domingo Piedra, who gazed at her with hunger in his eyes. If he kept her, it was only a matter of time until he possessed her. She had never before in her life hated and loathed a man, but she did Domingo. With a speculative glance from Domingo, both men disappeared around the front of the saloon.

While she waited with the remaining captives, the children were silent, some of the women quietly weeping. She stared at a dusty barn across the road, refusing to close her eyes because when she did, images of Lucius haunted her.

The men returned, striding toward her. Domingo cut her bonds. "You belong to him now. He's Coit Ritter." He stepped back and she gazed up into black eyes that gazed over her boldly and were filled with regret. She realized he had had no intention of losing her, and he was disappointed and angry at the outcome of the gambling. She shifted her gaze to the lean, silver-eyed stranger, who studied her with curiosity. He smiled and offered his arm; at the moment, she was thankful she was going to leave with him. She lifted her chin and took his arm, pausing in front of Domingo.

"You'll sell your soul someday for what you have done."

He frowned and blinked, then shook his head as if warding off a blow. "You can do nothing to me." Domingo experienced a chill as he looked down into her blue eyes.

"May your dreams be haunted and Lucius avenged," she added quietly.

Rage flared in Domingo, and he reached up to strike her. Instantly the gambler drew his revolver aimed at Domingo. "Don't touch my woman."

Domingo inhaled swiftly as he dropped his hand, his eyes raking over her again. He hadn't intended to lose her. He wanted to possess her. He cursed the fact that he hadn't done so back on the road, but he had wanted her to come willingly to him, and that took time.

The gambler mounted a horse and swung Hattie up in front of him. As they rode away from the saloon, he said to her, "We'll head north to the next town. I want to get you away from Domingo before he changes his mind. What's your name?"

"Hattie. Harriet Danby."

"He said he killed your son. What about your husband?"

"I came West to find my husband, but I suspect he too is dead," she said quietly. The thought of escape crossed her mind fleetingly, but she knew she couldn't escape Coit Ritter easily or quickly. she had seen the way the gun jumped into his hand, and she could feel the coiled muscles beneath the cloth of his sleeves as he held her.

At the next town he got a hotel room and took her to eat, buying them both large steak dinners. Hattie had little appetite and he ate quietly and quickly. Then he leaned back, studying her, asking her questions about her past. When he took her back to the hotel room, he turned her to face him. "You're my woman now," he said quietly.

She nodded, feeling neither grief nor fear. She felt nothing, as if all emotion and feeling had been taken from her.

He pulled her into his arms gently and held her. "I won't rush you, Hattie," he said in a deep voice, "but you're my woman."

"I would rather be with you that *him,*" she said, standing woodenly, wondering if she would ever have charge of her own life again.

"I'll tell you now. I'm not a marrying man." He leaned back to look down at her, then he swung her into his arms, and carried her to the chair. Sitting down and placing her on his lap, he turned her around so he could massage her back, his strong hands rubbing her tense muscles. Though she wanted to be free of him, she was grateful, suspecting he had enabled her to escape a far worse fate. As his hands massaged slowly and deliberately, the tenseness went out of her and when it did, all her reserves broke. Great, wracking sobs came, and he pulled her into his arms to hold and stroke her. Carrying her to the iron bed, he lay down on the blue coverlet beside her and held her close.

She clung to him, dimly aware of his warmth and

strength, his hands moving slowly over her. He sat up once and left her, only to return in minutes. "Take a drink of brandy."

"No—"

"C'mon. You need it."

She let him hold the glass and she placed her fingers over his cool ones, drinking the fiery liquid that burned as it went down. Coit had shed his boots and coat and shirt. His chest was smooth, the skin stretched tautly over corded muscles. His belly was a washboard of rippling muscles, and the tight trousers fit like a second skin. He refilled the glass and held it while she drank again.

She lay back, assaulted by another rush of grief. She barely noticed when he stretched beside her and pulled her close. The brandy swirled inside her, burning and warming her, fogging her mind. Coit's deliberate strokes changed to caresses.

"How long since you've been with a man, Hattie?" he asked in a husky voice, his breath fanning over her.

She felt befuddled and couldn't answer. She was aware he was treating her kindly, that his hands were stirring reactions and feelings she hadn't experienced in years, causing responses that seemed beyond her control.

"How long?" he asked, turning her face up to look into her eyes.

The room swam, her head spun as his hand stroked the length of her back and then returned to caress the nape of her neck.

"A long time," she whispered, watching him as his gaze dropped to her mouth.

"I thought so. That long time is over," he said softly, shifting so his mouth covered hers.

Just over a month later, Domingo Piedra crossed the boundaries of his ranch, twenty miles south of San Antonio. He ran his hand over the saddlebags bulging with coins. Only a few more years and he would quit traveling, build the house in town he dreamed about, and open a freight office. All his life he had wanted wealth and power; he wanted men to respect him and fear him, and he intended to fulfill his dream.

In another mile he neared the ranch house. As he looked over his land, his gaze stopped on a butte to his right. Two small figures on horseback were on top of it. The rider on the black horse plunged down the steep slope.

"Madre de Dios!" Domingo gasped as he watched, experiencing the vexation that only Catalina could provoke. He knew the rider remaining on top of the butte was her younger brother, Emilio.

Why hadn't Catalina been a son? His first child should have been a son, not a daughter who was self-willed and headstrong. Instead, Emilio, his son, was the woman. Five-year-old Emilio feared his father's return. He was afraid of his own shadow.

Domingo's disgust changed as he urged his horse toward the adobe house with walls that were two feet thick and vigas protruding at the top of them. He glanced at his daughter. Her black hair streamed behind her as the stallion reached the level ground. Catalina was foolhardy, taking risks, already at only seven years of age enjoying life.

Seven years old—soon half grown. In nine or ten years a husband would have to be found for her. When the time came, Domingo decided he would select the man who would be as wealthy and as strong-willed as Catalina.

A family was necessary if he was to build a reputation as an outstanding citizen, and if he intended to have a flourishing business in San Antonio as well as his ranch. He had gained the ranch because he had joined the fight for Texas at San Jacinto. According to the constitution of the new republic, every man who was in Texas in March 1836, who had fought for Texas and hadn't already received land from Mexico, was entitled to a headright of one league and one labor of land, 4,605 acres. Because it was limited to married men, Domingo had hastily wed Sophia, using her dowry to add more land.

Money could be made in Texas. It was growing, and San Antonio was the leading city as far as Domingo was concerned. Texas had officially become the twenty-eighth state in the Union on February 19, 1846. Mexico was still disputing the boundary with President Polk, but Domingo expected the United States Army to end the questions if necessary. In ten years the population had quintupled.

San Antonio's population had grown sufficiently to need a large bridge built across the river on El Potrero Street. For years Domingo had dreamed about building a house on Calle de la Soledad, where the Veramendi Palace was located. It had served as a governor's palace when Juan Martin de Veramendi was Governor of Coahuila and Texas. After the Mexican invasion in 1842, families like the Mavericks hadn't returned to Soledad, but had built elsewhere. Strangers lived there now, and Soledad was dusty with traffic from the increasing number of people and wagons, so Domingo was no longer interested in living there.

An Irishman, John Twohig, had built one of the first two-story houses along the river, a house that Domingo envied. The town was a mixture of styles. La Villita, the area southwest of the old mission, San Antonio de Valero, where Texas had fought for independence, was littered with crude Mexican jacales made of posts driven into the ground, tied together with rawhide, and chinked with mud. Beside them, more substantial houses of caliche and adobe had been built, including the Mexican general Martin Perfecto de Cos's house where, in the attack led by Ben Milam in the 1835 uprising, General Cos had signed papers of capitulation of Mexico to the Texans. Last year Irish immigrants had arrived in San Antonio; now German immigrants had begun to arrive, establishing settlements both north of and in San Antonio.

Domingo needed a family to give him respectability, so no one would suspect what he did when he was away, but he dreaded coming back to his pious wife, strong-willed daughter, and timid son. Memories of the woman named Hattie returned, and he swore under his breath, wishing for the hundredth time that he had possessed her. Her spiteful words and golden beauty haunted him.

Catalina raced from the house, dreading the homecoming. When her father was away, their household was peaceful, everyone contented, but the moment he returned, her mother became nervous and silent. Emilio was even more frightened of their father.

She turned west, hoping she was out of Domingo's sight because he hated for her to take the horse over jumps and ride in an unladylike manner. In a few moments she reined in near the river and jumped down.

"I didn't think you would go home," said a quiet voice. She turned to see her younger brother, curly black hair falling over his forehead, his brown eyes full of worry.

"I'll go soon," she said.

"I hate it when he comes home!" Emilio stretched his thin legs in front of him and sighed. "Now I'll have to ride with him. I hate wild horses and steers!"

She grinned at him. "Too bad we can't trade. You do my lessons for me, and I'd ride with Papa for you."

"It isn't fair, Catalina. Lessons are easy, but I can't ride well. You can do both. The lessons are as easy for you as riding. You ride like Papa. I would gladly trade and do your lessons, but he'll say I have to ride with him."

"When you're bigger, you won't mind."

"I hate it now. Sometimes I hate the ranch."

"It isn't the ranch. It's our family. Someday I'll have my own family, and it'll be a happy one. A man I truly love—"

"I heard Mama say Papa will decide who we'll marry."

"No! I won't marry and live like they do!" Her tiny chin raised defiantly. "I'll choose my husband."

"No, you won't." Emilio persisted, rubbing his thin nose. "Papa will pick your husband, like Grandmother picked Papa for Mama. You've heard Mama tell the story. You'll see."

She stared at him, all her good humor gone. "Serves you right to have to ride with Papa, Emilio!"

"You're like him. When you're angry, you're mean as a snake!"

She leaned forward, hissing at him. Startled, Emilio jumped. Catalina laughed. "The only good thing about Papa's arrival is we'll get to go to town soon. I love San Antonio."

"I'm going home," Emilio said. "I'm sure he saw us on the ridge."

"I'll be along in a minute."

In another ten minutes she jumped to her feet and gathered the reins, mounting easily. Someday she would have her own home and family, and they would love each other and be happy. With a sigh of resignation she realized she had many years before that day came. Emilio couldn't be right! When she grew up, she would marry a man she loved or none at all. Squaring her shoulders, she turned the horse toward the ranch house.

2

LUCIUS STIRRED AND GROANED AS PAIN RIPPED through him in a hundred different places.

"Lie still, boy. You're close to death."

He tried to open his eyes but couldn't. He tried to form words, but the only sound was another groan. Then oblivion returned.

Intermittently he became conscious of probing hands and soothing coolness on his body or his brow. Finally a day came when he opened his eyes and could see clearly. He stared at a tree, watching the leaves flutter. Coming from every part of his body was dull and all-consuming pain. He turned his head to look around him. Mild shock registered as he gazed at a tent made of hides. Where was he? Who was taking care of him? A twig snapped, and a man appeared who was broad-shouldered and dark-skinned with a patch over one eye. While one black eye stared back unblinkingly at him, Lucius studied a rugged face with a strong jaw, a hawklike nose, and a scar on one cheek. A black braid hung over the man's shoulder.

"Where am I?"

"You're better. I found you and brought you home with me."

"Home? You live in the tent?"

"Yes. I'm Ta-ne-haddle, Running Bird."

"I'm Lucius Danby."

"I'll get you a little broth to eat."

Lucius closed his eyes, weakened by the brief conversation. In a short time Ta-ne-haddle was back with a hot liquid that tasted good. Within minutes exhaustion returned, and Lucius drifted off to sleep.

The first time he sat up, his head spun and he gasped with pain. His body was wrapped in rags, but he seemed to still be in one piece. He thought of Ta-ne-haddle's scarred cheek and ran his hand across his own face, feeling the rough rags that swathed his head.

He sat in the shade of a birch on a bed made of branches. He couldn't see Ta-ne-haddle anywhere nearby.

"Stay in bed, boy, until I can help you." Ta-ne-haddle appeared from the trees, moving without a sound. He wore buckskins and a deerskin coat.

"You're not like I imagined an Indian looking," Lucius said, his jaw aching with each movement.

"You haven't seen an Indian before?"

"Not out West. I didn't think you'd be dressed that way. I'm from Boston. We were with a wagon train headed west when some men—" He paused, remembering.

"Now, drink this, Luke."

"It's Lucius." Lucius took a tin cup and drank something with a strange, inviting smell. It tasted good, but he didn't bother to ask what it was. "Some men jumped us. One of them dropped a rope over me and pulled me behind his horse."

"He shot you also."

"I was shot?" Lucius asked, amazed as he stared at his body.

"In the shoulder. You should be dead."

"But I'm not. I'll get the man who did this to me," Lucius said with the first stirring of anger.

Ta-ne-haddle paused and straightened up from gathering wood. His dark eye squinted as he studied Lucius. "Hate won't help you."

"They took my mother!" he snapped, remembering clearly the attack and all that followed.

"Let me tell you something, Luke."

"It's Lucius."

"Hatred is a bad thing to live with. You're alive. If you're smart, you'll go on with your life."

"You don't know this man. They took the women and children with them."

"How old are you?"

"Sixteen."

"When you get well, go back to Boston. This is a lawless frontier, uninhabited by the white man in many places. You're young and fortunate to be alive."

"I can't go back. They took my mother with them."

Again he received another squinty, one-eyed scrutiny. "You won't ever see her again."

"I'll find her if it takes the rest of my life," Lucius said between clenched teeth, the words having an eerie, hollow ring that sent a chill across his nape.

"Don't tempt fate," Ta-ne-haddle said. " 'What fates impose, that men must needs abide/ It boots not to resist both wind and tide,' " he quoted as he dropped logs in a pile and added sticks and brush for a fire

"Henry VI. How do you know *Henry VI?"* Lucius asked, staring at him in amazement.

"I'm a half-breed. My father was white, my mother Kiowa. I went to Princeton for one year."

"Princeton!" Lucius exclaimed, momentarily forgetting his problems as he stared at Ta-ne-haddle. His curiosity was stirred, but he didn't want to pry. The Indian's answers explained his dress and vocabulary, but why he was living a solitary life in the wilds?

"What are you doing out here in a tent?"

"What are you doing out here on the ground?" Ta-ne-haddle asked with an impassive stare.

"We were traveling west to find my father. He went west two years ago and was supposed to send for us. We never heard from him," Lucius said grimly, "so my mother took her savings, and we came west. The men who attacked the wagon train also took our one thousand dollars in gold."

"And how did you recognize *Henry VI?"*

"I read a lot."

"I'm going to remove some of your bandages and look at your wounds, Luke."

"Lucius. First, help me up. I want to stand." Ta-ne-haddle took his arm and steadied him. He clung to Ta-ne-haddle, feeling the powerful muscles, waiting until his head cleared and he could take a few tentative steps.

"Ouch. Everything hurts."

"Your collarbone is broken. You have some broken ribs. You're a man with two lives now."

"I guess I owe that to you," Lucius said. "Thanks for the care."

Ta-ne-haddle nodded. "Back to bed, Luke."

Lucius started to correct him about the name, but he bit back the words. Luke. Ta-ne-haddle said he was a man with two lives, and Lucius knew he would never be the same person again. "Luke it is," he said quietly. "Luke Danby survived. Lucius Townsend Danby didn't."

"The same as you, I've been caught between two worlds," Ta-ne-haddle said solemnly, poking logs and sending a spray of sparks dancing skyward, "and I don't belong to either. You have a choice. Go back to Boston where you're safe."

"Would you go back and leave your mother? And never know what happened to your father?"

Ta-ne-haddle nodded. "You'll never find her."

Their conversation ended, and in moments Ta-ne-haddle was gone from sight.

Later, Luke watched Ta-ne-haddle while he skinned a deer and placed it on a spit over a fire. The cooked venison was his first solid food since the massacre. That night as he slept, he was awakened by Ta-ne-haddle shaking his shoulder.

"Don't make a sound. We have to ride. You'll have to climb on a horse."

Ta-ne-haddle held his pony while Luke climbed astride. White-hot pain stabbed through him, but he sat still as Ta-ne-haddle got on the horse in front of him and they rode double, moving through the trees.

They rode until Luke felt he would fall off the horse. He hurt all over, he couldn't stay awake, wanting to yield to sleep and avoid the wracking pain. He knew they were in danger. They were moving faster now, riding down a stream, continually crossing it to come out beneath pines, then to swerve back into the water.

When they slowed, Luke gritted his teeth to keep from crying out in pain. To his relief, Ta-ne-haddle slipped to the ground. He helped Luke down and knelt beside him as Luke lay on the ground.

"What were we running from?" Luke asked, waves of pain receding. The cold ground beneath him was a welcome relief after the jolting horse. The night was silent with an occasional rustle, the faint whisper of their voices.

"Apaches. They'll kill us if they find us. I caused bad medicine for my people, and I'm unwanted by other tribes."

"Is there anywhere out here that's safe?"

"Probably not."

"Not a town?"

"Perhaps safer than here, perhaps not."

"Why aren't you back East or riding with your own people?"

"I have no people who are my own. My people refused me; I can't live in the East. I don't fit in either world."

"Looks to me as if you're trying to fit into one of the worlds."

"I would prefer to be Kiowa, but there is ill feeling. I'm a pariah."

Luke smiled and clamped his hand on Ta-ne-haddle's shoulder. "You're an angel of mercy."

"An angel," he repeated with the same solemn expression, and Luke wondered when the man had last smiled.

"Keep quiet and get up. I know a draw where we can hide."

Luke wanted to protest, but he struggled to his feet and moved behind Ta-ne-haddle. When they finally stopped, Luke was asleep the moment he stretched out on the ground. He awoke to find a blade pressed against his throat, and he looked up into Ta-ne-haddle's face. His heart slammed against his ribs.

"If you're not going back to Boston, you're going to have to learn to survive out here," Ta-ne-haddle said solemnly. "You better learn to sleep with one eye open. I could have slit your throat."

"I trust you, for Lord's sake!" Luke snapped, anger surging in him.

"Can you shoot?"

Beneath the bandages Luke could feel his cheeks heat with embarrassment. "No."

"Be'dalpago!" Ta-ne-haddle exclaimed contemptuously.

"What's that?"

"Kiowa word for whites. You're not going to last a month when we part."

"I damned well will!"

"I want to take the bandages off and see how you're healing. It may be time to leave them off." He began unwrapping and cutting away the bandages, and as Luke looked down at his body, he drew a sharp breath. He was covered with cuts that would leave scars. For a moment he thought of Elizabeth Chandler back in Boston. Elizabeth with her pale blue eyes, her quick smile. She wouldn't smile at him now. She would be horrified. Another twist of anger knotted his insides and he clenched his fist.

"Do you have a mirror?"

"No," Ta-ne-haddle replied. "I can tell you that you're not going to look the same. And if that's important to you, you head straight back to Boston as soon as possible."

"Will you forget Boston!"

"Shh!"

Instantly Luke clamped his mouth shut. He strained to hear any unusual sound, but didn't detect the slightest trace of one. To his amazement Ta-ne-haddle placed his hand over his lips, and motioned to him with a jerk of his head. They moved back through the trees to a shadowy spot in a draw that was thick with brush.

Ta-ne-haddle pushed him down and Luke squatted, peering through the branches, still unable to hear a sound. Ta-ne-haddle pulled out his knife and moved away, leaving Luke alone. He didn't know where Ta-ne-haddle had gone and he couldn't hear a thing except the wind sighing through pine limbs and an occasional bird.

Suddenly an Indian loomed before him, staring down at him with black eyes. Almost as swiftly, Ta-ne-haddle appeared behind the Indian, caught him around the neck, and plunged the knife into him.

"We take his horse and go."

"Are there others who were with him?"

"No."

"How do you know that?"

"Listen. Listen to every sound you hear. Watch for tracks. And learn to walk without noise. When we're in a safer place, I'll teach you to shoot."

Luke felt like a burden to Ta-ne-haddle as he fell into step behind him. "We just leave him behind?"

"We just leave him behind," Ta-ne-haddle repeated dryly. "You were planning a funeral?"

Embarrassed, Luke glared at the Indian's broad shoulders. Suddenly he stumbled and pitched forward. His face flamed in mortification while Ta-ne-haddle shook his head from side to side. "You belong in a city. A safe city."

"You weren't born creeping around without making a noise," Luke retorted swiftly. "If you learned to move quietly, I can too."

"First learn how to keep from falling over your own feet."

Two days later, the last of the bandages were removed, and Ta-ne-haddle placed a pistol in Luke's hand. "Luke Danby, your boyhood is over. It's time you become a man."

Within two weeks Luke was torn between running away and leaving Ta-ne-haddle or enduring his new life. He alternately hated the man, or was enveloped in a sweeping respect for him. Ta-ne-haddle was pushing him to do things that Luke found unnecessary. For instance, he had let him step into the deep part of a creek. Ta-ne-haddle watched him as he floundered around enough to swim to safety. Now Luke could swim.

He was beginning to use a bow and arrow with a degree of competence. He had argued about that too, but Ta-ne-haddle had convinced him there were times it would be disastrous to rely on a gun and have the sound of a shot carry to an enemy.

Luke had been bitten by a snake and discovered it was a harmless one, although the bite was painful and had frightened him badly. And he felt to his soul that Ta-ne-haddle had known he was walking into a nest of snakes and had deliberately kept quiet. He stared at the Indian's broad back, hating him, thinking of ways to slip off and run away. He could shoot better now, he could ride well enough. He grimaced, thinking about the damned mustang he had been forced to catch and ride. When the horse had thrown him time and again, Luke thought he surely had broken more ribs.

One night when he dismounted, Ta-ne-haddle motioned to him. "You get dinner, Luke."

"I can't shoot well enough with a bow and arrow to kill anything! And if I use a gun, Apaches will hear us."

"I hope you can live with hunger."

Luke swore under his breath and turned away to

hunt. Three hours later it was too dark to see game, and he hadn't bagged anything. He went back to camp empty-handed.

"We'll wait until you can provide something," Ta-ne-haddle said in that impassive tone Luke had grown accustomed to hearing. The half-breed stretched on the ground and in minutes was asleep. When Luke's stomach growled with hunger, he glared at the Indian, but in a short time he went to sleep and the problem was gone until dawn.

A day later, he was starving and no closer to having something to eat. And he suspected Ta-ne-haddle was eating. He had to be getting some sustenance.

"Are you just going to let me starve to death?"

"What would you do if an Apache killed me?"

Luke glared at him, knowing the Indian was right, but it didn't appease his hunger. "Dammit, I can't hit a thing."

"Practice."

"I can get something with a rifle!"

"Yep, you can bring up a nest of Apaches."

Luke snatched up the bow and arrows, and stomped off. The next day he finally shot a rabbit. He was so hungry his hands shook as he skinned it. He wolfed it down, alternately feeling satisfied that he had finally killed something and combating rage that Ta-ne-haddle had calmly let him suffer.

"If you're going to survive, you'll have to do better than a rabbit in three days."

"I know that without your reminding me!"

"We're close to a fort. You can get a stage home to Boston if you want," Ta-ne-haddle remarked impassively, biting off a chunk of meat.

Luke stared at the dancing flames and thought of Elizabeth Chandler. "I was going to be a lawyer like my father. I had his set of law books we were bringing West."

"If you go back, do you have family or friends?"

"Yes, but I'm going to find my mother," he said,

running his fingers over the scars on his face, feeling the deep anger that was always with him. "I want to learn what happened to my father."

"You don't think you're father is alive, do you?"

"No. He wrote regularly until he crossed the Mississippi. We've never heard from him since. It wasn't like him to go off without writing or without sending for us like he said he would." Luke poked the logs and watched a spray of sparks. "And I'm staying to find the man named Domingo."

"You better know how to draw and shoot if you do."

"I will."

"There will come a time when you can't go back."

"Why?" Curious, Lucius stared at him.

"The land, the wide spaces, and the freedom will get into your blood."

"Is that what happened to you?"

"Soldiers came and killed many in our tribe. There were four captives, and the soldiers took us back with them. I was fifteen and I loved a Kiowa maiden, Dancing Sun. They forced me to go with them because that was what my mother wanted. My grandfather was a powerful soldier, and he had ordered his men to bring us back. My mother was willing to go, because she never fully accepted Indian ways, but I had. I wanted to return to my tribe. My white grandfather saw to it that I couldn't. He sent me to school and had me tutored; life was easy and good in many ways, but my grandfather couldn't hold me. He offered me all his property and wealth if I'd stay and go to college and accept a white man's life.

"My mother died and that was the hold my grandfather had on me. I was twenty and I went back to my people. Dancing Sun had wed a warrior. I talked her into running away with me. We were caught. I'll never see her again. They sent her back to Gray Wolf, her husband, and told me I could never be part of the tribe, that if they ever saw me again, they would kill me. My people have made peace with other Comanche and Apache tribes, so I'm not accepted by any of them. I'm a man in limbo between the white man's world and the Indian's."

"Why don't you go East? Take your grandfather's inheritance. He didn't reject you. You rejected him."

For the first time Ta-ne-haddle smiled. "This is my land and this is my way of life. It was all I knew as a boy, and I can't give it up to live the white man's ways. I'm part of the land. My grandfather was a merchant. That's not the life for me, and wealth means little to me. I won't go back."

"Are you going to wander around forever? There are other women."

"You're young and decisions are easy. You haven't been in love."

"Yes, I have."

Ta-ne-haddle gave him a squinty look and shook his head. "You're becoming a man now. And a man doesn't love the same way as a boy."

"I can't think about women. I want to find the man called Domingo. He will pay and the woman in his life will pay."

" 'Eye for eye, tooth for tooth, hand for hand,' " Ta-ne-haddle recited.

"That's exactly the way it will be," Luke said bitterly.

3

April 1857

CATALINA PIEDRA SHOOK HER HEAD, HER RAVEN hair cascading over her back. She swept off the horse and sank down on a log beside a wide river. Smoothing her denim skirt, she shifted booted feet and stared toward the north. A breeze swept over the cottonwood trees that lined both banks. She glanced at the nearby outcropping of boulders. The big slabs of rock that jutted into the air were piled on ones that sank out of sight beneath the water's surface. Catalina shifted impatiently, then her heart skipped as she heard the approach of a horse.

In moments the rider appeared. A slender, golden-haired man tugged on the reins and dismounted. With joy Catalina viewed Blake Corning, her gaze drifting swiftly over his lanky frame, the faded denims, and a white shirt. Wishing he would pull her up and kiss her, she fought the urge to throw herself into his arms.

He stopped yards away. "Did anyone follow you?"

"No," she answered with a flare of impatience as she brushed off her blue skirt, moving a few steps closer to him. His chest expanded with his deep breath.

"You'll get me hanged yet!"

"I didn't hold a gun to your head to force you to come see me," she answered, disappointed by his concern.

"Let's walk, Catalina."

She fell in step beside him, aware of his height, his nearness, wanting him to put his arm around her.

"When do you go back to town?"

"Not until next week," she said, her gaze sweeping over the river, the morning sun making ripples in the water sparkle. They paused beside the outcropping of boulders in the shade of a tall cottonwood. "We have a week while Papa oversees rounding up the strays, and then we'll return again for the branding. There's a dance Saturday night."

"I'll be there. Will you?"

"Yes. Our whole family is going."

"Some of the men are staying home to guard things. Comanches are on the warpath." As Blake squinted at the sun, a breeze caught the unruly locks of his hair and tangled them over his broad forehead.

"As long as you don't stay home!" She danced in front of him. "You're too solemn, Blake. You worry like an old man."

He smiled and caught her around the waist, his features softening. "You should worry. If your pa catches us, he'll flay the hide right off me."

"I'll see whom I want to see!"

"Easy enough for you to say. You're his daughter." He drew her closer, and Catalina felt as if her heart had stopped beating. She was in love with Blake, the most handsome man she had ever known. He was nineteen, one year older than she, and it made her weak in the knees just to be near him.

"Catalina," he whispered, pulling her to him. She closed her eyes and tilted her face up.

"Come here, where we're not in such plain view," he said softly and tugged her hand.

Exasperated, she followed him, wishing he would kiss her. She raised her face again and felt his lips press hers while he hugged her to him. She flicked out her tongue, making him open his mouth, wishing he would be more forceful. His arms tightened, and she clung to him.

Suddenly he raised his head. "Gawdamn, horses!"

"We'll hide," she said, slipping out of his arms. Holding his hand, she ran toward the boulders, scooting beneath one. "You stay here. I'll send them away."

In spite of Blake's protest, she slipped out and ran up the slope to her horse. Sometimes she wished Blake would just stand up to her father, but she knew Domingo Piedra instilled fear in nearly all the men he knew.

She swung onto her horse and urged it to a trot in the direction of the men. In seconds she rode into view of Domingo and two of his men. She tugged on the reins and waited.

"Catalina, I've told you to stay closer to the house!" Domingo snapped. "We've lost a bull and he's a mean one. And there's talk of Comanches on the warpath. We're far enough from the ranch house that you could be in danger."

"It's a beautiful morning. Why don't I ride with you?" she asked, knowing he wouldn't allow it.

"You go home. Your mother won't want you riding with us all day, and soon we'll be a long ways from home."

He turned his horse. She watched until he twisted to look over his shoulder at her. As soon as he did, she wheeled her horse around and headed in the direction of the ranch house

After the men had ridden away, Catalina suddenly veered to the west, a smile breaking forth as she urged the horse to a trot.

Luke Danby shifted his weight on the warm rock and silently cursed his luck. Two days earlier he and Ta-ne-haddle had been ambushed by Mexican bandits as they headed north to San Antonio from Laredo. They had fought off their attackers, and in the ensuing chase they split up, agreeing to meet in San Antonio. Several hours ago Luke had stopped riding to rest. After a swim he had climbed up the boulders and stretched out, falling asleep. His horse was a half a mile downriver, out of sight of anyone nearby. Voices had awakened him, and he realized he was overhearing a man and woman. He heard the woman leave and knew the man was below. He didn't see any point in stirring up trouble needlessly, so he stayed where he was and hoped they would go away soon. He was getting tired of lying on the rock, and the sun had shifted so he was no longer in the shade.

"Blake!"

"I'm here," the man said

Luke was tempted to raise his head a few inches and get a look at her, but he knew better than to risk it. He heard her horse halt, then brush rustled, and from only yards below him her voice came up as clearly as if she had been talking to him.

"Papa's gone."

"Yeah, and I better go too. Your pa's not a man to reckon with."

"Don't be silly. He rode the opposite way, and he thinks I've gone home. They're looking for a bull. Blake, sit down."

Luke listened to the coaxing, breathless voice and thought if a woman sweet-talked him like that, he would sit down instantly. He conjured up a vision to go with the voice: a voluptuous, golden-haired woman with big blue eyes and ruby lips.

"I better go."

"Blake, c'mon. Sit down."

"Look, you won't get skinned alive if he catches us. I will. Aw, stop it, Catalina," he said, but there was no protest in his voice, and erotic possibilities of what the man wanted her to stop doing floated in Luke's mind. Catalina. He silently mouthed the name, listening in earnest now.

"Kiss me again, Blake."

"I shouldn't . . ."

Luke frowned, wanting to roll over the edge of the rock and tell Blake he would gladly trade places with him.

"Catali—"

His words stopped abruptly, and there was silence from below. Luke could imagine kissing a woman with a voice as tempting as honey. He wiped his forehead, feeling as if the sun had dropped halfway to earth and was broiling him.

He heard clothing rustle and he sat up, pulling out a cheroot. He remembered just in time that he couldn't smoke, or they would discover they weren't alone.

"Blake, oh, Blake, I love you."

"You're beautiful. The most beautiful woman in the world."

Luke shifted uneasily. He had never eavesdropped in his life, and his first experience was a particularly personal one that he didn't relish hearing.

"Want to swim, Blake?"

"Oh, Lordy! Catalina, your pa's somewhere on this side of the ranch. I'm going home before I get my neck stretched. I'll come back tomorrow."

"Blake, you can't go. We're alone now."

"Tomorrow. This time tomorrow."

"I may be here and I may not, Blake Corning."

Luke grinned. She was a feisty one, and if he were down there he would show her a thing or two. He wished with all his heart he could trade places with Blake Corning. He wouldn't go home and refuse the invitation to swim. Not if her pa and an army of men were on this side of the ranch.

"Now, honey, don't get in a huff. Come on, Catalina, give me a kiss and tell me you're not angry."

"You just go on home if you're in such an all-fired hurry."

Women! Ten seconds ago she had been begging Blake to stay. Now she was telling him to go.

"Catalina, please. Just one kiss. Come on. We don't have all day."

"Indeed, you don't. Good-bye, Blake."

"Come here."

"Blake!"

There was silence and Luke gritted his teeth, trying

to keep tormenting images out of his head. The first thing he was going to do when he got to town was find a pretty woman and kiss her. It had been a long time since the last one, and this woman's throaty, breathless voice was stirring him.

"You'll be here tomorrow."

"Yes. I love you, Blake."

Another long silence came and Luke shifted uneasily. Then he listened to more good-byes until one horse rode away. One stayed. Luke was tempted to lean over the edge of the rock when he heard her singing softly. He listened to the rustle of clothes, and realized she was probably going to swim. If she went out very far, she would be able to see him up on the ledge.

He shifted his weight carefully. He needed to get out of sight, but his curiosity was too great. He scooted forward, wanting one glimpse.

She was ankle-deep in water, walking into the river with her back to him. He caught his breath as he looked at her slender tan body and shapely curves, her bare buttocks. She turned, reaching up to let down her hair. Her breasts were high and full with dusky pink tips, her belly flat and her waist tiny. Luke felt on fire as he watched her, thinking he had never seen a woman as beautiful in his life.

She wasn't at all as he had imagined. She was tall, slender, dark-skinned, and had midnight hair. And she was more beautiful than he had dreamed possible. He felt as if his heart were pounding through his chest as he watched her. Blake Corning didn't have a grain of sense to turn down a swim with Catalina.

"Catalina." He whispered the name to himself. He licked his lips and ached, his manhood throbbing as he viewed her.

She sang softly, swaying her hips as she waded calf-deep. Luke was mesmerized, watching her hips, the slight jiggle of her luscious breasts. She turned toward the rocks, facing him fully.

"Lord!" he whispered, his ears roaring as he looked at her, slowly letting his gaze roam to her knees, and then back up to her face. At that moment she raised her head, and looked directly into his eyes.

4

NEITHER MOVED. LUKE FELT AS IF TIME WERE held in suspension, his heart, lungs, and blood ceasing to function, his body clamoring for physical release.

Then she screeched and dropped into the water. Throwing her hands up to cover her breasts, she sank in water to her chin.

Knowing he had probably scared the daylights out of her, he said clearly, "I didn't mean any harm. I was here when you came." He scrambled down the rock, holding his hands up in the air so she could see he didn't intend to hurt her. He expected her to start screaming with fear, and he didn't care to have her summon the father Blake Corning so feared.

"Son of a pig! Damn your eyes!" she snapped without a shred of fear in her voice. Luke lowered his hands and grinned, placing his fists on his hips.

"So the lady has a temper too."

"You sneaking sonofabitch!"

"Whoo! I should have known that a woman who begs a gentleman to kiss her wouldn't be a shy, mannerly miss." he said, beginning to enjoy himself.

"You dirty, lowlife skunk! How long were you up there?"

"Long enough, Catalina. Come out here and I'll oblige. You won't have to beg me to kiss you," he said, teasing her. "Matter of fact, I'll accept the offer of a swim in Blake's place."

She scooted farther away from the bank. "Don't you come near me, you varmint!"

"You do have a way with words." He sat down to pull off his boots.

"What are you doing?"

"I told you, I'll be glad to swim with you."

"The hell you will! Turn your back so I can get out and get my clothes."

"And waste a perfectly good swim?"

"Turn your back!"

He grinned and made a mocking bow. "Whatever the lady wants." He turned around and folded his arms across his chest, listening to her flounder out of the water and yank on her clothes, a clear picture coming of her standing nude in the river.

"Catalina?"

"I hope I never see you again as long as I live!"

"And I hope I see you again and again . . . just like I did today."

"Dammit!"

He turned around and whistled loudly, knowing his horse would obey and come to him. She hadn't finished dressing, and yanked her bodice closed over a tantalizing glimpse of flesh.

"You were supposed to keep your back turned," she snapped angrily. "I should have known better than to expect an eavesdropping scoundrel to show an ounce of respect for a lady."

"A lady? A lady who can swear like the toughest waddy I've ever known," he said with amusement, watching her fasten her bodice with angry tugs. He realized she still didn't have an ounce of fear in her manner or her speech, and he was intrigued by her, ensnared by her beauty.

"Catalina. What's your last name?"

"You don't need to know because we will never cross paths again, I hope. And you're trespassing on our land. Stay off if you don't want to get shot."

His horse came ambling through the brush, stopping obediently. Luke walked over and gathered the reins. Then he went to Catalina, halting only a few feet from her. Anger sparked in her velvety black eyes. Her lips were full, rosy, and a blazing temptation.

"You're wasting your love on Blake Corning," he said quietly, suddenly wishing he were going to stay in one place long enough to get to know her. He studied her intently and felt his breath stop as he was caught in a gaze that seemed to burn to his soul. She drew a deep breath and stared at him.

He was drawn to her like a tree to sunlight. His arm went out and caught her around her waist. She spun away from him and reached down where her boots lay to yank up a pistol and point it at him. She pulled back the hammer.

He watched her, his pulse pounding with desire. "Put the Colt away," he commanded quietly. "You need kissing by a man, not a boy." He mounted his horse and looked down at her. "Someday, Catalina, I'll kiss you whether you draw on me or not."

"Go to hell, gringo."

He grinned. "When I remember you standing in the river, I'm in heaven. Sheer heaven."

"You—"

"Save the fascinating words! Adios for now. Until we meet again. And we will meet again, I promise you," he added with all laughter gone from his voice. He turned and rode away, heading toward San Antonio, fighting the urge to turn around and look at her again. His back tingled because he suspected she was just fiery enough to take a shot at him, yet she too had been caught in something that had passed between them. He should have kissed her, but they would meet again. And when he kissed her, he didn't want her enraged and embarrassed. He grinned, then sobered as he remembered her standing in the water. He would never forget that moment as long as he lived.

He took a deep breath and felt his body heating with desire. He wanted to meet her properly. He wanted to kiss her, to have her beautiful body in his arms, yielding to him completely. He wondered who she was. Catalina. Beautiful Catalina.

His gaze scanned the area, and he reined in his horse to look behind him. There was no sign of her, and he wondered where the boundaries to the ranch were, where the ranch house was, who her family was. His thoughts shifted as he headed toward San Antonio.

This was the first time he had been far south, down to Laredo, back to San Antonio. There had been leads about the man named Domingo, but Hattie seemed to have vanished off the face of the earth. As time passed, Luke couldn't find anyone who knew the man called Domingo, and he and Ta-ne-haddle decided to leave New Mexico and head down through Texas.

He rode into San Antonio that evening, past missions that had been built long before his country had heard of George Washington. On impulse Luke entered the grounds to an abandoned mission, riding slowly past the last remnants of the defending wall. Over a century before it had given the friars and their flock protection from marauding Indians. Huisaches, tamaracks, and mesquites filled the grounds. Flying buttresses reinforced the stone granary walls. The mission, with its crumbling limestone walls and statues of saints flanking its open oak doors, was empty.

Luke dismounted and stepped into the cool shadows, wondering how many years it had been since he had darkened a church door. The stone floor was covered with dust and weeds that had blown in through the open door. He was Boston Protestant, and since the violent separation from his mother, his faith had suffered. He closed his eyes and said a silent prayer that she was still alive and in some kind of decent existence. He turned angrily and strode out, his thoughts slamming shut on the possibilities of what might have happened to his mother. He mounted up and angrily cantered away.

Luke followed a road that meandered along the course of the wide river that was clear and green. He

rode in on Calle de la Presa, crossing the Alamo ace-
quia built to channel the river water. He turned west
on El Potrero, or La Calle del Comercio, absorbing
the sights and smells of one of Texas's largest towns,
the site of the battle for independence at the Alamo.
Luke passed myriad shops: a tin shop, a cabinet-
maker, two shoemakers, a grocer, and a freighting
company. Wagons jammed the road, filled with people
in both sombreros and white cotton pants, and in tai-
lored suits and tall beaver hats. A parading troupe of
actors dressed in spangled tights, playing drums and
trombones, promoted their evening performance.
Doors stood open to adobe houses, or they had no
doors and he could see domestic scenes as he passed.

The battered old San Fernando Cathedral, where
Santa Anna had flown his red flag of "no quarter"
during the seige of the Alamo, stood on the west side
of the wide Plaza de las Islas. The main plaza swarmed
with freighting wagons, chickens, men smoking cigarettes while lounging in sombreros and serapes. Behind it, vendors sat with their wares spread on the
ground in the Plaza del Presidio. Luke's gaze shifted
to a cantina; he wanted to find a beautiful woman. An
image of Catalina rose like a haunting specter, making
his breath catch as he remembered every flawless detail. Catalina. He wanted to touch and kiss and possess her.

Fool, he admonished himself mentally. No doubt
her proper Mexican parents would protect her from the
likes of him, and he would never get closer than he
had today, but it didn't stop the desire or the vivid
mental pictures. She was the most beautiful woman he
had ever seen, and she was no dull, shy miss. He
smiled, remembering, feeling a stirring of his blood.
What a feisty one, and what a beauty!

He reined his mount and his gaze traveled over the
busy area with its vendors, the soldiers, and cowmen.
On the occasions when they rode into a town, Ta-ne-
haddle enjoyed himself and gave up all his solitary

habits, and Luke expected to find him in the nearest saloon or bordello.

Ta-ne-haddle couldn't be found in the first two cantinas Luke visited, and then he gave up his search when he found a pretty senorita. Two days later there was still no sign of Ta-ne-haddle, but Luke didn't have the slightest concern that the Indian hadn't eluded the bandits. After years of traveling with his Kiowa friend, Luke realized the wily Ta-ne-haddle was as much at home in the wilds as a mountain lion. In addition, his years of education back East made him doubly formidable, because his mind was shrewd and quick.

During his first two days in town Luke won over a hundred dollars in cart wheels, Mexican silver dollars. He had part of the money in a pocket, part in his boot. The rest was in a belt made of deerskin with pouches to hold coins flat against his body. Ta-ne-haddle had made it. Luke knew the Indian wore one and had a goodly supply of gold and Mexican silver if he ever needed it. It was replaced occasionally at faro, and a large part promptly spent on whiskey.

Luke was sleeping in a wagon yard; there was no need to spend money for a hotel room. He and Ta-ne-haddle would often bed down outside of town, moving on within a few days while Luke continued his hunt for Domingo. Occasionally, for one reason or another, they had stayed longer at a place. Luke had recently been sheriff in Madrid, New Mexico Territory, and earlier had practiced law in the territory.

In a town like San Antonio men named Domingo were numerous, so he had to spend some time in town. With the discovery of Catalina, he was happy to stay. So far his inquiries in saloons hadn't gleaned any information about her, but yesterday a blacksmith had given him a pitying smile and said, "She's the only daughter of one of the leading businessmen in town. You'd best forget about her, because her parents are protective and her father has a quick draw and a mighty short temper." Catalina Piedra. He had learned her full name. And it would be as easy to forget her as to forget to breathe.

Luke learned about the dance Saturday night, and he intended to go, because he wanted to see Catalina again as soon as possible. He stepped into the cool interior of a general store, and walked down an aisle to search for a roll of twine and some new rope. As his boots scraped the bare boards, his spurs jingled slightly with each step. He pushed his black hat to the back of his head as he gazed at the shelves of goods.

"Which one do you like the best?" came a question from the next aisle. It was the voice of a young boy, and the words barely registered on Luke.

"The blue. You know I always like blue," came a careless answer. Luke paused, his hand in midair, all thoughts of twine gone. He couldn't forget her throaty voice. His pulse jumped, and he listened with his head cocked slightly.

"I hope Mama likes this."

"Of course she will. Thank goodness, San Antonio gets the latest materials and fashions! Let's take the blue material. Tell Mr. Schatzel to put it on Papa's account. I'm getting something for myself."

"I thought he told you not to get any more material until summer."

"I'll handle Papa."

"I'll get this and I'm going to the back of the store to look at the books."

"Don't you ever tire of books, Emilio?"

"Never. You sound like Papa with that question."

"Go ahead, but I won't wait all morning while you read some dusty book of Mr. Schatzel's."

"I know you won't wait," came a dry answer. Luke smiled and listened to the boy walk away. Moving quietly to the next aisle, his heart slammed against his ribs as he looked at her. She was as beautiful as he had remembered. Instantly he mentally stripped away the multicolored yellow-and-blue gingham dress she wore.

Catalina walked down the aisle, touching the bolts of material, envisioning how each would look made into a dress. She ran her slender fingers over a bolt of deep blue grenadine, picturing it trimmed with lace. Then her hand strayed to a bright pink glacé silk, a color Mama wouldn't allow except for a party. Out of the corner of her eye she became aware of someone nearby, and she felt compelled to look up.

Her heart lurched and flames of embarrassment burned her cheeks. She detested the stranger and had hoped she would never encounter him again. San Antonio had frontier ruffians, renegades, gamblers, rustlers—this man looked as if he were all of those rolled into one, she thought as she had at that first encounter. He had enough scars to have withstood dozens of fights. He wore a gunbelt and had the insolent manner of a renegade. He stood with his hip canted against a shelf, his thumbs hooked into his belt, a faint grin curving the corner of his mouth while his gaze drifted slowly down over her. Every nerve tingled as his knowing gaze called to mind that moment when she had discovered him at the river.

Her embarrassment, something new to Catalina, stirred her fury. She placed her hands on her hips and glared at him as his gaze traveled upward with languorous deliberation, pausing over her full breasts. Adding to her fury, she tingled in a manner that until now only had happened when Blake looked at her. She wanted to hurl something at him, denounce him for the snake he was, but she couldn't in Mr. Schatzel's store. It would be reported immediately to her father and then to her mother.

His gaze finally met hers, and she glared at him with all the hatred in her being. " 'Morning, Catalina," he said in a soft drawl. The use of her name was so brazen, yet his deep voice caused another tingle of awareness in her.

She firmed her lips and flounced her head, turning her back to walk around the counter to the next aisle.

She heard the faint jingle of spurs and there he was, facing her again. She took a deep breath and glared at him. She wasn't ready to leave the store, but she didn't want to converse with this man.

"I'll tell Mr. Schatzel you're bothering me, and he'll call the sheriff."

"Will he, now?" the stranger asked easily, looking amused, and Catalina's anger climbed a notch. She had yet to meet a man she couldn't manage within a few moments' time, except her father, who invoked a fearsome respect in everyone. With an easy gait the stranger moved closer. His thick brown hair had a slight curl. A stray lock curved on his forehead above his thin, slightly crooked nose. He appeared tough, knowing, and confident. The thought crossed her mind that he might be on one of the wanted posters over at the stage office.

Stopping only a few feet from her, he looked down at her with the same faint smile. Her gaze was ensnared by green eyes that held and seemed to draw the breath from her body. His lashes were a thick fringe surrounding eyes that refused to allow her to turn away. His gaze dropped to her mouth and a shock rippled like a strong wind passing over her. He had told her he would kiss her sometime, and he looked as if he were going to do so right now in Mr. Schatzel's store!

"You remember what I said," he said with quiet satisfaction, in his deep-voiced drawl, his eyes boring into hers again.

She wanted to look elsewhere, to turn her back on him, to make some scathing remark, at least a denial. Instead, words failed her, and her heart thudded as if she were in the most enormous danger.

"*Hasta la vista,* Catalina," he said softly, tipped his hat, and turned to walk away.

Stunned, she stared at his back and broad shoulders. In both encounters she had felt caught in an invisible battle, and to her amazement she had felt he was in command both times, that she had lost a skirmish that she couldn't even understand.

She had been wrong in her assessment of him. He wasn't one of the lawless renegades that sometimes were too forward before they found out who she was. This man would be the same whether he knew her father or not, she suspected. And he hadn't forced his attentions on her beyond a few minutes' greeting that could be described only as polite and respectful by any observer. But he hadn't actually been either polite or respectful in the manner in which he had looked at her, or in his tone of voice, or in his heated gaze that stirred her in a manner that made her furious.

Only Blake had ever made her heart thud like that. Only Blake had made her tingle from head to toe. She wanted to stamp her foot and swear until she realized that she was letting the stranger get the best of her. She tossed her head and went to get Emilio, who stood with a bundle of material wrapped in brown paper under his arm while he thumbed through one of Mr. Schatzel's worn books in the back corner of the room.

"Emilio, we need to leave now in time to get home."

"We have an hour left."

"I'm going. I want to stop at Don Pelon's store. You better come along unless you want to ride home with Papa or walk."

Emilio closed the book and placed it on the shelf, his brown eyes studying Catalina with a scrutiny that made her irritable. "What's wrong? You look as if you pinched your fingers."

"I'll pinch yours if you don't stop asking foolish questions!" she snapped.

"Mr. Schatzel wouldn't let you buy any material," Emilio persisted, knowing how far he could go before he pushed her to the limit.

"No. I didn't see any material I wanted."

They hurried to the buggy in silence, but she was aware of Emilio's curious stare. He could stare all he wanted; she would never tell a soul about the disturbing stranger. Emilio took the reins and headed down El Potrero.

As they entered their house on Calle de las Flores, Catalina's spirits improved. The town house, made of weathered six-inch cedar boards, was decorated like the elegant German homes with red velvet furniture and brocade draperies, crystal candelabra, gilt-framed mirrors, and paintings. Catalina liked both their houses, but deep down, her first love was the ranch house.

Saturday night at half-past nine, Catalina felt on fire with excitement as their carriage passed the mansion of Jose Cassiano, only a little more elegant than the Piedra home. Next door to the mansion, they halted in front of Madame Bustamante's fandango hall on the west side of the Plaza del Presidio. Along with her family, Catalina entered a large hall lighted by tall white candles. At the back of the room was a pungent fire of burning mesquite logs that heated coffee, tamales, and enchiladas. Nearby tables covered in bright red cloths held dishes for the feast. At the opposite end of the room from the fire, on a platform made of planks placed on boxes, were two violinists and a guitar player. Benches and straight-backed wooden chairs lined opposite walls of the room for observers. Catalina felt a tremor of excitement as she searched for sight of Blake.

The men looked elegant in their dark, tight pants and brightly colored red or green sashes tied around their waists. For an instant Catalina glanced at her father, thinking he was as handsome as many men half his age. Beneath a wide-brimmed black sombrero, his swarthy looks were set off by his snowy shirt. His short jacket didn't hide the bright green sash around his still narrow waist, and the toes of his black boots gleamed with each step.

Her mother too was as pretty as many of the younger women with her large black eyes and dainty features.

Sophia's blue and white silk with its wide blue sash and blue ribbons for trim was a foil for Catalina's red crepe de chine, a color she liked to wear.

The women were dressed in their finest, and Catalina was assured she looked her best with her hair parted in the center, caught up over each ear with bunches of curls that cascaded down in back between her shoulder blades. Her red dress, trimmed in black lace, was her favorite.

Blake would be here, dressed in his good pants and a white chambray shirt with a string tie, not in the Mexican manner as the men in her family. Her brother was nervous, wanting to be home with his books and away from the crowd who intimidated him. If he would just relax and stop worrying about Papa, he would have as much fun as everybody else. She forgot Emilio as her gaze swept the clusters of people, watching for a certain golden head of hair.

"Ah, good evening. The most beautiful ladies of San Antonio have now arrived, so the party can begin." Friedrich Kreuger, Domingo's business partner, bowed low over Sophia's hand, his words tinged with a German accent from his native tongue. San Antonio's German immigrants were increasing in number each year. They were successful, industrious business men, and were changing the town. The house had been in a turmoil when Domingo had gone into business with him.

Catalina drew her breath sharply as he took her hand, his fingers running over her palm lightly. At the time the two men had formed the partnership and opened their freighting business, Catalina had been too young at fifteen and too preoccupied to notice Friedrich. Nor had he noticed her until this past year. Now she wanted to avoid him at all costs. Too many times she had caught him watching her with a lustful look that made her skin crawl. She loathed his touch, fighting the urge to yank her hand from his, resisting gently as he turned her palm up to kiss it, letting his tongue touch her flesh.

Pulling her hand away, she pressed it in the folds of her skirt, looking up into the mocking blue eyes that frightened her. Friedrich was wealthy, powerful, and the only man she had ever known that her father deliberately tried to please as much as possible. She had never known Friedrich to attend a fandango fete before. Usually the Germans went to their beer halls, and danced their polkas and waltzes to their own robust music. She had an uneasy suspicion that Friedrich might be present tonight because of her.

As swiftly as the thought came, she rejected it. She was eighteen and Friedrich was forty-two, older than her father. She glanced at Domingo, who smiled at her as he took Sophia's arm. "Shall we say hello to everyone before we dance?" he suggested. "Join us, Friedrich."

Without waiting for an answer, Domingo turned away and steered Sophia through the crowd, greeting each person. He too wondered why Friedrich was here tonight. As closely as he worked with the man, he would never understand his Teutonic mind, only that Friedrich had an uncanny knack for making a dollar. Friedrich had immigrated with almost no money. He began work in a small dry-goods store; within two years he owned the store. When Domingo had first approached him about a freighting and commission business, Friedrich had seemed on the verge of refusing, but had agreed to think it over. Within a day he had accepted. To his surprise, Domingo discovered Friedrich was as ruthless as any renegade he had ever known. If a man couldn't pay, Friedrich would take land and goods; he demanded a prompt settlement under all circumstances. Consequently, the company's fortunes were growing. Friedrich now had three parcels of land and cattle on all three. For once in his life, Domingo had found a man he respected, because he knew how merciless and shrewd Friedrich could be. And Friedrich still had control of the partnership.

When Domingo danced with Sophia, he looked over her head at Friedrich dancing with Catalina. His white teeth flashed in a smile, and Domingo realized that Friedrich was flirting with her.

Shocked, he swirled Sophia around as his gaze swept the dusky room filled with spectators and dancing couples. There were beautiful women in low-necked dresses, many in the simple Mexican dress of a scooped-necked white bodice and a brightly colored skirt. The constrictions of respectability and family gnawed at him. If he were at this party in another town without his family, what fun he would have! He sighed with a longing that no longer surprised him. All the years of his childhood as an orphan on the streets, he had dreamed of what he had now, respectability and wealth. But it was an empty dream. His family was a leaden weight, respectability tiresome. Sometimes he was tempted to get on his horse, gather the men who had always ridden with him, and disappear from San Antonio.

His thoughts shifted as Catalina danced past. He glanced at Ticiano, the man whom he had decided over a year ago would be the most likely husband for Catalina. Domingo had no intention of letting her follow her own whims. She would do as she was told. He had always expected her to marry someone of her own Mexican heritage, not a cold, harsh German like Friedrich. He noticed that Catalina was somber as she danced with the older man. The girl knew nothing of marriage, men, or fortune. She would obey him in this matter as she always had.

Domingo studied Ticiano, who was six feet tall. He had brooding dark eyes and a thin mouth. On more than one occasion Domingo had discussed marriage between the two families with Marcos, Ticiano's father, and he knew it was acceptable to Marcos as well.

"You're solemn tonight, my husband," Sophia said softly.

He looked down into her brown eyes. She was ethereal and cold, like a beautiful doll. She hated lovemaking, whimpering and blushing even after all these years, but there were moments when he wanted her and tonight was one. He had an urge to sweep her out the door and into the dark.

A nagging memory stirred. Hattie. He frowned, hating the way his heart raced whenever he thought of her. He still dreamed of her. Had nightmares would be a better description, he thought, because he always woke sweating and yearning for the golden-haired *gringa*, his manhood hard and throbbing until he had to wake Sophia for relief.

"You're frowning, Domingo. What troubles you?"

His gaze swept beyond her and he found a ready excuse. "Our son. Why won't the boy dance and talk to others? He sulks in a corner as if he is afraid of his shadow."

"He's afraid of your anger," Sophia said quietly.

"My anger?" he repeated in dismay. "I'm enjoying myself. The only thing to make me angry is the way he acts."

"He's afraid whatever he does will make you angry."

"If he would just act like a man!"

"You mean, if he would act just like you."

Domingo strode to the door, wanting to force the disturbing thoughts of Hattie out of his mind, wanting to feel a woman's softness against his body.

"Catalina is going to be beautiful," Sophia said, a slight frown creasing her brow.

Domingo laughed, his white teeth flashing beneath his thick black mustache as they walked outside. "You sound as if she carries a burden."

"Beauty and her temperament might prove to be a bur—" She looked up. "Domingo, what are you doing?"

"Hush, Sophia. I want you."

"It's shameful. We're in public."

"We're out of everyone's sight," he said and stopped her protests with his mouth as he crushed her in his arms.

The music wafted on the air, laughter and voices mingling with the faint jingle of spurs when someone passed nearby.

Luke noticed a couple moving into the shadows as he approached the hall. He could hear the music and laughter, and his pulse quickened over the prospect of seeing Catalina. Ta-ne-haddle was asleep in the wagon yard, passed out from a night in a cantina. The Indian's capacity to consume whiskey was enormous, but afterward he slept around the clock.

Keeping in the shadows along the walls, threading his way through the crowd in the warm room, Luke spotted Catalina in seconds. She danced in the arms of a tall, thin boy who gazed at her with a hungry look. Luke guessed most of the men in the room would like to be dancing with her. He wondered which one was Blake; if he heard him talking, he would recognize his voice.

While they danced, Ticiano smiled at Catalina. "Our fathers will be pleased to see us dancing. They intend to betroth us, you know."

"That's nice, Ticiano," she said politely, gazing beyond his shoulder.

He smiled, one corner of his mouth climbing higher. "And I may take you home with me tonight. And do whatever I wish."

"Good."

"I will claim your body and kiss—"

Her head jerked up, and Catalina's eyes narrowed while Ticiano grinned broadly.

"So finally I have caught your attention! What man do you watch?"

"I don—all right, I do! What did you say to me?"

"How flattering you are, Catalina. You haven't heard a word I've said."

"I'm sorry, Ticiano, but you know half the girls in San Antonio would hang on your every word, so what I do or don't do, shouldn't matter to you."

"It matters," he said, all humor leaving his voice. "I said, our fathers are about ready to seal our betrothal."

Catalina felt a sting of shock, then gave a shake of her head. "What foolishness. I haven't heard Papa say a word on the matter. You're teasing, Ticiano," she said.

"I'm not one to tease. My parents are having your family to dinner next Monday night."

"We've eaten with your family before."

"I don't think we'll have a choice in the matter. Thank heaven, I can abide by their decision."

"What's that supposed to mean? Don't talk in riddles, Ticiano."

"You have a sharp tongue, but not too sharp. You'll make a good wife. And you're the prettiest girl in San Antonio."

"A sharp tongue! Our dance is over now."

He laughed softly. "The music still plays. You can be a beautiful little witch when you're angry, but I know how to handle problems like you." He tightened his grip on her, his arm like steel around her waist as they continued to dance.

"Ticiano, I can create a scene."

"But it would embarrass you as much as it would embarrass me, so I don't think you will. And it would displease your father immeasurably. You don't often displease him, do you?"

"You're hurting my wrist."

"Relax, and I won't. Do what I say, Catalina."

She stepped quickly, the heel of her shoe coming down on his instep. He drew a hissing breath as the music ended. For an instant he looked angry enough to strike her, but then he gave her a thin smile. "Someday I will get to tame you," he said coolly. Her anger evaporated, and her heart missed a beat because she saw Blake headed their way.

"This dance is mine," he said, taking her hand and merely nodding in greeting to Ticiano.

"Blake, at last. I've wanted to be with you so badly," she said in rapturous tones, linking his arm through hers, and relishing the swift look of anger that surfaced in Ticiano's eyes. Turning her back on him, she moved with Blake to the dance floor.

"You want to get me shot?"

"Ticiano deserves whatever he gets."

"It's my hide he'll take his anger out on. What did he do to you?"

"He's cruel and heartless, and I despise being around him."

"Word's out that your families plan that you two will marry," Blake said gruffly.

"Why, Blake, you're jealous."

"Don't play with me, Catalina. Has your father said anything to you about it?"

"No. And I'll marry the man of my choice."

Their conversation ended as other couples began forming a circle around the room, then lining up facing each other. Her gaze drifted beyond Blake, and her heart seemed to stop beating. Directly across from her was the stranger she had met at the river. As Catalina looked into his mocking green eyes, she missed a step.

5

BLAKE DIDN'T SEEM TO NOTICE HER CONFUSION. Catalina was determined to look elsewhere as she danced, but each time they turned around the room, her eyes went back to the stranger's. As Blake danced her close to the spectators, she tried to keep her head averted, but Blake spun her around and she faced an amused, insolent glance that drifted over her body as if he were seeing her nude again. She drew a sharp breath and stepped on Blake's toe. She smiled up at him, trying to think of something to say that would get her mind off the disturbing stranger. "When will you come to town again?"

"Next week we have to come in to get supplies."

"Will I see you?"

He frowned as he gazed intently at her. "I don't think your pa likes for me to come calling."

"Nonsense. Of course, he does."

"He doesn't act like it."

"Papa's gruff and you know it. Don't be afraid of him, Blake. It just brings out the bully in him. Emilio is always afraid of Papa, and consequently Emilio is constantly in Papa's bad graces."

"Where is Emilio? I haven't seen him."

"He should be dancing, but he's probably off in some dark corner talking to Antonio Musquiz. That's his best friend."

"You look pretty."

"*Gracias.*"

Catalina smiled up at him, trying to ignore the pull

she still felt on her senses. Blake danced with his brow furrowed in concentration.

"Your pa is glaring at me for dancing with you."

"Nonsense. I've danced with many tonight."

"Dammit, that wasn't what I wanted to hear. I was late getting away from the ranch because one of the mares was foaling."

The music ended and dancers applauded. As the fiddlers commenced another number, Catalina looked up into the eyes of the stranger.

"This dance is mine," he said in a deep voice, stepping up and taking her in his arms to whirl her away before Blake could protest.

"You have the nerve of an old mossy-horn," she snapped, trying to look past him at Blake and wondering why Blake didn't interfere. Turning, the stranger moved so she couldn't see Blake. Anger flashed in her dark eyes and her lips were pursed in a pout, but she was in his arms, and he was enjoying himself.

"Catalina Piedra, we haven't been formally introduced and for someone I know in some ways so very well, in other ways we hardly know each other at all."

"Will you stop reminding me? If you had one ounce of gentlemanly courtesy, you wouldn't keep harping on a moment that was highly mortifying to me."

"What moment? I haven't said a word about any one moment in time," he said with an air of innocent curiosity, enjoying teasing her and watching the flush in her cheeks. She was fighting to be polite and mind her manners, yet he knew how completely and swiftly she could lose control. And how tempting she was all the time.

"You varmint," she said politely, smiling at him to fool any onlookers.

He laughed. "I'll have to admit, I like to tease you. You rise to the bait like a hungry fish after a fly. I never did finish my introduction. I'm Luke Danby."

"I can't say I'm pleased to meet you, because I'm not."

"How can I ever win your good opinion?"

"Frankly, I don't think you possibly can under any circumstances. You're better off staying out of my life."

"Not in the next million years," he said amiably, dancing near the door where a cool breeze came into the overheated room. "Are you in love with Blake?" he asked, knowing her answer and not caring about it, but merely trying to keep her attention elsewhere for a moment.

"Very much, as you should know from eavesdropping on our conversation. It was—I can't go outside!"

"We are outside, and it's about twenty degrees cooler," he said, stretching out his long legs and dancing her into the darkness.

"My father won't allow it."

"He probably won't notice, and we're here." He slowed, taking smaller steps, watching her in the moonlight as his eyesight adjusted to the darkness.

"This is improper and I have to go inside at once. Mama and Papa both will be dismayed that I'd do such a thing."

He stopped dancing and tilted her chin up. Catalina's pulse had quickened since the first moment he had stepped up behind Blake. Luke Danby. He was tall, rugged, green-eyed like a cat, and he didn't seem to care what anyone thought.

"I'm going inside," she snapped, fully intending to do so until she looked into his eyes. Her pulse jumped another notch and she caught her breath. She felt a pull on her senses stronger than before, as if he wove a spell that held her in invisible bonds. His mouth was well shaped, wide with a full underlip. The only men she had ever kissed were Blake and Ticiano. Ticiano's kisses were cruel and a little frightening. No man could kiss like Blake, she was sure. Yet at the moment as she looked at Luke Danby's mouth, a ripple of ex-

citement coursed in her, and her curiosity was stirred
by the notion of being kissed by him.

"Shall we find out?" he drawled softly in a husky
voice. It took seconds to register on her what he had
asked. Her gaze flew up to meet his and she felt her
cheeks burn. *Had the man read her mind?* His arm
tightened gently around her waist and drew her closer.
Her hands slipped up to his arms, and she noticed the
hard muscles beneath the sleeves of his white shirt.

She was intoxicated by a consuming attraction that
overrode judgment and anger. Boldly he pulled her
into his arms, watching her as he lowered his head,
his mouth seeking hers.

Every thought whispered to stop him, to say no, to
go inside. But she couldn't move. She could only raise
her lips to meet his, feel the soft brush that made her
heart slam against her ribs. His lips pressed on hers
firmly, opening her mouth. His tongue thrust into her
mouth and she was on fire. A breathless dizziness
washed over her, and a physical hunger came as
strongly as a surging tide. His arms tightened, crushing the breath from her lungs as he leaned over her,
fitting her to his hard length. Her heart pounded with
a roaring in her ears that drowned out all sounds of
music while his kisses demolished all awareness of the
world.

Finally he paused, looking down at her with a surprised, round-eyed stare that was filled with more curiosity than ever. And she couldn't imagine he could
have one degree more shock or curiosity than she. His
kisses diminished Blake's to nothing. *Nothing!*

"Put your arms around me," Luke commanded, and
she did so willingly, feeling caught in a spell. Her
heart was pounding. She wanted him to kiss her again
and again.

Luke lowered his head, spreading his legs and moving her closer against his body. She was fire and magic,
scalding him with her kisses. Her tongue played against
his and he couldn't get enough; he couldn't get his

breath. He shook with the urgent need for more of her, for all of her. His throbbing manhood threatened a complete loss of control, and as he kissed her deeply, bending over her and molding her softness to him, he remembered to the smallest detail her naked body: the luscious flesh and full, marvelous breasts. His hand slid to her throat and he caressed the nape of her neck. When he heard her faint moan, his pulse jumped, and he fought the urge to let his fingers drift down, down to that tantalizing softness.

He released her, feeling his senses battered by a storm he barely withstood. "Catalina," he whispered, knowing no woman had ever stirred him in such a manner as she had in the past few minutes. Her eyes were wide and black, and seemed to pull him down into a spellbinding darkness of molten heat. He heard her whisper something and step out of his arms.

He wanted to ask when he could see her again, but he knew her fiery disposition. Instead he asked, "Your father is Domingo Piedra?"

"Yes. And if he catches us, he might just put a bullet through your wicked heart."

He caught her arm and spun her around. "If you keep calling me wicked, I might have to live up to my reputation."

"Let's go inside," she said breathlessly, all the force gone from her voice.

He yanked her against him, one arm banding her waist while his other hand stroked her nape so lightly. "Wicked, Catalina?"

"Please," she whispered, her eyes closing as her head tilted back. In that instant he knew she was meant to be pleasured. They stood only yards from the door. She was fearful of her parents discovering she had stepped outside. Yet the moment he began to caress her, all her wisdom and caution vanished like moonbeams at dawn.

"Please *what?*"

Her eyes were closed, her mouth raised and lips

parted. She wanted to be kissed, and he wanted with every ounce of his being to kiss her, but this wasn't the time or place. He wanted her to remember him. He brushed her lips lightly, then withdrew. Her thick black lashes raised, and he felt as if he received a blow to his midriff. Her eyes were smoldering with fires that were as blatant as a prairie blaze.

He gazed into their inky depths. "Someday you'll be mine," he whispered, the words coming without conscious thought.

She blinked as if startled, and he reached up to caress her cheek. Her dazed expression slowly transformed, but there was a different note in her voice. Her fiery defiance was gone and she sounded somber as she said, "We better go inside."

"I want to meet your parents."

She drew herself up, and the angry note returned to her voice. "Never. My heart belongs to another man, and you overstepped your bounds tonight just as you did when you spied on us at the river."

He laughed. "Catalina Piedra. All I did at the river was stretch out for a nap and get caught in the center of a tryst. How the sweet hell was I to know you two would start romancing right under my rock?"

"*Caramba!*" She flounced away from him with a twist of her hips that made her skirt swirl. It caught on the rail of a mesquite fence surrounding the hall. "*Dios!*" she snapped, yanking it.

With a mocking grin Luke bent down to unhook the wayward skirt. He waved her on with a flourish. She thrust her chin high and yanked her skirts close as she hurried into the hall, hearing a deep, soft laugh float in the air behind her.

Inside, she looked frantically for Blake. The last few moments had unnerved her in a manner she had never before experienced. She didn't want the mocking stranger's kisses to be better—impossible! His kisses couldn't be better than Blake's.

"There you are," said Blake, taking her arm. "Who was that man? Have you been outside, Catalina?"

"I've been searching for you," she said. "Please, let's dance."

"Just what I was going to ask you," Blake said with a smile, leading her to the dance floor. "And then we eat some enchiladas. I smell them every time we dance down that end of the room."

"I think you notice enchiladas more than anything else."

"No, I don't. You're the most beautiful woman here tonight."

"Mil gracias," she answered pleasantly, her good spirits returning. She danced with abandon, relishing being with Blake, watching his eyes shine as he looked at her hungrily and let his hands stray across her neck and back and waist. He was handsome beyond measure with his thick golden hair and dark brown eyes. She wished he would dance outside with her and kiss her so she could forget her indiscretion. How she had allowed Luke Danby to kiss her, she couldn't imagine, nor did she care to remember or think about him. After the music stopped, Blake led her to the enchiladas and tamales.

"Finally you'll stop dancing," said Domingo as he joined her with Sophia beside him.

"Your parents aren't here tonight?" Sophia asked Blake.

"No, ma'am. Ma didn't feel up to coming to town, and they don't go to many fandangos. Pa says it hurts his feet to dance."

"I shall have to remember that excuse next time," Domingo said with teasing joviality.

While they talked, Catalina's gaze drifted around the room. Luke Danby was nowhere in sight, and she sighed with relief. He was disturbing just by doing nothing more than being present. She took a bite of steaming tortilla, and smiled up at Blake as they politely conversed with her parents.

Luke entered the hall, half tempted to go back to the hotel, yet at the same time he wanted to stay and dance with other senoritas. Catalina was getting in his blood in a manner that bothered him. The attraction that flared between them each time they were together was stronger than any he had known before, and could only lead to frustration. She belonged to one of the better Mexican families, and he knew how protective they could be of their daughters. Most likely her parents had already decided on her husband-to-be. Even if he could court her, Luke had no intention of settling down in marriage at this point.

He stood in the darkened shadows and looked around the room. There were other beautiful young women, dark-skinned and black-eyed, but none like Catalina. In a few moments he drifted into a cluster of men who had gathered to talk. When he had the chance, he asked one named Clemente Diego to point out the Piedras to him.

His new acquaintance turned to smile at him and thump him lightly on his shoulder. "You've met Catalina."

"*Sí.*"

Clemente laughed. "Forget her, my friend. Her father will decide on her suitors, and you are merely passing through town. I saw you win at faro at El Bebedero Cantina last night. You're a gambler. Domingo Piedra is a businessman. He does not like gamblers."

"I don't plan on gambling with him. I might want to call on Catalina."

"He'll never allow it unless you own acres of land, tons of gold, or a thriving business. Do you have any of the three?"

"Show me who he is and the mother also."

"Catalina's mother will be easy to win over, but it won't do you any good. Domingo is king in his family. And half the men in this room have tried before you. More than half. Probably all the men who aren't married."

"You just introduce me. Point them out to me."

"You're a stubborn fool, but I will do this favor for my new friend. In turn, you will include me in your game tomorrow night at El Bebedero."

"Done."

"I can introduce you to a senorita who will make you forget Catalina for a few moments," he said, winking.

"Maybe in a few minutes I'll take you up on that offer too."

"That's more like it, amigo. I'll get some aguardiente and we'll go where we can really have a good time. There's Catalina's mother, see the woman with dark hair."

"Ah," Luke said, knowing instantly which woman he meant, because her mother was a beautiful woman too, but in a much less earthy way. She looked delicate, like a china doll, but she was beautiful and looked too young to have a grown daughter.

"There's her father by the table with the food. He's the tall man with his back to you. You don't cross Domingo Piedra. He is a powerful man and so is his partner, Friedrich Kreuger."

"A German and a Mexican are partners?"

"That's so odd?"

"The cold Teutonic mind and the hot-blooded Mexican? That must be an interesting arrangement."

"It's a thriving one. They're commission agents and have a freighting business. Texas doesn't have banks, so the commission agents handle money as well as goods."

"So I've heard. *Gracias*, amigo. I'll be back soon."

"If you knew this senorita, you would be ready to leave now."

"Soon." Luke drifted through the crowd, watching Catalina dance and laugh at Blake. He felt a stab of annoyance, wanting to go claim her, but he controlled the impulse. He intended to meet Domingo Piedra, and he intended to win Domingo's permission to call on his daughter.

He sauntered up as Domingo stood talking to two men. Accepting a cup of coffee from the hostess, Luke listened to the men talking, hearing the heavy German accent of one, and guessed the man might be the partner, Friedrich Kreuger. When they spoke of the sale of Texas land after the Mexican war, he turned.

"With the sale of the western land to the United States, Texas has finally paid off its debts from the battles for independence," he said, moving closer to them as they turned to look at him.

"Friedrich Kreuger," the tall blond said and extended his hand.

"Luke Danby. I'm glad to meet you."

"This is Ernesto Golcher, who owns a ranch nearby."

Luke shook hands with a short, heavyset man whose skin was burnished by days in the sun.

"This is Domingo Piedra, my partner and a rancher."

"Welcome to San Antonio," Domingo Piedra said heartily as he stepped into sight and shook Luke's hand.

Luke gazed into the black eyes, and took in at once the thick black mustache and the faint scar that ran across the bridge of Domingo's nose from ear to ear. A face burned into his memory and soul like a brand. Luke's breath caught and he felt as if the floor had suddenly dropped from his feet. He had finally found the man named Domingo.

6

ABOVE THE ROARING IN HIS EARS, LUKE COULD remember the screams of his mother and the women, the crackle of wagons burning, the terrible moments when he was hauled across the prairie behind a galloping horse. For eleven years he had hunted the man who stood shaking his hand. The last time he had looked into the same pair of black eyes, he was near death because of Dómingo's cruelty.

Luke had to curb the impulse to leap at him and fasten his hands around his throat. Momentarily hate was a roaring flame, burning away awareness of everyone except this man. Slowly reason began to return, first with a shock that Domingo didn't recognize him. Then logic reminded him that Domingo hadn't known his name and if he learned it from the women, there would be no reason to remember it. And many men bore scars, yet Luke had thought of Domingo for so many hours on end, it was amazing that his hatred didn't convey itself to Domingo. But it hadn't. He smiled and shook hands firmly with Luke.

"What line of work are you in?" Domingo asked easily. "You seem to know Texas politics."

"The land in dispute involved what's now New Mexico Territory, where I was living when the sale was completed," Luke answered, hearing his voice as if it came from far away. Agonizing memories tore at him, and he wanted to shout at Domingo that he would get revenge in full measure. Instead, he continued in a quiet tone of voice, "I'm a lawyer and I practiced law in New Mexico recently."

"A lawyer?" Friedrich said with satisfaction. "How'd you become a lawyer?"

"I've studied law. In New Mexico Territory, if you're admitted to practice in a district court, which I was, you can practice law."

As Luke chatted with him, only some of his thoughts were on the polite conversation while they took his measure and made their decisions about him. The other half of his mind was mulling over another shock. Domingo Piedra, the man he hated and had hunted for years, the man who had destroyed his family and taken his mother, was the father of Catalina. And it changed everything. It made it so much easier to know where and how to begin his task of revenge.

Instead of finding a beautiful, unattainable young woman, because he knew wealthy families of Spanish descent were protective, he found a beautiful instrument for revenge. His chivalry and feelings of respect for her vanished, because the same blood ran in her veins as in Domingo Piedra's: bad blood. No wonder she had lost her ladylike ways at the river and called him names without a qualm. Whatever smooth veneer Domingo showed to the townspeople, his family had to be exposed to his rougher side. Did they know what terrible crimes he had committed? Had they agreed out of avarice?

Luke didn't care. Rage and hatred was overpowering. Catalina was Domingo's daughter. That was enough. He gazed at her across the room. He would seduce her, because it would ruin Domingo.

While his thoughts churned with the shock of discovering Domingo, there was an added shock. Domingo Piedra was highly respected by the townspeople; he was successful. He was an honest businessman and a devoted husband. The man was a Janus, one face good and one face evil. Luke suspected few men had glimpsed both sides. But he had seen both, and the golden side of good made the dark side of evil even worse. To succeed in a double role, Domingo had to be unusually shrewd, sly, and ruthless.

"Papa, I was sent to find you. Mama said to tell you Cousin Garcia is here and you—"

Behind the group of men, Catalina hadn't seen Luke at first, but when her gaze met his, her words ended abruptly. Her black eyes widened as he winked at her. She seemed momentarily flustered, then she gave a faint toss of her head and lifted her chin.

"Catalina, come meet a new citizen of San Antonio," Domingo said easily. "Mr. Luke Danby. Mr. Danby, this is my daughter, Catalina."

His fiesty, fiery daughter had to be very important to him. Luke waited as Domingo introduced them, then Luke took her hand and bowed low. *"Buenos noches, señorita,"* he said in fluent Spanish. "I see San Antonio is a city of beautiful women." He paused to look into her eyes. "I cannot recall seeing such beauty anywhere beyond the San Antonio River," he said easily, amused at the flash of anger in her black eyes and the pink flooding her cheeks.

"Our lawyer has a flowery tongue," Domingo said, and Luke smiled at the men.

"I'm inspired," he answered lightly, making a new discovery when he caught a look of burning anger in Friedrich's eyes. Luke was only mildly surprised. Friedrich looked years older than Catalina, but sometimes that made no difference. She was the most beautiful woman present tonight. He gazed at her, seeing the faint resemblances she bore to her father. Anger boiled in him like molten lava.

"Papa, Cousin Garcia is here now. Mama sent me to tell you. I'll leave you gentlemen to your discussion," she said with a smile and was gone quickly. Luke watched her, noticing how straight her slender back was, the slight sway of her hips as she walked. The same blood as the father's ran in her veins, and he thought after this night he would always view Catalina Piedra with contempt.

Conversation resumed about the money that had been spent to rid Texas of debt from the ten-million-dollar sale of New Mexico Territory to the United States, and then changed to speculation about the coming election with Sam Houston running against the incumbent Hardin Runnels.

"Runnels is a staunch advocate of slavery, Mr. Danby, in case you're not familiar with Texas politics," Domingo said.

"Sam Houston will oppose him?"

"Yes," Friedrich answered. "And I hope this slavery question dies down. According to the assessment rolls, there are about one thousand in Bexar County, with about two hundred of those in San Antonio. Of course, I feel rather far removed from it because I don't own any. Our German paper, the *Zeltung,* had pro-abolitionist sentiments in its editorials. We have several newspapers here, as you may have already learned, the *Zeltung,* the *Herald,* the *Ledger* in particular."

"What's your business, sir?" Luke asked politely.

"We, Mr. Piedra and I, have a freighting business. We're commission agents. We buy cotton, pecans, and hides and sell them in Mexico. Our freighters haul merchandise and return with Mexican silver. Actually, we handle money for customers in the manner of a bank."

"What's the name of your company?" Luke asked, assessing Domingo, noticing his height and the broadness of his shoulders, his still slim waist. He looked as tough as cactus and he must be older than Luke had guessed. When he wasn't talking, he stood quietly listening, his wide eyes half closed with a sleepy-eyed look that didn't hide his alertness. He was still formidable and the years hadn't softened him. He reminded Luke of a hungry wolf with soft, thick fur and appealing brown eyes; hidden were fangs and powerful muscles and a predatory nature. If he wanted revenge, Luke knew he would have to take great care. Once he had survived a bullet in the chest. He wouldn't the second time.

"Our company is the Citizens of Texas Freighters," Friedrich answered. "Anytime we can serve you, we'll be happy to do so."

"Thanks. I'll remember that."

"You were a lawyer in New Mexico Territory. What town?" Domingo asked.

"Madrid. A mining town. Have you ever been to New Mexico Territory?"

"Often in the past. I used to own a ranch in the eastern part. The Santa Fe Trail crossed my land."

"Then most likely I've crossed your land."

"I haven't been there for several years now. I sold the land. I have the business and the ranch here to keep me busy."

Luke noticed a slight frown on Domingo's face. When he could, Luke turned his head, glancing casually over his shoulder while Ernesto talked about the new Giddings-Doyle overland mail run that was expected to start in July from San Antonio to California. Catalina was dancing with Blake, smiling up at him.

Luke remembered Blake's fear of Domingo that first day at the river. In a moment he realized all the men were staring politely at him. "I beg your pardon. I was taken with watching a beautiful lady."

"Do you plan to stay in San Antonio long?" Ernesto asked.

"I think I'll stay and look around awhile, see if I'd like to settle here."

"Are you familiar with the town?" Domingo asked.

"No, but I intend to be."

"About one-fifth of our population now is German," Friedrich said. "It's a thriving city with large Mexican, German, and Irish populations, plus Frenchmen, Englishmen, and native Texans. As you can see, the ladies wear fashions that would be appropriate in the Eastern cities or Europe, as well as dresses that show the Mexican heritage. It's an interesting mixture."

Within minutes two more men joined them and then the group dispersed, men moving to join their wives. Before Domingo stepped away, he offered Luke his hand again. "Glad to have met you, Mr. Danby. If we can be of any service to you, we'll welcome your business. Come in and talk to me next week."

"I'll be by Monday," Luke answered, noticing the strong grip and the callused hand. Domingo didn't spend all his time in an office.

With a deep, burning rage Luke watched him walk away. The slight swagger to his steps and his height made him easy to keep in sight. So many years. Luke ran his fingers along a scar on his jaw, remembering clearly that terrible day and wondering what had happened to his mother.

He stood on the edge of the dance floor watching Domingo and his daughter, Catalina, dancing. Spoiled, willful, and beautiful, most likely she was the pride of Domingo's heart. She would be the first step in revenge, because her seduction would goad Domingo to fury. And Luke would enjoy every moment of it. His gaze drifted brazenly over her slender body, and his blood heated when he realized that soon he would possess her.

Blake gave her a rapturous, puppy-dog look of devotion that was foolishness. Blake didn't stand a chance with his lady. Her father would never approve. Luke could imagine right now what Domingo planned for her. He would expect to marry her to the man of his choice and probably one of the wealthiest men in San Antonio. Luke would wager every cent he had on that. And in another week he guessed he would know the Piedras sufficiently well that he would be able to name the most likely prospects.

It would ruin Domingo's plans if she were deflowered.

As she danced past and saw him, she tossed her head with a disdainful air. His pulse quickened. "Soon, senorita," he said softly under his breath.

He strode outside, mounted up, and rode back to the wagon yard. His eyes had adjusted to the darkness, and he knew Ta-ne-haddle would bed down in back under the stars. He poked his friend with the toe of his boot. "Come with me. We're moving to a hotel."

"You're drunk," Ta-ne-haddle said, staring up at Luke, coming awake instantly.

"Nope. I'll tell you as we go. We can get the horses tomorrow. We've paid for the night."

Shaking out his blanket, the Indian picked up a bottle of whiskey, and fell into step beside Luke. "How was the fandango?"

"Danced my feet off," Luke answered casually. "How's your head?"

"Having its own dance. Little devils are stomping and whooping inside my skull like a regular war dance. Why are we going to a hotel?"

"I want to impress someone with my wealth, something difficult to do if I'm sleeping in a wagon yard."

"You want to impress a woman."

"No, a man."

Ta-ne-haddle stared at him as they walked along in long strides. "You found Domingo," he said flatly.

"That I did. How'd you guess?"

"You're up to something."

"That's right. Revenge."

"A knife though the shoulders would end it."

"And he would never know why or who. No, he's going to know. And I want to know what he did with my mother."

"He probably couldn't remember if he wanted to."

"You never did see my mother. I was born when she was very young, and she was a beautiful woman. He'll remember."

"All children think their mothers are beautiful."

"Would you like a bet?"

"Nope, because he'll probably lie. Who is he? A cowman?"

"No. He's a successful businessman."

Ta-ne-haddle stopped walking and Luke had to turn to look at him. "Now more than my head aches. My heart aches because this is bad medicine."

"And what was it when he hauled me across the damned prairie? Or when he took my mother? And God only knows what he did to her. You should have seen him! He's well dressed, success oozes from him. I'm sure his wife and daughter adore him, people respect him and take his advice. He's an evil, wicked monster who presents to the world a righteous man who is good. I would be willing to wager all I own that he will go marching into San Fernando Cathedral in the morning to worship."

"You'll get yourself a pack of trouble if you gun down an upstanding citizen. 'The primrose way to the everlasting bonfire.' "

"*Macbeth.* You should have stayed back East and become a professor of English. I don't intend to gun him down."

"No, I guess that isn't your style. That's why we're moving to a hotel."

"Right. I want to impress him. He has a freighting company, but he and his partner are bankers also. Often freighting companies handle money like a bank. I'm depositing my gold with them."

"A knife in his back would be safer. Why do you want his friendship?"

"He has a daughter. Only one daughter and he must adore her. She seems willful and spoiled, no doubt pampered by him."

"He's Mexican, Spanish descent, has a fine business, and has a daughter. She's innocent in this."

"So was my mother. And so was I," Luke said bitterly.

They stopped in front of one of the fine new hotels. Ta-ne-haddle paused at the door. "I'm a Kiowa. They won't let me stay here."

"Sure they will. If you're worried, tuck your braid under your shirt collar. I'll tell them you're my brother."

When they entered their room, Luke sauntered to the wide window and gazed outside, his eyes accustomed to the darkness. Ta-ne-haddle stretched his blanket on the floor and lay down.

"Don't you ever get tired of sleeping on the floor or the ground?" Luke asked while he pulled a chair close to the window, and sat down, thinking about Catalina and Domingo.

"Beds are too soft. We've traveled together many years now," Ta-ne-haddle said. "I don't want to bury you before I leave San Antonio."

"He's here, and I'm getting my revenge. I've waited all these years."

"My people are fierce warriors. I've ridden with them to wrong injustices, but there is one thing I learned from my grandfather's books: revenge can be bitter fruit."

"I want to see if I can pick up the trail of my mother."

"You torment yourself there. So many possibilities and so many of them are bad. Better you don't know."

"No, it isn't. I'll find her. And she's alive! They didn't kill the women."

"You've seen yourself what happens to those captives. As a sheriff—"

"No one here knows I was a sheriff, and I'm not announcing it to anyone."

"Since when is it bad to be a lawman?"

"I think it'll make Domingo look just a little more closely at me. I don't want him to do that."

"You're sure he won't remember who you are?

"He couldn't. Do I look the same as I did when I was seventeen? And before I got all these scars? I was dressed in my Boston suit. And he shot me, so you know he thought I died. He dismissed all thought of me from his mind years ago. If you hadn't come along, I wouldn't have survived."

"True."

"Don't you ever want to settle?" Luke asked, for a moment forgetting his problems and thinking about his friend. "You're still a young man, only thirty-four years old now. You're strong, educated."

"You try to make a white man of me."

"Your people won't take you back. Why waste your life wandering around? I've seen the ladies; you've left more than one broken heart behind."

"Dancing girls, soiled doves. My heart was given long ago to a Kiowa maiden. She has my love forever."

"That's foolishness. The world is full of beautiful, loving women. In every town you can find them."

"Listen to the wise one. You'll lose your heart someday, my friend, and then you'll sing a different song. For your sake, I hope she will love you in return and others will not come between you."

"No danger. I don't want a woman tying me down, telling me her problems. Maybe I've been with you too long. I have to keep roaming around."

"When you're in love, you won't give a whoop and a holler what I'm doing or what we've done if it's another five years from now."

"Want to bet?"

"I could use a new pony. A nice sorrel gelding with a blaze and four stockings."

"And I would like to spend one week with you, instead of me, furnishing the game when we're traveling cross-country. You shoot it, dress it, and cook it.''

"Agreed."

Luke grinned. "Better get your knife sharpened. It'll be awhile though, because this is going to take a little time. First of all, I want all the gold I own."

"Oh, damn."

"You know, you drift from Indian to white to Indian with such swiftness, I sometimes feel like I'm with two people instead of one."

"I sometimes wonder myself. Tomorrow we ride out and dig up the gold, but if you want the advice of your elder, you'll stash away a little."

"Nope. I have to impress Senor Piedra. I'm going to lure him to take the bait like dropping a fly on a hook into a pond. I'll get the big one this time, and I'll gut him for what he's done."

Ta-ne-haddle laughed softly, and Luke turned to look down at him.

"We'll break out the firewater and celebrate. I remember how you were with your fancy Eastern talk and falling over your own feet. You can shoot the legs off a fly at fifty paces now."

Luke crossed the room and picked up a bottle of whiskey to uncork it. He handed it to Ta-ne-haddle. "This will blow your brains right out of your head."

"You've waited eleven long years and you've found your man. Get him. He deserves it. I saw what he did to you."

"Now you're Indian again."

"Revenge isn't the white man's way?"

"Okay," Luke said, taking a long, burning drink, then passing the bottle to Ta-ne-haddle.

"Luke, don't underestimate him."

"I won't. Few men could carry off a double life without discovery. I'm going to get each one of his family, his business, and then I'll have my revenge."

"Don't ever call *me* a savage," Ta-ne-haddle said solemnly. "Revenge can eat at a man and change him.

If you fail, the consequences might be worse than last time.''

"I won't let that happen," Luke said grimly and accepted the bottle from Ta-ne-haddle.

Across town Domingo sat in his large bedroom and pulled off his boots as he watched Sophia pause in front of the mirror to take down her hair.

"Did you notice tonight, Catalina was the most popular woman at the party. I think Friedrich wants to court her.''

"Friedrich! He's much too old," she said, looking at him with alarm.

"He isn't an old man. He's only a few years older than I am," he said, watching the long black locks of hair fall down her back and feeling the stirring of desire. "But I think we have more to gain from a match with Ticiano Flores.''

"Ticiano is cruel. I've known him since he was a baby and he can be cruel in the extreme," she said in alarm.

"Catalina needs a strong man. With her looks, we can make a wealthy alliance. And it will unite two huge ranches.''

"I want her to be happy." In the mirror Sophia saw him watching her. Hastily she put down her brush and crossed the room to get her white nightgown out of a drawer. She glanced at him and away quickly.

"Come here, Sophia.''

"I am tired, my husband," she said stiffly. Domingo stood up angrily and crossed the room to yank the gown out of her hands and take her in his arms.

"You give me excuses too many nights. I want a woman tonight," he said harshly, the old anger rising. Of all the lusty women he had known, he had married a woman who hated his kisses and bed and everything about it. Sometimes he wondered if she hated her own body. He kissed her, consumed by need, hating the memories that still taunted him of golden-haired Hattie.

Monday morning, dressed in his good black coat and trousers, his broad-brimmed black hat squarely on his head, Luke rode to the two-story stone building on El Potrero near the Main Plaza that housed the Citizens of Texas Freighting Company. Lined up in front were the familiar Mexican *carretas* covered in white cotton stretched over hoops, with their two huge wooden wheels and four yoked oxen waiting patiently to start.

A mule was tied behind Luke's horse, saddlebags bulging with the gold Luke had saved. He usually managed to win at gambling; he had held down a high-paying job as sheriff of Madrid, making nine thousand dollars a year. Sunday he had ridden out with Ta-ne-haddle to retrieve most of their gold. They had decided when they had ridden south to bury the gold near any sizable town, then dig it up when they moved on, so there was less hazard of theft or gambling it away.

Luke had stopped in the sutler's store and ordered a new suit and linen shirt. His plans were formed and the first step was to properly impress Domingo Piedra.

He tethered his horse and mule and dismounted, unfastening the saddlebags to place them across his shoulders, then unloading more to carry over his arm. Out of the corner of his eye he was aware of people stopping to watch him, but he worked as if unaware of the attention he was drawing. As he pulled the bulging sacks of gold coins out of the saddlebags on the mule, he dropped one. It jingled, and no one in earshot could be mistaken about the contents. Luke scooped it up and glanced around. People looked away or nodded except for one man who gaped open-mouthed at him and another who disappeared into the freighting office.

Luke's impassive features masked his satisfaction. It

suited him just fine to start rumors about his wealth. He strode into the building, his spurs jingling slightly.

"Good morning, sir," a man said and held open the door.

"Mr. Danby" came a greeting. Luke thanked the man for holding the door and strode forward to shake Domingo's proffered hand.

"Fred, help the man, will you?" Domingo ordered, and the man who had held the door stepped forward, but Luke shook his head.

"Thanks, but no. I'll manage."

Domingo chuckled. "My office is this way."

Luke entered an office that still had the smell of new wood. The floor was polished to a high shine and the broad oak desk was piled with papers. With deliberation Luke dropped each sack of gold on the desk. The clinks were loud in the silence. While Domingo went around his desk, he stared at the sacks, the gleam in his eyes clearly revealed. Barely able to keep his gaze from the mound before him, Domingo motioned to Luke to sit down.

"What can we do for you, Mr. Danby?"

"I want to deposit my gold for safekeeping as long as I'm in San Antonio," Luke said, with an effort keeping his voice pleasant. The bags of gold lying between them were what prompted Domingo's courteous manner. Luke had to fight the same strong urge he'd had at the dance to grab him by the throat and wring out of him what he had done to Hattie. He hated Domingo with an all-consuming anger he had never felt toward any other man.

Domingo's grin spread, white teeth showing against his dark skin, looking as if he were the most trustworthy man on earth. "A good idea. Wells Fargo won't send out that much gold without someone riding shotgun over it. And gold is a scarce commodity in Texas. Many a man would be happy to relieve you of it."

Luke returned Domingo's smile. "I'm aware of that. Before I put my money here for deposit, I want to know if my gold will be safe here. John French and Erasmus Florian are fine bankers with a guard. And I've heard about the Groos."

"Mr. Danby, I can promise you, your money will be safe," Domingo said. "We have guards here at night; I'm here or Friedrich is here during the day. We've never had a peso stolen. Not a peso. We use the same system as the Groos: our storage is in large dry-goods boxes bound with iron loops riveted to the wood. The boxes are too cumbersome to carry away, and attempts to break them open would create such a racket our guard would hear it. Let me show you."

"I don't need to see where it'll be stored."

"Of course. I'll have a man start counting."

Luke withdrew a folded slip of paper from his pocket. "Here's the amount to the penny, but I know it has to be counted." He passed the paper to Domingo and watched as it disappeared into Domingo's pocket. "How long will it take to withdraw my money if I decide I don't want to stay in San Antonio?"

"We can have your money within the hour you ask for it. But you won't be leaving anytime soon if you'll just give our city a fair chance," he said in warm tones, unable to resist glancing at the sacks of gold as he talked. "San Antonio is a wonderful city, growing by leaps and bounds. According to the last census we have over three thousand people. We have a good climate, the San Antonio River winds through town. We have the soldiers from earlier battles and the Texas Rangers to protect us from the Indians. Immigrants are coming to town in wagon loads."

"Did you come by wagon train?"

"No. I'm Mexican. I rode up here on my own as a young boy," he said with a disarming smile while he reached out to run his hand lightly over one of the bags of coins. "You must come to dinner with us, and let me tell you all about San Antonio."

"Thank you. I'd be glad to do so."

"Fine. When is a good time? Tomorrow night?"

Luke nodded, his pulse skipping. Things were moving so quickly. "Tomorrow would be fine."

"Now if you'll sign some papers, I'll get a man in here to count this."

Luke suspected Domingo wanted to count it himself, and he was sure Domingo would read the total on the slip of paper as soon as he was out of Luke's sight.

"Excuse me a moment, Mr. Danby, and I'll get my partner." Domingo left the office and when he returned, Friedrich was with him.

Luke stood up and shook hands, returning Friedrich's greeting. Behind him was their employee, Will Sanders, who was going to count the money. "We'll show you around," Domingo said, clasping Luke on the shoulder, "while Will gets things officially done."

At Domingo's touch Luke felt a tremor go through him. There were moments when years rolled away and he could remember with stark clarity every second of that horrible day. He forced himself to smile and relax, and caught Friedrich looking at him with curiosity. They showed him the store that Friedrich still ran and the warehouse with piles of hides and crates of goods. They stepped outside a moment, and Luke watched while a man lubricated an axle of a cart with crushed prickly pear.

"We can still offer a low rate because we use the Mexican carters with their oxen which are slower," Domingo said, "but we're thinking of going to the new faster wagons and mules."

"They've had fights with men killed by cart drivers who want to keep out the new wagons," Friedrich said, studying a cart, "but that's progress."

"What are the rates?" Luke asked.

"During good weather, between one to four cents per pound, but in bad weather the figure can double or triple," Friedrich said. "We can haul up to nine thousand pounds in a cart. Most of it goes to Indianola, Lavaca, or Matagorda Bay. We receive goods from Indianola most often.''

"There's a brisk trade to Mexico, and to the forts from here because supplies for the new frontier forts come through San Antonio,'' Domingo added, turning as Will Sanders handed him a written account of Luke's gold. They returned to Domingo's office, where Luke signed papers and Domingo and Friedrich signed them, stating how much gold they would hold on deposit. Luke folded his copy and tucked it into his pocket. As he shook Domingo's hand good-bye, he felt the same loathing at the contact he had before.

From the doorway of the freighting office, Domingo watched him go. His gaze drifted from Luke to the large wooden sign of the Pioneer Freighting Company across the street in the next block. He frowned and stroked his mustache. They couldn't discover who the owner was; Friedrich said he would give the matter his full attention. The company had grown swiftly, becoming competition during the past few months. Domingo went back to his office, pausing to step into Friedrich's office and close the door.

"I was just looking at the Pioneer Company. Have you learned anything yet?''

"No, I haven't. Tandy McQuire is a tough little Irishman who knows how to be tight-lipped about his business. Whoever hired him to manage the business has his full loyalty.''

"I say you let me send some of my boys one night. They can get the truth out of Tandy, I promise you.''

Friedrich's thin nose wrinkled in distaste. "There's no need for violence. We'll learn in time. No successful businessman will keep his ownership a secret for long.''

"Why wait? I could know the truth tomorrow.''

"No! I'll find out. I told you I would.''

"Do it before a month passes or we'll do it my way.''

Friedrich's face flushed, but he nodded his head.

"Did you see how much gold Danby had?" Domingo asked, changing the subject as he thought again of the bags of gold.

"Yes. Danby's a cool, close-mouthed man. And he has the coldest green eyes I've ever seen."

"He wants something here. I can feel that," Domingo commented, thinking no one could look more cold than Friedrich, who was like a man of ice without blood in his veins. The German was money hungry, ruthlessly ambitious. Yet he wouldn't resort to violence as Domingo often did. Instead he coerced people or trapped them into agreement that soon paid off. Next to Friedrich, Luke Danby seemed like a friendly fellow, yet Domingo knew better than to take on trust what appeared on the surface.

"San Antonio has an abundance of lawyers now," Friedrich said. "He'll have to be good if he gets any business. Ah, Domingo." He paused a moment, uncertain about how to proceed. "There's another matter I want to ask you about."

"What's that?"

"I'm getting older. I've been occupied, leaving my homeland, coming to a new country, getting started. I've spent all my time working. Things are finally getting easier."

"They should be much easier," Domingo said dryly, knowing how Friedrich put money away. He suspected what Friedrich wanted.

"It's Catalina. I'd like to call on her."

Domingo had already given it thought, weighing all possibilities with care, thinking about Ticiano and the huge ranch that would someday belong to the boy.

"I have to think of my daughter's wishes in the matter. I hope this won't change our business dealings."

Friedrich shrugged. "Change is inevitable. This cannot help but affect our dealings together." He gave a frosty smile. "Perhaps it will change for the better if we become relatives."

Domingo experienced a grim sense of foreboding.

He hadn't crossed Friedrich in all their time of working together.

"As much as I would welcome that, Friedrich, Catalina has been promised to the Flores family for years now. Ticiano and Catalina had grown up expecting to wed."

Friedrich smiled and leaned back in his chair. "I own most of this company, Domingo," he said softly, and Domingo went cold. "I could buy your part out easily, and you would have to go back to ranching at a time when San Antonio seems on the brink of fantastic growth."

Domingo licked his lips, suddenly hating Friedrich. He had known from the first that Friedrich was a shark, but they had operated amicably all this time. He rubbed his jaw while his thoughts raced.

"As a wedding gift, I would be willing to give you another share of the business."

Domingo digested his offer. He wanted the union with Ticiano, but if Friedrich was angered and forced him out of the freighting business, he didn't have enough capital available to start his own business and keep the ranch. And it would be years before Ticiano would inherit. "How large a share?"

"Another tenth."

Domingo knew Friedrich could dissolve the partnership and buy him out at any time. One tenth share would put him almost on an even footing. Another year or two and he could get rid of Friedrich. Time was all he needed.

"Domingo, I can see the anger burning in your eyes. Don't ever cross me."

"You call on Catalina whenever you like," Domingo said, momentarily loathing the golden-haired German. The business was too successful to give up at this point. And it held a promise of growing rapidly.

"I invite your family and Catalina to my house next Wednesday night for dinner."

"Thank you, Friedrich," Domingo said stiffly. Few

times in his life had he been forced to do something
against his will, and it created a deep rage. "We'll
leave for the ranch on Sunday, and I'll be gone for the
next week. Before I forget, there's a shipment of goods
coming in from Indianola. We need to let the Robert-
sons know the moment it arrives, because they have
customers waiting."

"It should be in today."

"I'll tell Will to notify us as soon as it arrives,"
Domingo said, leaving, his emotions boiling.

Mulling over the morning, thinking he should get
enough capital together to buy out Friedrich and be
free of him, Domingo went to his office. That caused
a nagging disquiet, because Friedrich had a keen mind
for business and his constant attention to work left
Domingo free to run his ranch as well. He mulled over
again the problem of Tandy McQuire, thinking of the
redheaded Irishman. He would have Juan follow
Tandy. Maybe something would turn up. If it didn't,
in a week he would send four of his boys to catch
Tandy alone at night. It wouldn't take long to get the
truth about the owner of the new company. Why would
the man take such pains to hide his ownership of a
legitimate business?

A thought struck Domingo like a blow, and his head
snapped around to stare through the open door of his
office to the hallway beyond. He shook his head.
Friedrich? Impossible! But the owner of Pioneer
Freighting was going to great pains to hide his name
from someone. There had to be a reason, and Domingo decided he would find out soon.

His thoughts shifted to the gold Danby had brought.
It was the most gold they had ever received for deposit. Luke Danby. A man to be reckoned with. If
only he stayed in San Antonio and continued putting
his gold on deposit with Citizens of Texas!

Mid-morning Tuesday, Luke visited John Settle's
shop to purchase a new buggy. At a cost of five hun-

dred dollars, he selected an elegant Premium Top Carriage built by G. and D. Cook & Company. Shiny black, it was handsomely carved, trimmed in black velvet and silk, with case-hardened axles and English-steel springs. Next he went to a tailor's and was outfitted in a new suit, and then he purchased a new team for his buggy. Ta-ne-haddle had ridden south, saying he would be back within the month. He didn't like the confining space of a hotel and he had no mission in San Antonio.

That evening Luke dismounted in front of the Piedras' one-story frame house with its high roof that sloped down over a wide porch flanked by live oaks. At the carved oak door, Luke raised a brass knocker and let it fall with a clang.

A butler opened the door and announced Luke's presence. When he entered the drawing room he realized he wasn't the only guest. He was introduced to some of San Antonio's leading citizens, combining three cultures, Mexican, Anglo, and German. He noticed Friedrich Krueger wasn't present. Catalina stood by the mantel, her pale yellow dress in contrast to her dark beauty. Her black eyes swept the room and looked into Luke's, an awareness flaring that made him draw a quick breath. With a haughty lift of her chin she looked away. Her father stood nearby, and as Luke gazed at both of them, his anger flared. Always his memories were too vivid.

Sophia Piedra smiled and came forward to greet him. She was as exquisite as her daughter, only in an ethereal way. Catalina's beauty had a strong sensuality—her full red lips, honey-colored skin, flashing black eyes, and lush breasts—while Sophia's skin was almost translucent, her gaze timid, her voice soft. He wondered how she reconciled her husband's evil deeds with her conscience, but then his deeds had brought wealth.

Luke greeted Sophia in return, allowing her to take his arm and introduce him to the guests. As soon as he could move away from Domingo, he drifted over to Catalina, who stood talking to two young women.

"We meet again," he said easily. "Good evening, Miss Piedra"

"Mr. Danby. Maria and Angelina, this is Mr. Danby. Meet Miss Garcia and Miss Fitzpatrick."

He nodded to both women and politely answered their questions, conversing with them while glancing occasionally at Catalina. In seconds she said, "Excuse me, I think my mother may need my assistance."

He was left with two women who seemed to hang on his every word, but Luke found it difficult to keep his attention on their conversation. At dinner he was seated across from Catalina, and he enjoyed the chance to openly watch her. She had avoided him all evening. If he was going to get his revenge through her, he had to win her over. He tried to exert all the charm he could summon, smiling at her when he caught her attention, otherwise ignoring her as much as she had ignored him earlier.

Catalina stayed with the guests because she didn't care to have Mr. Danby engage her in conversation. As badly as she wanted to do so, it was impossible to ignore him. At last she glanced around the room and didn't see him. He must have gone home. Then Ticiano took her arm, and they walked outside on a winding stone path through beds of flowers and trees.

"This is our second time to your house for dinner within the month. Our families are becoming closer," he said, pausing beneath a tall pecan tree.

"We aren't betrothed and I haven't heard a word on the subject. You don't want to marry me, Ticiano. Your parents wouldn't force you to do something you didn't want to do."

"I've given it thought," he said gravely, startling her. "I think I would like you for my wife. You're beautiful—"

"And sharp-tongued, you said only Saturday night."

"That can be cured."

"You're too mean, Ticiano. You don't mind hurting people or animals. My father's like you."

"He's a strong man."

"And often a cruel one. And he's never made my mother happy."

"Sometimes cruelty is necessary. And perhaps she has never made him happy. Did you think of that?" He turned her to face him. "We've known each other since we were children. You'll make a good wife."

She laughed. "You sound as if you've shopped all through a marketplace and made your choice."

"The fandango was a marketplace. Mothers dress their daughters to catch the young men of the town. Deny it," he said with a mocking grin.

She shrugged. "Perhaps that is part of the festivities, but my mother was not parading me like goods for sale."

"Bah. You know she was."

"It's a beautiful night, and I won't argue with you and spoil the evening," she said, inhaling deeply.

"Catalina," he said, his voice becoming deeper as he slipped his arm around her waist.

"We'll be seen," she whispered, looking up at Ticiano in the moonlight. He was cruel, handsome, strong. For an instant she raised her face. He bent his head to kiss her, crushing her in his arms.

In seconds she wriggled out of his grasp. "Enough! You will get me in trouble with Mama."

"No, I won't. Give me another kiss."

"No, Ticiano. We'll be in trouble. We shouldn't be out here now. You go back first."

"Give me a kiss or I'll take Juanita out and kiss her. She won't refuse me."

"Go ahead," Catalina snapped. "I don't care if you kiss every woman in the room."

He laughed softly. "I think you do care. You're becoming angry."

After a moment of silence, he turned away. His

boots clicked on stones in the walk. She stared into the darkness, thinking of marriage to Ticiano. It wasn't Ticiano she loved, it was Blake. Her parents had to see that, had to honor her wishes. She heard a rustle behind her.

"To think of all those kisses you gave up to observe propriety" came a lazy drawl, and Luke Danby stepped out of the shadows.

7

"YOU! EAVESDROPPING AGAIN!"

"To the contrary. I thought you were following me."

"You know I didn't follow you." Her cheeks flamed to think he had watched Ticiano kiss her and had overheard their conversation

"Ticiano, Blake, how many men are the lucky recipients of such wonderful kisses?"

"You scoun—"

"Save the name calling. You worry one minute what you mother will think, and the next you resort to language that would make her faint. I suspect you weren't worrying about what she would think when you sent Ticiano packing."

"You are the most low-down varmint!"

"Just remember, both times I've been minding my own business when you and a man appeared where I couldn't help but overhear and see you. I'm an innocent victim of circumstances you've caused."

"You're neither innocent, nor a victim. If you had a gentlemanly bone in your body, both times you would have slipped away without making your presence known. Much less doing the things you've done!" she added hotly, still embarrassed that he had seen her naked. His bold perusal now did nothing to soothe her.

"I could hardly get down off that rock and ride away without your knowing it. You and Emilio are the only two children, aren't you?"

"Yes." His change of topic disconcerted her, and she frowned as she stared at him. She had been intensely aware of him since his arrival and couldn't understand why. His scars gave him a rugged, harsh appearance, but she had to admit, he was a commanding man with his broad shoulders and lean body, clad in a flawless black suit and snowy shirt.

"Your brother is very different from you. I wouldn't have guessed he was your brother until we were introduced."

"We're different. Emilio is quiet and bookish. He loves to read. Something Papa detests."

"Too bad Ticiano didn't have my father. My father loved to read."

"Emilio and Papa don't get along, as you probably can see. Emilio doesn't cross him," she said, wondering how they had gotten into this personal conversation about her family.

He moved a step closer. "What do you like to do, Catalina, besides ride horseback and kiss?"

"For a moment I was beginning to think you could be civil, but I was wrong. And it's Miss Piedra to you," she said in haughty tones.

"I feel as if I know you well enough to call you Catalina," he said with a disarming casualness.

Each time he said her name it made her tingle, which only added to her annoyance. "I'm going."

"You can't answer my question," he stated with an air of innocence. "Or maybe there isn't anything else you like to do besides ride and kiss."

"Of course, there are other things I enjoy. I like to swim!" The moment she said the word, she wanted to throw her hands over her mouth. She clamped her mouth shut and glared at him, her cheeks growing warm while a mocking, lopsided smile pulled one corner of his mouth up.

"I know you like to swim, and I pray that heaven favors me with an opportunity to swim with you one day. That fellow who turned down your offer to join you in a swim needs help.'' Luke placed his hand on a tree limb over her head and leaned closer, hearing the swift intake of her breath.

''I'll swim with you any day, Catalina. Even in a river full of snakes.''

''You would bring that up,'' she snapped. His nearness made her breathing erratic, and his mellow voice seemed to envelop her in warmth.

''Who brought up the subject? Who mentioned swimming first?''

''For a moment I forgot that dreadful day, thank Heaven, and then you reminded me.''

''Did I say a word?''

''You didn't have to,'' she snapped with more force than before. She felt ensnared in an invisible web she couldn't escape. She knew he was teasing her, enjoying every moment of her discomfort, studying her as if he were imagining exactly how she would look without a stitch of clothing again, yet she couldn't turn her back and walk away. He was the first person in her life who could make every encounter a challenge. She groped wildly for some other topic of conversation. ''Do you like to read?''

''Love to, almost as much as swimming. Almost. Of course—''

''Do you like to ride?''

''Yes, indeed,'' he answered pleasantly, biting back his laughter. ''I'd have a difficult time out here if I didn't like to ride. As a matter of fact, we can go for a buggy ride tomorrow afternoon.''

''No.''

''Maybe you'd rather meet me at the river and swim?''

''Of course not.''

''Good. We ride. I'll bring my buggy around tomorrow.''

''I can't ride alone with you. My parents would never approve.''

"Want to wager on it?" he asked softly, leaning closer. The disconcerting twinkle in his eye and husky note in his voice ran across her nerves like invisible fingers.

"I can't wager with you, but I'm right."

"You can wager me a walk in the garden. That's harmless."

"Very well," she said, sure of her father's reaction, wondering why she couldn't ever control the situation when Luke Danby was involved.

"Shall we go see?"

"Of course," she said, relieved to return to the other guests. He disturbed her more than she wanted to admit.

They found her father standing just inside the door, and Luke stepped up to him. "Mr. Piedra, I've been talking with your charming daughter"

Domingo turned to face him, black eyes developing a gleam of speculation.

"Part of my decision to stay in San Antonio depends on whether I can build a satisfactory house," Luke said pleasantly. "I have furniture to move from the East. I'd like permission to take Miss Piedra out tomorrow and let her show me the homes of San Antonio."

Domingo blinked and rubbed his jaw. "Catalina—"

"I'd be proud to have her company, and I assure you we'll return promptly. I don't want a tour of the town by some dusty cowhand. I want a woman's view."

Domingo glanced at Catalina. "Perhaps Sophia and Catalina could show you around."

Catalina shook her head imperceptibly, astounded that Domingo would consider the question "Mama won't want—"

"As much as I would enjoy Mrs. Piedra's comments," Luke interrupted smoothly, "two women means two opinions. I'd like Miss Piedra to accompany me. I've trusted you with my gold for an indefinite time. Surely you can trust me with your daughter for an hour or two in a buggy?''

"Of course," Domingo said in a friendly manner.

Catalina stared open-mouthed at her father. He never would have approved such a thing before. Never. He had always told her she could not be alone with a man other than a relative.

"Excellent," Luke said with maddening cheer. "Thank you. I'm looking forward to exploring this town. In the meantime, you were going to show me the garden," he said, turning to offer his arm to Catalina.

She was torn between anger that he had won the wager and amazement at her father's swift capitulation.

"You do believe a man should honor his debts, don't you, Miss Piedra? Shall we discuss the matter while we walk? Excuse us, sir."

She took his arm, and they sauntered toward the door. His eyes held a twinkle, and suddenly she had to laugh. "You are a rogue."

Her smile took his breath away. She was the most beautiful woman he had ever seen, yet he reminded himself of his purpose, revenge rising like a specter.

"I only showed an interest in this fair city."

"Bah! If you have deposited your gold with Papa, he'll do all he can to keep it as long as possible. You know full well you appealed to what he wants most in the world."

"That's usually the way to get what you want from someone," he said. "And what do you want in this world, Catalina?"

"Probably a happy family," she said somberly, startling him. "When I wagered, I misjudged you and my father."

"I'm happy you did, because now I get to take you out tomorrow," he said, watching her steadily, curious about her remark. His fingers were on her wrist and he felt her racing pulse. His gaze went to her mouth and he ached to kiss her. Soon he would kiss her until she yielded to him totally.

Her cheeks became pink, and he gave her a mocking smile, suspecting she guessed exactly what was on his mind. He didn't want her to be angry with him tomorrow.

"Have you lived in town long?"

"For several years now."

"Do you want to live here always?" he asked as they stepped onto the porch. Sounds of splashing water came from the fountain, and voices grew dimmer as they wound their way past tall, exotic banana trees.

"Yes. I love San Antonio. It's exciting."

"More than the ranch?"

"The ranch is always there. It's truly home. Where's your home, Mr. Danby?"

"Call me Luke. We know each other that well. Massachusetts is where I was born."

"You have seen so many cities and states," she said with a wistful note in her voice.

"You'd like to see them?"

"Someday I will. Blake—" Abruptly she bit off her words. "When did you leave Massachusetts and come to Texas?"

"I came West long ago and maybe someday I'll go back. Maybe someday soon. Or I may just settle and stay right here in San Antonio. Maybe it depends on you."

"On me?" She slanted him a curious look.

"We'll see what houses you can show me tomorrow. If San Antonio doesn't suit me, I'll move on. No need getting tied down in a place I don't like, is there?"

"Men are fortunate. They can do as they please."

"If you could do exactly what you want, what would you do?"

"What a thought! I can't, so I don't think about it, but I would travel and see Galveston and New Orleans and Nashville and Boston and Philadelphia and San Francisco . . . all the wonderful cities I've read about."

He was surprised, because since he left Boston, he had met few women who could name that many cities, much less want to visit all of them. They had crossed the patio and stepped through a gate to a garden. Moonlight bathed the leaves with a silvery tint, and gave a lustrous glow to her skin. She was acutely aware of Luke, disturbed by him more than any man she had ever known. He didn't react like other men she knew. He didn't have Blake's uncertainty or Ticiano's forcefulness, yet he accomplished what he wanted without people being fully aware of what he was doing.

"I wouldn't think you'd like San Antonio after living in Boston."

"I don't know yet. I just got to town." He pulled her down onto a bench in the garden. "Sit down here. When it's important, I try to get what I want. Will you marry Ticiano or Friedrich?"

"Friedrich is older than my father," she answered with amusement.

"He wants you," Luke said, touching her hair with the slightest touch, but she felt it.

"That's ridiculous. I'm not interested in Friedrich. And I'm not marrying Ticiano."

"Why not?" he asked, leaning a fraction closer. Her heart thudded, the beat seeming to slow and pound in her ears. He was going to kiss her. Her lips parted, and she gazed up at him. His mouth was well shaped, a slightly full lower lip, a sensuous lip. She realized he had asked her a question and was waiting for an answer.

"You asked me something," she whispered.

"I asked why you're not marrying Ticiano," he repeated, and again she thought she detected a note of amusement. She realized she was leaning toward him, acting daft, smitten by his charms. She straightened up and took a deep breath.

"I don't love Ticiano," she snapped.

"I asked a simple question. Hold your fiery temper."

Disturbed, she gazed at him and felt that same mesmerizing pull until his words registered. She laughed and leaned away. "Me? I don't have a fiery temper."

"You're like red peppers when you're angry," he answered with a smile, touching her hair again. He was surprised she had laughed, and he was intrigued with her. He suspected she wanted to be kissed, because she seemed sensual even in her innocence. He let his fingers follow the curve of her ear and trail down her throat.

He ached to kiss her, but he forced himself to wait, to tantalize her. He would take delight in destroying her because she was Domingo's daughter, as much a part of her father as a branch is part of a tree. He would destroy Domingo bit by bit. One by one, his family, his business.

He continued to talk to her, touching her lightly on her arm, her hand, her throat, knowing that in spite of her aloofness, she was aware of each touch. They were interrupted by Sophia searching for Catalina. Luke took her arm and they joined the others. He wasn't alone with her again that night.

The next day he called before noon. Helping her into his new buggy, he climbed up on the seat beside her. As they drove away from the house, he made a thorough assessment of her: her blue gingham carriage dress with white lace at the throat and cuffs.

Aware of his attention Catalina's gaze ran over the matched pair of horses, the shiny new buggy, and she felt a ripple of excitement. As the horses began to trot, she directed him. "If you want to see some of the finest houses, turn here at the corner."

When he drove straight past the corner, she turned in the seat to look at him with raised brows. "You didn't turn."

"Did you think I actually wanted to spend an afternoon with you looking at houses?"

8

DISCONCERTED, SHE STARED AT HIM. "YES."

"That isn't what I intend. I brought a picnic basket. It's a beautiful day, and I plan to enjoy it. I can look at houses anytime.

'Papa will be livid," she said slowly, undecided whether she should be angry with Luke or not. As much as she hated to admit it, his plans sounded more fun than driving along dusty streets on a nice afternoon and looking at houses she had seen all her life. "And I think I should be too."

He winked at her. "Admit it, Catalina. I can see it in your eyes. You'd rather take a picnic out by the river."

With a laugh she nodded. "It only confirms my feelings. You're a rogue. This isn't what you carefully explained to Papa you planned to do."

"Hardly. Do you think he would have agreed to letting me take you off alone for a picnic by the river?"

"You know your answer. It's a beautiful day for a picnic."

"Tell me about your family. Are your parents from San Antonio?"

"My mother's family is. My grandparents came from Spain and settled here a long time ago. They're no longer living. My grandfather was killed fighting for Texas's freedom."

"And your father?" Luke asked, turning the horses to a narrow lane that wound down to the river.

"He's Mexican. He lived in Mexico City. Actually,

he was an orphan and I think he was on his own from an early age. He won't talk about his past. He met my mother in San Antonio. He saw her first at the cathedral and wanted to know who she was." She shrugged. "That's how they came to know each other."

"Your father said he used to travel in the territory that's now New Mexico."

"Yes. We had land there, but he sold it to go into business with Mr. Krueger."

Luke reined in the horses and jumped down. His hands closed on her waist and lifted her easily, his gaze locked on hers as firmly as his hands. When she looked into his cool green eyes that were impossible to read, Catalina's heart skipped.

"What's running through your mind?" he asked. "You have curiosity in your dark eyes?"

"Do you ever lose your temper?"

Releasing her, he laughed as he lifted a blanket and a basket out of the back of the buggy. He looked down into her black eyes, and for a moment he thought of the smoldering fury he had carried for eleven long years. "I've been known to lose my temper on occasion," he answered dryly.

As he took her arm, she glanced at him spectulatively. "I find that difficult to imagine," she said, wondering what had happened to him to cause so many scars.

"Let's leave the blanket here," he said, shaking the brown woolen blanket on the ground, "and walk down to the water's edge. The river is shallow here and we can wade."

She didn't protest as he expected she would. Instead she eagerly slipped off her boots, wearing her stockings as she waded into the water. They splashed, and it was impossible to keep images of her naked out of his mind. Finally he picked her up and strode out of the water.

"Mr. Danby, put me do—"

"It's Luke, and your feet are wet. I'll carry you to the blanket. Let me hear you say my name."

"Luke," she said with a shiver of pleasure. "But I can't call you Luke in town where people will be with us. You know it isn't proper."

"Nonsense. Say it again," he ordered, pausing near the blanket and looking at her in his arms. Her slender arm was wrapped around his neck, and her enticing fragrance made him want to continue holding her close.

"Luke," she whispered.

He swung her feet down and kissed her cheek lightly. "That's better," he said while she gazed at him with a smoldering look that set his pulse racing. He longed to crush her softness against him, to kiss her without stopping, but he made himself wait. He spread the blanket and unpacked the lunch, taking out grapes and oranges he had found in the market, claret wine from Smith & Burns, crackers, the specialty of Schelhegen & Schmit's bakery, bread still warm that he'd had made at the hotel kitchen. She ate little of the thin, cold slices of beef or the thick yellow cheese. They talked of a wide variety of subjects. While she told him about the Christmases of her childhood, he reached out to take a pin out of her hair. For a moment she didn't seem to realize what he was doing. Her lashes came down and her voice became breathless.

"Grandfather had firecrackers and let Emilio set off one," she paused, suddenly catching his wrist. "You mustn't take my hair down. You don't observe any rules of propriety, do you, Mr.—Luke?"

"Of course I do," he answered, pulling her wrist up and kissing it lightly. Her hand was slender, her wrist tiny and delicate. He turned her hand over and put his finger on her wrist, where he could feel her swiftly beating pulse. "Your pulse races."

"You're causing it," she whispered. He had set her on fire last night with his continual light touches; today only added to her mounting desire. She was all but quivering with the longing he was creating. She leaned closer to him. He sat beside her, his knees drawn up. As his fingers traced the line of her jaw, she looked at his mouth that was so tantalizingly near.

"Luke—"

"Yes?" he whispered, his hands moving methodically to take the pins out of her hair, watching the midnight locks tumble down. His pulse pounded now like an ocean surf. He slipped his arm around her waist and pulled her to him. Her lashes dropped, hiding her eyes while her hands slipped up his arms. She tilted her face up to his, and a faint moan came from her open lips.

He leaned forward the last few inches, brushing his mouth over hers. Her lips were warm, her breath sweet, her mouth incredibly soft. His arm tightened, his lips coming down firmly to part hers and to thrust his tongue into her mouth.

Passion seemed to explode deep within her. His kiss made her thoughts spin away into nothing. Her arms went around his neck and she was unaware that he moved her closer, leaning over her, cradling her head against his shoulder while he kissed her. Her heart beat in hammer blows as his tongue thrust deeply, playing over hers with searing touches.

Her raven hair tumbled over his shoulder and arm. Luke's hand caressed her throat, sliding down over her full breasts. She shivered with delight. She should make him stop; she didn't want him to ever stop! No man had dared touch her breasts. Blake would not, sometimes kissing her as if he were afraid of her. Luke touched, caressed, and drove her to a frenzy that she hadn't experienced before. He shifted, lowering her gently to the blanket while he stretched beside her, pulling her against his full length. She felt his throbbing maleness press against her thigh and her blood heated. She knew she should stop him, should have stopped him minutes ago, but her will was gone, melted away in an inferno he built with his hands and lips and hard body.

His hand followed the curve of her hip, then back to her breast. Through the gingham he could feel the hard bud as his hand drifted over her lush curves. His thumb brushed her nipple, drawing invisible circles. Catalina moaned, moving closer, tightening her arms around his neck, her hips thrusting against him. Suddenly she tore herself from his arms and sat up.

"No!" she exclaimed in a hoarse whisper, her breast heaving as she inhaled rapidly.

He ran his fingers across her ribs just below her breast. "Come here," he coaxed in a husky voice.

She scrambled to her feet. "We better go home."

He gave her a lazy smile, and his gaze drifted down languorously, as if he were mentally peeling away every stitch of clothing. He wanted her. She was a witch, Domingo's flesh and blood. If Luke destroyed her, he would destroy part of Domingo. Her black eyes widened, her breath came sharply while Luke unfolded his long legs and stood up.

"No," she whispered, backing up a step.

"Come here, Catalina," he coaxed, thinking he would soon have part of his revenge.

She fled and climbed into the buggy, turning to look at him. "I want to go home."

He debated whether to pull her out of the wagon and storm her protests, or to accept that now was not the time. Unless he rushed her too swiftly, sooner or later she would yield. Her young, healthy body had almost caused her to capitulate in the past few minutes. She liked to be kissed and touched. He gathered up the blanket and placed it in the wagon, sauntering back to her. Her cloud of black hair spilled across her shoulders. Her breathing was still ragged, her full breasts straining against her bodice. Her lips were red from his kisses. Disheveled, with stormy fire in her eyes, she was more beautiful than ever, and he was tempted to pull her down out of the wagon. He wanted revenge and her seduction was important.

Without a word he walked around to climb up beside her. "Here are the pins for your hair."

She accepted them, feeling the brush of his hand on hers. Burning with desire, she was in a turmoil of indecision. Half of her wanted Luke to continue what he had started and never stop. The other half of her was frightened of the reaction she had had to him. His kisses were better than Blake's, far better than Ticiano's. His caresses drove all reason from her mind, made her wanton. Yet she knew he wasn't in love with her, wasn't susceptible to her charms as Blake was. And she suspected she couldn't get the best of him as she often did in struggles with Ticiano. Ticiano was cruel, but he didn't frighten her. Luke Danby, for all his gentleness, had a streak of iron. He did frighten her, because she couldn't understand him. She felt powerless around him, as if she had to yield willingly to his wishes. And that frightened her, because she knew he wasn't in love with her.

She cast him oblique glances while she put up her hair. She had never known another man like him. Even now, if he took her in his arms to kiss her, she wouldn't be able to refuse him.

"We'll do this again soon. I'll ask your father."

"No," she exclaimed vehemently, and the mocking amusement returned to his features.

"Why such a violent protest?"

She drew a deep breath, causing her breasts to strain against her bodice. His gaze lowered, lingering, making her feel as if he were caressing her. "We shouldn't have kissed like that," she whispered.

"Why not?" he asked with a sardonic drawl that brought a prick of anger.

"You're too forward. You know that wasn't proper."

"Since when did you worry about what's proper?"

"Since I'm with you!"

"Don't try to salvage your conscience by getting

angry with me. You like kissing and you wanted to kiss.''

The conversation was taking a turn that was more disturbing than ever. Luke Danby was impossible to control or understand or disturb. He was always cool and aloof unless he was passionate. That added to her ire, because she could seldom control her emotions. "Even if it's so, it's ungentlemanly of you to say so.''

He emitted a deep, throaty chuckle. "I'm just making an observation of the way you are. If you don't want to hear about it, don't bring up the subject. How about next Wednesday afternoon?''

"No.''

"Are you afraid of me?''

"Good heavens, no,'' she lied, unable to look him in the eye.

"Then Wednesday it is. I'll ask your father when I stop by his office in the morning.''

"No, I don't want to go out with you on Wednesday or any other time.''

He pulled on the reins and stopped the team, and her pulse began to drum violently. She scooted away from him another inch.

"Why don't you want to go out with me?'' he asked, turning to her, placing his hands on her shoulders. "Haven't you had fun today?''

Unable to answer, she stared at him. She was aware of his every touch: his hands holding her shoulders, his knee lightly pressing hers. As he looked at her lips, she wondered if he might kiss her again, and the thought unraveled the last threads of logic in her mind. He looked into her eyes, and his voice lowered while he repeated his question.

"Haven't you had fun today?''

"Yes,'' she whispered.

"You're not afraid of me, are you?''

She was unable to answer him. She was afraid because he was impossible to maneuver or outguess, and his kisses melted her resistance.

He smiled, making creases deepen in his cheeks, and her heart fluttered because his enticing smile softened his harsh features. "Then we'll go out again Wednesday."

She nodded. Satisfied, he turned to pick up the reins and the buggy began to roll again. She was constantly astounded how he could get others to follow his wishes effortlessly. As they rode, she became more composed.

"You're still a scoundrel. You get your wishes without any effort, you don't act in a gentlemanly manner, you're blunt, and I'm not sure I really want to go out with you again."

"We've already settled that. We go out Wednesday and when we do, we can discuss my gentlemanly manners if you'd like. But when I came to the West, I found gentlemanly manners to be of little use."

"It would help where women are concerned." Suddenly she had to laugh at herself as much as at him. "You're a scoundrel and don't try to deny it, but I did have fun. And I shouldn't admit it to you, but sometimes trying to be a lady is stifling."

"I like to see you smile," he coaxed in a honeyed voice she couldn't resist. "That's more like it. A smile that could win battles."

She couldn't resist his coaxing. He was easy to talk to and as they rode back to town, she asked about his travels. With a squeeze of her hand, he said good-bye at her door, and she watched him as he climbed back into his buggy and drove away. Alone in her room, she thought about the afternoon, and her heart began to pound when she remembered Luke's kisses. Wednesday afternoon.

That night when her father came home, he announced they would leave the next morning to go to the ranch for the rest of the week. They had had cattle stolen by Comanches.

At the ranch on Friday, Blake came to call for an hour and when he left, she promised to meet him at their place by the river. Two hours later she climbed off her horse to run to him. He stood by a cottonwood, his brow furrowed in a frown. Sunlight made his hair look golden; he was broad-shouldered, deeply tanned from days in the sun. She ran to him and he caught her in his arms.

"Hey!" One look into her eyes and his smile faded instantly. As he bent his head to kiss her, she clung to him, annoyed by the memory of Luke Danby's kiss. She squeezed her eyes shut and kissed Blake wildly in return. She didn't want Luke's kisses to be more exciting. She didn't want to think of Luke when she was with Blake.

Blake released her abruptly and she saw his frown. "What's wrong?" she asked, suddenly getting a cold feeling.

"Your pa. He wants to buy mine out. Pa doesn't want to sell, but he thinks your pa will force him to sell."

"He can't force him to sell," she said firmly, thinking Blake was too much of a worrier.

"It makes me look bad."

"How on earth could it?" she asked, puzzled by his statement.

"Because . . ." He paused and took a deep breath. His cheeks reddened, and Catalina's curiosity was heightened. "I want to marry you. If I ask you now, your pa will say it's only because I want to make sure—"

She squealed and threw her arms around his neck to kiss him soundly. Finally he pushed her away.

"We have to have your pa's permission," he said soberly.

"He'll give it. He'll have to. If he doesn't, we'll run away."

"We can't run away." Blake swore and turned away, running his fingers through his hair distractedly. "I have to stick around to help Pa." He faced her with his hands hooked in his belt. "We have to have your pa's permission."

"He'll give it," she said, somber now, feeling a cold chill of dread. "He'll have to give it."

"I'll come calling tonight and ask."

They both knew the risks and Domingo's feelings. Blake reached for her and she flung herself into his arms. He kissed her passionately, his mouth hard on hers, yet when he finally released her, she stared up at him with a tiny, traitorous flame of dissatisfaction. She wanted him to make her melt as Luke Danby had, to touch her and set her aflame, make her quiver with longing. Instead he faced her solemnly, telling her what time he would be at her house, and then he mounted his horse and rode away. She stared at the trees for a long moment, then she kicked a rock, swearing to herself.

"Damn you, Luke Danby."

He had no right to interfere, with his wild kisses. When she married, Blake's kisses and caresses would mean more to her than Luke Danby's. She would completely forget that afternoon with Luke. And then she forgot everything except the problem at hand. She had few illusions about her father. He was a harsh man who was never interested in others, only in gain for himself. She mounted up and turned for home.

Blake came to call that night and asked to talk to Domingo. He was dressed in his Sunday best, a black broadcloth suit. His hair was washed and combed back, slick and looking darker. Without his hat he had a pale band of skin across his forehead. Catalina thought he looked so nervous he might bolt for the door, but her father politely motioned him to the library and closed the door.

"He wants to marry you," Sophia said.

"Yes. I love him and I want to marry him."

Sophia turned to look at her daughter, who seemed so young and so full of vitality. She couldn't remember what it was like; her own girlhood seemed so long, long ago. "Come with me, Catalina," she said softly and led the way to the front parlor, which was directly across the hall from the library. She closed the doors and faced Catalina, who had a wary look in her stormy expression.

"Catalina, you're headstrong like your father. Emilio is the gentle child. But in this, as in so many things, you will have to abide by your father's wishes. Don't do something foolish that will hurt Blake, because it is Blake who'll get hurt, not you. Your father will show no mercy to Blake if you both cross him."

"Papa wouldn't hurt Blake. Not if he's the man I love."

Sophia felt sad when she thought of how much Catalina had to learn about the evil side of life. Children were sheltered from so many heartaches. "Your father will do whatever he wants, Catalina. You'll have no more choice in the matter than I did. Your father won my mother over. She had lost her husband in a battle, and there were four girls in the family. She was happy to marry me to him. I had only met him once when we were married."

Catalina only half listened to history she had heard before. Sophia's first statement echoed in her mind, wiping out all else: *Your father will do whatever he wants. It would be Domingo, not Catalina and Blake who had to be pleased.*

She glanced at the closed doors. "Can we open the doors so we'll know when they're through talking?"

"You'll know," Sophia said sadly. She had heard Domingo talk about Blake. He would never allow Catalina to marry the boy. She opened the doors and went to her room, wishing she could turn the key and lock the door, to shut out the commotion that would follow. Catalina was as volatile as Domingo. Raising her voice to shut out all other sounds, Sophia knelt to pray before the altar in her room.

Catalina paced frantically. Suddenly the door across the hall was flung open, and Blake strode angrily toward the front door. His cheeks were red and his jaw set. Domingo stepped to the doorway to watch him with a brooding speculation.

"Blake!" Catalina cried, horrified that he would leave without talking to her, terrified of the outcome of his talk. She blocked his path, holding his arm. "What happened?"

"You ask him, Catalina."

She threw her arms around him. "I want to marry you! I will marry you!"

Blake pushed her away, and she felt as if something were breaking inside her. Hot tears sprang to her eyes. "No," she cried.

"Get out of my way. I have to leave your house and your property. We won't see each other again."

"No!" The protest was almost a scream. He pushed her aside and strode out of sight. The butler closed the door quickly behind him. She turned on Domingo, who faced her calmly.

9

"YOU CAN'T DO THIS!" SHE YELLED, RUSHING TO-
ward her father. Like a bolt of lightning his hand
raised, and struck her.

The blow sent her toppling backward and she
crashed into the wall. Her ears rang, her skin stung
from the blow. Stunned, she stared at him. His black
eyes flashed as he jerked his head. "Come in here,
Catalina."

She followed him into the room, and he slammed
the door. "You can't marry Blake Corning."

"I love him."

"You're young. You don't know anything about men.
You'll marry someone of your own station or better.
Someone who can care for you and add to our riches,
not take from them. I intend to buy out the Cornings
before winter. The boy is weak, spineless. He is not
the man for you."

"He isn't weak. He's sweet and good and I'll—"

Domingo hit her again, this time sending her
sprawling to the floor. Stunned, she shook her head.
But she couldn't control her tears.

"You'll marry the man of my choice. Do you understand, Catalina?" he asked harshly.

She gazed up at him, anger beginning to surface.
"And I'll have a marriage like yours. Mama is afraid
of you—"

"Enough!" he shouted, yanking her to her feet cruelly. As he strode across the room, she shook with
rage. Her mouth hurt where he had hit her, but all she

could think about was that she couldn't marry the man she loved.

"I'll run away."

"And I'll bring you back," he shouted, returning with a whip in his hand. She shrieked and ran for the door as a blow struck across her shoulders. With a cry she doubled over to protect herself as another lash came down in a stinging blow across her back. Again he struck her, and fury exploded in her. She turned to grasp the end of the whip, winding her hands around it and tugging. With a yank he jerked her to him and grasped her upper arms painfully.

"Don't defy me, or I'll beat you senseless. I'll have my orders obeyed. Do you understand?"

She broke free and ran from the room, ignoring his shout at her. She raced to her room and shut the door, wishing she had a key so she could lock herself away from him. Her back stung from the blows and tears cascaded down her cheeks as she stormed up and down the room, trying to think what she could do.

Domingo swore and threw down the whip. He strode down the hall, staring at her door impatiently. His emotions seethed. Anger changed to desire as his gaze shifted to Sophia's door, and suddenly he headed to her room. He kept a woman, Isadora Williams, and he could go to her house, but he didn't want to tonight. His breath came in short gasps as he flung open Sophia's door.

She twisted to look over her shoulder at him, and frowned. Why had he married a pale woman who hated to be touched? At the time he had wanted her dowry and her family's respectability, but he wished now he had waited. He closed the door and began to pull off his shirt.

She drew a deep breath and her frown deepened. "I'm praying, Domingo."

"Do you pray all day and into the night, Sophia? You should pray that you have more desire for your

husband. That you won't lie in bed like cold marble.
Do you know what some women are like?''

She stood up and backed away from him. "You hit
her, didn't you?''

He didn't answer. "Come here, Sophia. Some
women love to be touched, to be kissed. Let's see if
somewhere deep down you have a spark.'' He pulled
her into his arms to kiss her, blanking the past stormy
minutes out of mind.

Early the next morning they went back to San Antonio. Catalina spent a miserable week. She couldn't
run away, because she was afraid Domingo would kill
Blake. She couldn't talk to Blake until they went back
to the ranch. In the meantime, the welts and bruises
on her face faded while she stayed shut in the house.
On Monday of the next week, as they were eating dinner, Domingo announced that Luke Danby would call
on Wednesday for Catalina to show him around San
Antonio again.

Relieved to get out of the house, Catalina nodded in
agreement. In the turmoil of her worries about Blake,
she had forgotten Luke Danby. Later that night an idea
came to her that made her quiver with anticipation:
she would get Luke Danby to contact Blake and tell
him to come to town to meet her, and then the next
time she went out with Luke, he could take her to meet
Blake. Frowning, she wondered if she could trust Luke
Danby to keep her secret from her father. He'd kept
his own secret that he hadn't taken her to look at
houses the afternoon she had spent with him. Smiling,
she began to pace up and down with eagerness. She
would wear her best carriage dress of blue foulard with
narrow flounces of white lace at the hem, and try to
look her prettiest. She might have to give a few kisses
to convince him to do what she wanted. At the thought
she paused, remembering too clearly what it had been
like to be kissed by Luke. She tossed her head, trying
to get her thoughts back to Blake.

On Wednesday, he was waiting in the hallway watching her approach. Her worries momentarily vanished under Luke's intense scrutiny as she became aware of herself as a woman. In spite of his scars, he looked handsome in a white shirt and black coat and trousers. His black hat was pushed to the back of his head, revealing his thick brown hair above his forehead. Eagerness made her smile. Luke could help her see Blake. Luke's smile softened his harsh features, causing crinkles at the corners of his eyes and creases to frame his mouth.

"Good afternoon. I'm looking forward to a ride with a pretty woman," he said softly.

"Thank you. I'm looking forward to this afternoon too," she said, pausing in front of a hall mirror to put on her white chip bonnet and tie the blue ribbons beneath her chin. In the reflection in the mirror, Luke watched her, his green eyes appreciative and disturbing. He ushered her ahead as a butler held open the door. Luke helped her into his carriage. It was a glorious April day with shrubs in bloom, a clear, blue sky overhead, and a crispness in the air.

"Ready for another picnic?" he asked.

"Yes, I am. If my father knew what you're doing, he would be furious." she said lightly, feeling an undercurrent of excitement.

"He won't know. I thought you'd never get back from the ranch."

"I didn't expect to go, but Papa insisted, and so off we went. Have you looked around town?" she asked, wondering what he would do.

"Yep, I have and I like what I've seen."

"You should let me show you around and tell you about San Antonio, There are missions near here that were built over a hundred years ago. The Spanish intended to have a way station here between the east Texas missions and New Spain, or Mexico." She wore a narrow silver bracelet and he touched it lightly, his fingers brushing her arm. She tried to concentrate on what she was saying, to forget his touch. ''In the early eighteenth century, a Franciscan friar, Father Antonio Olivares, along with the new governor of the province of Texas, Martin de Alarcon, founded the mission San Antonio de Vallero, the Alamo. This was a religious and military outpost, and later the Spanish thought there should be families here, so sixteen families came from the Canary Islands and they built to the west, where the two large plazas are now.''

''I think I'll build a house and settle here. There are attractions in San Antonio I don't want to leave.''

His voice had lowered and he watched her as he spoke. He was flirting, and she didn't want to displease him, because it was important to get him to cooperate in her plans. And in spite of her preoccupation over Blake, Luke Danby's deep voice touched nerves like a wind playing over her. She smiled at him and answered softly, ''I'm glad you're staying. What kind of work will you do?''

''As soon as I can, I'll practice law. To be a lawyer in Texas, a man has to live in the state six months, he has to be over twenty-one, which I am, and he has to get a certificate from the county court showing he has a good reputation for moral character and honorable deportment.''

She laughed. ''And here you are taking me on a picnic while Papa thinks we're on business.''

Luke grinned at her. ''That's my good sense, not my moral character showing. It would be sinfully wicked to spend the afternoon kicking up dust instead of going to the woods to picnic.''

''So when you've qualified with your good moral character, what happens?'' she asked, enjoying the teasing sparkle in his eyes.

When I have those three things, I have to make application to a district court, or the Texas Supreme Court if I ever want to practice in the Supreme Court.''

''That's all there is to it?'' she asked, noticing his long fingers and strong wrists as he held the reins.

"Not exactly. If a judge is satisfied, he authorizes the new attorney to practice law in the district court and inferior courts until the next term of court. During the next term, three lawyers are appointed to examine the new attorney. If they're satisfied, they report to the judge, and then a new lawyer can practice in any district and inferior court in the state. At present, San Antonio has an abundance of lawyers, but I want to join them."

"You don't mind competition?"

He shook his head. "That's part of all business."

"You were a lawyer in Madrid?"

"Yes, among other things."

"What other things?"

"I was a sheriff," Luke answered, knowing that some people in town already knew about his past because they had traveled through New Mexico Territory.

Luke watched her as they rode away from town, following the trail that wound alongside the river. Catalina was friendlier than he had ever seen her. He wondered if his kisses had won her over so quickly and easily, but doubted it. She flirted with him, was charming to him, and as they waded in the river again, he decided she wanted something from him. She was too cooperative, too charming. Once he alluded to their first meeting, and for just an instant her black eyes flashed. Then she smiled and changed the subject, moving away from him with her back to him.

Once he guessed she wanted something from him, he had to hide his amusement at her efforts to please him. She was too feisty to easily become so adoring and acquiescent. They ate another picnic the hotel had packed, this time with some special treats; sugar cookies, thin slices of ham on fresh bread, wine, and grapes. He was thankful there was an abundance of foods in San Antonio. It was a cosmopolitan place with stores that carried merchandise unavailable anywhere else in Texas except Galveston.

He stretched out on the blanket with his hands behind his head. His hat and coat had been tossed aside. She sat with her back to him, idly telling him about an army experiment using camels. Luke reached up and began to withdraw the pins from her hair again.

She twisted around to smile down at him. "The last time you did that, I went home looking as if I'd been caught in a windstorm."

He suspected if he pulled her down to kiss her, she wouldn't protest. She wanted something, he was as certain of it as if she had come right out and asked him. But what was it? Deciding it was time to find out, he yanked her down to him.

It caught her off balance, and she flung out her hands against his chest, her breasts pressing against him.

"Luke!"

He silenced her words, pulling her head down so he could kiss her. After the first moment of shock she responded, her tongue playing against his with a flaming abandon that made his body react. While he kissed her, he rolled her over on her back, wrapping one arm around her, leaning over her to kiss her passionately. His other hand drifted down the bodice of her dress, touching her full breasts, feeling her nipples push against the soft material. He unfastened the buttons from her throat until his hand could slip beneath. He stroked downward, his hand seeking the soft fullness of her breast.

"Luke!" She gasped his name, sat up, and scooted away an inch, fastening her dress quickly. He caught her hands, and shoved aside the fabric still gaping open to kiss her flesh just below her collarbone.

"You mustn't!"

"I think you like to be kissed," he drawled quietly, leaning forward to kiss her throat, "almost better than anything else."

Catalina felt bombarded by a force she couldn't combat. Everything had been going so well, but she couldn't control him when he started to shower kisses and caresses on her.

"You made me think this is just what you wanted," he murmured, trailing kisses from her ear and throat to her mouth.

He set her on fire with his burning kisses, and she couldn't resist parting her lips, letting him kiss her again. Finally she pushed him away while she tried to get her breath. He was the most disturbing man. He always jumbled her thoughts and intentions.

"I want you to do something for me." She hadn't intended to blurt it out like that. She was going to work up to it subtly, but Luke's kisses made wisdom and flattery vanish. His brows arched, and she thought she detected a sardonic gleam in his eyes.

"What would you like me to do?" he asked, stroking her shoulder, her nape, sitting so close his hip pressed against hers as he faced her. His long legs were stretched out beside her and she didn't have any place to put her right hand except in her lap. She was acutely conscious of his nearness and her nervousness increased. The conversation wasn't going as she had rehearsed a dozen times in her room.

"I'm having trouble," she said, watching him. "Blake Corning asked to marry me. Papa refused him and told him never to come back. The next morning we had to come back to town. There's no way I can see Blake. Papa won't let me go to the ranch without him, and frankly, I don't think he'll go for a long time. If you would tell Blake to come to town and meet me, you could take me to see him. He could come out here and you could bring me and leave us alone and—"

Luke threw back his head and laughed. "So that's why you've been like honey all afternoon."

She blushed, trying to control her temper, once again thinking Luke Danby was an infuriating man. "I've had a lovely time today, but since you and I have become such close friends, I thought you would do this for me," she said sweetly.

"Why in blue blazes would I bring another man to see you? If Blake Corning wants to see you alone, let him figure out his own way to do so."

"Does this mean you're refusing to help me?"

He leaned close, his twinkling eyes level with hers. "Does this mean you're going to stop being sweet and charming?"

"Indeed, it does," she snapped, her anger rushing in full force. "I should have known. All you want is to kiss me."

"Oh, no," he drawled, running his finger down her arm. "I want more than to kiss you."

Shocked that he would dare tell her such a thing, she looked into his unfathomable green eyes. She was caught in the heated look she met. He wanted more than kisses; his desire showed in his hungry gaze and it made her burn like fire. He pulled her to him. She pushed, struggling, twisting her face so he couldn't kiss her.

He kissed her throat, holding her easily with one hand. Their silent struggle intensified as she wriggled and pushed uselessly against his chest, but oh, how tantalizing he was! His arm was a band of steel around her waist, holding her while his fingers worked at her bodice.

"No! You scoundrel! I should have known bet—"

He kissed her, catching her mouth with his, his tongue probing deeply while his hand stroked her breast. Sensations came like storming waves, battering her anger and her resistance. Her struggles ceased and his fingers unfastened more buttons. His hand slipped beneath her bodice to cup her breast. His thumb flicked over her nipple, and she thought she would faint from the feelings he stirred. Intoxicated by the new sensations, her arm slipped around his neck and she forgot everything else. Her mind ceased to function as she yielded to Luke.

Luke felt her become pliant in his arms and then her hips began to move in an age-old rhythm. He cupped her full breast, playing with her, caressing her, listening to her soft moans while he grew hard with desire, wanting to shove her down and take her now. And he thought she would let him. He opened his eyes a fraction as he kissed her, wanting to watch her.

Her eyes were closed, and perspiration beaded her brow. Soft moans came from her while she clung to him more tightly than before. He lowered her to the blanket, kissing and stroking her as he finished unbuttoning her dress. He pulled her up to peel it away.

Catalina felt cool air rush across her shoulders and gasped, twisting out of his reach. Her dress fell to her waist and Luke looked at her full breasts that showed plainly through her dainty lace chemise. She wanted to fling her hands over herself, to yank her clothing back on, but the expression in his features held her. Never had she seen a man look at her with such blatant desire. It made her immobile, unable to breathe, her heart feeling as if it had ceased to function. As if in a dream, she watched Luke reach out with both hands to push away her chemise and caress her breasts, his thumbs drawing lazy circles over twin peaks. She threw back her head, gasping as sensation overwhelmed her. She knew she should make him stop, but she was powerless to do so. She wanted him to go on forever.

Aching with desire, Luke watched her, knowing he could wreak his revenge now. He leaned forward to touch her taut nipple with his tongue. She cried out softly, winding her fingers in his hair and pulling him closer.

Suddenly she rolled away and stood up. Gasping for breath, she yanked up her clothing to cover herself. She was breathtakingly beautiful, making Luke inhale deeply, his heart thudding.

"No! You'll take me, and I'll be ruined for the man I marry."

Luke stood up, unfastening his shirt. "You want to be kissed and touched."

"No," she whispered, watching him intently as he pulled his shirt out of his trousers and tossed it down on the blanket. His broad chest was muscular and covered in dark brown hair. His shoulders and upper arms were laced with scars. She hadn't seen a man without his shirt before except her brother. Her mouth went dry and she couldn't stop looking at deeply tanned skin, bulging muscles, broad shoulders. He moved toward her and she backed up a step.

"You would destroy me," she whispered. "You know a woman must be pure for her marriage bed."

"And you know women have gotten around that since the beginning of time," he said, moving closer.

With a little shriek she tried to run toward the buggy. Luke caught her, pulling her against him, kissing away her protests. He fondled her until she put her arms around him. She yielded, clinging to him, allowing him to kiss and caress her while her hands roamed across his chest.

This time when she broke free, she snatched up her clothing and ran to the buggy. He followed more slowly. She stood facing him, her back to the buggy, her clothes held before her, leaving her shoulders bare. Her black eyes were wide. Frowning, Luke paused. His heart lurched when tears spilled from her eyes.

He wiped them away while she trembled in his arms. "You know I want you and you make me do sinful, wicked things."

"You're worried about your feelings for Blake," he guessed. Her eyes flew open in surprise, and he saw he had been right. "You don't love him as much as you think you do," he said flatly, drying her cheeks. "Your father's right. Blake Corning isn't the man for you. If you were in love with him, you wouldn't want my kisses."

"I don't," she cried.

"Catalina," he said gently, "that's not the truth. You do want them. Look at me," he commanded. Her dark eyes met his and he asked, "Now tell me you don't want my kisses."

Her eyes closed, and she frowned as if she were in pain. "I shouldn't. I don't love you. I don't want to love you. You don't love me."

Luke felt a twist in his heart, and then he reminded himself that she was Domingo's daughter. The first step in his revenge was only a breath away from success. "You don't love Blake Corning," he repeated persistently, "or you wouldn't want my kisses."

"I do love him," she cried, her chin raising. "And I'll find a way to see him whether you help me or not. Whether or not Papa beats me senseless, I'll see Blake."

Shocked, Luke stared at her. "Your father wouldn't hit you."

"Oh, yes, he would."

"You're lying," he said flatly, staring at her piercingly, his emotions undergoing an upheaval.

"I'm not lying. Look!" She spun around, revealing her bare back. There were still two faint lines across her shoulder blades that had turned an ugly yellow. Luke's notions of a spoiled, adored daughter vanished. He stared in horror at her bruises. Domingo was a monster, as brutal to his daughter as to strangers. The knowledge cut like a knife, and as Luke gazed at her back, he wanted to beat Domingo to a pulp for his cruelty to her. With another jolting shock, he realized his anger was because Domingo had hurt her, Catalina. Hadn't Luke coldly intended to seduce her?

In that moment he realized he couldn't deliberately hurt her, and Luke's plans for revenge by using Catalina disintegrated.

She faced him as she yanked her dress back on and began to button it. "He won't let me see Blake. He says he is buying out the Cornings, but I'll see Blake. I thought you would help me."

"I'm not going to help you see another man," he said flatly, still digesting her revelations, catching tantalizing glimpses of her flesh as she struggled with her clothes.

This time she looked startled. "You don't really care about me, so why won't you help?"

"Maybe I do care," he said, still trying to absorb the changes of the past few minutes. Domingo was cruel to his daughter. He didn't care if he broke her heart with his orders. "If you love your father, how can you defy his wishes?"

Rebellion flared unmistakably in her features. "My father is a harsh man," she said quietly. "Every man who knows him fears him."

As he listened to the pain and anger in her voice, Luke realized his snap judgments had been wrong. Domingo had hurt Catalina and Emilio as well. He reached out to fasten the last buttons of her dress.

"Let's go back and talk. We don't have to be home for another hour," Luke said quietly. "I won't kiss you if you don't want me to."

"I don't know what there is to talk about unless you'll help me meet with Blake."

"It's a beautiful afternoon, you're upset now. There's no need to go home yet," he said quietly.

She eyed him with uncertainty. "I guess you're right." He dropped his arm around her shoulders, hugging her, looking down at the top of her black hair as they walked back to the blanket spread near the riverbank. He sat down and pulled her down to face him, pouring them both another glass of wine.

"I shouldn't drink wine. Mama would be horrified."

"I promise I won't tell," he said, handing her a glass. "You said your father is a harsh man. Has he ever struck you before?"

"Yes." She gazed at the river. Her hair was disheveled, falling over her shoulders and curling on her back. She seemed to almost forget his presence as she talked. "He's always been cruel and strong. Emilio is afraid of him, as is Mama, and they won't cross him.

They hide from him.'' She fell silent and Luke waited, letting her talk freely at her own pace.

"Yes, he's hit me before, many times, because I defy him. I tried to snatch the whip out of his hands!'' she said bitterly. "I think I might have tried to hit him with it, he makes me so angry, but my defiance simply enrages him. Mama says I'm like him.''

Luke couldn't resist. He wrapped his arms around her to hug her gently. "You aren't like him,'' he whispered, torn now with conflicting emotions.

"I love Blake. I want to marry him. I don't want a husband picked out by Papa. I don't want a marriage like my parents'.''

"Your mother isn't happy?''

"No! She's afraid of him and she does just what he tells her. She barely knew him when her mother made her marry him.''

Luke tilted Catalina's chin upward, seeing clearly that even though she was Domingo's child, she was as much an innocent victim as those he had taken captive.

"You don't truly love Blake Corning,'' he said quietly.

"I do. I love Blake with all my heart.''

Luke shook his head. "You can't if I can kiss you until you forget him.''

"I can't help it if I like to be kissed,'' she cried, rubbing her brow.

Amused, Luke stroked her back. "You wouldn't like it so much if you were in love with him. Everyone else would pale in comparison.''

"How do you know that? Have you ever been in love?''

"No, I can't say I have been, but I know that. I won't ever marry until I find a woman whose kisses make everyone else's fade from memory.''

She studied him, tilting her head to one side, aware of his well-shaped mouth, his appealing thick eyelashes. "Have you kissed a lot of women?''

Keeping his features solemn, he seemed to ponder her question. ''Well, I haven't kept count, but I've kissed several.''

''Am—am I as much—never mind!''

''Go ahead. As much *what?*''

Her cheeks turned pink and she looked down, touching his sleeve slightly. ''Am I as much fun to kiss?'' she whispered.

He gazed into her velvety eyes. ''You're more fun to kiss,'' he said, realizing it was the truth. Her kisses were fiery, special.

She looked up at him, and as he gazed into her wide, black eyes, the moment changed imperceptibly.

10

HIS DESIRE FANNED TO LIFE. HE NEEDED TO touch her, to taste her sweet kisses, to feel her softness crushed against him. She seemed to experience the same desire, because her eyes widened. He slipped his arm around her waist, drawing her to him. "You're very special," he said in a husky voice, wanting to hold her close. He leaned down to taste her mouth again.

She felt a burst of longing deep within her. She did like for Luke Danby to kiss her more than anyone else she knew. Moments later she scooted out of his arms, facing him with a frown. "You don't think I love Blake."

"No, not enough to marry him."

"I do love him. Maybe I'm just—I don't know the word—bad to like someone else's kisses."

He stroked her cheek lightly, wanting to touch her constantly. "You're not bad. You're just not absolutely, totally in love with Blake."

She bit her lip, drawing her knees up to her chin. Luke watched her, feeling unsettled. He had intended to seduce her to get revenge, but now he suspected it wouldn't hurt Domingo. The only person who might be hurt by a casual seduction would be Catalina. He reminded himself she was still Domingo's child, his blood ran in her veins. But it was becoming increasingly difficult to remember that.

"Even if I don't marry Blake, I don't want my father

to select my husband. My father doesn't know what
love is.''

''Perhaps it'll work out that the man who loves you
will satisfy your father's requirements.''

''Ticiano. Ticiano thinks his father and mine have
already made an agreement.''

''Could you love Ticiano?''

''No. He's cruel.''

''You must like to kiss him.''

Her cheeks reddened and she gave him an angry
glare. ''Don't remind me of your eavesdropping.''

''Just an observation,'' he answered dryly.

''I liked to be kissed,'' she snapped with a haughty
toss of her head.

''How can I resist?'' he drawled and pulled her to
him swiftly to kiss her before she could voice a protest. She clung to him, yielding and responding with
abandon for long moments before she scooted out of
his grasp.

''You surprised me!''

''And you liked it,'' he answered with amusement.

''One minute you're a friend,'' she said angrily,
standing up and brushing off her skirt, ''someone I
can talk to about my problems, and the next minute
you're a scoundrel. I need to go home. I don't want
to meet Papa coming home from work when we arrive.
She blushed as she fumbled with pins and caught up
long locks of her hair. ''I let Ticiano kiss me because
I like to kiss,'' she said quietly. ''The same reason I
let you kiss me. Maybe that's why I am bad.''

He stood and tilted her chin up. ''You're not *bad*.
You're a normal, healthy young woman.''

She laughed suddenly, and her black eyes flashed.
''You sound like old Dr. Birdwell. And do you really
think that, or are you merely trying to convince me so
I'll kiss you again?''

He leaned closer to her, enjoying her smile. ''I'm
merely trying to convince you so you'll kiss me
again.''

Her heart skipped and she forgot about her worries, knowing he was teasing her, yet becoming aware that he was about to kiss her. She leaned away. "I have to go home now."

He picked up their things and helped her into the buggy. As they drove back to town, they talked about what kind of house he wanted and where he wanted to build. When they rode along El Potrero Street, Luke pulled on the reins and halted in front of a small one-story adobe building. He jumped down.

"This won't take a minute more. I want you to see the new office I rented."

He lifted her down easily and unlocked the door. She stepped into a cool office, where there were hooks by the door for his hat and coat, a potbellied stove, a desk and a safe, a glass-enclosed bookcase.

"It's nice."

"It's brand-new. I just got everything moved in yesterday afternoon. It'll take awhile before I can get started."

"You'll succeed," she said, turning to face him, thinking he looked handsome and forgetting that not too many days earlier, she hadn't thought he was handsome at all. His green eyes were unusual, and in moments of passion, they seemed to grow darker, like the color of deep river water. Impulsively she stood on tiptoe, "Good luck, Luke Danby," she said and kissed him lightly on the cheek.

His arm went around her waist instantly, tightening to pull her to him as he turned his head to kiss her full on the mouth. He leaned over her, kissing her until she forgot where they were or why she had kissed him. Finally he released her and she stepped back. She felt dazed, disturbed at how deeply his kisses could always affect her, how badly she wanted more. And she thought he looked dazed and disturbed.

"We better go," she whispered and stepped outside quickly, glancing around to see if anyone might be watching.

At the door of her house, as she told him good-bye, she caught his hand. "Are you sure you won't talk to Blake for me and help me to see him?"

He gazed into her dark eyes and was reminded again how young she was. He had been near her age when the wagon train had been ambushed. "I'll think about it this week, and you think about whether that's what you really want. You might be placing Blake in danger."

She frowned and bit her lip, gazing into space. "I'll think about it," she answered solemnly, and then she was gone. He strode back to his buggy, knowing he wouldn't ride out to get Blake to come meet her. He glanced back over his shoulder at the house and was again dismayed at the discovery about the Piedras. They weren't a happy family, and Domingo must be as cruel to them as to others. And there was no way on earth now Luke could harm Catalina. He didn't care to explore why he felt so strongly about her.

The next week Luke sat in his office going over a law book. His door was open, letting in warm spring air. He tuned out the sounds from the street: the occasional shouts of children, dogs barking, the clops of horse hooves and creaks of wagon wheels.

"Luke!"

Catalina stood in the doorway. Her cheeks were flushed and her eyes filled with worry as she gasped for breath.

"Come quick! You have to help!"

"Come in here, Catalina. What's wrong?" he said, standing up with a scrape of his chair.

She dashed across his small office and caught his arm. "Please come now before Blake gets hurt."

"What makes you think Blake will get hurt?"

"He's been to our house, hunting Papa. He said Papa hired Dade Phelps to burn down their place. He's going to kill Papa."

Luke strapped on his gunbelt and jammed his hat on his head. "Do you know where Blake is now?"

"He said he would find Dade Phelps. I saw Blake go into the Paloma Cantina. Please stop him from doing something foolish."

"You go home," Luke ordered, striding down the street. The Paloma Cantina was only three blocks away. Catalina rushed along at his side.

"I can't go home until I know Blake is safe."

"You can't go into a cantina."

"I'll wait outside."

Without a word Luke strode through the open door into the cool, dusky interior of the almost empty cantina. Blake Corning was facing a man who leaned against the bar. Two other men were watching Blake closely. Their hands rested near their guns.

"You did it, Phelps, and there's no use denying it. Three of Pa's men are willing to testify to it, but I aim to get justice right now. You don't come burn us out," he snapped. His face was smudged with soot and his cheek was scraped raw.

"Sonny, you're tossing around a lot of false accusations."

At that moment Mario Echevarria, the Bexar County Marshal, entered the saloon. Luke stepped back, moving along the wall, relieved to see him.

"What's going on here?"

"These men burned down our place," Blake yelled. "And I know Domingo Piedra sent them to do it."

Dade Phelps laughed and started to turn.

"Dammit, arrest him!"

"We've been in this cantina all day long," Dade said, smirking at Blake.

"You damn liar," Blake shouted and drew his pistol. Instantly Dade Phelps drew and fired. The marshal shouted for him to stop as he drew, and suddenly guns appeared in the hands of Dade's two cronies. Luke drew and fired. One of them spun back against the bar and crumpled on the floor. Luke fired again, and it was over. Blake, as well as Dade and his men, lay still on the floor. The marshal pitched forward and lay still.

Catalina screamed from the doorway and ran into the room to kneel beside Blake. Luke was there in a second, catching her arms and spinning her around.

"Get the doc quick."

With one fearful glance at Blake, she ran from the saloon while Luke knelt beside Blake and turned him over. His pulse had stopped and blood soaked his chest, pooling on the dusty plank floor.

"He's dead," Luke said grimly, standing up as a man knelt over the marshal.

"The marshal's dead," a man said. "That was fancy shooting, mister."

Luke ignored the comment as he stepped to the bodies near the bar. All three were dead. "Five men killed," he said, thinking, what a waste. And Catalina would be heartbroken over Blake. Now she would fancy herself in love with him more than ever. He stepped to the door as she came back, running beside the doctor.

Luke caught her with his arm, pulling her to one side. Her dark eyes searched his and she tried to push past him. "No!"

Luke released her and watched her kneel beside Blake. Sobs shook her shoulders and he waited while she gave vent to grief.

A crowd was gathering, people murmuring over what had happened, speculating about Blake's accusations. "We're going to need a new marshal," a man said.

Someone pointed at Luke. "Ask the lawyer. He's faster with a gun than anyone I've ever seen, and he knows the law as well."

Luke barely heard them as he watched Catalina. He went to her and took her gently by the shoulders. He pulled her up and led her out of the saloon with his arm around her. They walked the three blocks to his office, where he led her inside and kicked the door shut behind him. He pulled her against his chest while she sobbed.

"I loved him. I really did love him, Luke."

"I know, Catalina," he said, speaking softly to her and stroking her head. "He's the first man you ever loved."

"Papa did this. I heard Blake. Papa sent those men to burn down the Cornings' house."

"You don't know that for sure. It would be a sin to blame your father if he's innocent."

"He isn't innocent," she said bitterly, wiping her eyes. "I know my father. When he wants something, he gets it by any method he has to use."

"Don't be too hasty in judgment. Blake might have been guessing," Luke said, wondering why he was bothering to help Domingo in any manner. "I'll see what I can find out, but if it was your father, there's nothing you can do about it now."

"I hate him!" she cried, breaking into fresh sobs. Luke held her again, stroking her head, thinking what an odd turn fate had taken. He had expected to destroy Catalina's reputation, now he wanted to protect her. He hated that she was hurt, wishing he could have done something more to try to protect Blake.

Someone knocked, and Luke released her to open the door and faced Emilio. "I'm looking for Catalina," he said with concern.

"She's here," Luke said, motioning Emilio inside.

"You're supposed to come home. Mama is worried about where you went. Someone said Mr. Corning was killed."

Catalina covered her face to cry, and Luke squeezed her shoulders. "I'll take her home. My buggy is in back. Lock the door, Emilio."

He herded them through the back door to his buggy and soon stopped in front of the Piedra's house. Before she climbed down, Catalina caught Luke's hand. "Please find out who burned down the Corning house."

He nodded and saw Emilio watching him with a

worried expression. "I'll come by tomorrow and see you," Luke said.

"Thank you, Luke," she said solemnly. He patted her shoulder and wondered since when he had become such a brotherly friend. What he felt for Catalina wasn't brotherly.

He sat across the aisle from the Piedras at the mass said for Blake Corning, and he stood across the grave from them. Catalina cried quietly while the others stood solemnly. Afterward, Domingo Piedra left without giving his regrets to the remaining Cornings. When Luke had a chance to speak to Catalina, he leaned down so only she could hear. "I'll take you for a carriage ride next Friday."

She nodded, looking up tearfully, and he wondered how much more firmly Blake would have a hold on her heart because of his senseless death.

On the following Monday morning Luke looked up from his desk as three men entered his office, Friedrich, Judge John Roberts, Tomas Lopez. As soon as they had all shaken hands and been seated, Judge Roberts spoke up. "We've come to see if you'd like a new job. San Antonio needs a marshal."

"I hadn't figured on becoming a lawman here." Luke smiled, leaning back in his chair. "I haven't bought a home yet."

"We heard you're planning on building one soon," Friedrich said. "We know you've been looking."

"We heard about the Corning shooting and how you helped get rid of those Phelps boys. We need someone who knows the law and who can uphold it with a peacemaker if necessary."

"The pay is good," Friedrich added, studying Luke. "In addition to your regular salary there are some fees you can collect. All in all, you should earn as much as Marshal Echevarria, twenty thousand dollars last year."

Luke knew many sheriffs and marshals earned high wages. He had earned a large wage in Madrid, and it was a much smaller settlement than San Antonio. So he wasn't surprised at the sum and he wouldn't have voiced his surprise if he had felt any. He ran his finger along the edge of his desk. "I'll have to give it some thought, gentlemen. I appreciate the offer, but it would mean I'll have to stay in San Antonio, and I haven't absolutely made up my mind that's what I want to do."

"I'll make the appointment," Judge Roberts said, "but I have to know if you're willing. It's not far, Mr. Danby. Come walk over to the courthouse with us."

A few minutes later, Luke's gaze swept over the familiar two-story building with its tall chimneys, the outside wooden stairs leading to an upstairs door, five large windows in the upper floor and four downstairs. They showed him around the marshal's office with its large oak desk. The lower floor also held the city court and the city department. Upstairs he saw the district courtroom.

"The Old Bat Cave," Luke remarked, chuckling as he recalled what others had called it.

"Judge Jefferson Devine was the first presiding judge," Judge Roberts said as Luke gazed at the large courtroom, the whitewashed canvas ceiling. The judge pointed up. "Thousands of bats roosted between that canvas and the roof, but they're gone now."

Luke walked to the window and looked down at the jail, constructed of irregularly shaped stones. A high wall imbedded with glass surrounded it.

Once they were back on the street, all three men faced him. "We can't wait too long for an answer," Friedrich said curtly.

"I know you can't," Luke said, weighing the possibilities in his mind. He wanted to be free to pursue Domingo and to flee San Antonio quickly if necessary. As lawman, he might have advantages over Domingo, but it also might hamper him. If he destroyed Domingo without due cause, as a United States Marshal he would be a hunted man. On the other hand, if he took the job, he would be near Catalina for a long time. He rubbed his fingers on his knees and glanced at the three men, who sat quietly waiting. "I'll be glad to take the job."

Smiles appeared on all three faces. As they congratulated him, Judge Roberts told him the procedure they would follow for his appointment, and he invited him to the Roberts' house for dinner to celebrate on the following Saturday night. Luke walked them to the door and watched them walk away, wondering what he had gotten himself into. What would Ta-ne-haddle say? He knew the half-breed would simply accept it and go, just as he had done when Luke had been sheriff in Madrid. Periodically the Indian would reappear and stay a few days, then leave again without warning.

Luke had never owned a house before, but he thought he should now. He wanted to take all the time necessary to get Domingo, and he had had to change his plans about what he would do to get revenge. He had no intention of deliberately hurting Catalina after discovering Domingo had caused her so much grief. He sat back down at his desk, and was staring at his law book when a shadow fell across the desk. He looked up into a pair of dark eyes.

Ta-ne-haddle stood in front of him; Luke hadn't heard him enter the office. He leaned back and smiled. "Pull up a chair. I was just thinking about you."

Ta-ne-haddle sat down facing him, produced a cigar, and proceeded to light it. "I hear you're becoming Marshal of Bexar County."

In all the years he had known him, Ta-ne-haddle never ceased to amaze Luke. "How the hell do you know that? I just accepted the job about ten minutes ago."

Ta-ne-haddle blew smoke into the air and smiled. 'I overheard three gentlemen who left here with smiles on their faces. I heard the last marshal was killed in a gunfight."

"Yes. So was Blake Corning. The man Catalina loved."

"Miss Piedra? And have you ruined the lady's reputation yet?"

"No."

Ta-ne-haddle studied Luke and Luke stared right back at him. "Something's changed."

"Maybe," Luke said, brushing a smudge of dust off his knee, aware of Ta-ne-haddle's scrutiny.

"You're in love with her."

"No, I'm not. But I don't want to hurt her. Her father has done enough of that."

"Ahh. Revenge is more complicated than you'd expected."

"Don't sound so happy about it. I'm still at the hotel. Stay with me tonight."

The Indian nodded in silent agreement. "So now what do you do to get revenge?"

"I don't know, but I'll get him. Blake Corning accused the Phelps of burning down the Corning house following Domingo's orders, because Domingo wanted to buy them out. Sooner or later he'll overstep the bounds of the law and get caught. At least I hope to be there to catch him. If not and too much time passes, I'll take matters into my own hands."

"And get your neck stretched for your foolishness. An arrow in the heart would settle matters quickly."

"It won't be so simple when I'm United States Marshal sworn to uphold the law."

"You wouldn't be the first to break the law."

"I know. C'mon, let's go over to one of the exchanges and get some joy juice."

"Best suggestion I've heard since I hit town," Ta-ne-haddle said, standing up. Together they strolled to the Main Plaza and one of the old Mexican establishments that had been repainted in gaudy colors and turned into drinking places called exchanges.

Smoothing her hands on her blue muslin dress, Catalina stared out the window. She felt like a prisoner in her own house. She wanted to go to the ranch, to ride to the Cornings and see for herself if the house was burned to the ground as Blake had said. Her father had sworn he had not hired the Phelpses, that he had merely made the Cornings an offer for their ranch. He said the Phelpses may have tried to implicate him, because he had fired one of them several years back.

She hoped he'd had no part in the treachery. She mourned Blake, and her memories became more golden with the passing of time. Startling her out of her reverie was a knock at the bedroom door. A maid stepped inside.

"Senorita Catalina, your father wishes you to come to the library."

"Very well," she said with a sigh, having lost interest in day-to-day activities in the house. It was the last week in May now. Friday she would go out with Luke, and it would be a welcome break. She descended the stairs and found her father seated on the long black leather settee.

"Close the door, Catalina."

She did as he asked and moved to a wing chair facing him. He leaned forward, rubbing his broad jaw. "I know you are still mourning Blake Corning, but he is dead and life goes on. Friedrich has asked for your hand."

"It took a moment for the announcement to register. "No," she whispered, aghast over his declaration.

11

"No! I won't!"

"I know this is a difficult time for you, Catalina, but you're the age to have a husband, and Friedrich will be a good one. I had thought Ticiano—"

"No!" She jumped to her feet. "I refuse. I'll run away first. I won't marry him."

"Yes, you will," Domingo said in a controlled voice. "Sit down."

"No! You can beat me or do what you want. I won't marry him."

"You'll marry Friedrich, or I'll put you in a convent in Mexico. One where you cannot run away."

She drew her breath sharply. The last thing she wanted was to stay in a convent shut away from the world. She stared at him as anger and fear mounted. "Please, don't make me do this. I would prefer Ticiano to Friedrich."

"Friedrich will make you a good husband. His wealth grows daily."

She took Domingo's hand. "Please, I beg you to reconsider. Ticiano is wealthy and he wants to marry me. He's Mexican as we are, not German."

Domingo stared down into her black eyes, feeling a tug of conscience for what he was doing to his daughter, but later she would become accustomed to Friedrich. He thought of their business. Easily Friedrich could buy out Domingo, but if he married Catalina, he wouldn't do that.

"We're all Texans. Our past heritage is not as important as the future, and if you have Friedrich for a husband, so much more will be secure."

"You mean your business will be secure," she cried, standing up and gazing down at him.

"That's enough, Catalina. Friedrich has invited us to a party at his house next Friday night. Soon he will propose and you are to accept graciously."

"Never."

Domingo came to his feet in one lithe movement and slapped her hard, sending her toppling onto the sofa. She twisted to cry and he stood over her. "Do not defy me unless you want to spend your life locked away in a convent, away from your precious horses and San Antonio, away from your friends." He wound his fingers in her hair and jerked her head so she had to face him. She cried out as he pulled her hair cruelly. "Do you understand?"

"Yes," she whispered, frightened, horrified about her future.

Domingo released her. "Go to your room."

She fled to her room and threw herself across the bed, sobbing uncontrollably. She didn't love Friedrich, she detested him. He was older, and she hated his lascivious touches. She shivered with revulsion when she thought of Friedrich kissing her.

The next few days were a nightmare. Her mother wouldn't listen to her pleas. Sophia stayed shut in her room. Emilio accepted Domingo's orders and expected Catalina to do likewise. She knew Luke had been appointed Bexar County Marshal, and when he came to call, she met him eagerly. He looked as handsome as ever in butternut pants and a leather vest over his white chambray shirt, and the thought occurred to her that as soon as she was betrothed to Friedrich, she could no longer go out with Luke. Or dance with other men, or ride with them, or do so many of the things she loved. If only it had been Ticiano or Luke Danby—

She tilted her head and studied him. Domingo had talked of Luke's gold on deposit at the freighting company. If Luke had more gold than Friedrich . . . Her thoughts leaped at the possibility, and she slanted him a curious look as they rode across the plaza.

"What's going on in that pretty little head?" he asked lightly, his gaze raking over her green pique carriage dress and white straw hat.

"I'm thinking how much I'm enjoying the ride. It seems forever since the last time we were together."

He gave her a sharp look that made her blush, but she smiled at him and batted her eyes while she pondered this new possibility. She would much prefer to marry Luke. He was closer in age, interesting, kinder, and more fun, much more fun to kiss. She hated for Friedrich to touch her. The more she thought about it, the better the idea became. Domingo would only consider Luke Danby if Luke were wealthier and more powerful than Friedrich. Somehow she couldn't imagine someone wealthier than Friedrich, but she had to find out.

Soon she realized they weren't taking their usual direct route out of town, and she turned to Luke quizzically as he headed down a lane where there were scattered new houses. "We're actually going to look at houses today?"

"Yes, we are for a few minutes," he answered in his deep voice. "At least, we're looking at one house in particular." He reined to a halt in front of a sprawling single-story home. It was built of limestone with arched windows, louvered shutters, a porch across the front with fancy woodwork, and a high, peaked roof.

"What a beautiful house."

Luke jumped down and came around the front of the buggy to lift her down. "I'm glad you think it's pretty. It's mine. I just bought it." He took her arm and led her up the walk. Her heart jumped at the prospect. His home was as impressive as Friedrich's. She didn't want to marry anyone now, but if she was going to be forced into a marriage, it would be better with Luke Danby. Her lifting spirits momentarily sagged when she realized it wasn't just a matter of wealth. There was more to it than that, or Ticiano might have been as good a choice as Friedrich. Ticiano's family was enormously wealthy and owned many acres of land that Ticiano would inherit, yet Domingo had still preferred Friedrich. The thought disturbed her because there was some reason for Domingo favoring Friedrich so strongly.

She couldn't combat the unknown. She smiled at Luke as he led her inside, knowing if any of her parents' friends had seen her enter, they would have been shocked that she was allowed to go home with Luke Danby. She shook her head, dismissing that worry from her mind as highly insignificant.

"What a beautiful home," she exclaimed, looking at the large empty rooms with long windows that let in light.

"I've bought a bed and a chair, a few pieces of furniture, and I'll add to them soon. I'm going to move here from the hotel tonight. This is the front parlor." He took her arm to lead her through double doors into an empty courtyard. "The house is built in a square and each room opens into the courtyard. I'm having plants put in tomorrow."

"It's beautiful and it's huge," she exclaimed sincerely, impressed by the size. "You'll be able to get a good breeze through each room."

"Let me show you my bedroom," he said, drawing out his words and watching her, making her tingle with an undercurrent of excitement. He led her across the courtyard and into a large room with windows on the south as well as on the courtyard. A four-poster mahogany bed and a leather chair were the only furnishings. Books, boots, a washbowl, and pitcher sat on the floor, a small mirror beside them. "Here's where I sleep."

Images of Luke stretched on the bed came to her mind: his long, lean, muscular, healthy body. She drew a sharp breath, looking up to find him watching

her with a mocking smile. He moved closer, turning
her to face him, holding her arms lightly. "I think,"
he drawled in a husky voice, "after today, whenever I
go to bed, I'll remember today and you standing here
in my room." He tilted her chin up. "Will you remember today, Catalina?" he asked, his gaze dropping to her mouth and making her pulse drum.

"Yes," she whispered, her breath stopping as his
head lowered and he brushed her lips lightly. He
straightened up, giving her a smoldering appraisal, and
then he took her arm. He led her through each room
and told her his plans. His tantalizing brief kiss had
only made her want more, and she was acutely conscious of each touch of his hands.

She praised his choice until he began to study her
too closely. In the hall he turned her to face him. "You
like my house?"

"I think it's wonderful."

"For someone who only weeks ago was constantly
calling me a scoundrel, and a few days ago was in
mourning, you're mighty enthusiastic."

She debated whether to try to cajole him into pro-
posing or to come right out with what she wanted. To
come right out with it might scare him away forever.
She smiled sweetly, running her fingers lightly along
his arm. "I always have fun with you. Today is a glorious spring day, I know I'm going to have a delightful
afternoon, and you've just showed me your wonderful
new house. Why shouldn't I smile and be happy?"

He shrugged, but the intentness in his green eyes
didn't diminish, and she felt a twinge of unease, because he had an uncanny knack of guessing what she
was thinking. They climbed back in the buggy and
rode out to another spot along the riverbank, where
they had a picnic lunch. When Luke pulled her into
his arms, she acquiesced. Melting against him, she
wound her arms around his neck and raised her lips to
meet his kiss eagerly.

After a moment he leaned away and studied her

again, and she felt as if he could read her every thought. "You want something from me, Catalina. And I want to know what it is."

"Me? What would I want from you, Luke Danby?" she asked, and prayed she sounded insulted and innocent. "You can take me home if you think I want something."

To her amazement he moved away and began to gather together their things. "What are you doing?" she asked, not meaning to sound quite so sharp.

"I'm going to take you home."

She watched him in consternation. Every other afternoon he had kept her out as long as possible, kissing her, trying to win her over. Now he acted as if he was thoroughly ready to be rid of her.

"Luke, do you have to go back now?"

"No, I don't," he said, pausing.

"Sit down and let me talk to you," she pleaded. She could talk more freely to him than anyone she had ever known, including Emilio. Luke set the basket down and dropped down beside her, taking his hat off. He ran his hand through his thick brown hair that revealed glints of gold in the sunlight.

"What's troubling you, Catalina?"

For the first time he wasn't easy to talk to. She didn't know what to say without blurting out her dilemma. "Do you want to get married?"

"Maybe someday, but not anytime soon," he answered, looking more curious than ever.

She bit her lip. "How come you didn't want to kiss me today?"

Amusement sparkled in his eyes, and he slipped his hand across her shoulder to stroke the nape of her neck. "I did want to kiss you. I just had an idea something was bothering you."

"We don't have to go back this early, do we?" she asked in her most cajoling voice, her black eyes an invitation.

Luke knew she wanted something from him, but he

couldn't guess what. At the moment it didn't matter. He drew her to him, her soft body pressed against his while she slipped her arms around his neck and clung to him, returning his kiss eagerly. She moaned and twisted against him, stroking his neck, winding her fingers in his hair as her heated kisses drove him to a frenzy. Moving sensuously against him, she caressed his back. His hands sought her buttons and soon he had her dress and chemise pushed to her waist. Her lush breasts quivered as she offered them to him. She lay back on the blanket and closed her eyes, yielding to his kisses.

She was too eager. She spoke no words of love, as he had heard her give Blake. There had been no words of love on his part either, and he was suspicious. Never before had she given so freely, and he wondered if he tried to possess her, would she let him? He pushed his hands beneath her skirt to caress her silken thighs, his manhood throbbing with desire. She gasped and caught his wrists, frowning before she released his hands.

She lay on the blanket with her mass of black hair framing her face, her tantalizing breasts bare, her dark eyes watching him. He pulled off his shirt and saw a flicker of both longing and uncertainty in her expression.

"Luke, will you marry me?"

Stunned, he paused. This was the last thing he expected. On the other hand, he didn't care about her reasons for yielding. He just wanted to take her. "You're an enticing, beautiful woman, Catalina," he said in a husky voice. He pulled her up where he could sit close to her and look into her eyes, trying to keep his gaze from drifting lower, but unable to keep from kissing her throat. "Why the proposal when only weeks ago you were heartbroken over Blake?"

"I realized I didn't love him. I—"

"Don't lie to me," he said harshly, suddenly loathing protests of love that didn't truly exist.

"Papa is going to make me marry Friedrich," she burst out, looking down to pull her dress to her chin.

He stared at her, confounded. She sat with her clothes pulled to her jaw, her big, luminous black eyes wide, her brows arched in question, a hopeful expression on her face.

Luke laughed out loud, as much at himself as at her. "Dammit, I knew you wanted something."

Luke, I do care for you! I can't marry Friedrich. I detest him."

"So I'm a better choice then the detestable Friedrich," he snapped, his curiosity rising. "What about Ticiano? He wants to marry you."

"Papa has eliminated Ticiano."

"And why wouldn't he eliminate me?"

"He might not if you're richer and more powerful than Friedrich!"

"Particularly since I've bought a house," he said. Domingo stood between them like a vast chasm. He wouldn't deliberately hurt Catalina, but he still intended to get his revenge. "No, I'm sorry, Catalina, but I'm afraid I can't supplant Friedrich. Anyway, if your father didn't approve of me, you're so young you can't go against his wishes."

"I hate this," she cried, staring into the distance. "I don't want Friedrich to touch me!"

Luke ached to pull her back into his arms, but he knew he shouldn't. He agreed with her about Friedrich. The man was cold and ambitious. "How soon is the wedding?" he asked quietly, wondering what he could do to help her.

"I'm not even engaged, but I know I will be. We're going to his house for dinner tonight, and then we're going again to a party next Saturday night."

"So am I. It's going to be a large party. Probably an announcement of your engagement."

She looked as if he had struck her, and he felt a twist in his heart for her. She was too young and full of life to be bargained off in a loveless marriage. He had to laugh at himself. Only a few weeks back he had been intent on destroying her.

Her long black locks spilled over her bare shoulders as she held her dress up beneath her chin. Luke reached out to take it out of her hand. Her dark eyes flickered and changed. She licked her lips and tilted her head back, watching him through narrowed eyes that made his pulse drum wildly. He pulled down the dress, trailing his fingers across her taut nipples, hearing her gasp of pleasure.

"How beautiful you are," he murmured, cupping her breasts, drawing circles on them with his thumbs.

She squeezed her eyes closed and tears sparkled on her lashes. "I don't want to marry a man I don't love. My parents did that, and it's been terrible all through the years. I want someone I love to kiss me," she whispered. Her eyes came open wide to stare at him, and he could easily guess her thoughts.

"You're young," he said gently. "I can't marry now. I may not stay and I don't want to be tied here."

Her cheeks turned pink and she sat up angrily, pulling her clothes around her. "You're laughing at me."

"Not at all," he answered solemnly, knowing he had hurt her, yet knowing there was no way he could wed her. His hatred for Domingo was too deep, too lasting. "There are things I need to do before I settle down."

"Take me home now."

"I don't want to part when you're angry," he said, turning her to face him.

"If only Blake were alive! There will be someone—"

Her words cut through him like a knife. He didn't want her to wed Friedrich, but the thought she would go ask someone else to marry her stung more than he would have dreamed. He frowned at her, pulling her collar closed and fastening it beneath her chin.

"Don't go do some damn fool thing to stop Friedrich."

"I don't want to marry him."

"Make the engagement long, Catalina. Things change and things happen."

She lifted her chin and turned to climb into the buggy. As they rode in silence, a storm seethed inside him. He was caught in a trap he hadn't expected. His feelings for Catalina were strong and he wanted her. He wanted to protect her and he ached to possess her. Her checks had bright spots of pink, her jaw set in a determined line. She was fiery and her emotions were close to the surface, so easy to read. No matter how many times he went over it, he came back to the same decision. He couldn't marry her. But the thought of her marrying Friedrich was abominable.

While they were still on the edge of town, he halted the team with a yank of the reins and took her in his arms. Looking down into her questioning eyes, he lowered his head for a bruising kiss. Frustration and deep rage burned in him.

Catalina's breath was squeezed from her lungs. The first moment of surprise changed to wonder at the way he kissed her, as if she were the only woman in the world. She clung to him, trembling with eagerness from the passion in his kisses. He released her abruptly, gazing at her with heated green eyes.

For a second, he was tempted to tell her about her father, why he couldn't marry her, yet he couldn't. He picked up the reins and they rode back to town.

"Go out with me next Tuesday afternoon," he said brusquely. "I can't get away from my job until then."

She nodded, brushing his hand with hers before he climbed out of the buggy and helped her down. She gazed up into unreadable eyes that had darkened; a frown creased his brow, adding to his angry expression.

"What's wrong, Luke?" she asked softly.

"I don't want you to marry Friedrich."

She felt a mixture of pleasure and annoyance, and she blushed when she thought about asking him and being refused. "Catalina, there are more reasons for me to say no than you can imagine," he said gently. "You don't really know me."

Her embarrassment deepened, yet at the same time he sounded sincere. There was no teasing as he did so often, and she wondered about him and his past. She nodded, but she didn't understand. Luke Danby was a mystery to her. And a delight. She wanted him, and this afternoon made her realize how deeply.

"Good-bye, Luke," she whispered and hurried inside.

With reluctance she dressed for the family dinner with Friedrich. She was relieved the whole family would be present because there might not be much chance for Friedrich to talk to her, and even less for him to touch her. She smoothed the folds of her dark brown silk dress and picked up her shawl, draping it around her shoulders.

Dinner was bearable and to her relief there were twenty guests at Friedrich's lavish table. He was a charming host, attracting other daughters in the room who blushed and were coy with him, paying him undivided attention. Why had he singled her out? Catalina wondered. He was handsome with a straight nose, a square jaw, large blue eyes, and his thick golden hair, but he held no interest whatsoever for her.

She tried to avoid his glances, and the evening went well until he joined her as she stood in a group of people near the large stone fireplace. "I want to show you a new flower in my garden, Catalina. It would be perfect for your dress. Come with me. Everyone will excuse you for a minute."

There was no way to protest, and she strolled at his side as he folded his arm through hers and held her close beside him. They wandered down the back steps, where torches flickered over an immaculate yard laid out with precise beds of flowers.

"You look beautiful tonight," he said.

"Thank you. Mr. Krueger, we shouldn't get so far from the house. Mama will come searching for us."

He laughed and tightened his hold on her arm. "Nonsense. I'm not a young blade. She'll trust you with me, and I'm sure your father has talked to her about me."

She bit her lip, knowing each step led her closer to difficulty.

"You're not going to ask why your father has talked to her about me?"

"I know why," she blurted, feeling trapped. "I don't want to marry now."

He laughed softly and turned her to face him. "You're young and romantic. I can be a good husband, and I can give you everything you want. In turn, I want a beautiful, healthy, young wife who can give me sons."

"Your proposal is overwhelming, but—"

"No buts, Catalina. You father has given me permission. He'll see to it that we marry."

"You would want me against my wishes?" she whispered, knowing his answer.

"I think once you're married, you'll change. A child would hold your interest."

She knew she should be tactful, but Friedrich was blunt and frank and it was her nature to be. "I don't want to marry now."

He smiled, holding her upper arms tightly. "Your wishes are a small matter. Woman have always done as their husbands and fathers wanted. When we marry I will give you a diamond necklace." He pulled her to him abruptly, his mouth coming down on hers wetly and forcefully. His kiss was loathsome. She struggled in his arms, pushing him away violently.

"No!" She wiped her mouth with the back of her hand.

He caught her arm, yanking her to him again, his fingers biting into her flesh. "You're young and I'll make allowances, but I will marry you, Catalina."

He held her in an ironlike grip with one hand while he kissed her as forcefully as before. His other hand roamed over her roughly, and she shivered with revulsion. Pushing and twisting, she turned her head. "Please, let me go. I'll be disgraced if I go back to the party all rumpled."

He released her a fraction still holding her upper arms. He placed his hand over her breast. "Be still," he hissed forcefully. "You'll be mine. You have no choice. The wedding should be by Christmas."

With a cry she yanked free of his grasp and brushed past him, running into the shadows. Stopping, she leaned against the side of the house. Her breath came in gasps. She hated Friedrich for what he was doing. She knew her mouth would be red from his kisses. Knowing she would bring down her father's wrath, she walked around to the front of the house and called to the butler.

"Please tell Senor Piedra that I became sick and went on home."

"And your name, miss?"

"Miss Piedra. I'm his daughter."

"Shouldn't you wait—"

"No. The night air is refreshing. I'll be all right. Just give him the message," she said and hurried down the steps to the street. As she walked the long distance to Flores Street, her nerves began to settle. She would have to find a way to escape marriage to him. If she could convince him how much she loathed him, surely he would give up. No man would want a wife who despised him. Many young women would be delighted to marry Friedrich. They found his age an added attraction, his wealth impossible to resist, his golden looks exciting. Why he would single her out of the others who willingly wanted him, she didn't know. Catalina decided to make a list of them, and point this out to him the next time they were together.

She heard the clop of hooves and looked over her shoulder, her heart jumping in fright that Friedrich might have come after her. A broad-shouldered man rode down the dusty road and she was tempted to turn and run. She moved closer to the houses, trying to stay in the shadows, her steps speeding up.

"Catalina!"

Relief washed over her, and she whirled around as Luke rode up. "Where are you going?"

"Home. I left Friedrich's party. Papa will probably be furious. I told the butler to inform them I'm ill."

"Shame on you," he teased, dismounting and lifting her into the saddle. "I don't want to wrinkle your pretty dress."

"Climb up here. My dress will iron."

He mounted behind her, and his arms went around her as he picked up the reins. Instantly, encircled in his strong arms, she felt better. She leaned her head back against his shoulder, wishing Luke wanted to marry her the way Friedrich did.

Luke drew a sharp breath. Her body was pressing his, and he was responding in a manner she had to be aware of. She smelled sweet, and her softness tormented his senses. He urged his horse forward, and soon he reined up in front of her house and helped her down. His hands dropped away from her waist as they stood facing each other. "I'm glad I came along."

"Luke, Friedrich is horrible."

"I'd think you'd find him handsome and attractive. He's one of the wealthiest men in this town, if the rumors I've heard are true."

"That's right. Otherwise my father wouldn't be afraid of him. He has nothing but contempt for anyone weaker than he is. I hate Friedrich and I won't want to marry him."

"Are you engaged yet?"

"No! And we'll never be."

"Something sent you dashing from his house. He kissed you," Luke said, surprised at the anger it stirred in him. The thought of Friedrich kissing Catalina made he want to ride straight to Friedrich's and hit him. He slipped his arm around her waist, drawing her close, stepping back into the shadows of a live oak.

"Luke, I can't kiss," she whispered, her cheeks flaming. "He hurt my mouth."

Luke swore softly. "I won't hurt you," he whispered, brushing his lips on her cheek, the corner of her mouth, down to her throat.

Catalina closed her eyes and wrapped her arms around his neck. Unable to resist the sweet torment, she turned her head so that her lips met his. The gentle, featherlight pressure of his mouth against hers was tantalizing and she pressed harder, forgetting the faint hurt as Luke kissed her.

He tried to remember her bruised mouth, but she tasted sweet with her heated kisses that made gentleness evaporate. Finally he released her, gazing down at her solemnly. He wanted her, more than he had ever wanted a woman before in his life, and the knowledge shook him deeply. His past rose like a ghost to haunt him, and came between them. He reluctantly took her arm to lead her to the door, his body aching with a need for her.

"I'll see you next Tuesday."

"I'm glad you came along."

"So am I, Catalina," he said solemnly as he rode away. He felt a knot in his chest when he thought of her marrying Friedrich. He didn't know Friedrich well, but if tonight was an example of how he would court Catalina, what kind of beast would he be to marry? More important, Luke thought about his own feelings for Catalina. She was becoming more necessary to him all the time.

Luke stopped at his office and picked up a book to study, then locked up and rode to his house. When he slammed the door, he found Ta-ne-haddle in the courtyard, a lamp burning as he carved a horse out of a bit of cottonwood.

"Something happened tonight," Ta-ne-haddle said.

"Yes. I saw Catalina. She walked home from Friedrich's house. Friedrich told her he would marry her, that her father had agreed. Damn them!''

"Who! Catalina and Friedrich?''

"No, of course not. Friedrich and Domingo.''

Ta-ne-haddle stopped whittling. "Perhaps revenge has become a bitter pill to swallow,'' he said, studying Luke.

"Perhaps, but I can't forget or let him get away with all he's done.''

"As Edmund Burke said, 'You can never plan the future by the past.' ''

"Stop quoting to me!''

"You're in love.''

Luke glared at him, hearing the words as they seemed to swirl in the air in an echoing chorus. *In love with Catalina.* He couldn't be! It was only because she was beautiful, exciting, sensuous enough to drive a man loco. Nothing more. He had never truly been in love. When it came time to part, he had always been able to leave women. Yet he knew his arguments had a hollow ring. He swore softly and strode across the courtyard impatiently, knowing that blocks away Catalina was getting ready for bed. He knotted his hands into fists without realizing what he was doing. Ta-ne-haddle glanced at him once, then went back to his whittling.

Finally Luke took off his coat, and sat close to an oil lamp to study his law book.

Catalina's door burst open and she rolled over to sit up as Domingo entered with a lamp in his hand. "Why did you leave Friedrich's tonight.''

"I felt ill and I told the servant to give you my message,'' she said firmly. "There was no need to disturb all of you.''

"Friedrich was angry.''

"I can't help it if I became sick.''

"What's wrong with you?''

"My stomach hurts.''

For an instant Domingo had an urge to strike her. He thought she might be lying, but there was a chance she was telling the truth. She had grown up with a mother who constantly complained of ailments.

"Next time I hope you feel better. You owe Friedrich an apology."

"Yes, sir," Catalina said, thinking she owed Friedrich nothing.

Domingo closed the door with a bang, and Catalina's thoughts shifted to Luke and the encounter tonight. She smiled and scrunched down in the bed as she remembered his kisses. She wriggled in bed, conjuring up a clear image of Luke without his shirt, his muscular chest bare, appealing in spite of so many scars. He was exciting, charming, inscrutable. Luke Danby. Her pulse drummed and she smiled in the darkened room.

Because Matthew McDermott's horses had been stolen early Tuesday morning, Luke had to cancel his ride with Catalina.

When Saturday came, she dressed carefully, thinking constantly of Luke, wanting him to be pleased when he saw her.

Domingo knocked on the door of her room and entered just before they were to go. "Catalina, tonight I don't want you to leave without us. If you become ill, tell me," he said, his dark eyes raking over her.

"I feel fine. There should be no need," she said, determined she would not allow Friedrich to see her alone.

"Good. In a short time Friedrich will ask you to marry him. You know what your answer must be."

She nodded, her mind still mulling over possibilities to escape such a marriage.

"Shall we go?"

"I'll be down in another minute," she said. As soon as he closed the door, she spun in a circle, the full skirt of her wine-colored moiré billowing away from her ankles. She wore a wine-colored velvet ribbon around her neck and flowers in her hair. Her dress was trimmed with ecru lace, and she studied herself for long moments. Thinking of Luke and how his green eyes flashed with unmistakable desire, she smiled in anticipation. Instead of seeing her image, she saw Luke's slender face, his prominent cheekbones, and thick brown hair. "Luke," she whispered, realizing he could excite her more than Blake. She liked to be with him more than Blake. Her eyes focused and Luke's image vanished as she studied herself with curiosity.

"I love you, Luke Danby," she whispered in surprise, trying the words aloud, wondering if she did love him. He was becoming more and more important to her. Was it because he was a friend and she could trust him? She knew that wasn't all, not when his kisses made her lose all control and caution. With a smile she turned away to go to the party.

In a short time the Piedras were greeted as they entered the ballroom of Friedrich's house.

12

FRIEDRICH CAME FORWARD AT ONCE. HIS GOLDEN hair gleamed in the candlelight, and his full mouth revealed white teeth as he smiled. He shook hands with Domingo, kissed Sophia's hand fleetingly, and turned to Catalina to take her hand in his. He raised her fingers to his lips, but she slipped her hand out of his grasp adroitly.

"I hope you don't have to flee my party tonight," he said in a deep voice.

"I won't if I'm not disturbed as I was last time," she said evenly, smiling sweetly as his eyes flashed. She moved ahead while he greeted Emilio, but within seconds he was again at her side. Soon he had to leave to greet new arrivals, and Catalina sighed with relief.

She was soon surrounded by six young men and enjoying herself immensely. As she laughed at a story Werner Gates told, she felt drawn to turn her head. As Luke stepped through the doorway, she smiled. He winked without a change in his expression, but the quick exchange made her feel warm with anticipation. He looked handsome as he stood head and shoulders above most of the crowd. His white shirt was a contrast to his burnished skin, his thick brown hair waved over his forehead.

He couldn't see her well for the crowd surrounding her, and then his attention was distracted as Friedrich greeted him and introduced him to Marta Zachweger, who took his arm.

Along with the others in her circle, Catalina laughed

at something Ticiano said, but she hadn't heard a word. The sight of Luke's arm linked with Marta's disturbed her. Luke Danby was becoming special to her; she had faced the fact clearly. He was fun, exciting, charming, but there was always something mysterious about him. His cool, quiet manner made him impossible to fathom. She was accustomed to a father who shouted to the world what was on his mind. She vented her own feelings freely, and she was impressed by Luke's quiet control.

"Catalina?"

"I'm sorry." She saw Ticiano's brows arch as Werner repeated his question to her. Ticiano turned his head to look over his shoulder in the direction she had been looking, and he gave her a long, curious stare. All the time she talked with the men around her, she was aware of Luke and where he was in the room. Finally a moment came when she was alone. He left a crowd and crossed the room to her, his gaze drifting over her languorously in a manner that brought a blush to her cheeks, but she saw the pleasure in his eyes and she was happy.

"Buenos noches," she said, lapsing into Spanish as she did occasionally because often Sophia spoke in Spanish.

"Hello, Catalina," he said in a deep voice, smiling down at her. "You're more beautiful each time I see you."

"Thank you," she said, pleased by his compliment.

"How did you get away from all your admirers?"

"I don't think they know I'm gone."

"Yes, they do know. They keep glancing at us. Let's walk outside," he said, taking her arm and they strolled out on Friedrich's back porch. The sun was slanting low in the west and Catalina stood by the porch railing. "Congratulations. I heard you caught a horse thief today."

When he nodded affirmation, she added, "It sounds

dangerous and exciting. Are you ever afraid of anything, Luke?"

He laughed. "Of course." He leaned down, his arm braced on the column. "I'm afraid of beautiful black eyes and rosy lips."

She smiled at him, slanting him a look. "When you start to practice, you'll probably win every case with your glib tongue."

"If I win, it's because I can out-argue my opposition."

"So that's why I never win arguments with you. I thought it was your charm. It's just stubbornness."

"I like it better when you think it's charm," he said in a husky voice, stepping closer to her. His knee pressed hers as he touched the neck of her dress. The high, demure collar fastened just beneath her chin. His touch sent her pulse racing, and she wished they were alone so he could kiss her.

"There you are," came Friedrich's voice, and he stepped out to join them. He took her arm. "It's time to eat. Shall we let Catalina lead the way?"

As Friedrich took Catalina's arm and led her inside, Luke had to curb an impulse to yank her away. He was seated at the opposite end of the table from her. If the situation were less serious, Luke would have been amused at the obvious distaste in Catalina's expression whenever Friedrich tried to capture her attention. As it was, Luke suffered a smoldering anger while trying to carry on polite conversations with the women seated on either side of him. In a few minutes he began to watch the ladies at the table, and soon singled out what he was seeking in Elke Ludvig, a golden-haired woman recently widowed. She obviously was interested in Friedrich, barely able to keep her glances from returning to him constantly. She was three seats away from him, yet several times during dinner she was able to capture his attention.

As soon as dinner was over the ladies adjourned to

the front parlor while the men remained behind for another drink and to smoke. Luke studied Friedrich, amazed that Catalina wasn't in love with him. He'd seen women openly eyeing the golden-haired German, beautiful young women flirting with him, mothers trying to win his friendship. Friedrich was wealthy and handsome and intelligent. Yet Luke suspected Friedrich could be as hard and ruthless as Domingo. He had asked Ta-ne-haddle to see what he could find out about Friedrich, since he was constantly amazed at the Kiowa's ability to come up with information about people. Ta-ne-haddle never seemed to make an effort to become friends with townspeople, yet shortly after his arrival at any town, he knew a great deal about most of the people.

As the men rejoined the ladies, Luke strolled over to Elke Ludvig, who stood with a cluster of people beside an imported rosewood piano. When he had an opportunity, he leaned down to speak quietly to her. "I've heard Friedrich has an impressive collection of guns. Would you like to have him show them to you?"

She gave him a curious glance and shrugged her shoulders. "Of course, Marshal Danby," she replied with a strong German accent. He took her arm and crossed the room to where Friedrich and Catalina stood talking. Catalina's features were stormy, her dark eyes flashing with anger as they approached.

"What a marvelous dinner you served," Luke said.

"Thank you. I have a fine cook who has mastered some of my German recipes."

"Thank goodness! It was wonderful to taste German food again," Elke said, touching Friedrich's arm lightly.

"I made a promise without consulting you," Luke said, and Friedrich turned curious eyes on him. "When I discovered Elke was interested in unusual guns, I told her you'd be willing to show her your collection."

"Of course," Friedrich said, looking pleased and curious. "We can all go look."

"I'll keep Catalina company," Luke said easily, catching a flash of anger from Friedrich. "I know how much she fears guns."

"Is that so? I haven't heard your father mention it."

"He surely hasn't told you everything about me," she replied, her black eyes sparkling with devilment. Friedrich looked at Elke, who was waiting expectantly, and nodded to Catalina. "If you two will excuse us, please."

As they parted, Luke steered Catalina through the door. They walked down the steps and out of sight around a clump of wisteria. She spun in a circle, laughing and clapping her hands together. "Thank heavens you got me away from him."

He smiled at her, thinking she was marvelous. She was so many things he wasn't and couldn't be: exuberant, volatile, playful. "I thought it was time you escaped his company. Has he proposed yet?"

"Dios, no. Don't bring it up."

"Maybe he won't."

"He may not tonight, but he will soon. My father wasn't imagining their conversations about it." Her laughter vanished and he wished he hadn't asked. He glanced over his shoulder to make sure they were hidden from view. "I wanted to sit by you at dinner. You look too beautiful to resist, Catalina."

Her pulse drummed crazily as she watched him. She reached out to catch his hands and hold them in hers. "Thank you."

"I've asked your father if I can take you out to help me select material for my new house next Tuesday."

"And? Did he agree?"

"Of course," Luke drawled.

"I don't know how you always get your way without any fuss or commotion."

"I don't *always* get my way," he said.

"For instance?" she asked with a tingling anticipation. "When haven't you gotten your way?"

"Right now. I'd rather take you home and kiss you soundly. Barring that, I'd like to kiss you right now."

"And what's stopping you?" she whispered while her heart thudded.

He tilted her chin up. "Only common sense," he whispered and pulled her close, feeling the cool silk brush his hands, the rustle of her skirts, the warmth of her. He lowered his head to cover her mouth, parting her lips.

Desire burst within her. In spite of many kisses with Blake or Ticiano, Luke had awakened sensations she had never experienced before. She was amazed at the intensity of her desire for him, and it seemed to build each time she was with him. She relished pressing her body against his hard length; she had to fight an urge to let her hands drift over him as freely as he did her.

"Blake said I'm wild. I embarrassed him."

Luke kissed her hard. He didn't want to hear about Blake or think about Blake making love to Catalina. And in spite of her declarations of innocence, he felt sure Blake had. She was too sensuous to be innocent, and too demanding. She was a burning flame, like an awakened woman. He'd known virgins and they had been shy and reluctant and modest. Catalina was none of those. And she set him on fire with her hips grinding against him, her full, fantastic breasts pressing against his chest. He released her abruptly. "We should stop. I can't go back to the party now."

Catalina knew why. She had felt his manhood press against her. The pressure had made her quiver with excitement, and curiosity about Luke was rampant. She wanted to kiss him and touch him. Most of all she wanted him to kiss and touch her, to drive her wild as he could so easily do. She ran her fingers across his cheek. "How did you get scarred?"

Her question jarred him back to reality. There was no way he could tell her the truth and have her see the depth of her father's brutality. And he couldn't reveal his hatred or his intentions. Never. Domingo was a wall between them, and Luke knew he wasn't free to love her. Not now, not tomorrow, not ever. She might have her quarrels with Domingo, but he was her father, and she seemed loyal to him and probably loved him in spite of his cruelty. Luke kissed her fingers lightly, regret rising in him over what had to be. "I was in a bad fight once. I almost died."

"Oh, no." She threw his arms around him and hugged him, and he smiled as he disentangled himself.

"Catalina, you sound as if you're going to cry over me. Everything is very wonderful or very terrible for you, isn't it?"

She shrugged. "Perhaps so. And nothing is very terrible or very wonderful for you, eh?"

"I don't show my feelings like you do, but there are wonderful and terrible things in my life," he answered solemnly.

"What wonderful things?" she asked, wanting to hear him say that she was the most wonderful thing.

"Wonderful—you, Catalina."

"Ahh, Luke," she said with satisfaction. "I'm wonderful?"

"Very, very wonderful and special," he said solemnly, with another aching twist of regret. "Some time I want you to meet a friend of mine. He's a Kiowa, Ta-ne-haddle. He saved my life once."

"When you were in the bad fight?"

"Yes. A long, long time ago."

"Catalina!"

"That's my father."

"Go ahead. Answer him."

She kissed Luke quickly on the cheek and stepped around him to hurry toward the house. "Here I am. I was walking . . ."

Her voice trailed away. Luke jammed his hands into his pockets, feeling caught in a dilemma he hadn't ever expected to have happen. He cared for Catalina more than any woman he had ever known. He clamped his jaw shut angrily, and went inside to find his host and thank him for the evening. As he was leaving he glanced over his shoulder to see Catalina's back turned to him, her dark hair shining, parted in the center, fasted in loops of braids over each ear with tiny flowers and ribbons. She stood in another circle of men who gave her their undivided attention. Luke left, mounting his horse to ride home, suffering a longing he had never known before.

Catalina finally realized he had gone without telling her good-bye. She expected her family to leave soon. Most of the guests had gone. Suddenly her father was at her side, his hand clamping on her shoulder.

"Friedrich has asked if he could accompany you home, and I gave my permission."

She almost cried out a protest, but one look at his dark, threatening eyes and she held her tongue.

"I told him he must bring you straight home."

"Mama agrees to this?" Catalina couldn't resist whispering.

"She agrees. Friedrich is an old and dear friend, and will soon be my son-in-law."

She drew a sharp breath and would have protested vehemently, but Friedrich appeared at that moment. The men talked as Friedrich accompanied her parents and the last guests to the door. He turned to face her and she knew it was highly irregular for her to be at his house so late at night. If her reputation was compromised, she would have to marry him.

"Papa said you're taking me home, and we should go right away."

Friedrich smiled. "Of course. My servant is getting the carriage. Come here, Catalina, I want to show you something."

He led her to the library with its shelves filled with books. With only one lamp the room was sparse, dark, and gloomy. Friedrich handed her a box, and she held it disdainfully.

"Open it. It's a gift for you."

"For me?" She longed to refuse, yet she knew she

shouldn't. She raised the lid and gazed at the sparkling diamond necklace.

"Friedrich, you shouldn't. It isn't proper."

"No, it isn't," he said, taking it from her hands and closing it to place it on his desk. "But it will be proper when we become engaged. It's yours as soon as we announce our engagement."

"Thank you," she said stiffly.

He yanked her to him suddenly. "I want to announce our engagement next week, Catalina."

"No! I don't want to wed," she said, her hands pushing against his chest, feeling his powerful muscles. He was broad-shouldered with a barrel chest, and she was defenseless against his strength.

"You will. Your father has already given me permission. I want you to say yes without having to resort to force."

"No," she gasped, struggling to get out of his grasp. "You're supposed to take me home."

"I will, I will." He pinned her to him and kissed her, his mouth as forceful as before. He pushed her backward and they went down on the sofa. Catalina fought him as he shoved her back against the cushions. He held her arms behind her, his leg holding hers down so she couldn't kick him while he kissed her brutally. His hand unfastened her dress, reaching beneath the soft material to squeeze her breast. Catalina relaxed momentarily, enduring his caresses, waiting for the moment his hold relaxed. Suddenly she burst into fury, kicking and wriggling away from him, running to the door. He caught her, slamming the door and spinning her around.

"I won't marry you! Take me home!"

"If I possess you now, you won't be able to refuse," he said in his harsh German accent, and her blood went cold with fear.

"I'll make your life a living hell if you force me into this marriage," she said, looking him in the eye.

His blue eyes narrowed, and she braced for him to hit her.

"Go ahead, strike me, but the first chance I get, I'll put a bullet through your heart."

"I should have found a good German girl—"

"A good German girl would act the same if you treated her as you have me. I won't endure your cruelty and domination like my mother has endured my father's. I loathe your kisses and your touch."

"You slut!" he snapped, yanking her closer with his fist wound in her hair. "You'll marry me and you'll do what I want or I'll throw your father out of the business."

"Go ahead. My father is a wealthy man. He can open his own business."

"You ignorant little chit. Your father doesn't have half the wealth I do. I'll ruin him if you don't acquiesce right now. Apologize to me."

"Never," she snapped, her fists clenched, her head aching where he was pulling her hair. She loathed him, and wanted to escape from him. And she saw he was debating; she knew the moment he made the decision to take her by force. He reached up with both hands to rip the front of her bodice. She kicked with all her strength, then jerked her knee high to hit him in the groin. He doubled over and she ran, throwing open the door, oblivious of her torn dress.

She raced out the front door, yanking up her skirts to run down the center of the street. Friedrich wouldn't risk the humiliation and ire of the townspeople by running after her. Then she realized he could come on horseback and get her easily. She glanced around and veered to the right, dashing beneath the high porch of a neighboring house. In seconds she heard the pounding of a horse, and Friedrich appeared in the road. He slowed his horse, then stopped, looking all around.

13

CATALINA HELD HER BREATH, SCOOTING BACK. Her hands and knees were smudged with dirt and her skirt dragged in the dust, but she was oblivious of them. Friedrich looked around slowly, and she froze.

He rode closer to the house, and her heart lurched. If he caught her, he could carry her back to his house. She debated whether she should try to break free and run, and decided to wait until she knew he had spotted her. He rode closer and dismounted. She heard his feet approaching, and she prayed he couldn't see her.

His boots swished in the grass; the sound grew louder and finally began to fade. She let out her breath slowly, watching him walk back to the road, leading his horse behind him. He disappeared on the other side of the road, and she heard him thrashing the bushes.

She slipped out from behind the porch and tiptoed around the house to the back. Watching for Friedrich, she tried to stay in the shadows. With a pounding heart she gathered her skirt, slipped between the rails of a fence, and hid behind the trunk of a tree. She heard the horse and peeked around to see Friedrich return to the house where she had hidden beneath the porch.

Thankful she had moved away, she watched him disappear under the porch.

Forcing herself to walk carefully, trying to be as quiet as possible, she crept away in the shadows. The flesh on the nape of her neck tingled, and she shivered

as if it were a winter night, but she kept walking quietly.

Soon she slipped through another fence. At the
sound of hoofbeats she pressed against a tree trunk.
In minutes Friedrich rode slowly past.

Her mind raced. Friedrich was a ruthless, determined man. And a powerful one. If she didn't get
home soon, he could still claim to have possessed her,
and her ruined reputation would force her into the
marriage. Any minute now the realization might occur
to him, and he could go confess to Domingo that he
had seduced her. Her disheveled appearance would
only confirm the lies. She bit her lip, trying to decide
what to do. She could climb into her bedroom window
and claim she had been home for hours, but her father
might not believe her.

Luke. She could find Luke and he could take her
home and tell her father they had been together. Friedrich wouldn't come forward if he saw Luke's buggy at
the house.

She heard hoofbeats and Friedrich rode back, turning into the lot across the road to dismount and search
for her again.

"Catalina!"

The anger was clear in his tone. It might be only
minutes until he found her or rode to her home. Pan-
icky, she angled off across the back of the lot, holding
up her skirts to run. She had to find Luke, get him to
take her home.

Skirting some lots, cutting across others, she raced
along until she saw his house and the empty lots surrounding it. She tried to smooth her hair in place,
pinning up curls that had fallen. Yellow light glowed
in an upstairs room. She held up her skirts, crossing
uneven ground.

Suddenly a hand clamped her arm. She was spun
around, and another hand clamped over her mouth to
smother her scream.

Catalina gazed into the dark features of an li. Her breath caught and held as terror shook her.

"I'm a friend of Luke Danby's," the man said, and she went weak with relief.

He released her. "Sorry if I frightened you, but I saw you walking along. You're Catalina Piedra, aren't you?"

"Yes. How did you know?"

"Luke's told me about you. I'm Ta-ne-haddle."

The Kiowa who saved his life."

"He told you?"

"He said he was in a terrible fight once, and you saved his life."

"Come along and we'll get him," he said, taking her arm and leading her across the yard and through the back door. "Luke!"

"Tell him to hurry, please," she said, and Ta-ne-haddle called again. She tried to straighten her clothing and fasten what buttons hadn't been torn. Removing her wide, silk sash, she pulled it around her shoulders like a shawl and knotted it over her breasts. She heard a footstep and a jingle of spurs, and turned to see Luke. She flung herself into his arms and he caught her.

"What happened?"

"Take me home, and I'll tell you on the way, but we have to hurry."

"It was Friedrich, wasn't it?" Luke asked. A fierce note had come into his voice even though the tone hadn't raised so much as a fraction.

"Yes. Please, let's go."

"Ta-ne-haddle is getting my horse right now," he said and she saw the Indian had gone. As they went outside, she poured out what had happened, pausing while Luke mounted, lifting her up in front of him. Ta-ne-haddle waved them on and disappeared into the shadows.

"I'm afraid Friedrich will realize he can go to Papa and say I succumbed to him willingly, and then I'll have to marry him. Will you tell Papa you brought me home, and that I've been with you, riding home?''

"Yes, I will," Luke answered firmly.

"Luke, don't do anything to Friedrich. I wasn't hurt."

"I won't promise, Catalina. Nor will my new deputy, Hans Kaupman. He's an immigrant. The Germans are a close-knit group, and they're not going to be happy to discover Friedrich's activities."

"There are wicked men the world over, just as there are good men," she said, and he looked at her sharply. She was straightening her dress, and he wondered what would happen if she were to learn how evil her father was. Luke suspected it might not come as a shock, and he felt protective toward her, wanting to shield her from the knowledge as well as a loveless marriage, above all, from what he knew he must do to Domingo. The opposing emotions in him made him silent while she worked hastily to straighten her garments. She smoothed stray hairs into place and when he stopped in front of her house and dismounted, lifting her down, she asked him, "How do I look?"

"Just as lovely as you did at the party," he said in his mellow voice, smoothing a stray tendril away from her face. For a second she forgot her problems, because his touch and warm voice made her aware only of him. His gaze drifted down and his fingers smoothed the sash over her breasts.

"Luke," she whispered, tingling from his touch. "We must go inside. I'm afraid Friedrich will arrive at any moment. He might have already been here."

"I'd like to pull that bit of silk off and kiss you," he whispered.

Longing stirred within her, and she couldn't resist reaching out and stroking his arm, wishing they could be alone for hours. "We have to go inside," she whispered, thinking Luke was becoming the most handsome man she had ever known in spite of his scars.

He took her arm and they headed up the walk. She

was conscious when she brushed against him where his hand held her arm, light touches that were volatile. And then awareness yielded to the problems at hand, and fear came.

Her heart pounded violently. Her father would be displeased, both with her saying she returned with Luke, and with the fact that she had once again gone against his wishes. When they reached her house, light spilled from the front windows and the front door was open. Catalina stepped inside the lighted hallway.

"Papa!"

Domingo appeared from the parlor. He had a drink in his hand, his coat was gone, his shirt unfastened at the throat. He squinted his eyes as he looked at them.

"Luke brought me home," she said, waiting for Domingo's anger.

"I forgot my hat," Luke said with ease, "and when I went back to get it, I saw that you and your family had gone, so I asked Catalina if she would like me to accompany her home. I'd like to sit on the porch and talk to Catalina for a few minutes if I may."

Domingo gave her an angry glance as he scowled, but he looked at Luke with speculation. "Of course. I suppose I can trust the town marshal. I'll be in the parlor."

Domingo and Catalina seldom hid their emotions, and their expressions gave away many of their thoughts. Luke guessed that it had just occurred to Domingo that Luke might also be a candidate for Catalina's hand, and Domingo was too shrewd to alienate the marshal. Also, Domingo didn't know the full extent of Luke's worth, and that would keep him from refusing Luke any reasonable request.

Luke led Catalina to the far end of the porch away from the parlor. "Your father can hear us," he said softly into her ear. "I wanted to sit out here where Friedrich can see us. It should prevent him from going to the door to talk to your father."

"Of course," she answered softly, unable to resist letting her fingers brush his hand.

The touch was little more than the breeze playing over his skin, but it made Luke intently aware of her. She was more sensuous than any woman he had ever known. She constantly touched him and liked to be touched. He leaned back in the chair next to hers, propping his feet on the porch rail and tilting his chair. "Would you like to go to a bullfight Sunday? I'll ask your father if I can escort you."

"I like the bullfights! Of course, I will if he allows it," she said enthusiastically. "My father goes often, but Mama and Emilio have never enjoyed them."

"I paid a peso and saw my first one last Sunday," he said, his voice a deep rumble in the night. He reached out to stroke the nape of her neck lightly, and the caress made her pulse race wildly.

"Did you like it?" she asked, barely aware of her question, far more conscious of the desire his strokes kindled.

"Better than the cockfights on the Plaza. Mostly, I prefer the horse races along the Alameda."

"We can see both on Sunday afternoon," she said, longing to feel his arms around her. She studied his profile, his firm jaw and thin nose with a slight crook. He had tossed his hat down, and a lock of hair curled over his forehead.

"I can't decide whether to have more furniture made here in town or to order it. Do you know what your parents did?"

They talked about furniture, and Luke tried to keep the same casual tone when he heard the approach of hoofbeats. He stood up and sat on the porch railing, where he was silhouetted by the light in the window inside the house. When Friedrich halted in front, Luke sauntered down the walk to meet him.

"Danby. What are you doing here?" Friedrich asked.

"I left my hat on your porch and went back to pick

it up,'' Luke said evenly, clenching his fists and trying to resist the urge to yank Friedrich off the horse. ''I told Domingo I saw the guests were going, so I brought Catalina home. We've been sitting here on her porch ever since with Domingo inside where he can hear us.''

Friedrich sat as still as a statue, and Luke waited, knowing that he still could cause trouble if he wanted.

''I'll be glad to tell Domingo you were concerned about Catalina's welfare and wanted to make sure she was home safely, that you didn't realize she left with me,'' Luke said quietly. ''So you can go on home now.''

With a jerk of the reins Friedrich wheeled his horse around and rode away, urging the horse to a canter. Luke strolled back to the porch as Catalina came down the steps. He was tall, commanding, and exciting. She wanted him to come back and sit with her and talk for hours, but she knew he wouldn't. Luke always seemed to have some kind of reserve with her. She sensed he was fighting to control his emotions, but she couldn't understand why. Unless he didn't want to marry and was afraid he might be trapped into it. Whatever the reason, she wished he would lose his iron control. He excited her as no man had, and he was quickly becoming more special than any other man, including Blake. Blake seemed like a sweet boy in comparison to Luke.

''I'll ride on home now,'' he said quietly, holding her shoulders lightly. She knew Domingo was probably watching them, yet she longed to feel Luke's arms around her, if only for a moment.

''Good night, Catalina,'' he said in a husky voice that made her tremble with longing. He mounted up to ride away, sitting straight and tall in the saddle.

Catalina took a deep breath and rushed upstairs without looking back, expecting at any second Domingo would order her downstairs for a stormy confrontation.

He stood in the parlor doorway watching her go. She had probably insulted Friedrich, yet Luke Danby must be interested in her, and Luke Danby was a man of means. If only he could learn more about him, he might make a better suitor than Friedrich. And Friedrich's threats to buy him out tormented Domingo. He was unaccustomed to anyone holding power over him. Friedrich might have a bad accident one dark night soon, and Catalina could wed Ticiano or Luke Danby or any other wealthy suitor.

His thoughts shifted back to the evening. Catalina's young friends were beautiful; he had watched them all evening, his desire rising. The constraints of family life and the freighting business and the daily grind were constantly annoying. There was far too little pleasure in his life, far too much responsibility. More and more now, he was tempted to take some of his gold, give everything else to the family, and just leave them.

Swearing softly, Domingo picked up his hat and went striding out the back door. He had a new woman he kept in a small house on a back street, Monica Fitzgerald. She had blond hair and blue eyes, and there were moments he imagined he held Hattie. After all these years he still dreamed of the golden-haired captive. He wondered if she were still alive. Deep down he suspected she wasn't, but he closed his mind to that abruptly, trying to think of Monica, wanting release from his pent-up frustration.

On Monday morning when Domingo arrived at the office, Friedrich wasn't there. It was the first time Domingo could recall that Friedrich hadn't informed him of his absence beforehand. Friedrich was seldom absent, and never once to Domingo's knowledge had he been late.

That afternoon Domingo was busy at the dock, where they were loading wagons headed west, when Juan Todaro, one of his employees from the ranch, appeared in the doorway, motioning to Domingo. He handed a checklist to Will Sanders and stepped to the door.

"I have to see you alone, boss," Juan said quietly.

In his office Domingo closed the door. "What's happened?" he said, standing with his fists on his hips, his patience worn thin by the chores of the day.

"You wanted me to find out who owns Pioneer Freighting Company, your competitor."

"Yes. Who is it?" Domingo asked, moving around his desk to sit down, curiosity gripping him.

"Your partner, Friedrich Krueger."

"*What?*" Domingo said, coming to his feet immediately. "You can't be right."

"Yes, I am. I followed Tandy McGuire. He met Friedrich this morning at dawn. They went into Tandy's front room, and the windows were open. I couldn't hear all they said, but I heard enough. Friedrich owns the company."

His temper soaring, Domingo swore. He wanted to beat Friedrich into the ground with his bare fists. His mind raced over what to do. And he knew what he wanted first: to bring Friedrich to his knees and teach him a lesson he wouldn't forget.

"Tonight I want you to get five of my boys. Take Manuel, Jake, Durango, Enrique, and you. Give Friedrich a beating he won't ever forget. He won't ever cross me again. And then burn down that damn freight office."

"He'll go to the law and say you did it."

"How many women can swear all five of you were at Miss Bea's Sporting House all night long?"

Juan's dark eyes glittered. "No problem, but what about you?"

Domingo's mind raced over the possibilities. "I'll spend the evening with the marshal and my family. If he's not available, I'll have someone reliable." He walked to the safe and opened it, looking at the bags of Mexican silver. He took three of Friedrich's and thumped them on the desk. "Here. Take one bag to Miss Bea. Tell her to keep half and use the other half to pay her girls. They'll get more than their usual three dollars a trick tonight."

"*Si.*" Juan nodded, his eyes on the bags of gold.

"This bag is for you. Don't make any mistakes. Divide the other bag with the boys. Good work, Juan."

"*Gracias. Buenas tardes,*" he said, lapsing into Spanish as he picked up the bags of gold and slid them beneath his shirt, making his chest bulge. He grinned and was gone.

Impatiently Domingo paced the floor, running his hands through his thick black hair while he swore with rage. He wanted to kill Friedrich for his deceit. He was tempted to send one of his boys and kill Friedrich some dark night in the future, but Domingo weighed the consequences and possibilities. Friedrich was ruthless, daring, and shrewd. If he learned he couldn't cross Domingo, he still might be useful.

On impulse Domingo took his bags of cartwheels from the safe and half of the remaining ones of Friedrich's. He packed them into a small crate and called to one of his men to load them into his buckboard. Domingo rode home and had a servant unload them, placing them in his safe at home. He rode back to work, shutting himself in the office while he mulled over the future.

In the middle of the afternoon he heard footsteps and Friedrich entered. Fighting to control his temper, Domingo leaned back in his chair and glared at him. He saw anger in Friedrich's expression in turn.

"I'm dissolving our partnership," Friedrich announced coldly, his face flushing.

Curious as to what had prompted the sudden change, Domingo leaned back in his chair. "Isn't that rather sudden? Yesterday we were making plans for expanding."

"Yesterday I expected your daughter to marry me. Catalina is a headstrong strumpet—"

Domingo was up instantly, his chair crashing against the wall. Just as swiftly, Friedrich drew a derringer and Domingo halted in his tracks. "Sit down, Domingo. And keep your hands on the desk. I'm buying your part of the business or you can buy mine. I give you a choice."

"You bastard," Domingo ground out the words, his temper soaring. "You know I don't have the money available to buy you out."

"Then I shall have to buy your share," Friedrich replied with an icy smile.

"You filthy *ladrón. Basurero.*"

"While you promised Catalina's hand in marriage, you allowed her to ride unchaperoned with Danby. I don't care to marry used goods."

"Damn you, he's the town marshal. All he did was escort her home."

"I've drawn up the papers to dissolve this business." Friedrich flung them down on the desk. "I've been generous with your share. Sign them, or have the money on my desk by tomorrow. And Domingo, I know you're not a subtle man. Don't try to kill me. You'll only end up at the end of a rope. I intend to tell Danby that you've already threatened me. And—I kept two boxes of those cartwheels clearly marked with the men's names you robbed. I'll turn you in if you try anything."

"You agreed to the thefts! You were as much a part as if you had ridden with me and my men."

"It will come down to my word against that of you and your men—and I have a better record than you. I didn't burn down the Cornings' house. You're in no position to give me trouble, so don't try." With the gun still poised, he backed out and left abruptly.

Crossing the room and kicking the door shut, Domingo swore steadily. He doubled his fists, striking the chair and sending it sliding across the room against a wall. He wanted to smash something, to go after Friedrich and kill him with his bare hands. He didn't want to sell his share of a lucrative, growing business. He could start his own, but it would mean starting over, and he didn't have enough capital available now. He swore, hating the confinements of his life, the loss of control. He snatched up his hat to go. He should be able to overtake Juan on his way to the ranch. And he would have Juan and his boys kill Friedrich. How he longed to join them, but he would have to have a strong alibi. Weaving his way alongside a herd of cattle on a drive through town, Domingo stopped at the courthouse to invite Luke to dinner. If he dined with the marshal, that should be sufficient accounting of his whereabouts.

Twenty minutes later, Luke closed the door to shut out the dust from the herd headed down El Potrero. The rumbling of their hooves was loud enough to almost drown out the sound of the soldiers drilling and the band playing on the southeast side of the Plaza, and the shouts of the cowmen added to the noise. Luke stared thoughtfully after Domingo. He couldn't understand what had prompted the invitation to dinner. He wasn't openly courting Catalina, yet Domingo had pressed him to come. Luke shrugged. He seemed to receive more invitations since he had been sworn in as Bexar County Marshal.

Ta-ne-haddle drifted into the office as silently as a shadow, and gazed all around him. He was bare chested and wore fringed buckskins, moccasins, feathers in his braid, and a silver chain he had fashioned around his neck. His body was bronze, all hard muscle, and Luke thought again that it was a shame Ta-ne-haddle had lived such a solitary life. He was handsome and intelligent, his body fit and full of vitality. He had long ago told Luke how he had lost his eye in a fight with Dancing Sun's husband, but Luke thought it hardly detracted from his commanding appearance with his high cheekbones and a beak of a nose. "Very nice place."

"And you could have one too if you would go back and finish your education."

Ta-ne-haddle grinned. "You think a Kiowa could be

sworn in as marshal in any county in the West? They don't even count us in the United States Census. We're non-people.''

Luke grinned. ''Pull up a chair, non-person, and tell me what you learned.''

Ta-ne-haddle sat down in a straight-backed chair. ''I learned that Friedrich Krueger owns part interest with Domingo in a freighting business. Krueger's past is obscure, but there's a brother in Houston. Also, a closely guarded fact, he owns a newer business, competing with himself and his partner, the Pioneer Freighting Company.''

''You're sure?'' Luke said, digesting the startling discovery. He didn't listen for Ta-ne-haddle's answer, and Ta-ne-haddle didn't give one to the useless question.

''Domingo doesn't know.''

''Obviously not.''

''Thanks. I'm invited to the Piedras for dinner tonight.''

''I'll see what else I can learn,'' Ta-ne-haddle said, and stood up. ''The Williams Exchange and Billiard Parlor is a good place to get information,'' he said, striding from the room as noiselessly as he had entered and closing the office door behind him.

Luke sat quietly thinking about the implications of the latest bit of news. And then his thoughts shifted to Catalina. He would see her tonight. He felt a skip in his pulse, a sense of hopeless longing that was futile. Always Domingo stood between them and never could he explain to her why.

Thoughts of Catalina made him remember the weekend. He would like to confront Friedrich and repay him for what he had done to her. He pushed back his chair and strode purposefully down the hall into the sunshine, listening to the band as the soldiers did their daily drill.

He discovered both Friedrich and Domingo were gone from their office. He searched for Friedrich and finally found him at the lumber yard, where he talked to workmen as they stood by a tall pile of freshly milled lumber. While Luke removed his marshal's badge, which had been fashioned from a shiny, Mexican cartwheel, the owner appeared.

"Afternoon, Marshal. What can we do for you today?"

"Otto, you can hold this for me. For the moment I don't want to act in an official capacity."

14

"Sure, Marshal. Whatever you say," the balding German said with a puzzled note.

Luke walked over to Friedrich, who had stopped looking at lumber and was watching him with curiosity. Luke halted a few feet away, his fists clenched. He stood with his feet planted apart; his legs, enclosed in black pants, were taut with bunched muscles.

"I'm not the town marshal for the moment, Krueger."

"I see you're not, Friedrich answered with a faint smile. "I expected to see you before now." He stood with his coat off, his shirt sleeves rolled up to reveal hard muscles.

"This is for a lady," Luke said quietly. He swung his fist to hit Friedrich on the jaw. Friedrich dodged but not quickly enough. The blow caught him on the jaw, but he jabbed with his right and snapped Luke's head back. Luke swung again, remembering how Catalina had looked, knowing what the results of the evening could have been if she hadn't managed to escape from Friedrich. In seconds he realized Friedrich was accustomed to fighting, as he matched blow for blow. They exchanged punches, staggering against piles of lumber until Luke pulled back his right fist and drove it full force against Friedrich's jaw. Friedrich slammed against a stack of lumber, and then slid to the ground limply.

Luke gasped for breath and wiped his bloody jaw. He drew himself up, shaking his head to clear it and

walked over to Otto holding out his hand. "I'll . . .
take my badge." he gulped for air. "Send me a bill
for damages."

"No damages, Marshal," Otto said in awed tone.
"That's a mean right you throw."

"Yeah, sure," Luke said, barely hearing him for the
ringing in his ears. Jamming his hat on his head, he
staggered away. A crowd had gathered; there were
murmurs and some calls of praise. A few shouted
questions about what had Friedrich Krueger done, but
they parted and let him pass.

He wove his way across the street, ambling back to
the Military Plaza and Bat Cave.

"Luke." He paused and swayed when he heard his
name called.

Looking like a vision in a pink gingham dress, Catalina scrambled down from the Piedra buggy while the
driver climbed down slowly. She ran over to grasp
Luke's arm.

"You're hurt. Someone came to tell Papa you were
fighting with Friedrich, and I knew it had to be over
me."

"Shh, Catalina. Go home. You'll start a hell of a
bunch of rumors," he muttered, the world spinning
crazily.

"Let people talk! You shouldn't have fought him.
That miserable sonofabitch—"

"Catalina, not now. People will hear you."

"Let them hear," she exclaimed more loudly.
"Friedrich Krueger is a varmint!"

"Lordy, get me in Bat Cave before I faint," he managed to get out the words, hoping she would forget
Friedrich for a moment.

"Don't faint. *Madre de Dios!* I've sent for the doctor. Come on, lean on me and I'll help you to your
office. Oh, Luke, I didn't want you to fight him. You're
hurt."

"I think you're right," he mumbled, wiping a trickle
of blood off his jaw.

"You're angry."

"Not at you," he murmured. "Smell sweet, Catalina. Soft, sweet. Want to kiss you, but I can't."

"I know you can't now. You better be quiet, Luke."

"I better be quiet."

"There's some people gathering around your office."

"Oh, Lordy."

She waved her hand. "Here comes Doc's buggy, thank goodness!"

She stepped through the crowd, and someone took Luke's other arm to help him. They led him to the chair in his office. He sank down, leaning back and closing his eyes.

Catalina ran outside to pump a bucket of water and bring it inside, wringing out a cloth to wipe Luke's forehead. In seconds Dr. Milton Ellison, tall, lanky, and sandy-haired, shooed out the onlookers and closed the door.

"What happened, Marshal? Someone resist arrest?"

"No sir. Little disagreement with a man. I wasn't wearing my badge. Had nothing to do with marshaling."

"Just a fight, huh? Who's the lucky fellow?"

"Friedrich Krueger," Catalina answered, biting her lip. "Will Marshal Danby live?"

Dr. Ellison snorted. " 'Course he'll live. You've seen a man who's been in a fight before. Where's Krueger?"

"He's at the lumber yard," Catalina answered before Luke could say a word. "I think they fought over me," she whispered.

Luke groaned. If she didn't stop, by nightfall rumors would be so rampant, he would have to marry her to save her reputation. "No, sir," he snapped.

"No sir, *what?*" Dr. Ellison asked.

Luke opened one eye and saw Catalina hovering over him, looking worried and distraught. He couldn't deny what she had said, because it would be ungentlemanly. He gave up and fell back with his eyes closed. Catalina shrieked, making him open both eyes.

"I'm all right," he said hastily.

"Madre de Dios, I thought you had fainted," she cried and knelt down beside him to take his hand.

"Ouch!" Luke said as she crushed his sore hand in hers. Instantly she released him.

"Miss Piedra, why don't you step aside and let me check the man over for broken bones."

"Of course."

"Better still, step outside."

"Of course," she said and left. In a few minutes Dr. Ellison closed his black bag with a snap. "You'll live. I better go look at Krueger."

"Doc . . ."

Yeah?"

"Let me pay you, and don't tell people we fought over Catalina."

"I won't tell. You can pay me when you feel better."

"Thanks."

As soon as he was gone, Luke pulled himself to his feet, went down the hall to glance through the door at the crowd, and waved at them. A few waved back, and to his relief they all began to move away. Catalina came inside and tears glistened on her lashes, giving a twist to Luke's heart.

"Don't cry," he said as he took her arm to lead her back into his office.

"You did that because of me, and you're hurt."

"Not one blow bothered me as much as your tears. Don't cry over me, Catalina."

She smiled and blinked and stood on tiptoe to kiss his cheek. He wanted to hold her, but he couldn't because his ribs hurt. He put his arms around her lightly. "I can't kiss you."

"I shall always hate Friedrich."

"I started this, not Friedrich."

"You did it for me."

"I have to sit down. My head is spinning. Friedrich's had his share of fights. He gave me some mean punches."

"I don't want to hear about Friedrich or ever think about him again." Suddenly she spun in front of him, almost toppling him over. "But, one more thing about Friedrich, Papa said I won't have to marry him."

Startled, Luke forgot his aches momentarily. "What changed his mind?"

"I don't know and I don't care. I couldn't have married Friedrich Krueger. I would have run away first."

Luke grinned in spite of the ache it caused. "You probably would have," he said, touching her shoulder. "I'm invited to your house for dinner tonight."

"I know. Will you feel well enough to come?"

"Wild horses couldn't keep me away."

She slanted a sensuous look at him that made him want to kiss her. "We've having several people tonight. The Garcias are coming and the Schmidts. I hope you feel better by then."

"I've been through this before. By tonight it'll be worse."

"Oh no. I still wish you hadn't done this."

"Forget it, Catalina."

"Mama's waiting. I'll go now."

In another hour Luke closed his office and went down to the floating bathhouse on the San Antonio River by Nat Lewis's grist mill. Luke had paid three dollars to bathe daily for three months instead of the single rate of ten cents a bath. He intended to soak his sore muscles for an hour if he had to pay Mr. Hall extra for the time and hot water.

That night he was still sore, but the hot bath had helped. His pulse jumped when he saw Catalina. She was devastatingly beautiful in a simple white chambray low-necked blouse and a bright red gingham skirt. Red flowers were tucked behind one ear. A silver chain dangled around her neck, the links glittering against her olive skin above the rise of her full breasts. As he realized that the low-necked Mexican blouse leaving her shoulders bare also meant she wasn't wearing a chemise or anything beneath, the thought set his blood pounding. It was an effort to look away, to carry on a normal conversation.

Domingo was his most charming, and Luke wondered why he had been invited. Twice he caught Domingo watching him speculatively, and he guessed that Domingo expected him to ask for Catalina's hand in marriage. The idea disturbed him, because more and more his life and Catalina's were being drawn together. He cared for her more than he wanted to admit. He had wanted to possess her since the first day at the river, but it ran deeper now and he wouldn't deliberately hurt her. But there was no way on this earth could he marry Domingo Piedra's daughter.

Disturbed, he excused himself and left early, but the party seemed to be going strong as he walked outside to mount his horse.

"Luke."

Catalina stood on the porch while a servant stood by the door. Luke motioned to her to join him and he took the reins, leading the horse while Catalina walked beside him toward the wide, dusty street.

"Are you all right?"

"Yes. I'm going to the office. We have a prisoner in jail and I need to relieve one of my deputies."

"You're the marshal. Let your deputy stay at night."

"He just married recently," Luke drawled dryly. "I figure he'd like to be home in bed. I would if I had just married."

A tingle raced through Catalina at his words. He stood close to her, looking down at her with his hands resting on her shoulders. She swayed closer.

He dropped the reins and moved Catalina around so the horse was between them and the house. "Now no one can see us."

She smiled up at him, moonlight playing over her

features. He leaned down to kiss her, ignoring his bruised mouth or the ache her kisses caused.

"Luke I'll hurt you. We—"

Luke silenced her protest. All evening he had wanted to kiss her. His tongue played in her mouth, tasting her sweetness, fueling the fires within him. He reached up to untie the red ribbon that was a drawstring for the neck of her bodice and he pushed it down, cupping her breasts that were bare.

He groaned as he bent his head to kiss her flesh, breathing a faint scent of rosewater, feeling her nipples grow taut as his tongue flicked over them. He wanted her with a burning, overpowering need, and he fought for control.

He released her and watched as she stepped back, pulling her blouse into place and retying the red ribbon.

"I better go back now," she whispered.

He knew he was on the brink of disaster. He should use more control around her, but it was impossible. With regret he watched her walk away.

At the courthouse he set the two oil lamps where he could get the best reading light, took down a heavy volume from the top of his desk, and opened the book to read.

Domingo settled back in his chair, telling his friends about the latest battle between the Mexican drivers with their oxcarts and the new drivers with their wagons and mules. While he listened to Antonio, his thoughts drifted from freighting problems. He was sorry Marshal Danby had to leave early, but it wouldn't be bad, because the marshal had been here and when he left he knew everyone else was prepared to stay for hours.

Now was about the time when his men would attack Friedrich. Actually, the marshal had played right into his hands today with his fight with Friedrich. People would think Friedrich had died from his injuries caused in the fight. Most important, Friedrich would learn too late that he shouldn't have tried to cross his partner.

He glanced at Catalina as she entered the room and realized Luke Danby had kissed her. Her mouth was red, her cheeks pink. Well and good if the marshal had enough wealth. Otherwise it would be Ticiano who would claim Catalina. Perhaps, he mused, he should stop Catalina from riding around town unchaperoned with the marshal.

Luke shifted in his chair. He was uncomfortable and growing weary of reading. The town had grown so silent that a scraping noise made Luke lift his head. He heard a low moan and tilted his head to listen, staring at the darkened windows and the blackness outside. There was a rustle and another moan. Frowning, Luke took down his gun belt from a peg and buckled it around his waist. He moved cautiously toward the hall and heard another scrape. He rested his hand on the butt of his gun. He had made an enemy this morning, and he had been using more caution ever since.

With only a faint jingle of his spurs, he walked quietly to the door. When he heard another moan, he frowned, trying to sort out the sounds. Cautiously he stepped into the hall, glancing down the hallway toward the open door at the end of the darkness outside. Luke's breath caught in his throat.

A man lay sprawled on the ground, half over the threshold of the door and into the hall. He groaned as Luke reached him in long strides and knelt beside him.

"Friedrich!" Stunned, Luke didn't know where to touch him to help. The man was beaten almost beyond recognition. "Let me help you inside and I'll get the doctor."

"No." Friedrich tried to move, gripping Luke's arm to pull him closer. "It was Domingo. His men—"

"Let me get a doctor," Luke said grimly. "I can carry you into my office." He turned Friedrich over and picked him up. Carrying him into his office, he placed him on the floor. He pulled off his coat and covered him, his stomach churning at the bloody pulp of Friedrich's face. Friedrich moaned and motioned Luke down.

"Get to my safe at my house. In upstairs bedroom. Domingo robbed wagons we sent out . . . knew had silver. He did this . . . get him. One of his men dead at my house. Dissolved partnership today . . ."

Shocked by his statements, Luke knew time was running out. Friedrich was bleeding profusely from several wounds. "I'm going for the doctor. I'll hurry." As much as he disliked Friedrich, he hated Domingo more. Now he knew why Domingo had invited him to dinner tonight. He had a solid excuse for his whereabouts while his men beat Friedrich to death. Luke mounted his horse and urged it to a gallop, rushing the short distance to pound on Dr. Ellison's door.

It opened and Mrs. Ellison stared at him. "It's the marshal," she called, holding up a flickering candle. "Come in. He'll be ready in one minute."

"Tell him to make it faster than that. Friedrich Krueger may die."

She turned away to get her husband's black bag, coat, and hat, and in seconds Dr. Ellison appeared. "You tie into Krueger again today?" he asked, squinting at Luke.

"No, I didn't," Luke answered. "I found him trying to get to my office to tell me about the men who beat him."

Doc Ellison looked Luke over and nodded his head. He mounted up behind him to ride with him as they rushed back to his office.

Luke helped Dr. Ellison clean and bandage Friedrich's wounds. "We need to get him home. I'll have to get my buckboard."

"And I need to get my deputies. He said there's one man dead at his house.

"You go to my place. Tell Mama to get my buckboard and her brother, and come over here. We'll manage the rest.''

"Okay. I'll go get my deputies then." Luke mounted up and rode first to the Ellison's house. In minutes he stopped at the small frame house where Deputy Hans Kaupman lived with his new bride. Luke thumped on the door and waited until the tall German opened the door.

"Ja?"

"Hans, sorry, but I need you.''

"Give me five minutes. Come in,'' he said and was gone to Luke's relief, thankful he could rely on good men. In three minutes' time, Hans was ready and they rode to wake Deputy Lucio Carabajal. The three men rode to Friedrich's house. The back door was open and Luke led the way with his hand on the butt of his pistol. An oil lamp burned overhead in the parlor, which was now a shambles. The furniture was smashed and bloody, the floor smeared with blood. A man lay sprawled near a corner of the room, a knife protruding from his back.

"You two see about the body. I want to look upstairs.'' Luke pulled out a Lucifer and struck it. The match flared and the smell of sulphur filled the air as he found a candle and lit it, then carried it before him. In the front bedroom he found the safe. It was unlocked and when he opened it, he found two bags marked with individual's names, other bags in plain wrappers, a box of coins.

He heard the buckboard stop in front, and he hurried to light a lamp and turn down the covers on the bed. In minutes his deputies carried an unconscious Friedrich in and put him in the bed.

"Doc,'' Luke said quietly as they all started to file out of the room. "Do you think he'll live?''

"He's hurt badly, but he's healthy and strong. I think three or four days and we'll know. You know who did it?''

"Yes. He told me.''

"Low-down skunk, I'll tell you that much. Krueger must have done something mighty big to provoke that kind of beating."

"Yeah. Thanks for all you've done."

"You better get some sleep yourself. You know some people are going to blame you for this. You're lucky he lived to tell people who did it."

"You know?"

"Yeah, and if I hadn't heard it from him, I wouldn't have believed it. Domingo Piedra. He said Domingo robbed the silver shipments that the agent Frank Schulter had sent on his stages that left weekly for Eagle Pass. And the dead man downstairs, Manual Rodriquez, is one of Domingo's men."

"I know. I'll issue a warrant for Domingo, and we'll bring him in tomorrow."

Dr. Ellison shook his head, running his hand through thinning sandy curls. "Never can figure people. A lot isn't enough. Always want more. I know Domingo's tough and a hard man to deal with. There's been talk in the past, like burning out the Cornings, but no one has ever really known. Now they do."

"We might know only the slightest bit of Domingo's activities," Luke said, and Dr. Ellison gave him a curious glance. He started downstairs. "Call me again when you need me. I'll stop here tomorrow and Mama will get the ladies organized to come sit with him." He chuckled. "They'll be lined up to the street. He's the town catch."

"One of my deputies is staying tonight."

"Yep, he told me. Good thing. Friedrich won't be able to lift a finger for several days. Good thing he got help when he did or he would have bled to death. Wonder how he knew you were in your office."

"It was one of the few lights on the plaza. He might have tried to make it to the Plaza House. I don't know how he got as far as he did."

"Nope. Willpower does amazing things. 'Night, Marshal."

"Thanks again. 'Night, Doc.''

Luke and Hans left, parting ways when Hans turned for his house. As Luke rode slowly along the dusty lane, his thoughts were in a turmoil. Tomorrow he would arrest Domingo for ordering his men to beat Friedrich and for the robbery of the gold. And instead of feeling satisfied and victorious, all he could think about was what it would do to Catalina. As he headed down the wide street that was so busy in the daytime, nearing the freighting office, he heard a horse whinny and drew on the reins to stop, listening with undivided attention as Ta-ne-haddle had taught him to do.

He heard the thud of a hoofbeat. Curious, he dismounted and led his horse to a hitching post. He glimpsed someone moving in the shadows in the next block. It wasn't the time of morning for anyone to be at work. Edging close to the buildings, Luke moved carefully so his spurs wouldn't jingle.

Sounds of men whispering could be heard. There had to be several of them. Luke drew his pistol and pulled back the hammer as he crept forward to look. The street appeared deserted, but ahead in the middle of the next block was the Pioneer Freighting Company. Luke drew a sharp breath, suddenly guessing what might be happening. He ran around the building to the back side of the block on Carcel, and saw a man with a torch ride along the side of the Pioneer building. With a flash of fire, the man threw the torch through a window. Luke began running toward him, reaching out to aim and fire.

15

THE MAN REACHED UP TO THROW THE TORCH through a window. A crash of falling glass sounded as the rider wheeled his horse around. With a shout Luke began running toward him.

Men and horses seemed to appear from the darkness. One galloped out the back of the building, where the loading docks were, his horse leaping from the platform.

"Let's go, boys," someone yelled.

Luke paused to aim, squeezed the trigger, and a man toppled from his horse. Luke fired again and another man dropped to the ground as the others raced away. Luke swore when he saw the flames leap and dance inside the building. He broke into a run for his horse. He yanked the Henry from its boot and fired, hoping he could wake the townspeople. He mounted and rode for help, pounding back to Hans's house to wake his deputy again.

"What the hell?"

"The Pioneer Freight Company is on fire. Sound the alarm." Luke wheeled his horse around and galloped for the home of the fire captain.

In a few minutes while the church bell tolled, the Ben Milam Company volunteer fire department with its two-wheeled hook-and-ladder truck arrived. Trying to control the fire, men passed out leather buckets to start two bucket brigades. Luke yanked off his coat to help beat out the fire where they could. Heat and smoke choked him, his ribs ached, and anger made him work furiously, knowing they couldn't save the business. The best they could hope to do was keep the fire from spreading to the neighboring buildings, to bring it under control and let it burn itself out. Finally he had to step back with the others and watch as the roof fell in with a crash, and smoke and sparks spiralled high in the air.

"Luke!"

He spun around and saw the slender figure standing in dark shadows behind him. He strode over to her, his emotions as wild and fiery as the raging inferno behind him. "What are you doing here?" he snapped.

"I had to come and see what was happening," Catalina answered breathlessly.

"Where's your father?" he asked tersely, wanting to shout that Domingo was the cause of the conflagration.

"He and Emilio came to help. I've been in the bucket brigade. All of us came except Mama. She's terrified of fire. Are you all right?"

"Yes." He glanced over his shoulder as the fire burned under control now. People ringed the ruins, still throwing buckets of water on it and beating the ground. He took Catalina's arm and pulled her away from the crowd.

"I need to talk to you."

"I'll have to go home with my family. It can't wait until Tuesday?"

"No, it can't even wait until tomorrow."

With her brow furrowed, she gazed up at him. Her hair was caught behind her head with a ribbon, and she wore a simple denim skirt and shirt. Suddenly Luke's emotions underwent an upheaval. Rage changed to despair at having to hurt Catalina. He wanted to hold her and protect her. Here he had waited eleven years to find Domingo and bring him down. Now that he finally could achieve that goal, it held no satisfaction because of the slender girl standing in front of him. He loved her. He admitted it to himself, yet Domingo still stood between them and always would.

"I'll slip away at five o'clock this morning. Can you meet me?"

"I don't want you going anywhere alone. I'll wait behind your house. Are you sure your parents won't be up?"

"No, they won't be."

"We better get back before your father begins searching for you."

Luke gave her arm a squeeze before they parted. He hoped he didn't cross paths with Domingo. He hated what Domingo had done, hated how it would hurt his family when the truth came out. Emilio, Catalina, Sophia—all as innocent as Hattie had been.

Luke knotted his fists and swore, searching through the crowd for Doc Ellison. He found him climbing onto a buckboard.

"Doc, wait up," Luke called, running to catch up with him.

"It's been a busy night, son. One disaster after another. We're taking the bodies over to the funeral parlor."

"Do you know who they are?"

"Yes," Milton Ellison replied evenly. "I wondered when you'd ask. They're Domingo's boys. Work on the ranch for him. Who owns the Pioneer Freighting Company? All Tandy McGuire will do is swear and beat at the flames."

"Friedrich owns it," Luke replied, and Dr. Ellison swore.

"Looks like you have your work cut out for you. We have a full-fledged feud on our hands. I don't envy you, Marshal. I think a lot of people have known this was coming for some time now. See that Domingo gets what he deserves."

"Yes, sir, but it's going to be hard on the family."

"That it will. Emilio and Catalina are young enough

to survive. Sophia will survive too in her own way. I don't think she's ever loved her husband.''

He turned away and the buckboard began to roll. As the last of the flames crackled and died, Luke watched Domingo mount his horse with Catalina and Emilio on horseback beside him. Flames silhouetted Catalina's dark hair streaming down her back, and Luke swore bitterly. He loved her! The child of his most bitter enemy in the world, his nemesis he had sworn to destroy. He swore again and strode angrily toward the fire captain to talk to him about the fire.

When he finally reached the hotel, he was bone-weary, more sore than ever, but he washed up, changed clothes, and left to meet Catalina. He dismounted far behind the house and walked noiselessly through the shadowy yard. He watched the back door until Catalina stepped outside.

''Cat!'' he whispered, but the sound carried in the stillness of the night. She ran toward him swiftly.

''Luke?''

''Here I am.'' He glanced again at the house. All seemed dark and quiet. He took her slender hand to lead her toward his horse. He helped her up before him, holding her close with his arm tightly around her waist. She snuggled closer, and he felt a tight pain in his chest because of what he had to do.

He rode to his house and led her inside through the back door. The back parlor was now furnished with a desk and leather sofa, shutters on the windows. He had left an oil lamp burning, and in its soft light Catalina looked as lovely as ever. Her hair was tied behind her head with a blue ribbon, and she had changed to a pale blue cotton shirt and a blue gingham skirt.

He took her cape and drew her down on the sofa, her slender fingers warm in his. ''I had to see you. Are you certain your family is asleep?''

''Yes,'' she whispered.

Luke touched her ear lightly. Her eyes were wide and trusting, her lips rosy. He loathed what he had to do, and he was amazed he found himself in such a predicament.

"Something's wrong, isn't it?" she whispered, catching both his hands and holding them in hers.

"Yes. I have to tell you something that you won't want to hear. And it may mean you won't want to see me again."

"No, that's impossible," she said forcefully, throwing her arms around his neck. She was soft, marvelous. In spite of the ache in his ribs, his arms banded around her and he turned his head a fraction to kiss her hungrily. As always, she responded instantly, her tongue thrusting over his and setting him aflame.

He wanted her. Images of her standing nude in the river flashed in his mind, and he held her with one arm while his other hand ran down her side over the tantalizing curve of her hip, down her smooth, warm thigh, back up slowly to the fullness of her breast. She moaned in his arms and arched closer to him.

Desire was a white-hot flame burning Luke as he turned and pulled her into the crook of his arm, letting her head rest on his shoulder while he kissed her. Need drove him relentlessly; he knew he should stop, but he couldn't. His senses were intoxicated with her beauty, and desire consumed him. His knee was bent, his foot on the sofa so Catalina could lean back against him. His arousal was swift and throbbing while he unfastened the buttons of her blouse, pushing it open to view her high, firm breasts. He glanced in her black eyes that smoldered with desire.

His heart seemed to thud against his ribs as he slipped his hands over her silky smooth skin up to the tantalizing fullness of her breasts. As he cupped them, he leaned down to kiss her, trailing his tongue over her flesh, listening to her soft cries of pleasure that set him wild.

Lost in the tempestuous pleasure she evoked, he gave himself over to loving her, finally sliding her down on the sofa and moving above her. She moaned

softly, clinging to him and kissing him passionately.
Clothing was a barrier between their bodies; he burned
with a scalding longing for her, all else forgotten momentarily.

He groaned and pulled away, sitting up beside her
to look at her. Her bodice was pushed to her waist and
her breasts were bare, nipples taut from his caresses.
Her beauty seared his senses and he couldn't break
away or stop touching her. His hands roamed over her,
sliding beneath her skirt to feel her silken thighs.

Catalina wanted him more than she had ever wanted
any man. Luke awakened feelings no other man had,
and she stroked him with unbridled passion. She pulled
his shirt out of his trousers and slid her hand beneath
the soft chambray to feel his muscular chest. She let
her fingers drift down over his thigh, his lean body
and long, sinewy legs a wonder to her. Her hand
stroked upward, touching him intimately, the first time
she had touched a man in such a manner, and her pulse
raced with excitement.

"I love you, Luke," she whispered.

As he groaned again the sound was muffled against
her throat. Then he knelt beside her to peel away her
clothing. With her heart pounding, she watched him,
seeing a hungry look on his face that made her melt
with eagerness. She wound her fingers in his hair as he
gazed at her while she lay bare. His intent gaze was a
scalding caress that made it impossible for her to lie
still. She gasped and pulled on his shoulder. Coming
to her feet as he stood up beside the sofa, she helped
him pull his shirt over his head. She ran her fingers
over his marvelous chest while he unfastened his trousers. With trembling urgency she watched as he pulled
off his boots and undressed, and Catalina reached for
him, touching him, his body bare and heated and hard.

Luke watched her through half-closed eyes. She was
as beautiful as he had remembered. And as insatiable
as he had suspected. She was a lusty woman, and her
delight in his body was as evident as her desire for his

caresses. Longing made his fingers tremble while he drew her to him, and then she was in his arms, kissing him wildly, her soft, luscious body moving against his, her slender arms wrapping around him. He kissed her, moving down her throat, between her breasts, to her thighs, wanting to drive her wild, to see how much he could pleasure her.

To his amazement she pushed him down and knelt over him, watching him as she lowered her head to kiss him as he had her. "I love you, Luke Danby. With all my heart . . ."

He wound his fingers in her hair and stroked her, letting her kiss him for another moment. Then rolling over, he moved above her between her thighs. "Catalina . . ."

She reached for him and his words stopped. He lowered himself, thrusting into her softness, feeling the barrier that made him look at her with surprise.

"You're a virgin," he said, the deep timbre of his voice making her quiver.

"Luke," she gasped, her eyes squeezed tightly while she pulled his shoulders.

He thrust into her warmth, the pounding of his heart drowning out her cries as her hips moved beneath him in a timeless rhythm.

Catalina felt a brief sharp pain and then as Luke thrust, slowly filling her, sensations swept her on a giddy spiral of rapture, making her meet his thrusts wildly. Ecstasy burst within her, and she cried out his name, clinging to him while his hips continued to move, and in seconds he gasped her name and release came.

Finally he lowered his weight to lie on top of her, holding her and murmuring endearments. He shifted then, turning on his side to face her as he held her and gazed at her solemnly.

She knew in that moment that he wouldn't marry her. He wasn't in love with her. She could feel a puzzling, invisible barrier still between them, and it subdued her. She adored him and she wanted him forever. What she had felt for Blake had been nothing, nothing compared to this.

Luke stroked her face, kissing her lightly on the cheek and throat. "You're beautiful, so exciting," he said in a husky tone, his thick lashes raising. Deep green eyes focused on her, and she stroked his chest and firm jaw. "I hope I didn't hurt you. I didn't know—"

"No, you didn't hurt me," while silently she added, *yet*.

Her body was liquid fire, her molten responses a dream. He loved her. Deep down he knew he always would, and it brought an immeasurable sadness to him. He swore softly and crushed her against him in a hug, wanting her, knowing a dark shadow separated them, because someday he would have to confront Domingo and when he did, one of them would kill the other.

As Catalina lay listening to his heartbeat, she let her hands roam freely over his magnificent, virile body, wanting to touch him constantly. In minutes she felt his manhood grow thick and press against her as she continued to stroke his warm body.

"Minx," he whispered and turned to kiss her. "Catalina, we have to talk."

"Go ahead. I'm listening," she said playfully, letting her hand drift up his thigh to his throbbing shaft.

His head came down, his mouth covering hers fiercely, his tongue thrusting into her mouth in a demanding kiss. Her playfulness vanished as she wrapped her arms around him and yielded herself to another flurry of caresses and kisses, until again Luke possessed her. This time was even better and she cried out in unison with his deep voice as they reached a rapturous peak.

Exhausted, she lay in his arms while he stroked her and told her how wonderful she was. But he never said he loved her, and she began to feel a strange premonition of disaster. Finally he moved away to pull on his trousers and boots, and she gathered her clothes to dress.

He felt caught in more turmoil than he had ever known in his life. Everything seemed simple and clear before. Right was right and wrong was wrong, but now he was in love with the daughter of his worst enemy. Now he had to destroy her father, destroy her world, and he loved her with all his heart.

She looked at Luke, her big, black eyes widening, and she threw herself into his arms to hug him tightly, sending a sharp pain through his sore ribs, but he didn't care.

When he released her, she drew her breath sharply. She spent little time analyzing people, but it was clear something was terribly wrong. Instead of looking happy as he had only moments before, his expression was solemn and his eyes clouded with worry. He was too somber, and she felt her heart lurch.

"You don't want my love," she said.

He shook his head. "I want your love and all of you, but something stands between us," he stated so sadly she was frightened.

With a small cry she came up to hug him. "No."

He extracted himself from her arms and fastened the last of the buttons beneath her chin. "Catalina, I have to tell you something that I dread saying, and then I have to take you home before your parents find you're gone. "I can't marry you, because of things from my past." His chest heaved as he drew a deep breath. She was so beautiful with her wide, black eyes that always seemed to lure him closer. Her hair was a midnight cloud over her shoulders. Her mouth was an invitation to kiss, and he felt torn with the conflict that raged in him.

"Catalina, I'm a United States Marshal, and I promised to do my duty and uphold the law." Abruptly he moved away from her, afraid he would reach for her if he sat close to her another moment.

"What does that have to do with us?" she asked, knowing she must hear, but dreading it if it disturbed him so deeply. "Tell me, Luke,"

"ABOUT MIDNIGHT I WAS IN MY OFFICE WORKING late and I heard a noise. It was Friedrich Krueger. He looked half dead from a beating. I got the doctor and Friedrich will live. Friedrich told me your father's men did it." He turned to face her. "One of the men who worked for your father was shot and killed in Friedrich's house. Two of his men were shot and killed tonight by me as they set fire to the freighting office. That freighting office is owned by Friedrich. Friedrich told me that he dissolved their partnership yesterday."

Stunned, she stared at him, her expressive features changing from amazement to fright to dismay. "You have to take him to jail? My father in jail? You can't do that to him. He wouldn't destroy Friedrich." Aghast, she stared at Luke. As cruel and ruthless as she knew her father could be, she couldn't imagine him doing the things Luke had accused him of. And it would hurt her mother and Emilio.

She remembered the accusation Blake had made about her father having the Corning house burned. Painful thoughts and memories swirled in her mind. "He couldn't have done that."

"He'll have a chance to prove his side," Luke said grimly, hating to see the pain he was causing. He wanted to put his arms around her and promise her everything would be all right.

"He hasn't always been good to us. I think he and Mama hate each other. He's been cruel," she said quietly, "but he's my father."

She sank onto the sofa, staring beyond him. He waited to let her realize all the implications, but finally he couldn't stand watching her, and he crossed the room to kneel in front of her and take her hands in his. Her hands were as cold as ice and her gaze shifted to him blankly for a moment. She blinked and then frowned.

"You knew when you kissed me and loved me," she whispered, staring at him and he could see her anger build.

"I didn't plan that to happen. It just did."

"You know you did," she snapped, jumping up and yanking her hands out of his grasp. "You knew all the time and yet you kissed me . . . take me home, Luke Danby!"

"Catalina, I didn't plan this," he said firmly.

"You told me from the first that someday I'd be yours. Well, you got what you wanted, now take me home so you can arrest my father," she snapped, confused and hurt. If her father had done those terrible things . . .

Sharply her mind jumped to Luke's kisses. He couldn't really love her and arrest her father. Tears blurred her vision and she stormed angrily to the door. Luke's long arm shot out and held the door closed while he slipped between her and the door.

"I love you," he said quietly, knowing it was the truth, knowing how hopeless it was, and that she wouldn't believe him.

"You can't possibly," she snapped. "You wanted me and you got what you wanted. Get out of the way."

He gazed into the angry black eyes that were brimming with tears. With an ache he stepped aside and held open the door for her and let her sweep past him.

"I can walk home."

"No," he replied with a quiet note of steel in his voice. "That you can't do." He picked her up and placed her on his horse. She started to protest, but he mounted swiftly and caught her tightly around the waist. "Be quiet, Catalina. I'm taking you home," he ordered.

She clamped her jaw shut, trying to keep from crying while she was with him. She wanted to turn and beat on his chest, but she knew it would be as useless as beating on a tree trunk. Near her house, he halted, and she jumped down quickly.

"I can get the rest of the way alone. Damn you, Luke Danby."

He wouldn't answer, watching her turn and stride away with her head held high. He hated hurting her and he knew Ta-ne-haddle had been right. A boy doesn't love like a man. He had never felt for any woman what he did now for Catalina. As he turned his horse, his thoughts swirled with a confusing jumble of emotions.

For all these years he had dreamed of revenge, the destruction of Domingo. He still had to try to find out what had happened to Hattie, but beyond that . . .

Luke rubbed the scars on his jaw, remembering that terrible day. He had waited so long, yet now he couldn't kill Domingo. Revenge was hollow, and his desire for it had turned to ashes. When he arrested Domingo in the morning, Luke knew it would destroy whatever Catalina felt for him. His thoughts kept returning to her. He loved her and wanted her unbearably. He returned home and paused in the doorway, staring at the sofa, seeing Catalina stretched on it nude, her body glowing with vitality, offered to him.

He groaned and slammed his fist into a wall in an uncustomary burst of anger. He rubbed his knuckles, staring stonily into space. During the short time until dawn he paced the room. He went over and over what he had to do, and finally he made a decision to leave San Antonio. If he resigned as marshal and left Texas, he wouldn't have to be the one to destroy Domingo. It would be someone else. He still couldn't marry Catalina, as much as he loved her. Now she hated him, and hatred was too ingrained in him to forget what

Domingo had done to him and the others; his scars ran deeper than something physical. She must never find out the full extent of Domingo's wickedness, or that he was the cause of Luke's scars.

The prospect of leaving her cut deeper than his worst wounds ever had, yet it seemed the only possible solution. He heated water, took a quick bath, and dressed in his suit. He packed his few possessions. The house he would close and either come back later or sell. In the light of early morning while the town's quiet was broken by the occasional crow of a rooster and the steady clop of his horse's hooves, Luke went to Hans's house just as Hans rode into sight.

"Short night," Hans said sleepily. He saw the bulging bags on Luke's horse. "Are you getting ready to travel?"

"Yes, I am. I wanted to talk to you about that. I have to make a withdrawal from the freighting company and when I do, I want Lucio to accompany me out of town because I'll be carrying a fair amount of gold. I'm turning in my badge today."

"You're *what?*"

"I have to leave San Antonio," Luke said in a deadly quiet voice, and Hans clamped his jaw shut and bit back his next question. Luke knew his deputy eyed him with curiosity as they rode along. "I'm going to the freighting office as soon as it opens. When I get back, we'll get the warrant for Domingo's arrest."

"I've been hearing rumors about him—and a few about Krueger, for that matter—ever since I came to town. To tell you the truth, some of the German families in the community are pretty upset with Friedrich Krueger. He's a bad apple from the rumors, but no one knows anything definite. If they do, they won't talk openly about it." They rode quietly for another block and then Hans asked, "Do you think Domingo will come peacefully?"

"I don't know," Luke said, wondering if Catalina would warn her father. Even if she did, he guessed that as this point Domingo would try to brazen it out, proclaiming his innocence as he had done successfully in the past. "He has a quick temper and a quick finger from all I've heard."

The moment the freighting doors opened, Luke stepped inside, asking for Domingo. He came forward with a smile on his face, but it was a smile that didn't reach his dark eyes. Fury seemed to spark the air between them, and Luke guessed Catalina had revealed Luke's conversation to her father.

"I came to make a withdrawal," Luke said coolly. "I want all my gold."

"Of course, let me get Will Sanders," Domingo answered calmly, making Luke aware of the deviousness of the man. "Have a seat in my office. Is this because of something we've done?"

"No. I've made other plans and I need my gold." For a moment they gazed into each other's eyes again, and hatred burned through Luke. He realized Domingo didn't want to release the gold, but he would have no choice.

In minutes Domingo came striding through the door and Luke was struck how like her father Catalina sometimes was; full of vitality, fiery, physically commanding.

"I hope we haven't done anything to displease you. You aren't headed for a competitor to make a deposit?"

"No, I won't go to a competitor."

"That's a lot of money to carry around town, Marshal. But I guess if you're marshal, you feel safe," Domingo said, barely hiding the threat. Luke suspected one of Domingo's men would be sent after the gold before sundown.

"No one can be sure about safety."

Will Sanders came in carrying the bags of gold, and plunked them on the desk. After he had counted the money before Luke, Domingo pulled out a piece of paper for him to sign.

Luke dipped the pen into the inkwell and scrawled his signature. He laid down the pen, looking across the desk at Domingo, whose eyes narrowed a fraction. "Thank you. Will you be here in the office all morning?"

"Yes, I will."

"I need to see you again in a few hours. I'll be back." Luke picked up the bags of gold and strode toward the door.

"Why are you coming back? Tell me now what you want," Domingo said in a mocking tone.

Luke turned at the door. "I'll have to wait until I see a man, and then we'll talk."

He went outside and mounted, his saddle bags bulging, aware of a few people who stared at him. He rode to his office to place the gold and the bag of cartwheels in the safe, and turned to his two deputies on duty. "We'll need every man this morning. Get Ulrich and Troya here. Lucio, you stay here and guard the office. Hans, you find out how Friedrich is doing. I'm going to see Judge Roberts to get a warrant for Domingo Piedra's arrest."

He didn't feel a shred of satisfaction in the announcement. All he wanted to do before he resigned was find out about Hattie. And he felt a smoldering anger that Domingo would cause so much grief in the world, to his family as well as to strangers.

Two hours later he rode back to his office to get a deputy. Before he turned the corner at the end of the block, he saw Catalina riding down the street. Her expression was stormy, her straight black brows drawn closer in a frown. She had changed into a brown riding habit, and she rode alongside him, reining up her horse to face him from several yards away.

"Marshal, I warned my father what you intend to do to him." Anger tinged every word, her cheeks were bright with color, her eyes flashed fire. And in spite of all their dilemmas, all Luke wanted to do was pull her into his arms and kiss her until she yielded to him again. "Do you know what he said?"

Luke couldn't blame her for her defiance; he admired her for her spirit. He shook his head and answered quietly, "No, Catalina, what did he say?"

"That he's innocent and he'll prove it. He said you had been misled and lied to, that you would set him free before sundown. And I, Luke Danby, never want to see you again."

"Never is a hell of a long time," he said quietly as she began to ride past him. With a twist of the reins his horse pranced close to hers, blocking her path, making her look at him.

"I didn't want to hurt you," he said, constriction knotting his heart. "I do love you, Catalina."

"You have a poor way of showing it," she snapped, raising her chin defiantly and urging her horse past him. Luke moved back and let her go, looking at her stiff, straight back. Her words stung like a slap in the face, but he couldn't change the circumstances or what he had to do. Feeling as if he had lost something infinitely precious, he turned around and rode to his office.

Catalina rode toward home. She couldn't see for the tears that streamed from her eyes. Her father was innocent—or so he had said; at first his anger had been monumental. Her father always managed to get through accusations; she knew there had been many others. She was shocked over Luke's charges, but an unsettling worry persisted that Domingo possibly might have been guilty of Friedrich's beating and fire and more, because she knew in her heart Blake had not lightly accused her father of sending his men to burn down their house.

It was Luke Danby who made her cry. How could he have made love to her, and then said he would arrest her father. He had clearly told her he wouldn't marry her. His declarations of love couldn't be true. A nagging thought argued that there was something in

his past that still affected him, because he always kept
a barrier around his innermost feelings and thoughts.
She didn't think he had ever completely lost his cool
control.

Whatever happened, she had fallen in love with him.
She thought of their lovemaking. The memories were
indelibly etched in her heart and made her ache with
longing for him while she silently raged over him.
When she dismounted and went toward the house, she
heard a rustle in the bushes.

"Catalina." Emilio's head thrust up from behind a
bush. Hastily she wiped the tears from her eyes.
"You're crying. What did Papa say?"

"He said it was all lies."

"Do you think so?"

She looked beyond her brother, who had a book and
had been hiding behind a bush to read. "I don't know,
Emilio. I hate Luke for his accusations, yet what if
he's right? There have been so many insinuations. I
don't think Blake would have blamed Papa without being absolutely convinced of his guilt."

"I think he did it," Emilio said, a muscle working
in his jaw. "We both know about the gold that time,"
he said, facing her.

She remembered when she was fourteen years old,
she and Emilio had slipped out of the house after they
were supposed to be in bed asleep. It was a hot summer night at the ranch, and Catalina talked Emilio into
going outside where it was cooler. Because of the danger of Indians, they weren't supposed to leave the
house, and when they heard horses approach the barn,
they had hidden beneath the hay inside. They heard
Domingo and Juan talking about the gold they had
taken by robbing a stagecoach.

Long after the barn was silent Catalina and Emilio
had stayed hidden, and then they had rushed back to
their rooms. The next day when they could be alone,
they had made a pact they would never tell what they

had heard. Domingo was capable of robbery. Was he capable of worse?''

"What will happen to Mama?" Emilio asked.

"I don't know," Catalina answered, confused, hurt, and fearful.

"She doesn't love him.''

"I know. I don't know what will happen to any of us, and I wonder if he did it," she admitted, feeling a strange conflict. As harsh and cruel as Domingo had been he was still her father, and it was impossible to want something terrible to happen to him. Suddenly tears came again and she turned away. "I don't know what will happen," she exclaimed, her thoughts jumping to Luke.

"I can't cry over him," Emilio said harshly. "He's been too cruel. I've had to take his beatings, sometimes for nothing more than having a poor aim. And he has been unbearably vicious to Mama.''

"I better go in, Emilio, and you had too. Mama will need you and you'll be more comfort to her than I will.''

Catalina wiped her eyes and together they went inside the house. She left Emilio and closed herself in her room. She walked to the window and stared outside, thinking of Luke's house and the moments with him earlier. Her tears fell unheeded.

Luke, flanked by Hans and Troya, entered the freighting office and asked for Domingo. When Domingo came forward to meet them, his dark eyes flashed with anger. Luke was ready to reach for his pistol. He knew Domingo was a fast draw, so he moved his hand to his waist, close to the butt of his Colt.

"Domingo, I have a warrant for your arrest. You're suspected of sending your men to beat Friedrich Krueger and to set fire to his freighting office. There are also some stage robberies we need to ask questions about.''

"I didn't send any of my men, and you know where

I was last night. You spent the evening at my house. This is a poor way to repay my hospitality.'' His voice was friendly, and Luke imagined Domingo felt certain he would be able to walk away free from the charges. ''I'll go with you, Marshal, but I'll be back here by late afternoon.''

Luke nodded and stepped aside, watching Domingo carefully. The four men walked back to the courthouse, the deputies beside Domingo, Luke behind him. People stopped to stare and those in their path stepped aside silently, nodding to them as they passed.

As soon as they were in Luke's office, he turned to Hans. ''Will you boys step outside and leave us alone?''

Curiosity flared in Hans's blue eyes as he left with the others. Luke waited until the door had closed behind them. Domingo sat in a wooden chair, his right ankle on his left knee. He wore a fine brown broadcloth suit and snakeskin boots. He looked healthy and prosperous and fearless.

''You wanted to see me alone?''

''Yes, I do.''

''It's either to apologize for what you just did, or to apologize and ask for Catalina's hand in marriage. Am I right?''

''No, it's neither. ''Luke came around the desk, his heart beginning to thud while he tried to control his emotions. ''Look at me, Domingo.''

There was the faintest flicker of surprise in Domingo's black eyes, and then it was gone.

''You and I have met before. Eleven years ago.''

Domingo frowned, staring at him. ''Where did we meet? he asked gruffly, coming to his feet.

''In New Mexico Territory near Raton Pass,'' Luke said quietly, feeling the anger rising in him as he finally had his confrontation with Domingo. He saw the flicker of some kind of recognition in Domingo's eyes when he said Raton Pass, and it was all he could do to keep from slamming his fist into Domingo's jaw.

"You robbed our wagon train," he said, rage burning in him.

Slowly Domingo grinned and shook his head. "You're loco. I'm a rancher and a businessman, not a thief."

"You see these scars on my face?" Luke said quietly. His pulse jumped when he saw Domingo's fists clench and his eyes narrow.

"Dios! You lie!"

"You thought I was dead. Well, I didn't die, Domingo. Do you remember what I told you that day?"

"I was never there. You're crazy," he said, but his voice had sharpened and his calm facade had vanished. Perspiration beaded his brow while he studied Luke intently. "It's a trick." he snapped.

"No, it's no trick," Luke said, so clearly remembering standing in the hot sun, facing Domingo, hearing the women scream and cry while Domingo laughed. And the grinding pain of being hauled behind Domingo's horse.

"I—"

"Go ahead and say it."

"I shot you," Domingo whispered, staring transfixed at Luke.

"Yes, you shot me. I told you that you better kill me. Remember? And you remember the woman who screamed at you not to hurt me?"

To Luke's amazement, all the color drained from Domingo's face. He stepped back, knocking the chair to the floor. *"Dios!* You're Hattie's son!"

"You sonofabitch!" Luke snapped, unable to resist slamming his fist into Domingo's jaw and send him crashing across the room. In two long strides Luke reached him to yank him up by his shirt front. "What happened to her?"

17

"I DON'T KNOW WHAT HAPPENED TO HER," Domingo answered, rubbing his jaw. "Do your men know about this?

"Where is she?" Luke demanded, his pent-up frustrations building.

"I don't—"

Luke hit him full force on the jaw again, snapping Domingo's head back, slamming him against the wall. Springing back, Domingo swore and hit Luke. He staggered backward, gained his footing, and yanked his gun from his holster as Domingo had his half out of the holster.

"Stop right there and raise your hands." Luke straightened up. "Unbuckle the gun and toss it over here."

Domingo did as he asked, tossing the Colt and belt contemptuously. Without taking his eyes from Domingo, Luke caught the revolver with his free hand.

"Where's my mother?"

"I don't know anything about her."

"You knew her name was Hattie." Luke flung both gun belts behind the desk. "I won't stop until you tell me what you did with her."

"You think you're going to beat the information out of me?" Domingo asked scornfully, and Luke knew he never could.

"I'll trade with you. You tell me what you did with her, and I won't say anything to the court about the wagon train. That will lessen your charges and give you a chance.''

''How can I trust a man who swore he'd kill me?''

''You don't have much choice. What did you do with her?'' With hatred and anger he gazed into Domingo's black eyes.

''I lost her in a poker game.''

Luke felt as if he had received a blow to his midsection. He had known Hattie could have been used by Domingo and his men any way they wanted, but even after all this time it hurt to hear Domingo admit what he had done.

''Who won?'' Luke asked, trying to control the violent urge he had to smash Domingo to a pulp. He thought of Catalina and tried to bank the fires of rage that consumed him.

''How the hell would I remember after all these years?'' Domingo snapped, rubbing his jaw where Luke had hit him. A trickle of blood was still at the corner of his mouth, and he wiped it away with the back of his hand.

''You remembered her name after all these years.'' Luke rejoined. ''Tell me, Domingo, or I'll talk enough to have you hanged.''

''His name was Coit Ritter. He was a gambler and a gunfighter. I don't know where they went.''

''If it weren't for Catalina—'' Luke broke off the words abruptly. ''I know the evil side of your nature more than anyone else in town. I hope you hang.'' Luke strode to the door.

Before he could yank it open, Domingo said, ''Danby?''

Luke turned around. ''Yes?''

''I never knew her last name. You don't look like her.''

''No. I look like my father.''

''How'd you find me?''

''I've been searching for a long time,'' Luke said softly and opened the door. ''Hans.''

As his men filed back into the office with curious glances, Luke retrieved his revolver and removed his badge. He handed it to Hans. ''I'm resigning from office. Until such time the judge appoints the next marshal, you'll protect the town, Hans. Good luck,'' he said, handing over the badge.

''You're leaving town?'' Domingo asked, dismay evident in his voice.

''Yes. And may our paths never cross again, Domingo.''

''That's why you drew out your gold. Why did you buy a house here?''

''I intended to settle here. Now I can't.''

''Why not?''

Wiping blood off his lip and putting his hat squarely on his head, Luke turned his back and strode out. Mounting his horse, he rode to his house to get the rest of his things. In an hour he was riding west from San Antonio.

Dazed, tormented by too many haunting memories, he felt one ache stronger than any he had ever known. Catalina. He missed her more than he dreamed possible; he thought of her constantly, he longed to talk to her. She was like dancing firelight: beautiful, lively, necessary. He hated riding away and leaving her. He was leaving part of himself behind as well.

He rode hard, knowing Ta-ne-haddle would find him sooner or later, as he always had. And while he rode, he reflected on the long-awaited confrontation with Domingo that left bitterness and a faint hope. Domingo had wagered Hattie to another man in a poker game. Every time Luke faced the fact, it hurt. He thought of his gentle mother with her pale beauty and Eastern upbringing, and he prayed she hadn't been treated too badly and that she was still alive. Coit Ritter. He had heard of the man once or twice when he had been in Durango and Santa Fe and Taos. A gunfighter with a formidable reputation as a fast draw and a sharp gambler.

Domingo had recognized Hattie's name instantly, far quicker than he had remembered Luke. It had been a shock to him. Why? Eleven years ago was a long time. Luke's swirling thoughts always revolved back to Catalina and as he kept a watch for Comanches, he agonized over every mile that separated him from the love of his life.

Catalina finally picked up her parasol and went downstairs to get a servant to fetch their carriage. She would go to the courthouse and see what was happening to her father. For the past hour Sophia had been kneeling before the altar in her room, praying softly for the three of them, Emilio, Catalina, and herself. Never once had Catalina overheard Domingo's name cross her lips.

Catalina told Emilio where she was going and climbed into the carriage. In minutes she stood in the same office where Luke had kissed her, and it hurt badly to remember. Her gaze went around the room, now empty of all deputies except Hans. She glanced at the desk and saw Luke's badge lying there. The shiny bit of silver fashioned from a Mexican dollar caught the rays of sunlight that slanted through the wide window.

"Where's Marshal Danby?" she asked Hans.

He frowned and his blue eyes were troubled. "He quit this morning, turned in his badge after—" His face turned red and he shuffled his feet. "He left."

"Left?"

"Yes, ma'am. He left town."

"Where did he go?" she asked as shock buffeted her.

"I don't know. He just up and left."

"Maybe he'll be back," she said without knowing what she had replied. She was stunned that Luke was gone and had quit his job as marshal.

"He was a good man to work for, and I wish he hadn't gone."

"You're sure he's gone? What about his house?"

"He said a lawyer friend, Nate Webster, could sell it later. He took all his gold and left. I think he's gone for good from the way he talked." Hans tilted his head and looked at her with curiosity. "I thought you might know more about him than any of us."

"Why?" she asked sharply, blushing and wondering if someone had seen her with Luke in the early hours before dawn.

"He had a long, private talk with your pa before he left. They exchanged blows, because we heard them. I thought maybe why he left had something to do with your family."

"I don't know why they would fight," she said, puzzled and curious, but far more shocked over Luke's leaving. "May I see my father?" she asked, her thoughts filled with questions.

She was ushered in to talk to her father while Hans stood off to one side. The place seemed unreal to her, even though she could reach out and touch the cold iron bars.

"I've had my lawyer over," Domingo said, talking in a low voice, "but I'll have to stay in jail for the time being. Catalina, I want my family away from the trouble. My lawyer can take care of me. Promise me you'll take Emilio and your mother to the ranch."

"You may need me."

"No," he said in a jovial tone, smiling at her. "I'll be set free. They can't prove I did this. I've seen two people cross Friedrich, and he made them pay dearly. If he survives, I don't want trouble from him. Go to the ranch where it's safe."

"It's like we're leaving you."

"You won't be far away. Let Juan stay at the house with the staff of servants. He can come tell me any information I need from the family. You'll be safer, and I won't have to worry about you."

There was a long pause between them, and she stared into the black eyes so like her own, wondering about him and what he had done. As if he could read her thoughts, he said, "I didn't do what they said, Catalina."

She wondered if she could believe him. She nodded her head. "You should be set free soon, then. I'll go home to pack." There didn't seem to be any more to say, so she left with Hans.

"I'll be back to visit my father."

"Yes, ma'am," Hans replied politely as he held the door.

She swept out, climbing into the carriage. While they rode home down the wide street, her emotions waged a stormy battle. Luke had resigned his job because of her. All the fury she had vented on him underwent a transformation, and was replaced by pain. She loved him. He had quit because of her. Why hadn't he told her he would resign as marshal? If he didn't have anything to do with her father's arrest or trial, there wasn't any reason for him to go. There wasn't a reason as far as she knew, but Luke had told her they could never marry. He had always held something back from her. Something from his past, far removed from what was happening in San Antonio, was an obstacle that stood between him and marriage. Whatever it was, she knew he had quit to keep from hurting her further—*and that meant he cared!*

If he had gone forever . . . Her heart felt squeezed in two at the thought. He would have to come back sometime. The prospect that she might not ever see him again sent her spirits plummeting.

"Luke," she whispered. Why hadn't he told her he resigned? The question ran continually in her mind. It would have made all the difference in the world to her if she had known.

The carriage stopped in front of the back door of the house and she rushed inside to find Emilio in the parlor. She closed the door.

"You're crying over Papa," he said.

"No, I'm not. He's in fine spirits and he's talked to

Mr. McLean, his lawyer. I'm crying over something else.''

''You're in love again.''

''Emilio!''

''Well, there was Ticiano a long time ago, then Blake. Who is it now—Marshal Danby?''

''How'd you know?''

''I know how much you've been seeing him, and I've listened to you tell me about him by the hour. Marshal Danby's nice. I'm glad it's him. He's an improvement over Ticiano even though he's not as handsome.''

''Will you listen? Papa said Friedrich might harm us.''

''Mr. Krueger is about to die.''

''He may survive. Papa made me promise that we'd take Mama and go to the ranch. He said Juan will stay here with the servants and will come get us if Papa needs us.''

''Won't it look like we're deserting him?''

''He said no. He said he wouldn't worry as much. I promised him.''

''I thought Friedrich Krueger was too near death to be a threat to anyone.''

''He may get well; he might hire someone else.''

''Like our father has,'' Emilio said bitterly.

''We don't know for certain,'' she said quietly, the words having a hollow ring while her mind drifted momentarily to Luke and wondering where he might be right now.

''When will we go? Catalina? Did you hear me?''

''Sorry. We should tell Mama and go tomorrow,'' she answered, looking at Emilio's worried face. Suddenly she noticed how much taller he had grown in just the past few months. He was almost six feet tall now, slender, his voice changing to a new depth. ''We'll pack this afternoon. That's what I promised Papa.''

* * *

Domingo stood in front of the narrow window and stared through the bars, his mind working. He was still shocked over Luke Danby's revelations: Hattie's child. That boy he had dragged across the mesquite and no-pals was the marshal. Domingo's mouth curled in a derisive grin. What rotten luck. Luke had hunted him all these years and he had finally found him. *How the hell had the boy survived?* He had shot him, had seen the body jerk from the impact, the red spurt of blood. The scars would never allow Danby to forget. They were formidable, and to a young man, scars could be devastating, although it hadn't been a drawback to Luke Danby. Even Catalina seemed taken with him, and she had her choice of the most handsome men in town.

He shifted his feet, staring into the distance. Hattie Danby. Luke had looked as if he wanted to kill him. Perhaps Catalina prevented him from trying. Domingo smiled again as the irony of the situation struck him. Perhaps the marshal was in love with Catalina, and that was what had stayed his hand and made him resign. The fool. He hadn't learned his lesson well out there in the brush. There was little place in the world for softness. It was a good thing he had left town; if they crossed paths again, Domingo intended to make sure Danby didn't stay a threat.

Domingo's thoughts drifted to his own problem. He might not be able to clear his name with the townspeople. If he didn't . . . he was ready. He took a deep breath, feeling an edge of excitement. He wouldn't mind riding again, taking what he wanted when he wanted it. The daily grind of an office and his family were weights like chains that pulled him down, robbed him of his youth. He would show these people—he would teach them to respect Domingo Piedra—and when he tired of riding with his men, he could go west to California and start a new life. His family would have the ranch, they would be provided for sufficiently. His gaze wandered over the rough, odd-shaped

stones that had been used to build the jail and its surrounding wall. Because of the spaces between them,
it would be so easy to remove them and escape. He
jammed his fists in his pockets impatiently.

If Friedrich died and couldn't testify—with the marshal gone, McLean said they had a good case. And
Domingo would help his odds of winning and walking
away a free man. If his men made themselves evident
in town, no one would come forward to testify against
him. No one. He prayed Friedrich died and as soon as
he could talk to Juan, he would see to it that he did.
Why hadn't they finished the job that night?

He moved restlessly. He hated the jail. It was a cage
like one he had seen long ago on the Main Plaza. It
held a wolf that had paced back and forth with hungry
predator eyes. Domingo understood how the wolf must
have felt. When he got out, some people would pay
dearly.

Hattie. His thoughts turned to her. Where was she?
Was she alive? Hattie Danby, one of the most beautiful
women he had ever known.

Domingo stared at the sunny street outside, where
a boy was running after a dog, scattering chickens in
their path. Domingo hoped with all his heart that
Friedrich didn't survive.

Across town Friedrich shifted in bed and groaned.
Immediately a cool hand soothed his forehead, and he
opened his eyes to see Amelia Jacobs, his neighbor's
daughter, seated close to the bed. For a moment her
golden hair and blue eyes were a blur, then he could
focus on her.

"Lie still, Mr. Krueger. I'm Miss Jacobs from next
door. You'll be fine, Dr. Ellison said. I'm spelling
you, and in another hour Miss Rische is coming to sit
with you. We won't leave you alone."

He nodded and closed his eyes, wanting to shut out
the world while anger and pain tormented him. Catalina and Domingo Piedra. They would regret they ever

met him. He would teach them both a lesson. He thought of Marshal Danby and his scarred face, and wondered if he would be as badly scarred after this. He wanted to swear in rage; he wanted to take his rifle and blow Domingo off the face of the earth. And Catalina—he would bed that wench without benefit of a marriage.

He groaned and heard Amelia's cheery voice. "Poor Mr. Krueger. If you want anything, you tell me. If you need Dr. Ellison, he said to tell me, and Mama will send for him right away. I have a glass of water here if you'd like a drink."

Friedrich opened his eyes and focused on her. She was beautiful and empty-headed. He let her hold the glass to his lips, and she leaned over the bed, giving him a delightful view down her gingham dress.

He would have to find a wife, and this time he would be more careful. She must be a willing and grateful fiancée. So many mothers had all but thrown their daughters at him, and Lord knows, enough daughters openly flirted with him. Yet he had been taken by Catalina's dark beauty. And she wasn't empty-headed, he'd have to hand her that, but perhaps an empty-headed woman would be easier to manage. It would have to be a *quiet,* empty-headed woman, because he didn't want to listen to years of idle chatter.

"Thank you. I'll sleep."

"Oh, of course, Mr. Krueger. I'll just sit right here and be as quiet as a mouse. If you want anything, you just say so. Dr. Ellison will be back this afternoon. I won't be here then. You go to sleep now, y'hear?"

He heard and he intended to do so at once.

The next Tuesday Ta-ne-haddle stood in the office, looking at the silver badge still lying on the desk. "We don't have a marshal right now, just deputies," Hans said. "Sit down."

"How long has he been gone?"

"A week now."

Hans leaned forward to brace his arms on the desk. "He still has a house here. Judge Roberts thinks maybe he'll come back."

Ta-ne-haddle shrugged. "Where's the Piedra family?"

"I heard Domingo tell them to go back to the ranch. Friedrich Krueger has threatened them."

"How is Krueger?"

"Getting better by the day," Hans said quietly with a glance over his shoulder. "You wouldn't know *he* has a worry in the world," he said with a jerk of his head toward the jail. He studied Ta-ne-haddle. "Can I ask you something?" When the Indian nodded, Hans asked, "I know you're close friends with the marshal. Do you know where to find him?"

"I can find him."

"Can you talk him into coming back? He's made a lot of friends here, and he's done a good job in the short time he was in office. We all liked working for him."

Ta-ne-haddle shrugged. "I'll tell him what you said."

"You don't act like most Indians I know," Hans said, looking at him curiously.

"Did Friedrich act like most Germans you know?"

"*Ach, Himmel,* no!"

"Everyone's different. Some of us a little more different than others."

Hans grinned. "Sorry I asked."

"If you want Luke to come back, I need to get some information from Piedra. May I see him alone?"

Hans looked at Ta-ne-haddle sharply. The half-breed waited, staring back inscrutably while he saw the battle that waged in Hans. He wanted to trust Ta-ne-haddle because it might mean Luke's return. On the other hand, how could he trust an Indian alone with a prisoner? Ta-ne-haddle could pass a weapon to him easily.

"That's irregular. You know it could cost me my job if he escaped."

"Domingo Piedra may have some knowledge that will help me know which direction Luke rode."

Hans eyed the knife in the scabbard at Ta-ne-haddle's waist.

"Make it quick."

"Thanks," Ta-ne-haddle said, going ahead as Hans motioned him on. Domingo was the only prisoner. The Indian moved to the cell where Domingo sat smoking a cigarette as he went over some ledgers. His appearance had changed; he wore the familiar white cotton pants and shirt that so many Mexicans wore to stay cooler, but out of a business suit and a stiff white shirt, Domingo looked more the renegade he truly was.

"Domingo," Ta-ne-haddle said, feeling a sense of revulsion, remembering how near death Luke had been when he had found him.

Domingo looked up and his eyes narrowed at Ta-ne-haddle's familiarity. "Who the hell are you?" he asked, eyeing with contempt the Indian's bare chest and braided hair, his buckskin pants and moccasins.

"A friend of Luke Danby's," he answered in a low voice. "I want to ask you something."

Domingo's glance flicked over the scabbard at Ta-ne-haddle's waist, and he stood up slowly to walk to the bars. "Yeah, redskin?"

"What did you do with Hattie Danby?"

Surprise flared briefly in Domingo's expression, and then his mouth curled in derision. "I don't know who you're talking about and if I did, I wouldn't tell you." His hands rested against the bars.

"You're in a cell. I'm not. You have a house in town, a business in town, and a ranch. You want them to still be there when you come out of this cell, don't you?" Ta-ne-haddle asked quietly, and Domingo's chest expanded with a deep breath.

"You damned dirty redskin. Deputy!" he shouted.

"He's stepped outside."

"And left you alone with me?" Ta-ne-haddle stood

within a foot of the bars, close enough for Domingo to reach out and touch him, yet he faced Domingo's black-eyed stare without stepping back. "What did you do with her?"

"How'd you know about Hattie?" Domingo asked, his tone changing to coolness.

Ta-ne-haddle shrugged.

"If I tell you, how will I know you still won't do something to my places?"

"You'll have to take the word of a damned dirty redskin," Ta-ne-haddle said pleasantly, enjoying the clamping of Domingo's jaw. With an effort Domingo relaxed his shoulders and shifted his weight. His feet were planted apart, his hands were on the bars only inches from Ta-ne-haddle.

"I met Hattie Danby in a saloon. She was with a man who had taken her captive on a wagon train. She—"

"Don't lie to me," Ta-ne-haddle commanded softly.

Anger showed for a fleeting second before Domingo lunged, grabbing Ta-ne-haddle by the neck and banging his head against the bars.

18

SPOTS SWAM BEFORE TA-NE-HADDLE'S EYES, BUT he had expected Domingo to grab him, and he had wanted one chance to get at Domingo. With all the force he had, he jerked his knee up between the bars. Domingo was standing close to the bars, his knees spread apart when Ta-ne-haddle's knee slammed into his groin. He yelled, doubling over and swearing as he fell on the floor and rolled back and forth, his knees drawn high.

"I hope I busted you open," Ta-ne-haddle said quietly.

With a roar Domingo lunged at him, grabbing through the bars, but this time Ta-ne-haddle stepped back out of reach.

"When that deputy gets back, It'll have his tail and yours."

"No, you won't. It'll be my word against yours that I touched you. You fell and hurt yourself."

"No one will believe a lying Injun."

"Marshal Danby's deputies will. They want him back."

"Redskin, don't get in my path when I get out."

"I say the same to you Domingo Piedra. We have an old score to settle."

"I don't know you."

Even as he spoke, though, Ta-ne-haddle saw the realization dawning on Domingo. "You're the one who saved Danby's life. It's because of him, you hate me."

"You are a devil-man and bad medicine will follow your tracks."

"I'll get you, redskin. I'm going to peel your hide off and then give you a ride like I gave Danby. That's a promise."

"What did you do with Hattie Danby?"

"I sold her to a brothel in Chihuahua," Domingo lied, burning with rage, wanting to get his hands on the implacable Indian standing so close, yet out of reach. He vowed he would get the redskin and make him pay. Waves of pain still washed through him.

Ta-ne-haddle left to find Hans, who was standing in the hall. "Thanks, Deputy."

"*Ja.* I hope you find Marshal Danby and persuade him to come back."

"I'll try," Ta-ne-haddle answered. "Your prisoner fell and hurt himself while I was talking to him."

Hans's brows arched and a stricken look came over his face. "You didn't kill—"

"Oh, no. I just saw him fall. Hurt his privates, I think."

Hans blinked and nodded, staring at Ta-ne-haddle.

"He'll tell you I did it, but you know there were bars between us and only a fool would get close enough to get hurt by a prisoner."

"Yeah," Hans said as Ta-ne-haddle left.

In the street the Indian leaned against the wall of a tobacco shop, standing quietly with one knee bent, his foot propped against the wall. Ignoring him, people came and went, and he listened to snatches of talk, occasionally catching something about Domingo and Luke as well as Friedrich. After an hour he ambled across the street to the San Antonio Bar, where he stood outside for a time, then went in to order redeye. He sipped it lowly, aware that he should keep his wits about him.

Ta-ne-haddle knew why Luke had resigned and left—for Catalina's sake. For eleven years he had wanted to kill Domingo. Now when he could prosecute him and see him hanged, he had resigned and left town. It had to be for her sake, and Ta-ne-haddle had long suspected once Luke lost his heart it would be lasting.

He had to protect Catalina, because Friedrich might have his own plans for revenge. Overhearing the random gossip, Ta-ne-haddle was relieved to learn Catalina had gone to the Piedra ranch. By noon he had learned that Friedrich had made enemies in town with his heavy-handed ways and tight business dealings, particularly with his own people. Tandy McGuire had been so enraged at Domingo the morning after the fire, he had tried to storm the jail and shoot him.

The last was interesting information to Ta-ne-haddle, and that night he drifted silently through the shadows to a tall cottonwood behind Friedrich's house. He climbed high in the branches, where he could watch the street and the house. Near midnight he heard the approach of a horse. Within minutes it halted almost directly below him, and a rider dismounted. As the man moved stealthily into Friedrich's house, Ta-ne-haddle slithered down the trunk. Keeping in the darkest part of the yard, he opened the door cautiously, and stepped inside. Knife in hand, he slipped through the darkened house to the foot of the stairs. There he heard voices.

"You have to wait until I'm well. We'll burn them out. Take the horses and turn them loose."

"Why not make it look like a Comanche raid?"

"I want Domingo to know who did it," Friedrich said.

"Okay. I'm getting good men together. We can be ready to ride this weekend."

"No. I want to be part of it. You should understand that."

"Yeah, but I want to get Piedra for what he did."

"And I want Catalina."

"What about the wife and son?"

"Let the woman defend herself the best she can.

Kill his son. Can you do it, Tandy? You're not a man of violence.''

''When I think of my company—your company, sir, but I had a part in it. All my savings were in that business. My future.''

''We'll rebuild. Domingo Piedra won't stop us.''

''Yes, sir. I'll be back tomorrow night.''

Suddenly Tandy's boot heels strode loudly toward the stairs. Ta-ne-haddle shrank back, kneeling down in the darkened corner between the stairs and the wall, holding his knife ready as he heard Tandy descend past him on the stairs. The Irishman barged through the door and outside. Settling back on his haunches, Ta-ne-haddle waited for another quarter of an hour. He moved carefully through the back door and across the yard toward Luke's house.

At dawn he had to make a decision. Domingo had said he left Hattie in Chihuahua, so Luke should have headed south. Yet Domingo could have lied. Ta-ne-haddle was in a quandary about which direction to go. He headed southwest toward Chihuahua. As soon as he was out of town, he began to watch for a trail. All day long he couldn't pick one up. He knew Luke's habits, had taught him how to travel and camp. Usually it was easy to pick up his trail, but this was cold.

Two mornings later he sat astride his horse, staring thoughtfully toward the south. He had a feeling he was going the wrong direction, that Luke might be headed back to New Mexico Territory. And if he was, he would follow the Pecos River, then turn north at Franklin. Suddenly he turned his horse and headed back to the northwest, urging his horse to a gallop on the stretch of open land, keeping a sharp watch for a sign of Comanches or Apaches.

Ta-ne-haddle began to inquire in the settlements he passed through, and a week later someone had seen a man who fit Luke's description. The man waved his hands. *''Sí. Muy macho hombre. Ojos de verde.''*

A little over two weeks later, Ta-ne-haddle spotted

a lone rider descending a slope. As he rode out of sight, Ta-ne-haddle urged his horse forward. By mid-afternoon he caught up with him.

Luke was waiting, sitting at the riverbank. "I wondered how long it would take you to catch me."

"Too long." Ta-ne-haddle dropped to the ground and knelt to drink deeply and splash water on himself, letting his horse drink. In the broiling sun Ta-ne-haddle's body glistened with as much sweat as Luke's.

"Catalina Piedra is in great danger."

Luke's eyes narrowed and his chest rose as he inhaled swiftly. "What makes you think that?"

"Friedrich is going to get revenge. I followed Tandy McGuire one night and heard him talk to Friedrich. They'll burn out the Piedras at the ranch. Emilio is to be killed. Friedrich wants Catalina."

Luke was already mounted, swearing under his breath. "How long ago did you learn this?"

"Too many days ago, but Krueger has to get well enough to ride first."

"Oh, hell, let's get going!"

When they slowed later, Ta-ne-haddle told Luke that his deputies wanted him to return, that no replacement had been appointed as marshal. "I headed toward Chihuahua." When Ta-ne-haddle told Luke about his experience with Domingo, Luke swore.

"I wonder if he told either of us the truth. He told me he lost Hattie in a poker game to a gambler named Coit Ritter. They were in Santa Fe. Leaves me a hell of a choice," he said as they entered a stretch of brush and trees that indicated a stream. As soon as they found water, they stopped to drink and let the horses drink, because they both knew they had miles to cross without another one. As Ta-ne-haddle knelt beside the muddy water, there was a flapping of wings and a dark shadow loomed. An owl swept down on a branch of a tree near them. Ta-ne-haddle stood up and looked at Luke, gathering his reins to mount quickly.

"We go."

"You and your damned bad medicine. It's a bird."

"It's a sign of death. We ride quickly."

Luke mounted grimly, knowing the Kiowa's feeling that an owl was an omen of disaster as well as a sign of intelligence. His Eastern background made him shake his head, and tell himself there was nothing more to it than a bird flying to water, but deep down he had spent too long with Ta-ne-haddle not to be sobered by the Indian's premonitions.

During the next day Luke rode silently, driving himself because he was afraid of what he would find. The sun was a ball of blazing fire scorching the land and the men, but they kept up as fast a pace as possible without harming the horses. Luke prayed for the first time in years, praying that Catalina would be safe when he got there.

Catalina found the ranch both a haven and a prison. She wanted to get back to town to know every day what was happening to her father. There had been one delay after another. Juan promised to let them know when he would come to trial, which should be any day now. There was still no new marshal; she had heard that Friedrich was on the mend, growing stronger each day.

The ranch foreman had cattle stolen by Comanches one night and went to Catalina with the news. The following day some cattle were lost in quicksand at the river, and again Catalina was consulted about what to do because it had been happening regularly.

Within a few days she began to shoulder some of the responsibility for the ranch. And she took charge of running the household. Juan appeared and said her father's trial was set for the following Tuesday, the eleventh of August. Her father had asked her not to come to town until then.

They would stay in town throughout the trial, and then everything would be settled. To her surprise, Emilio had taken over more chores, riding out with the men in the morning instead of shutting himself in the house to read. Sophia remained closed in her room, reading and praying, living a solitary life.

Catalina stepped outside to supervise the servants' work. They had washed the lace curtains and were placing them on curtain stretchers in the sun to dry, hooking the lace over the rows of tiny nails that would keep the curtains from shrinking. She heard the pounding of hooves and looked down the road. A spiral of dust was rising from riders approaching the ranch.

"We better go inside until we know who it is. Maria, come help me close the gates. If they're friendly or if it's Juan, we can open them again."

"Comanches?" Maria asked in whispered horror.

'Comanches don't ride up the road to the house," Catalina said dryly. "Hurry."

"*Sí,* senorita," the diminutive maid cried. She helped Catalina push the heavy gates shut, let down the crossbar, and rushed back to the house. Catalina went to the roof, stepped into hot sunshine, and put her hand up to shield her eyes. There were two men riding hard, and fear gripped her. Something must have happened to her father.

She raced outside to swing open the gates as the riders approached. Both wore wide-brimmed black hats, both were broad-shouldered, but one formed a silhouette she couldn't possible fail to recognize.

"Luke!" Her breath caught in her throat. She wanted to run to meet him, but she checked herself, her heart pounding with eagerness and excitement.

They slowed before they reached her. His hat shielded him until he was close; then she saw the unmistakable longing in his expression. In a lithe motion he dismounted, tossing his reins to Ta-ne-haddle, who rode on past with a wave that she barely noticed. She couldn't take her eyes from Luke, gazing into the green depths that held a look that took her breath. As he strode toward her, he watched her with such intensity that her heart began to thud, and she flung herself into his arms.

He crushed her to him, and his mouth came down with a savage hunger, his tongue thrusting into her mouth in a hot demand that made her want to faint. She slipped her arms around his neck, closing her eyes, and clinging to him rapturously.

Finally he released her, gazing down at her.

"Thank heavens you came back," she exclaimed with joy.

"You're in danger here," he said. His voice was quiet and solemn, contradicting the heated look in his eyes. "Let's go up to the house where we can talk."

Luke watched her as he talked and saw the change he expected in her expression. With a quick intake of her breath, disappointment flared.

"I thought you came because . . . of us," she said, watching him intently.

He still hurt as badly as he had that day he left. "Let's talk."

She wanted to hold him, to have him kiss her, but that wasn't why he had come. She had been foolish to jump to that conclusion at the sight of him. She proudly lifted her chin and straightened her shoulders, refusing to let Luke see how badly he was hurting her.

Inside, she asked Maria to bring water and food, and they went to the front parlor, where she sat down facing Ta-ne-haddle and Luke. Both men were bronze, their bodies hard and fit. Their clothes were rumpled and dusty, and she realized they had ridden long and hard. Luke had a stubble of dark whiskers on his jaw, but in spite of dust and whiskers and his solemn countenance, she adored him and was thankful he was here.

"Ta-ne-haddle, tell her what you heard."

Even though it directly concerned her safety, Catalina had to struggle to keep her thoughts on what the Indian said. Luke sat only a few feet away. He had taken off his hat, and his thick brown hair waved over his forehead. He looked as if he had slept in the saddle. His long legs were stretched out in front of him, and for an instant she was unable to keep her gaze from raking down the length of him. She remembered exactly how his sinewy legs had felt against her own. Her cheeks grew warm when she saw Luke watching her with smoldering desire. She tried to make an effort to concentrate only on Ta-ne-haddle, but it was difficult. And at the moment the only fear that gripped her was worry over when Luke would leave her.

When Ta-ne-haddle finished, she laced her fingers together. "Papa had warned us about Friedrich. We'll be careful and we should be safe. We go into town next week for the trial."

"Ta-ne-haddle and I have talked this over," Luke said, leaning forward with his hands on his knees. The stormy look in his eyes made her pulse drum with excitement, because it meant that in spite of the mysterious barrier between them, he wanted her. "We think they'll make their move before the trial. If your father proves his innocence, it will be more difficult to retaliate."

"That's true," she said, trying to follow Luke's logic and not get lost gazing into his green eyes.

"And it would shatter your father's confidence if you were burned out, the ranch destroyed," Luke added grimly.

She nodded, following his reasoning. "I'll summon the men and we'll keep everyone we can spare close to home until we go to town for the trial."

"Good. Catalina, I hate to tell you, but I think all three of you are in terrible danger. You could leave with us and let me hide you somewhere."

"Mama would never agree."

"Ta-ne-haddle overheard Friedrich order Emilio shot."

His words finally broke through the spell woven by Luke's presence. And icy chill shook her. "How could he? Emilio's never done a thing to Friedrich."

"No, but he's your father's only son."

"Suppose you took Emilio away and hid him?"

"Ta-ne-haddle could do that," Luke said, "but will Emilio leave you and Sophia?"

"No, he won't. And Sophia won't go. I don't know if I can get her to go to town for the trial."

Luke ran his hand through his hair distractedly. "If you're divided between the ranch and town, it'll be even more difficult to protect the three of you."

"I know, but she thinks Papa . . . she thinks he's guilty. She's retreated from the world. Emilio and I hardly see her."

"I want to ask you to do something for me."

"What is it?" she asked curiously, wondering if he had any concept how much she would be willing to do for him.

"Let us stay here with you so we can help protect you."

"Of course," she said, her heart lurching at the prospect of Luke staying under the same roof for days. He talked to her the same way he would talk to a stranger. Whatever obstacle lay between them hadn't changed. Yet he had to care to go to all this risk for her.

"Good. We need to learn the ranch hands' names and the layout of the ranch. We need to set up some means of warning and defense, because I know Friedrich and Tandy McGuire will attack. The night of the fire Tandy was almost out of his mind for the first hours. I had to help Hans keep him from killing your father that night."

She shivered and saw Luke watching her closely. "I know how to shoot as well as Emilio."

"Where is Emilio?"

"Riding with the men. He's taken over some of Papa's chores, thank heavens."

"Why thank heavens?" Luke asked.

"I would have to if Emilio didn't," she replied simply. "I'll show you to your rooms and have the servants draw baths for you. I'm sorry, would you care for a drink?''

Luke nodded. He was bone-weary from travel. They had slept in the saddle for the past two nights, riding hard to get back to San Antonio. And he was bedazzled by Catalina. In a soft red-and-blue checked gingham with her hair tied simply behind her neck with a strip of leather, she looked lovelier than ever. There was a glowing vibrancy to her that he didn't remember from before, and he ached to pull her into his arms and kiss her.

She crossed the room to a table and picked up a brandy decanter. Luke went to stand beside her. ''Only a little for both of us. I'll do it,'' he said. Taking the decanter from her, his hand brushed hers. The sweet scent of roses from her skin made him want to leave the decanter and take Catalina into his arms.

They followed her down the cool hallway. It was protected from the heat by its thick walls, and Luke noted them with satisfaction. Tandy and Friedrich had talked of burning out the Piedras, but this house wouldn't burn. They paused at the big kitchen with its wide back door that was open, allowing in a shaft of sunlight. The large hearth built in an adobe wall served as an oven. Smells of boiling meat with chili peppers assailed him, making his mouth water. Luke studied Catalina while she instructed two maids to get water for baths, and then she led them down a long hall to show them each to a bedroom.

''I'll tell Mama you're here. I'm sure she'll join us for dinner.'' She paused before an open door. ''Tane-haddle, you may have this room.''

He nodded. ''I'll sleep outside, but I'll bathe here,''he said, eyeing the tin tub in the corner. Suddenly she stood on tiptoe to brush his cheek with a kiss. ''Thank you for getting Luke,'' she whispered. She turned to take Luke's hand. ''You're in the next room.''

He followed her into a masculine bedroom with

carved, dark, Spanish-style furniture. "This will be yours, Luke. You're between Ta-ne-haddle and Emilio."

Luke closed the door and turned to face her. Her pulse raced as he reached for her, pulling her closer. He held her upper arms while gazing into her luminous black eyes. "I'm dirty and I'll get your pretty dress dusty if I touch you."

"I don't care," she whispered.

He leaned down to brush her lips lightly with his. She closed her eyes, relishing the touch of his mouth as her lips parted, tongues touching with blatant desire. Then she was in his arms. He bent over her, molding her soft curves to his whipcord-lean body, his throbbing shaft pressing against her through the barriers of clothing. He groaned as he kissed her deeply, and Catalina trembled with desire, her hips thrusting against his.

With a deep breath he released her. "Be very careful," he warned, his fingers following the low neckline of her dress down across her shoulder, over the soft rise of her breasts. He wanted to push the gingham out of the way, to caress her. "Don't leave the house without letting one of us know."

"I won't," she answered breathlessly, and he knew she wanted his caresses as badly as he wanted to touch her. At that thought he stiffened. He knew full well that Domingo couldn't risk letting him live: he could turn Domingo in for old crimes. It was only a matter of time before Domingo tried to kill him again. When it happened, he would have to kill Domingo, and Catalina would never forgive him for it. She had been enraged when Luke had merely done his duty as marshal and arrested her father.

That knowledge didn't stop his wanting her more than he had ever wanted anyone or anything in his life. He ached to pull her into his arms now, and his fingers drifted along her slender neck, touching her silky hair.

"Put someone on the roof for a lookout. I don't

think they'll come during daylight hours. I think it'll
be at night, but I'd feel damn foolish if they rode up
in broad daylight and caught us unawares.''

''I will,'' she answered, tingling from his tormenting touches that were a tantalizing agony. He looked
marvelous, strong, and virile; his green eyes burned
with desire as his gaze lowered to the low neck of her
bodice. She touched his jaw, and his gaze flew up to
meet hers, revealing his blatant need.

''You look beautiful,'' he said gruffly.

''Thank you. I'm glad you came,'' she whispered.
As she drew fingers lightly over his cheek, Luke remembered how she had caressed his chest, his legs.
He doubled his fists and fought to control the urge
to reach for her again. She went to the door, paused
to gaze at him solemnly, then without a word she
left.

By the time they sat down to eat, Emilio had returned. Sophia joined them, sitting quietly unless
asked a direct question. Catalina had dressed in a favorite: a low-necked peasant shirt with a red drawstring and a bright red gingham skirt with flowers
behind her ear. She thought Luke looked more rugged
and handsome than ever in his white shirt and jeans.
After days without a haircut, his wavy hair hung long
on his neck. She wondered again about his scars and
whom he had fought so long ago.

Happiness bubbled in her because he was here.
Danger was a distant threat that had shrunk simply
because Luke was present. Now she felt safe. He was
always so in command of the situation that she couldn't
imagine it getting out of hand.

After dinner, she and Emilio took Luke and Ta-ne-
haddle to look at the ranch buildings: the bunkhouse,
the cook house and storage house, the barns, all the
outbuildings. Luke met with the men at the bunkhouse, and they worked out a plan by which only a
few men would be gone far from the house at a time.
Half the men spoke only Spanish, and she was sur-

prised that Luke conversed easily in Spanish while making arrangements. They agreed to stand watches, one on the roof of the house, the highest point at the ranch, another a few miles down the road, another at the back of one of the barns. A signal of three shots would warn the others, and all the women and children on the ranch would proceed to the main house and hide in the parlor, where they could close the heavy wooden shutters and barricade themselves in. Ta-ne-haddle left to ride to town and see what he could learn.

Finally they were through, and went back to sit in the parlor and talk. Sophia joined them, sitting quietly while Catalina and Emilio told Luke about the history of the ranch, their childhood, about Tejanos relatives on Sophia's side who had fought at Goliad and San Jacinto, all receiving a league and labor of land for their efforts as Domingo had for participating at San Jacinto.

Luke sat back on the leather sofa, his long legs stretched out, boots crossed at the ankles, the same smoldering speculation in his eyes when he looked at her as earlier. Catalina's pulse beat a little faster, her breath came a little quicker, and an inner excitement sparked the night. She knew Sophia would wait until Luke went to bed, so when he finally excused himself, Catalina waited only seconds before she stood up.

"Mama, I thought of something else I should tell Mr. Danby," she said hastily, and hurried from the room to catch up with Luke in the hallway.

"Luke!"

He turned and watched her walk toward him. His bold gaze drifted downward and lingered there, as if undressing her mentally, and her heart skipped a beat. "I wanted to thank you again for coming."

"I'm glad I got here in time," he said. Though he was drooping from exhaustion after the way they had ridden, all evening he had felt a racing excitement at being with Catalina again. Her dark, flashing eyes were a blatant invitation, and every time he looked at her full, rosy lips, he remembered her kisses, her golden body beneath his, with absolute clarity.

"Your mother was a very proper chaperone tonight," he said with amusement.

"Yes, and if I'm gone long now, she will send Emilio to search for me."

Luke looked down at her, seeing her beguiling black eyes with their hidden promises. "Come here, Catalina," he said in a husky voice, leading her to his room and closing the door.

"Luke, if Mama finds I'm shut away in your bedroom with the door closed—"

He turned around and leaned back against the door. Spreading his legs, he pulled her into his arms. Possessing her soft mouth with his, letting his passion show freely, he slid his hands down the sweet curve of her back and pulled her hips closer against him until he fitted her between his thighs. She moaned softly, clinging to him for a moment in wild abandon. Erotic images of her came to his mind, and he reached beneath the low neck of her bodice to free her breasts. Cupping them in his large, rough hands, he watched her as his thumbs flicked over her nipples. She stood, hips pressed against him, her head thrown back and lips parted, her eyes closed while she moaned softly.

"Catalina," he whispered, taking her breast in his mouth, his teeth teasing her lightly.

She gasped with pleasure, her hands stroking him, down across his flat, muscular stomach to his throbbing shaft that bulged against his tight pants. She broke away and pulled her bodice into place, giving him another brief glimpse of tantalizing charms.

"Luke, Emilio or Mama will come searching for me," she exclaimed with glittering eyes. Her heart pounded violently with desire. "If it's Mama—"

"When all this is over, we'll talk," he said, knowing he couldn't ride away and leave her ever again. There had to be a solution.

"I'm so glad you're here," she whispered. Drawing her fingers over his rough cheek, she stepped into the hall.

"Catalina," Emilio called.

"I'm coming." She wrinkled her nose at Luke and her dark eyes sparkled mischievously. "See, I told you. They're trying to keep me pure and innocent. Little do they know it's far too late."

She left him staring after her in amazement that she would so cheerfully admit the last. Then he laughed and closed the door. Leaning his forehead against it, he shut his eyes, thinking about the seconds earlier when he had held her. He needed her desperately. Weariness finally caught up with him and he crossed the room, pulling off his clothes as he headed for the bed. In seconds he was asleep.

Ta-ne-haddle returned the next day and sought Luke at once.

Luke was cleaning a rifle, checking over the extra rifles kept at the house when Ta-ne-haddle entered the library and closed the door. "Catalina said you would be somewhere in the house."

"What did you find out?" Luke asked, unable to read anything from Ta-ne-haddle's impassive features.

"Friedrich Krueger has recovered rapidly. He's up, able to ride, and they've started rebuilding Pioneer Freighting. He's closed the company he had with Domingo, and since Domingo is in jail there's nothing he can do about it."

"Damn. There'll be a feud between the two men until one kills the other."

"That may be sooner than you think. I'd say this family is in big danger anyday now. They'll come before Domingo's trial."

"You're right. You don't need to stay through this. None of this is your fight."

"I stay."

"Okay. You had your chance. I think I'll double the watch until time for them to go to town."

"You better have half the men escort them to town."

"I'm going with them."

"You still better have a lot of men. You don't know how many Friedrich will have, but he's efficient. I expect he'll be a formidable man to fight."

"I expect you're right."

"They want you back as marshal."

"I'll have to work out things with Catalina."

The Indian smiled. "I think I'm going to get my new sorrel gelding. White face and stockings. Don't forget."

"Our bet. You were right as you usually are. I'm in love."

"I kind of thought you were," Ta-ne-haddle remarked dryly.

"As long as you're doing nothing except thinking about a horse, why don't you clean that rifle?" He tossed one to Ta-ne-haddle, which he caught with ease. "If I stay here and they don't hang Domingo, he'll come after me. If I kill him, she'll never marry me or forgive me."

"Have you told her what he did?"

"No, and I never will. And don't you either. I want your word on it."

"You have it, but she may be more resilient that you think."

"If the woman I loved told me my father had done something like that to her, I think I'd have a difficult time living with it."

"She's an intelligent woman; then she would understand why you had to do it if you kill him in self-defense."

"You like her, don't you?"

Ta-ne-haddle flashed a rare grin, and Luke thought again how handsome he was and what a shame he had never found another woman. The dark patch over his eye only added to his rakish appearance. "I like her, and I think you need her."

"We'll see. One thing here, they can't burn down this house."

"No, but they're building a new freighting company, and they dynamited some rock for a deeper foundation."

Luke's head came up. *"Dynamite?* Lordy. I better think of somewhere to send the women if they try to dynamite the house."

"Friedrich wants Catalina, so they might not do that."

Luke worked grimly, his mind running over details of defense.

Two nights later Catalina tossed restlessly. The night was hot, the earth baked dry from days of heat. She got up and walked to the window. The knowledge that Luke lay only two rooms away kept her tossing and turning every night. How easy it would be to go to him and make love as they had before! As she gazed into the darkness, a shadow moved. There was not a breath of air, not a breeze to stir anything. Her eyes narrowed and she leaned forward, standing in the open window and staring. She turned and ran swiftly and quietly down the hall to Luke's room, opening the door and closing it behind her.

His naked body lay stretched in bed, the covers thrown away in the heat. For an instant she was lost. She forgot her fear, the danger, her suspicions. Desire swept through her like a summer storm. She drew her breath sharply, moving slowly to the bed.

His manhood began to throb and harden. "Catalina," he said in a husky voice, stretching out his arm, and she couldn't keep from coming down to kiss him.

With a groan he pulled her over his warm body, his hot shaft pressing against her.

"Luke, there's danger," she gasped, twisting away from a kiss that almost made her forget her reason for coming to his room.

Instantly she felt his muscles tense and he held her at arm's length. "That's why you're here," he said flatly.

"I almost forgot why I came."

His head snapped around and, catching her to him roughly, he looked into her dark eyes. "Lord help us both," he said painfully and kissed her hard, his mouth bruising on hers, as if he couldn't get enough of her. Abruptly he released her. "What happened?"

"I couldn't sleep, so I went to the window. I saw a shadow move, and I think it was a man. There's no wind to stir shadows."

"My sharp-eyed beauty," he said with satisfaction. "Warn Emilio and get the women."

"I might have imagined—"

"It won't hurt to move quickly. If it's a false alarm we can all go back to bed. Hurry!"

As she started to turn away, his hand closed around her wrist. He yanked her to him to kiss her hard and for just an instant, she yielded to inclination and let her hands drift over his marvelous body.

Abruptly he released her. "Someday . . . hurry, love."

She rushed out of the room, her heart thudding, his endearment ringing in her ears. *Love*. Luke cared. Whatever it was between them, he cared!

Within minutes the women were silently scurrying into the house, huddling together in the front parlor while Emilio closed the shutters to the windows and Catalina gave instructions.

"Senor Danby says if they use dynamite, we're to go to the kitchen, and one of the men will go with us to the root cellar. Who knows how to use a rifle?" Catalina asked, passing out weapons to each woman who answered in the affirmative. "Maria, you and Luisa go to the kitchen. Make sure you shoot only at an enemy. Our men will be firing from the house as well as the outbuildings on the roof.

"Dorotea, you and Hortensia go to the last bedroom where my mother is and protect her."

Catalina shouldered a rifle. "Arnaldo," she addressed Dorotea's fifteen-year-old son, "come with me. We'll go to the roof." They hurriedly climbed up the ladder, and she stepped out into fresh night air that was only a few degrees cooler than the house.

"Catalina, get below," Luke snapped.

"You may need us. We can shoot as well as some of the men."

"I want you downstairs where you're safe," he said, proud that she was brave enough to fight, yet wanting her as far removed from danger as possible. "Catalina, please, go downstairs," he asked. "Then I won't worry."

She smiled at him in the moonlight. "But I would be worried about you. No, we share our worry and the danger."

He shook his head. "Stubborn, stubborn . . . this is no place for a woman."

"You should be getting ready, not arguing with me."

He was tempted to scoop her up and lock her safely in a room downstairs, but he understood why she wanted to fight too well. "Dammit, I don't want you up here. You better not get hurt."

"Nor you, senor. I might not ever speak to you again." she snapped. Some women he had known would be whimpering and crying with fright, not ready to fight and joking about it.

"Go ahead, Senorita, have it your way."

"I intend to," she said blithely, the sense of danger once again diminishing next to the excitement that Luke stirred.

"Here they come!" one of the men yelled, and the first shot rang out. Bedlam broke loose. Men suddenly appeared out of shadows, racing toward the ranch, shots ringing out. Luke ran to the edge of the roof to fire at their attackers.

A rider vaulted the fence and galloped toward the house, then three more. A fusillade of shots rang out, and two riders fell from their horses.

A stick of dynamite was thrown, arcing in a spiral. Luke saw its bright fuse and yelled, rushing across the roof to throw himself over Catalina as the explosion came.

19

THE EXPLOSION DEAFENED HIS EARS AND MADE
the roof shake beneath them. A chunk of wood struck
Luke a glancing blow on the back. He had to stop
whoever was throwing dynamite sticks at the house
before they succeeded in blowing up everything.

"Get the women away from the house, Antonio,"
he yelled. Catalina fired her repeating rifle steadily,
and Luke ran across the roof to kneel beside her. "Get
downstairs," he yelled over the gunfire.

"Never!" she yelled in return, raising slightly to
shoot. Luke swore as he saw another stick of dynamite
arcing toward the roof. A blast rocked them and rocks
struck him forcefully.

"Get the hell out of here, Catalina!" he yelled,
crouching as he ran across the roof to the ladder.

As he exposed himself, someone fired at him, and
he leaped back into the protection of the doorway. A
woman screamed inside the house, and in seconds he
saw Antonio herding the maids toward the root cellar.
Catalina wasn't with them! A volley of shots brought
his attention back to the immediate danger, and the
spiral of another fiery stick of dynamite was hurled in
his direction.

Covering his head, Luke threw himself on the
ground. The third blast ripped up the ground only
yards from him. Rocks rained on him, but as the last
bits showered down, Luke streaked toward the back to
vault the adobe wall.

Catching one of the saddled horses, he mounted and

rode to the west. Riding wide of the house, Luke moved through the live oaks when suddenly a man stepped into his path from behind a tree. As the man drew on him, Luke fired his Winchester, and the man sprawled on the ground while Luke passed him.

Behind a line of men firing on the house, Luke searched for the one with the dynamite. In seconds another streak of fire glittered in the dark night. Luke aimed and shot the stick, hitting it in mid-air. With a loud blast and a shower of sparks, it exploded harmlessly overhead. In the flash Luke spotted the bright glow of a Lucifer's flame, revealing a canvas bag at the man's feet. The bag was open, a stick of dynamite plainly showing. Raising the Winchester to his shoulder, Luke aimed and fired at the canvas bag. The shot set off the dynamite.

The blast made Luke's horse paw the air wildly while dirt and rocks pelted him. As soon as Luke brought his frightened horse under control, he raced toward the house, where he saw a man run from the west, vault the wall, and vanish inside the house.

Catalina was his first thought. It could be Friedrich after her. He urged his horse forward, feeling its muscles bunch as it leaped the adobe wall, and then he raced toward what was left of the house. Luke jumped off the horse and dashed inside when a woman's shrill scream, heard clearly over the gunfire, sent a chill across his nape.

In the kitchen Emilio stood facing Friedrich, who had a gun drawn on him. Sophia screamed again and threw herself in front of her son as Friedrich fired. In the same instant Luke squeezed his trigger. Instantly Friedrich sprawled facedown, and Luke ran to Sophia, who had already slumped to the floor, blood pouring from her wound.

"My mother," Emilio whispered, kneeling beside her, shock and grief making him pale.

Sophia had been shot through the heart, her hand still closed on her beads. Luke yanked off his vest and placed it over her before putting his hand on Emilio's shoulders.

When Emilio stood up, Luke said, "We have to fight, Emilio. There are others." He thrust a rifle into Emilio's hands. "Can you fight? You don't want to lose Catalina too."

With tears streaking his cheeks, Emilio nodded, moving to a window. Luke went to the kitchen door, kneeled down, and peered outside. In seconds two men rode past, carrying burning torches. The orange flames danced brightly in the dark night. Luke fired at the men, who returned the shots, one landing with a dull noise in the wood beside Luke's shoulder. Down the hall behind him, tongues of flame licked through an open door.

"The barn is burning!" someone yelled. Emilio sprinted through an opening that an hour ago had been the kitchen wall. He raced toward the barn while Luke aimed and fired at a horseman, who fell to the ground. Another rider yelled, and the attackers began to turn away. The pounding of hooves was swallowed in the night.

Fires crackled inside the house as furniture burned, and the barn was a blaze that lit up the surrounding area as brightly as day. Great billows of smoke rolled skyward while horses whinnied and men yelled, trying to control the raging orange flames.

Luke saw the slender figure come around the corner of the house. Her skirt and bodice were ripped, her skirt was burned in patches, her black hair hung down over her shoulders, and her face was smudged with dirt with a bad scrape on one cheek. She carried the rifle in the crook of her arm, and sadness welled up in him over what had to be done.

"They're gone, Luke. Hurry, and maybe we can save the barn," Catalina cried.

"You're hurt," he said, tilting her face up to look more closely at her cheek. "Damn that Tandy!"

"I'm all right. Hurry!" she urged, taking his hand.

Catalina," he said gently.

"The animals are out, and we're needed to fight the fire." As his arm wrapped around her protectively, she suddenly knew something terrible had happened. "Emilio?" she whispered, going cold all over.

Luke shook his head. "I'm sorry. It's your mother. Friedrich shot her."

"Oh, no!" She reeled with shock; all she could think of was her pious, gentle mother—killed in a battle. "No!" she cried, tears coming.

Luke held her tightly while he stroked her head. Catalina burst into sobs and clung to him. She raised her face after a moment. "I have to tell Emilio."

"He knows, Catalina. Your mother stepped into the path of the bullet when Friedrich tried to kill Emilio."

"Oh, no! Emilio will suffer doubly. He would rather have died than have Mama hurt." Rage sounded in her voice. "Friedrich!"

"He's dead too. I shot him, but I was too late to save your mother."

"Everything is gone. Mama is gone," she said in a daze. "The house is destroyed." He glanced beyond her. One corner stood intact, the roof still covering what he guessed were two rooms. The rest had been blasted so badly it would have to be rebuilt.

"You have a home in town and your family still owns the land. Your father will rebuild."

"I'll have to go into town and tell Papa," she whispered.

Luke gave her shoulder a squeeze, realizing that Catalina simply assumed the task would be hers. At that moment Emilio appeared. His face was smudged and black, his cheek scraped raw and his hair singed. He stopped yards from Catalina. "Do you know?" he asked in a hoarse voice.

She went to him and they hugged each other, crying quietly. Luke left, striding toward the fire. He ordered two of the men to load the bodies into a buckboard to carry the dead to town for burial.

He surveyed the devastation. He hadn't dreamed Friedrich and Tandy would come with so many men. The ranch was a shambles, but Domingo could rebuild. And now the prime witness in Domingo's case was dead.

At the thought Domingo would probably go free, Luke clamped his jaw together tightly, shoving worries about the future out of mind while he thought about what needed to be done now.

Three hours later, the fires were smoldering embers. The barn was gone. Luke was on horseback beside Catalina and Emilio while Antonio drove a buckboard with the bodies of the dead and Ovidio drove another wagon with the maids.

The first gray light of dawn streaked the sky as they reached San Antonio and parted with Antonio, who took the bodies to the undertaker. The rest of them turned down Nueva Street toward the Piedra home.

A block away Luke saw figures moving, and wisps of smoke drifting into the sky. With grim foreboding he glanced at Catalina and Emilio riding stonily beside him. A few feet in the lead Ta-ne-haddle turned to give Luke an impassive stare, and it was enough to confirm Luke's suspicions. Luke squeezed Catalina's shoulder before tugging on her reins. "Catalina, you and Emilio have another disaster to face."

"What are you talking about?" she asked, and then her head snapped around in the direction of her house and Luke knew she had guessed. "No! Emilio, the house—" She urged her horse forward and Luke rode beside her, inwardly raging at Tandy McGuire, who had escaped and carried out his vengeance by destroying the Piedra home in San Antonio as well.

The house had been burned to the ground. Men still threw dirt on the smoldering ruins, picking through to salvage what was left. The acrid smell of smoke filled the air.

In a daze Catalina dismounted, staring at the ashes. A few pieces of furniture had been saved and stood to one side in the yard. Luke's arm went around her shoulders, and he held her close against his side. "You and Emilio can stay at my house," he said gruffly.

"All gone. Our homes, Mama . . ." She looked up at him. "It's all gone. Papa won't rebuild all this. There's too much lost. And he'll kill Tandy McGuire."

"Emilio," Luke said, looking over her head. "We'll go to my place. You both can stay there as well as the servants you want to keep with you."

"Thank you, sir," Emilio added solemnly. "Tandy McGuire did this, didn't he?"

Luke dropped his arm from Catalina's shoulder and stepped in front of Emilio. "There's been too much killing. It has to stop," he said, thinking his words had a false ring. Hadn't he lived with revenge and murder in his heart for eleven years?

"He'll have to pay for what he's done."

"Then let the law make him pay," Luke said.

"Will you go back and be marshal?"

The question hung in the air, and Luke glanced at Catalina. She was watching him closely. Emilio and Catalina were volatile, particularly Catalina. They were their father's children, and capable of strong hate and violence.

"If I become marshal again, will you promise me, both of you, that you'll leave Tandy McGuire to the law?"

Catalina stared at him, thinking about his question, realizing it meant that he might stay in San Antonio. Numbed by the events of the night, she couldn't think about a future that had changed drastically within a few hours' time, but she wanted Luke to stay. She nodded. "Emilio, please?" she asked.

Reluctantly he nodded. Luke's arm tightened around her shoulder. "Let's go to my place," he said to both of them.

His dark, empty house was stuffy and hot from being shut up. "Even though it's dawn, everyone needs sleep. I'll show you where the bed linens are as soon as we open these windows."

Within the hour everyone was ready to settle. The maids were behind the house in the servants' quarters. Along with Ta-ne-haddle, Emilio had gone to sleep in the courtyard, where it was cooler. Luke had shed his shirt and stood in the doorway to Catalina's room.

"You're sure you'll be all right?"

"Yes. I have to get accustomed to the changes in our lives. And I have to do so now. Today I'll make arrangements for Mama's wake and service."

He crossed the room and pulled her close again. "I'm sorry, Catalina."

She clung to his broad shoulders tightly, feeling as if he were a bulwark of protection. "If you hadn't been there, he would have killed Emilio as well as Mama. And if you hadn't come, we wouldn't have been as prepared to fight him." She raised her head and tears sparkled on her lashes. "I owe my life to you, Luke Danby."

He loved her and wished there were some way he could shoulder her burdens. He kissed her tenderly, then pulled her to him to hold her again. "Would you rather sit up than try to sleep?"

"I won't sleep, but you can and you should. You fought hard tonight. And your hands are burned."

"I'm all right." He went to the armoire and pulled out one of his shirts to use as a nightshirt for her. "Here. It's too hot for a wrapper."

"All my clothes are gone," she said with a wide-eyed stare.

"You'll get new ones. Don't worry about it now. Get ready for bed, and I'll come back with a glass of brandy and sit with you. I know you can't sleep."

A faint smile of gratitude curled at the corners of her mouth, and she nodded. He left and washed up at the pump outside, letting the cool water run over his head. It was hot and still, a night and dawn he would always remember. He went back down the hall and knocked on her door. Daylight shone through the open door to the courtyard and through the open windows behind her. She stood in the doorway in his white shirt that came to her knees, her shapely legs bare from the knees down. After the sorrow of the night, he hadn't thought he would experience the stirrings of passion, but the sight of her shapely curves outlined by the light set his blood to racing.

He took her hand and led her to a chair, pulling another one close and setting the brandies on the table between them. As they sipped the brandies, his muscles began to relax.

"Would you rather sit on my lap?" he asked in a husky voice.

Instantly she was in his arms, holding him tightly while she cried over her losses. Luke held her, trying to keep his thoughts on the problems at hand and not on the softness pressed against him. Her flesh was so warm through the thin layer of chambray.

Silently he swore and tried to concentrate on Tandy McGuire and the multitude of things he would have to do if he got his job back as marshal. Finally Catalina's breathing was deep and even; she had fallen asleep in his arms, her raven hair spread over her shoulders and his arms.

His heart twisted with longing. He kissed her head lightly, wishing things were different, wondering what had actually happened to his mother. Had Domingo lost Hattie to Coit Ritter as he had said, or had he sold her to a brothel as he had told Ta-ne-haddle?

Luke hurt for Catalina, because he knew how devastating it was to lose a parent. His arms tightened around her. Hers tightened around his neck, and she snuggled closer. He looked down at her sharply, but her breathing was steady, and the reaction had been in her sleep. He gazed beyond her through the open window into the courtyard, and wondered what would happen to them all.

As streaks of bright sunshine slanted through the open door, Luke finally stood up and carried her to bed. He laid her down carefully. With his heartbeat drumming, he drew in his breath sharply as he gazed at her beauty. His shirt was tangled, pulled inches above her knees, and she was so lovely it was an effort to keep from kneeling beside her and waking her with kisses. He turned away abruptly, and closed the door.

Luke slept less than an hour, then went out to pump water in the courtyard and saw Ta-ne-haddle was gone. Emilio slept, covered with a sheet, his dark hair barely showing. Emilio bore little resemblance to Domingo. Luke's thoughts jumped: he would have to face Domingo again. Domingo—who would never want Luke to live and be a constant threat to him.

Luke pumped water and bathed while he worried about the problem of Domingo. He dressed in fresh clothing, a white shirt, jeans, a leather vest, and boots. He started to the kitchen to fire up the stove when he heard hoofbeats approaching at a gallop. He swore as he headed for the front door and opened it. Hans was riding hard for his house.

"*Ach, Himmel!* Thank goodness you returned. I heard you had. Judge Roberts has already been to see me. We want you to come back as marshal."

"I intended to come in this morning."

"Domingo Piedra broke out of jail."

"He *what?*"

"He heard about his home being burned, and heard Friedrich killed his family."

"How the blue blazes did he hear that? It isn't the truth!"

"Someone was yelling about it outside the jail, calling taunts to him. Ulrich was on duty and he ran out to see who it was, but it was dark and he couldn't find the person. It set Domingo wild. Then he got quiet, Ulrich said, and he started complaining of pain, and all of a sudden Ulrich thought Domingo was having an attack or convulsions. He unlocked the cell.''

Luke groaned, guessing the rest, wondering what Domingo would do and where Tandy McGuire was.

"Domingo hit Ulrich and tied him up, and I found him a few minutes ago. Domingo's been gone about an hour.''

"An hour!''

"Lucio has gone after him.''

"Lucio's alone?'' Luke asked sharply.

"Yes. We didn't know you were in town at first, then someone told me that they heard you were at the Piedra ranch. If it was burned and everyone—''

"Emilio and Catalina and many of the employees are alive. Friedrich was killed,'' Luke said, his thoughts running over what had happened.

Domingo had almost had victory in his hands with Friedrich's death. To turn outlaw now was a surprise. Luke had guessed Domingo would gamble he could bluff his way through the trial as he had so many times in the past. A thought struck Luke forcibly—a lion never likes a cage. Domingo might be tired of his family and his respectable life. The predatory instincts are permanent in most wild animals.

"I have to tell Catalina and then I'll catch up with you.''

"*Ja*. Thanks Luke, for coming back.''

Grimly Luke went down the hall to Catalina's room and rapped lightly on the door. When there wasn't a sound, he opened the door. She had rolled over, her face hidden by a curtain of black hair, one arm stretched over the side of the bed. His nightshirt barely covered her bottom, her long brown legs were stretched out, and Luke had to clench his fists to keep from reaching down to stroke her silken legs.

He yanked up a sheet to cover her. "Catalina,'' he said softly.

When she didn't stir, he shook her shoulder. She was warm, strands of her hair playing over his hand,

and his body reacted to her. She rolled over sleepily, gazing at him through narrowed eyes, and it took all his control to keep from scooping her into his arms to kiss her. She blinked and stirred.

"Good morning, Luke," she said solemnly.

"I'm sorry to wake you, but I'm leaving and I thought you should know why."

She frowned. "Something's wrong. Something else has happened."

He sat down on the bed beside her, aware of her hip pressing against his, the languorous, sleepy-eyed expression she had. He touched her shoulder lightly, feeling her delicate bones.

"Go ahead and tell me."

"I wish I could protect you from it."

She placed her hand on his arm, gazing at him with her large black eyes. "Go ahead. What happened?"

"Your father broke out of jail a short time ago."

"He escaped?" She sat up swiftly, the sheet falling to her waist. His shirt was unbuttoned at the throat, revealing the curve of her breasts, and her dusky nipples were revealed by the thin material, an even greater temptation to him. Luke felt as if the temperature in the room had soared. His arousal was swift, longing swamped him.

"I'm going to the office. I'm taking back my badge if they want me, but it may send me against your father."

"Why would he do that? He'll be a hunted man. After Friedrich did so much to us, I thought everyone's sympathy would be with Papa," she said in a puzzled voice, running her fingers through a sheaf of thick midnight hair. Her gaze met his squarely, and he guessed her thoughts were following the same pattern as his had earlier. "Did he know about Mama and the houses?"

"Yes, he did. Hans said he went into a rage at first, and then Ulrich, a deputy, thought he was having an attack of come sort. He tricked Ulrich, and he's gone.''

"He didn't want to come back to us," she whispered as the implications of his escape settled on her. The night had been one blow after another, and this was one more that severed the last frail tie with her childhood. Domingo wanted to be free of them. By his choice he had made the decision which side of the law he wanted.

"He's an outlaw."

"If he contacts you, see if you can talk him into coming back," Luke said, barely able to keep his thoughts on Domingo. He couldn't resist catching a silky lock of her black hair and letting it curl around his fingers, letting his knuckles rest against her warm shoulder. In her disheveled state she was more appealing than ever, and his arousal was disturbing. "If he'll give himself up soon, people will accept he went a little crazy after learning about your mother and your homes. A month from now, they won't be so forgiving.

"Catalina, I tried to walk away and not hurt you where he was involved. I was drawn back for your protection. You and Emilio need me in the days ahead, but if I stay, I'll take back the badge. And I'll uphold it.''

"Why do you have to do that?" she asked with a frown. "You can stay here and practice law. You don't have to be marshal.''

"They want me and need me," he said, unable to tell her that Domingo would try to kill him.

"No! You and Papa will—one of you will hurt the other. Luke, please, you quit once. You don't have to go back.''

"I do if I stay in San Antonio. And I promise you, I'll try to bring him back alive.''

She turned her head away, her black hair swirling to hide her face. "Please, don't do this.''

"Catalina, I have to," he said grimly.

"I don't think he ever really wanted us, but I don't know why he's run away. He has money, land . . . he can rebuild."

"Maybe there isn't as much money available as you think. He may have put it in the business or in land," Luke said gently. "I'll see what I can find out if you want. If you'd like, I can go with you to the undertaker's to make the arrangements."

"Thank you, but I'll manage." She ran her hand across her brow, and he tilted her chin up to look directly at her.

"What's wrong?"

"Everything. I can't pay the men at the ranch or the servants who came with us last night."

"I can. Keep them on the payroll for now. I'll see what I can find out."

She threw her arms around his neck, startling him as she squeezed against him. He closed his eyes and held her tightly, wanting her desperately. Her warm nipples seared him where she pressed against his chest. Her slender waist enticed him, and he let his hand drift down over the full curve of her bottom, wanting to yank away the barriers of clothing between them and push her down on the bed with him.

"Luke, you're good to us," she whispered against his neck, and he tried to control his flaming urge to make love to her. "I'm sorry I was so angry with you. You care or you wouldn't be doing all this for us."

"I care," he said roughly, crushing the breath from her lungs in his steely hug. Abruptly he released her and walked to the door. "I'm going back as marshal."

She frowned as he left. Catalina felt caught in something that was twisting her heart in two. Her father had turned his back on them, breaking out of jail and riding off. It hurt even though it wasn't a terrible shock. And it pitted Luke against him. And Domingo against Luke. Would her father hurt Luke?

Her mind jumped ahead to what she had to do. They couldn't live with Luke indefinitely. She had to find out if any money was available. If it wasn't, she had to find out what they could sell to maintain the ranch. She and Emilio could run the ranch, it was all they knew. She washed and dressed quickly to hunt for Emilio. He was at the pump in the courtyard, splashing water on his face and chest, his thick black curls plastered to his head.

"Emilio, we have another problem."

He turned wide, dark eyes on her. "Another?"

"It's Papa. He broke out of jail and has run away."

Emilio stared at her open-mouthed. "He's an *outlaw!*"

"I don't think he'll come back to us," she said firmly.

Emilio blinked rapidly and sat down on a stone bench close at hand. "No, he won't," he said in amazement. His voice changed and bitterness replaced surprise. "No, he's always done as he pleases. He probably would prefer the life of a cutthroat renegade to facing prison or ruin. I'll bet we're penniless, Catalina."

"That's what I fear. We have the ranch, the land where the house in town was, and maybe something in the freighting business."

"The freighting business is entangled with complications from his partnership with Friedrich. There may be nothing for us when it's settled."

She bit her lip. "We should think about the ranch and what we can do to rebuild and live there." She paused a moment. "I can't believe he would do this. Why would any man prefer the life of an outlaw?"

"Have you ever understood our father?"

"No, but sometimes I think I came closer to understanding him than I did to understanding Mama."

"That's because you—" He snapped off his words abruptly.

"Go ahead and say it. I'm so much like him. Maybe I am, but I hope I don't have that wild streak in me that he does."

"You don't," Emilio said instantly.

"Luke is going to return to his job as marshal."

"Then he'll have to hunt our father."

"Emilio, don't hate him for it."

"Hate Luke? I like Luke and hate our father! Luke Danby saved my life. And if he had been a second sooner, he would have saved Mama's life." He turned wide brown eyes on her. "If he gets in a gun battle with Papa, he won't survive. I've never seen anyone who can draw and fire as fast as Papa."

"You haven't seen that many men," she said stiffly, hating to hear her own fears voiced aloud.

"I've ridden with him. I've seen him practice with the men. There's no one as quick. And our father will never abide by rules of society. If he wants something, no one will stand in his way. Including his children."

They looked at each other, both dry-eyed, she realized. She felt beyond tears, numb from the shocks and losses, but knew they had to do something to sustain themselves and do it quickly.

"I'll try to find out today if we have anything. I think we should sell the land where the house in town is."

"You don't think he'll ever come back," Emilio said.

"Do you?"

"No. He won't. Emilio, I think you should learn to use a pistol."

"If I practice for the next one hundred years, I'll never be able to handle one like Luke or Papa."

"Don't be absurd. If you practice you can."

"They're driven to it. There's something inside Luke Danby that drives him."

"How do you know that?" she asked, amazed at his pronouncement. She gazed into Emilio's thickly lashed brown eyes and thought her brother was almost beautiful with eyes like a girl's.

"Don't you think I'm right?"

"Yes," she said, thinking about Luke momentarily.

"But I know him much better than you. How did you guess?"

"I observe people and life, Catalina. Some people are observers and some participants. You're a participant."

"You sound as if you are moving back to the subject of books, and we have so much to do," she said, her thoughts returning to the problems at hand. "The servants are coming to town today to work here, and Luke said to let them stay. He'll pay them and the men at the ranch for the time being."

"He's a good man, Catalina. Whatever happens, remember that."

"I know he is," she said, suddenly laughing for the first time since the disastrous night. Her cheeks heated while she thought of how exciting Luke was.

"If he has to arrest our father, you must forgive him, because it's his sworn duty," Emilio added somberly.

"I know. You'll go with me to make arrangements about Mama, won't you? Next, I'm going to look up the land records and see exactly what we do own." She left him, hurrying back to her room, her thoughts already moving ahead on what she had to do.

As he left the judge's house, Luke was marshal again and he was going after Domingo. Domingo's jailbreak had caused a subtle change in the relationship between Catalina and her father, Luke suspected. He had been tempted to turn his back on San Antonio, the job, Catalina, and search for Hattie, but he couldn't do it.

Catalina shouldn't be alone during the worst crisis in her life. A muscle worked in his jaw when he thought about the possibilities. Domingo could have left his children penniless except for the land. He suspected Domingo would never have fled leaving a fortune behind.

And when the time did come for a decision, Luke didn't know which direction to search for Hattie. It could be more hopeless years. Had Domingo left her in Franklin, or handed her over to Ritter in Santa Fe?

Luke swore under his breath. He had to find Tandy McGuire. Two men on the run, both determined to kill each other, and Luke needed to find them both.

As soon as he reached the office, all his regular deputies were waiting as he had instructed. After listening to their welcome greetings, he gave them instructions. "We'll need extra help. For the next hour I want each of you to see how many reliable men you can find— no trigger-happy hotheads, no one who bitterly hates Tandy or Domingo—good volunteers to go after them. Hans, I'm going to leave you in charge here."

The disappointment was obvious on Hans's face, yet when he stopped to think about it, he would see that Luke had to have someone dependable in town.

"Hurry up, men," Luke said. "Be back in an hour because Domingo is hours ahead of us."

They scattered, and Luke settled down to look at records to learn what had transpired while he had been away. An hour later he glanced up to see Catalina in his buggy, driving past on the north side of the courthouse. He pushed away a ledger and hurried outside to wave to her.

"I didn't expect to see you out this soon," he said, bracing his hands on the buggy. She looked lovely in spite of the blue denim skirt and chambray bodice that were smudged with dirt, torn, and burned.

"I've been to see Mr. Morley, the undertaker, and make arrangements for the service. Emilio went with me and now he's gone to the lumber yard."

Luke gazed up at the strained look on her face. She was trying to keep a tight control on her emotions. He stepped up into the buggy with her, causing her to scoot over on the seat as he slipped his arm around her shoulders.

"Are you all right, honey?" he asked in a husky voice, wishing he could do something to stop her pain.

Catalina looked down at her fingers locked together

around the reins. His endearment almost undid the control she was trying to exercise. She wanted to fling herself into his protective arms, but she knew she had to shoulder her burdens and take care of Emilio as well as herself. Luke was being wonderful to them, yet the time had come when she had to take charge of her life. "Thank you, Luke, for all your help."

"Are you going home now?"

'No. I'm going to look up the land records. Why are you smiling?"

"I suspected you'd take charge. Not many young ladies would."

"Well, they'd starve, then. We have to do something."

"I'll feed you," Luke said with a note of obvious admiration. He reached up to smooth strands of black hair over her ear.

She smiled in return, and Luke's spirits lifted. She'd get through this crisis better than he had expected. And along with his admiration came desire. In spite of all the trials of the night, she looked beautiful. "Before you go home, go by the dry-goods store and pick up some material. You can take it to a dressmaker and have some new dresses made."

"I can't pay for it."

"I already have. Tell Emilio to go to the tailor's and the sutler's store and a boot maker. Both of you need clothes—"

"We can't let you do that."

"You can't stop me. I'm doing what I want, so don't argue," he said quietly, but with that steely note she had occasionally heard him use. She hugged him tightly, burying her face against his neck, and he felt tears on his skin.

"Hey."

"I wasn't going to cry, but you're so good to us."

He extricated himself from her grasp, pulling out a handkerchief and wiping away her tears. "You can cry all you want," he said, dabbing at her tears.

"You can be so good."

"People have been good to me. I wouldn't be here if it hadn't been for Ta-ne-haddle." The scrape on her cheek still stirred his anger. "I'm riding out soon with some men after Tandy. I'll leave right after the service for your mother."

She knew what he left unspoken. "You're not going after Papa?"

"A couple of my deputies and some volunteers will do that."

Catalina was torn with both fear and anger. She gazed into his thickly lashed green eyes, his commanding features, and her heart beat faster. As she placed her hand lightly on his knee, she saw the flicker in his eyes. For the first time since the tragedies of the night, she began to lose the numbness and shock, and longing for Luke tore at her emotions. "Luke, be careful. My father knows how to use a gun extremely well."

"I know, Catalina," he said.

The realization that Luke might be killed overrode all else momentarily. She ached to have his strong arms around her, to have him safe, to hear him laugh and to be able to laugh herself.

"I feel like I won't ever laugh again," she said, fighting back tears, for once in her life striving to control her emotions.

He tilted her face up. "You will. I can promise you that time will help," he said tenderly, looking into her black velvet eyes that mesmerized him. If he didn't move, he knew he might yield to the urge to kiss her, so he dropped down out of the buggy with an awkward jump.

"I promise you, you'll laugh again soon. You'll make it through this time, Catalina, because you're strong."

"I hope so. Luke, don't go after Papa," she asked, the words rushing out. "If you kill him, I can't forgive you," she said in a low voice, fear showing in her expression.

He nodded, aware of the consequences long before she told him. "I may be gone awhile. I put some silver in the drawer of the chest in your room for you to use while I'm gone. Don't protest, Catalina. I'm doing what I want to do."

She opened her mouth to protest anyway, and he stepped up to kiss her briefly. He had meant only a light kiss to stop her protest, but the moment he felt her soft mouth, he was lost. He kissed her hungrily, his arm tightening like an iron band around her waist. He released her brusquely and stepped down, turning away before she could argue.

The buggy began to move, and he looked at her as she left. Her back was straight, her head held high, and he wanted her to an extent he hadn't dreamed possible. And Domingo, the shadow that had always loomed between them, became less important to Luke than having Catalina. She couldn't forgive him if he killed Domingo. He couldn't let Domingo gun him down, but Luke wanted her and he wanted her forever.

"You're back in office," Ta-ne-haddle said, striding toward him.

"Yes I am. And she told me she won't ever forgive me if I kill him. I'll have to bring him back unharmed."

"So you've given up revenge."

"I gave that up long ago. As soon as her mother's burial is over, I'm going after Tandy and my deputies will go after Domingo. Then again, from reports we've received, both men and their gangs are riding in the same direction. I think Domingo is after Tandy." He gazed across the plaza, which was filling with large hay wagons and freighters. "I hope we get Domingo, because I want him to stand trail. As long as he's free, I'm a threat to him. He'll come after me."

"You could take her and go away. She has nothing to hold her here now."

"She has Emilio. And even if I took them both, I can't spend my life running away from Domingo. The first time our paths cross, he'd try to gun me down, and I'd defend myself. So one of us will kill the other. This way, if I can bring him back alive to stand trial, perhaps justice will relieve me of the problem." Luke studied Ta-ne-haddle. "Are you leaving town soon?"

"Nope. I've been down to the bathhouse."

"I'll feel better if I know you'll be here while I'm gone. Tandy may still try to hurt Catalina and Emilio."

"I'll watch them. They'll be all right."

"Thanks," Luke said as he saw a bunch of men striding down the street toward the office. "Looks like here come some of my volunteers to hunt Domingo and Tandy."

"You don't need me here," Ta-ne-haddle said, striding away while Luke headed for his office.

Sophia Piedra was buried the next morning in the cemetery west of the cathedral. As soon as the service was over, Luke kissed Catalina good-bye. By nightfall he had caught up with Ulrich and Troya, his two deputies, and a group of volunteers who had picked up a trail an hour out of San Antonio.

The next day a blazing sun climbed over land covered in mesquite and cactus as they headed northwest toward the rolling hills. Luke took the lead when he saw something on the ground in the distance. As he rode closer, his fears were confirmed: it was a body.

His stomach knotted as he drew in the reins and climbed down. He recognized the familiar cowhide boots that Lucio wore. He had been dragged across the ground, a rope around his ankles. The rope had been cut and lay carelessly on the ground. And Lucio had been shot, a bloody wound in his chest. Luke felt sick; Domingo had done it deliberately to taunt him.

Rage and sickness boiled in him as he fetched a blanket off his horse to wrap the body. The other men rode up, but a drumming in Luke's ears drowned out their questions until he saw Ulrich looking at him with a strange expression.

"You all right, Marshal?"

Luke nodded, spreading the blanket. Ulrich helped him wrap the body, and they tied it behind one of the volunteers' saddles. The man turned back toward San Antonio to take the body home.

"Let's mount up," Luke snapped, and swung up into the saddle. His chest swelled with rage. He wanted to go after Domingo and gun him down as he deserved, but he had promised Catalina he would try to bring him back alive.

Hours later they reached the clear, green Medina River. After watering the horses and drinking, they rode along the riverbank toward the north. As they rode down a wash, Luke discovered a body, a man shot twice. In seconds Ulrich found Tandy's body.

"Domingo did the job for us," one of the men said.

"Tandy McGuire deserved a fair trial," Luke said quietly, controlling his mounting rage. He gazed down at the tracks in the dusty ground, following them where they turned to the northwest. "None of these men have families in town, so let's bury them here. Then we'll go after Domingo," he said, knowing he couldn't turn back in spite of Catalina. Determined to catch Domingo, because now he would hang without question, Luke urged his horse to a faster pace.

Before dusk they reached the rise of an escarpment and climbed to the plateau, a rocky, hilly, highland covered in feathery mesquite, white limestone rocks, buffalo grass, low-branched husiaches, and pale green cactus. Before nightfall Luke spotted riders in a valley between two hills, but in moments they were lost from sight. If he had been alone, Luke would have kept after them, but he knew the men needed to stop for the night.

"We'll ride before dawn," Luke said, hoping he could take Domingo alive, hearing the echo of Catalina's words, *"If you kill him, I can't forgive you."*

Sleep was difficult because he kept thinking of Lucio and Domingo, and by dawn they were back on the trail again. Tracks began to be fresher as the distance between the two groups of men narrowed.

Four days later Luke spotted tracks at a stream near a pass between rugged hills. As Luke rode along slowly, his gaze sweeping the rim of a hill, he said quietly to Ulrich, "Those tracks aren't over an hour old. They could be up on that rim or down in the canyon waiting."

"Do you think they're directly ahead?"

"Yes," Luke said, dismounting to study the ground. He picked up a mesquite branch and saw where it had been freshly slashed from a tree. He spotted signs of a branch having been swept over the ground to hide tracks. He walked that direction for a moment while Ulrich followed.

"What is it, Marshal?"

He looked up at the rim and the empty blue sky beyond. "I think they're waiting up there for us. Someone tried to cover tracks with this branch." He scanned the rim, and felt an eerie certainty that Domingo was waiting for him. He took a deep breath. "If we go through the pass, we'll ride into an ambush. Let's go this way, up over the rim."

"It'll take a hell of a lot longer. We may lose them."

"We might," Luke said, picking up the reins, "but we'll be alive. Knowing Domingo, he'll be up there waiting."

"How do you know so much about Domingo Piedra?" Ulrich asked, staring at Luke with curiosity.

"We crossed paths once long ago," Luke said curtly and motioned to the men to gather around. "I think Domingo and his men are up on the ridge. Keep your rifles ready."

Luke rode slowly forward. His gaze roved constantly over the cedars. As they climbed, he could see for miles in the distance. His skin prickled: he was being watched. Each cedar tree became a trap, a possible cover for Domingo or one of his men. Domingo was waiting. Luke could feel it in the charged air. There wasn't a breeze, nothing to disturb the trees, and sweat trickled down his back.

When he and his men reached the top of the ridge, they rode in single file with Luke in front. All his senses were alert; he listened for the slightest unusual noise, his eyes scanning the terrain. He wanted to take Domingo back to San Antonio to face the charges against him, to let the law mete out justice.

Luke's horse made faint rustling noises moving through the brush, the slight clop of hooves on the limestone and caliche. Suddenly he caught a swift movement out of the corner of his eye. A rope dropped over his head and yanked him off his horse.

20

EVEN AS THE ROPE SNAPPED TIGHT AROUND HIM, Luke yanked out his knife. With one vicious swing he severed the rope, jerking on the reins to ride behind a cedar. Shots rang out and his men scattered. He dropped off his horse, his blood pounding. How close he had come to having a repeat of what Domingo had done years ago! He burned with anger while he crouched and moved through the brush.

A shot made a dull thunk in a tree trunk behind him. He fired, catching a glimpse of Domingo. He disappeared behind trees and Luke angled toward where he saw Domingo drop out of sight. Gunfire blasted the air. From behind a cedar a man pitched forward and sprawled on the ground.

One of Luke's volunteers was spun backward by a blast, tumbling over the ridge out of sight.

"*Vamos, hombres!*" came a deep bellow that Luke would recognize anywhere. Domingo jumped on a horse, urging it forward.

The thought that he had come so close only to lose Domingo now sent Luke into action. Without thinking, reacting violently out of rage, he crouched and ran in a zig-zagging line at Domingo, who was only yards away. Domingo turned to fire and Luke made a dive for a cedar, his hat flying off from the shot.

He didn't feel the impact of hitting the ground, but rolled and came up firing. Domingo turned, looking down with hatred as he aimed at Luke. Luke yanked the trigger; the shot hit Domingo's revolver, sending it flying from his hand. He swore, turning to ride down on Luke while shots rang around them as their men fought each other.

Luke dodged, but Domingo leapt off his horse and kicked Luke's rifle. It discharged into the air as Domingo landed on Luke, and they fought for control of the weapon. Luke flung it aside, slamming his fist into Domingo's jaw. The blow jerked Domingo's head back, then he lunged at Luke. The two men went down, rolling to the rim of the canyon. Domingo ended up on top, pushing Luke, trying to choke him.

Spots danced in front of Luke's eyes as he struggled, his breath cut off. Domingo's black eyes had a murderous gleam. "You die, Danby."

Dirt was crumbling under Luke. In seconds his head would be pushed over the rim; then Domingo could finish him off. The world swam, but rage sent power surging through him, and he slammed his fist into Domingo's jaw. Domingo was flung back, and Luke rolled to his feet, snatching up his rifle to aim with the barrel pointed between Domingo's eyes.

Domingo froze, looking up, expecting the shot. As his chest heaved while he tried to breathe, Luke remembered Catalina. He heard men riding away, some of his men galloping past after them. He stepped back and motioned with his rifle.

"Get to your feet and get your hands in the air. It's over, Domingo. I'm taking you in."

Domingo's eyes narrowed. He got up slowly, raising his hands, looking at Luke with contempt. "You dumb *buscadero!* You don't learn, do you?"

"Unbuckle your knife and toss it down at my feet," Luke ordered in a raspy voice. "Careful, Domingo." He kicked Domingo's knife in its scabbard over the ridge.

Suddenly a rider burst through the bushes. Luke spun around, diving to avoid the shots aimed at him. He came up and fired as Domingo yanked the man off his horse. The man jerked from the blast and fell forward while Domingo slipped down Comanche fashion, using the horse as a shield, as he disappeared in a cedar brake. Luke fired at him, running for his horse, and vaulting into the saddle to pound after him.

In moments he saw Domingo break into the open, his horse's mane and tail flying as he raced away. Luke started to fire, but stopped. At this distance his only option was to shoot to kill.

"Soon, Domingo," he said, reining in, looking at the cloud of dust that drifted in the air. He turned back to tend to his injured men. They had three men who needed medical attention and wouldn't be able to defend themselves from Comanches, so they made a travois, and turned back to San Antonio.

Catalina had heard his horse and then his voice. She pushed away from the desk where she was writing and ran to meet him, her new red calico skirt swirling around her legs. He came through the front door, stepping into the cool hallway.

Luke!" He was covered in dirt, his face smudged with blood, his clothing disheveled, but he looked wonderful to her. She flung herself into his arms. He caught her up in his arms, lifting her off the floor, and held her tightly as he inhaled a sweet rose scent and relished her softness.

"Your father escaped. We had to bring the injured men back."

"Was anyone hurt badly?" she asked, still clinging to him, her voice muffled against his throat.

"Doc Ellison said they'll pull through. Jim Corners was hit the worst. Dale Bixby died," he said, letting her slide down so her feet were on the floor. "Lucio was killed," he said, remembering too clearly every detail, knowing that was the fate Domingo intended for him if he got the opportunity.

"I heard Lucio was killed, as well as Tandy and two of his men," she said. "Papa did it."

"We don't know for sure. He's entitled to a trial."

"I know he did it. And now he'll hang. And you'll have to bring him back." She flung her head back to look up at him. "I hate what you do! You don't have to be a marshal!"

"Yes, I do," he said, thinking how good it was to come home to her as he stroked her face. "I have a job I have to do," he said, but he didn't give thought to his words. She was the most wonderful person in the world, and he wanted her desperately. He had dreamed of her each night, and longed for her as he rode. His gaze dropped to her full red lips and he leaned down, crushing her to him. His mouth opened hers and his tongue thrust over hers to kiss her passionately.

She tightened her slender arms around his strong shoulders, pressing against him, feeling his arousal. She trembled with excitement and happiness that he was home again. Finally he released her and she stroked his stubbly jaw.

"We're not going to argue now," she said, squeezing him and placing her head against his chest.

"No, we're not because I'm about to drop from exhaustion. We ran into a party of Comanches and had to stand them off. I haven't slept for over forty-eight hours."

"Shh. I'll see that the maids get water heated for a bath, and then you can eat and sleep to your heart's content."

He shifted to look down at her with a smoldering hunger that banished her light tone. He gave her another squeeze, "After I bathe we'll talk."

"*Sí,*" she answered quietly, walking down the hall beside him until she told him good-bye at his door. Luke took one look at the bed and went straight to it to stretch out. He fell asleep instantly, not waking until morning, when he heard a cheerful voice.

"Luke. Luke Danby," Catalina said playfully only inches from his face, her black eyes sparkling with happiness.

He groaned. His muscles ached and he was still groggy. She looked like a vision in a pale blue gingham skirt, a white chambray bodice, her black curls falling over her shoulders. A scent of flowers assailed him, and he reached for her, slipping his arm around her waist.

"You're beautiful."

She yelped and wriggled in his arms, twisting against him. "And you're dirty."

He grinned as he rolled over on his back to look up at her. "Okay. If I let you go now, can I hug you when I'm clean?"

"It's a promise," she whispered, the laughter in her eyes changing to a sensuous hint of promise that made his blood heat. "There's a bath ready for you and food on the table." Her smile faded when he stood up. He ran his hand through his hair. He was rumpled and dirty, but his body was hard muscle and burned brown by the sun. She drew her breath sharply, wanting him to hold her again, not caring about dirt. She looked up to meet a mocking gleam that made her blush. He tilted her chin up and looked at her mouth, and Catalina felt on fire as the depths of his green eyes grew stormy.

"It's been far too long, Catalina," he said in a husky voice that made her want to melt into his arms. His arm slipped out, circling her waist. This time she forgot how dirty he was or that she had on one of the few pretty new dresses she had made.

Luke pulled her close, crushing her softness, wanting to carry her back to his bed right now. He leaned over her, his swollen shaft throbbing as he pressed against her hungrily, taking her searing kisses with his tongue deep in her mouth. He wanted to make her cling to him, to make her cry out for him. Erotic images of her lying nude before him, of her soft body moving beneath his, fanned his fires to a blazing heat.

Finally she broke away. "Luke, the servants are heating water for your bath. They'll be here . . ."

Her mouth was red from his kisses, her eyes wide and black as midnight. Her skin looked petal soft and smooth. He couldn't say anything or get his breath; he shook with a slight tremor, he wanted her so badly.

She drew a deep breath and fled from the room. Catalina had seen the desire in his expression. It set her aflame with longing. The largest problem in her life was her passion for him. She was aware of him wherever he was when they were together.

Luke watched her go, his body throbbing with desire. The barriers between them that once had been so unbreakable had been shattered by Domingo himself. Yet there was no way Luke could tell her the full extent of her father's evil doings. Never would he do that, but some day he would have to tell her part of what had happened.

As soon as his bath was ready, he settled in the tub of steaming water. When he emerged, he fumbled for a towel and felt warm fingers place it in his hand.

Catalina knelt beside the tub, on his eye level while she gazed at him solemnly. "I knew you'd need a towel."

Luke couldn't give her a coherent answer. Her hair was freed of pins and ribbons, falling softly over her shoulders; her heated gaze strayed over his chest and shoulders. She was sensual, inviting. With a groan he stood up, sweeping the towel around his waist and reaching for her.

Catalina came into his arms in a rush, not caring that he was wet. Her hands slipped over his warm, wet skin and she stroked him while he stepped out of the tub and splashed water on her skirt and feet.

His fingers hooked in her scoop-necked bodice, and pulled it down to her waist. His eyes blazing with desire, he cupped her full breasts in each of his hands, her olive skin golden against his darker skin that was burnished from the sun. He ran his thumbs back and forth across her nipples while he watched her. Catalina closed her eyes, tilting back her head, and reached out eagerly to run her fingers along his thigh, pushing the towel away. He leaned down to kiss a full breast, to tease her lightly with his tongue and teeth, to stroke her silken skin.

With ease he scooped her up in his strong arms and carried her to the bed, placing her down on it as his weight came down on one knee. He kissed her slender throat, and moved downward to stroke and kiss, to drive her to the frenzy he felt. Once again he paused over her, his gaze drinking in her beauty.

"You're lovely and I need you, Catalina."

His words were headier than caresses, and she quivered with pleasure. His body was a perfection of honed fitness and vitality. His thighs, covered in short brown hair, were muscular and strong. His manhood revealed his need. With a small cry she pulled him down, wanting him to possess her. "Please," she whispered.

"I want you to always be mine," he exclaimed. He bent down to kiss her. Her flesh was dusky, slightly damp with perspiration, as smooth as silk. He gave her little nips, caressing her, until she moaned and writhed, reaching for him.

He thrust slowly into her soft warmth, trying to exert control and pleasure her. As her hips moved in fiery rhythm, his control vanished. He was lost to violent need, wanting to prolong the ecstasy. He cried out her name with his shuddering release, and in seconds she gripped him with her knees and hands, gasping and murmuring his name until she gave a muffled cry of rapture.

He stretched out on top of her, holding her tightly for long moments, kissing her heated flesh. "Catalina, love." He stroked her and kissed her and rolled over to face her.

"Thank goodness you're back. I missed you," she said. "I've been so afraid for you."

"Just keep waiting for me. I'll always come back to you."

"I don't want to wait," she said, running her hand

over his firm buttocks and along the back of his thigh. She couldn't get enough of his marvelous body, and his lovemaking sent shivers of delight through her as she drew her fingers along his thigh.

He caught her hands and pulled her toward him. "Lovely Catalina, how thankful I am you like to swim."

"It still embarrasses me to think about that," she said primly, and he dumped her on the bed, straddling her to look down at her. "Little liar," he accused. "You weren't badly embarrassed then, and now . . ." His gaze drifted down over her.

"Maybe so," she said breathlessly, her teasing humor swiftly changing to need in an impossibly short time. "Luke . . ."

He kissed her hard and she yielded, returning his passion. Thoughts spun away on a dizzying tumble of sensuous touches and kisses as her passion flared as bright and hot as a flame.

That night they faced each other across the table while they ate, and she told him her progress in settling matters. Luke heard only half of what she said because his thoughts were on how beautiful she looked. He wanted to carry her right back to bed. She wore her new red calico, and her hair was parted in the middle and tied behind her head with a red ribbon.

"Luke, are you listening to me?"

"Of course."

"What did I just tell you?"

He waited until a maid had finished serving them coffee and apple pastry. As soon as they were alone, he gazed at Catalina across from him. The soft glow of the oil lamp highlighted her cheekbones and glinted in her midnight hair. "You told me that you want to go back to my room after dinner."

"I did not. I knew you weren't listening," she scolded, but her eyes sparkled with excitement. Catalina felt as if laughter were bubbling up inside her all evening. The afternoon had been ecstasy; she loved Luke with her whole heart. He was exciting, charming, kind, intelligent, fun—a marvel to her. And when she thought of his powerful, masculine body, her heart beat like a drumroll. If only Emilio weren't returning to town from the ranch tonight, and she could be alone with Luke all night.

"Catalina," he said, "let's sit in the courtyard. When do you expect Emilio?"

"I don't know," she said, letting him take her hand, acutely aware of his slightest touch. "Luke, I want to show you the records I've found and my figuring."

"Mmmm," he drawled, leading her to the courtyard.

"I have some questions about what Emilio and I should do."

"Do you, Catalina?"

She knew he was taking her to the darkened courtyard to kiss her. Though she had waited days for him to return so she could get his opinion on her decisions about land and sales and rebuilding, she forgot all about business as he looked down at her with unmistakable desire.

They stepped into the darkness of a hot summer night. Luke drew her to him while he leaned against the wall and spread his long legs apart, fitting her close between them. She felt his hard arousal, and her desire flashed like summer lightning. She wound her slender arms around his neck as he leaned down to kiss her. In seconds kisses weren't enough. His callused hands untied the drawstring in her bodice, and he drew it down to her waist. As earlier, she wore nothing underneath.

His light touch made her tremble. Her hips thrust against him while she arched her back so he could fondle her. She gasped with pleasure, letting her hands drift down over him.

"Catalina?" came a call.

"There's Emilio," she said yanking up her blouse

and fumbling with the ribbons, and tieing them in a knot. Luke laughed and reached out to retie them.

"Stand still, honey."

His fingers were warm and she ached to be alone longer with him. Instead, she looked up as Emilio entered the courtyard.

"Ah, Catalina and Luke." Emilio strode to Luke and shook his hand. His grip was firm, his hands no longer soft like a girl's. Luke looked at him closely, realizing Emilio had added another two inches in height sometime since he had met him, and he hadn't even noticed when. His skin had darkened from working outside, his voice had deepened, and Luke realized the changes in Emilio might go as deep as those in Catalina.

"Sorry to interrupt," he said, glancing back and forth at both of them.

"No," Catalina protested a little too quickly. "Let's go to the parlor so we can go over our plans with Luke."

Luke draped his arm across Catalina's shoulders and she walked between them. In the parlor she pulled a ledger out of the desk. "Emilio found this at the ranch. It's accounts of costs at the ranch. The freighting company is closed up, but will you help me get inside tomorrow and get my father's accounts?"

"Yes. You can't disturb Friedrich's belongings until we know if he has heirs, but when I left, no one had come forward. I think the town is still reeling from the sudden outburst of violence."

"I've checked the land records and I have what I found in the safe, saved from the ranch fire. It's not very much," she said calmly, having already decided what she would have to do.

"Emilio and I have almost one thousand dollars in cartwheels, one hundred in gold." It was less than Luke had guessed, and he mentally swore at Domingo again.

"We thought we would try to sell the property in

town, but we'll rebuild at the ranch," she said, her mind ticking off plans in an orderly manner. She glanced at Luke to find him leaning back in the wing chair, his long legs stretched out while he studied her in a lazy, simmering appraisal that lingered on her breasts. She tried to keep her voice normal as she continued, but she could feel her cheeks heat. She slanted a glance at Emilio, and to her relief he was writing figures in a ledger. "Emilio has already been getting estimates on costs for the . . . ranch house and barn. Of course . . . we have to have . . . the horses."

Emilio looked at her sharply, and she realized she must have said something she shouldn't have. Luke had a mocking glint in his eyes, and the corner of his mouth raised slightly.

"What are you talking about, Catalina?" Emilio asked. "We have to have horses. Any simpleton knows that." He arched his brows at her and glanced at Luke with curiosity. He then gave Catalina a shake of his head before he went back to writing. She blushed and glared at Luke, who didn't hide his smile this time. He winked at her.

"You were saying, Catalina," he drawled, "you have to have horses."

"I meant we have to have a barn for them," she snapped, thinking there were moments when Luke was wonderful, and moments when he was bold enough to set her brain spinning. "I want to pay you what I owe you for staying here," she added briskly.

"Not even two-bits."

"It isn't right for you to pay our servants and all our bills, and keep us under your roof."

Leaning forward, he drew his finger lazily down her shoulder to her elbow. "As long as that's the way I want it, you forget about it."

"I don't want to have to move out," she said, her voice becoming breathless and losing its forcefulness because of his touch, "and this isn't right."

"Lord, you're stubborn," he said, and Emilio laughed aloud.

"You see, Catalina. Even Luke thinks you're stubborn."

Exasperated, Catalina announced, "I'm about to put all this away. Neither of you is being helpful."

"What did we do?" they both chorused with innocence, looked at each other, and tried to hide their smiles.

She snapped the book shut and started to set it down, but Luke caught her wrist. "Come on, tell me the rest. Emilio and I won't tease you."

"You two!" Mollified, she opened the book and continued, listening to Luke's opinions and talking them over with him. As he leaned forward to study her figures, his knee pressed hers, and his fingers drew invisible lines on the ledger, lines she could feel through the thin ledger book. Close up, he smelled clean and soapy. His jaw was clean-shaven, firm, and well shaped. He paused at one set of figures, and she saw it was her tally of how much of his money they had spent while he had been gone.

"No more about repayment," he said. "Both of you promise me."

Reluctantly they agreed, and he nodded with satisfaction.

"The ranch is Papa's, as well as the lot in town. I want to sell the lot in town. Can I do that since Papa might come back?"

"That's not the problem as much as you and Emilio are underage."

"I'm not old enough. I'm a woman. Everywhere I go, I run into obstacles because of my age and my sex."

"Not at this house, you don't," he teased, and Emilio groaned.

"Maybe you two should go back to the courtyard and be alone."

"Will you help instead of teasing me?" she snapped

at Luke, blushing furiously. "I figure if we can sell the lot in town, we might have enough to get me through this year, and then the ranch will earn enough to sustain itself."

"How many men can you count on staying with you?"

"There will be eight," Emilio answered quickly.

"And I'll live there soon," Catalina added.

"It's too dangerous with your father gone," Luke said somberly.

"Because I'm a woman again, dammit!"

"Never swear because you're a woman, Catalina," he said.

"You two do need to be alone." Emilio snapped the ledger shut, put it under his arm, and stood up. "I'm going to bed."

"Emilio!"

He kept going right out the door to the hallway. She gave Luke a wide-eyed stare. "Will you listen to me, and stop embarrassing me."

"Yes, ma'am. If you're through, we'll fol—"

"I'm not through."

"Then go right ahead. I'm just sitting here."

"You're not just sitting there."

"I thought I was."

"You know what I mean."

"Now what have I been doing wrong, Catalina?" he asked innocently, his green eyes full of devilment.

She had to laugh at him. "You're causing me trouble and embarrassment. You're flirting."

"Is it doing me any good?"

"Maybe," she said and leaned forward, licking her lips, letting her voice slow to a sultry drawl. "And maybe some day when you are involved in business, I will get sweet revenge."

"I hope so." He grinned. "Go ahead, honey. Tell me some more about your plans."

Happy, feeling an undercurrent of invisible sparks between them, she tried to get her thoughts back to the problems. "Emilio doesn't like working on the ranch, so he could go to work for one of the merchants or commission men in town, and I could take over the ranch. Emilio is a bookish sort of person. He isn't the type to cope with all the emergencies that come up on a ranch."

"You have everything figured out, don't you?"

She could hear the amusement in his voice and she turned to face him. "You're laughing at me *again.*"

"No, I'm not," he said tenderly. "Well, maybe I'm slightly amused. You forgot something important."

"What's that?" she asked, thinking he had the thickest eyelashes she had ever seen on a man.

"You'll get married."

"I might not!" she answered stiffly.

"Catalina Piedra," he drawled in a voice that played over her like a caress, "you know you'll marry some day, and all these plans will have to change."

"What my father does will make a difference to men. I passed Ticiano today and he was very cold."

Luke's amusement instantly left him and he gazed at her intently. "Ticiano snubbed you?"

"No, he spoke to me, but it wasn't like it has been before with him. And it may get worse," she said, facing Luke squarely, bringing her worries into the open.

She saw the sympathy in his eyes, and she hated it. "I don't want your pity, Luke Danby."

He squeezed her shoulder. "It isn't pity. I hate the circumstances you're in."

"Back to my plans. We need to find out about Papa's freighting business—" She tossed down a paper. "Why did he do this? All my life, I've wondered why he would be so cruel—"

With a scrape of his chair Luke turned and pulled her onto his lap, holding her tightly. "You can't control other people. You can't help what your father does."

"I know that. I'm afraid of what he'll do." She

looked up suddenly, her eyes filled with concern. "But I don't want you facing him across pistols. I don't want you to kill him, and I don't want him to kill you."

"I'll do what I have to do."

"But you won't give up being marshal?"

"No."

She blinked and looked away. "It hurts every time I see you ride away. Every time, Luke."

The calico was warm and soft, her skirt bunching against him. Luke kissed her lightly as he looked down into her velvety black eyes. "Most of the time I take the census. I collect fees from the saloons and bordellos. I have to make a few arrests of drunks and disorderly people. I have the most routine job in town a lot of the time."

"And when it stops being routine, it becomes the most dangerous," she whispered, her eyes drawing him closer, her lips raised to his. He bowed his head, kissing her full on the mouth, wanting her. He wanted her forever. In a rare moment for him he tossed aside his cool logic as he yielded to impulse and went with his emotions.

Raising his head, he gazed down into her velvety black eyes. "Catalina, will you marry me?"

21

SHE SAT UP SHARPLY. HER HAIR SPILLED OVER HER shoulders, and the oil lamp bathing her skin with a golden glow made him want to stroke her.

"Always before you held back. Never has there been talk of a future or marriage," she exclaimed, her heart seeming to stop.

"No, there wasn't," he said solemnly, "but I love you and I want you for my wife."

Words she had waited to hear! Yet now she suspected they were said out of pity, not love. "You ask me this to protect me and Emilio."

His eyes widened in surprise. "The hell I do," he said quietly. "I asked *you,* not Emilio. And I asked you because I love you," he said, suddenly feeling as if a burden had lifted. Domingo wouldn't stand between them any longer. "If I pitied you, I'd take you in as I have, but I wouldn't propose, Catalina."

"Then why the sudden change of heart?" she asked, knowing how cautious and reserved he was. "Why didn't you propose before when my father was wealthy and I could have easily accepted?"

"I had my reasons," he said evenly. "And they're buried now with the past."

She stood up and walked to the mantel in agitation. Words she had wanted to hear, yet for all the wrong reasons. "Luke, my parents had a bad marriage. It was unhappy for all of us in the early years. I have to be very sure," she said, trying to use wisdom when her heart cried out to accept. "I love you, but I won't marry you until I know it isn't out of pity that you ask. If you love me, you'll wait for me to be certain.''

"Lordy." He crossed the room to her, slipping his arms around her waist. "I love you. It's that simple. It has nothing to do with houses or money.''

"If that's the truth, you can wait for me to get back on my feet," she said with dignity. He realized how much she had changed from the volatile girl to a woman who thought things through before she acted.

He drew her to him. "I'm glad you feel strongly about what's happened, but I love you. I don't want to wait. Do you realize you could be carrying our child now?''

She inhaled swiftly, her breasts straining against her bodice. "I don't think I am.''

"Catalina, I love you and I want you.''

"If you do, you'll wait," she said firmly, wishing he were sincere, but afraid it was prompted out of pity. She threw herself into his arms and clung to him. "You've always held back. You told me you had reasons we couldn't marry. You never lose control.''

"I did this time. The reasons for holding back are gone. You'll see, I mean it when I say I love you," he murmured, leaning down to kiss her, crushing her to him. Now that he had asked her, he wanted her more than ever. He was determined he would get his way about this.

"We have to stop," she said later, moving out of his embrace.

"I want you alone for weeks," he said gruffly, his eyes dark with desire as she stepped out of his arms.

"Good night, Luke," she said quietly, sounding disturbed and subdued. As she went down the hall to her room, Luke followed slowly. Stopping in the doorway of his room, he propped his arm overhead and gazed after her. Pity was the last thing he felt for Catalina. She needed loving, demanding, scalding loving, not pity. Luke shifted impatiently and swore under his breath. If only she could see how badly he wanted her!

He would convince her soon what she needed and really wanted, what her body was made to do beneath a man's loving hands.

Catalina closed the door to her room, her emotions stormy. How much she had wanted to say yes! How wonderful to be Luke's wife. Her problems would dissolve instantly, and she was tempted beyond measure. If circumstances had been different, though, she wasn't sure he would have asked. There was still something he was keeping from her.

Whatever his reasons for holding back, they had changed, but he still wouldn't be open about them. She knew little about his past, only that he came from Boston. It seemed a closed subject and until now she hadn't cared to quiz him. She closed her eyes, thinking about his lovemaking. Her worries temporarily vanished as memories wrapped her in a cloak of happiness.

That night Luke was awakened by pounding on the front door. Swearing softly, he pulled on his pants and yanked up his revolver.

"Marshal!" came a call.

"Hans!" He unbolted the door and Hans stepped inside.

"Sorry, but there's been a holdup of a mail coach and three thousand dollars in gold taken. Two men made it back to town. It happened this afternoon on the run to Franklin. They think it was Domingo Piedra and his gang."

"I'll go to the courthouse as soon as I dress." He closed the door and turned to find Catalina standing in the shadows.

"My father," she said grimly.

"I have to go."

"Only one of you will live, Luke."

He hugged her tightly. She was right: someday he would kill Domingo Piedra.

In an hour Luke was riding away from town, once again tracking Domingo. This time he was gone three weeks until they ran into Comanches and had to turn back.

Luke returned at night, coming in after Catalina was asleep. He washed in cold water at the pump, dried off, and wrapped a large towel around himself before going to her room. The door was open to the court-yard, and he stepped inside. She lay sprawled in bed, her dark hair fanned over the pillow, her slender arms flung wide. He lowered his weight to the bed slowly, reaching to lightly caress her breast. She moaned and stirred, moving restlessly. He ran his hand down the length of her warm body, sliding it up again beneath the shirt. His pulse pounded as desire burned in him while his arousal was hard and swift.

"Luke!" She opened her eyes and her first surprised words were lost as he leaned over her, covering her mouth with his, stopping conversation for the next hours.

The next morning back at the courthouse, when he was finished with the business at hand, he turned to Hans, lowering his voice.

"Tomorrow there will be a mail coach through here. It'll be carrying five thousand in gold. They have two extra men riding shotgun, and they've asked us to pro-vide them with two more as far as Franklin. I think there's a chance Domingo will try to intercept and rob them."

"How will he know they're carrying anything worthwhile?"

"It'll be evident with so many men riding shotgun. He knows how much government gold goes through here."

"How many men do you want me to send with them and who?"

"Jim, Ulrich, Elmore, Troya. Put those four with the coach, Jim and Ulrich in front, Elmore and Troya in the rear. I'll ride in the coach when it leaves here," Luke said.

"Sir, may I ask you a personal question?"

"Go ahead."

"Why do you always leave me here?"

Luke gave him a level look. "You just married. I think your wife wants you to come home to her. The rest of us are single."

"She knew that when she married me. We talked it over and she agreed that I had a job to do."

"Someone has to watch the jail," Luke said, opening the stack of recently delivered letters, some months old in arrival. As he spread one before him and studied it, he forgot all about Hans's complaint.

"They've caught two of Tandy McGuire's men, and they want me to come up to Santa Fe and bring them back to Texas. It's a man named Thad Haley and another named Buster West. Bad men, both of them. I didn't know that was who rode with Tandy McGuire." He looked up at Hans. "I've heard Thad Haley robbed and killed the Cooper family. They rode with a gang that made raids into Texas and the territory, taking captives and selling them," Luke said stiffly, anger coming every time he read about someone taking captives. If he went to Santa Fe, it would give Catalina some of the time she had asked for. He wouldn't be gone long, and it was a job that had to be done before he could have a wedding and honeymoon. "I'll ride north and get them after we try to get Domingo. I want to see Domingo stand trial. Hopefully, I'll leave in a week for the Territory. Tell Ulrich and the others to be here in an hour, and we'll go over what we can do. That mail coach is due to arrive today or tomorrow."

Luke picked up his hat and jammed it on his head, striding to his horse to ride home for dinner. Emilio's horse was tethered in front, and Luke entered to find Emilio and Catalina both in the hall. While Emilio shook his hand, Luke placed his arm around Catalina. She looked beautiful in a simple Mexican-style white bodice and red skirt. All her fancy dresses had burned, but Luke liked the simple ones better. The soft fabrics clung to her shapely curves and tiny waist, and she was no longer corseted, covered in layers of clothing, buttoned to her chin in silks.

"You two come in and we can talk while we eat." The house was cool, the dining area open to the enclosed courtyard, a breeze blowing through the house.

Over crisp tortillas covered in peppers, chunks of tomato and cheese, and steaming beef, Emilio said, "I fired two men, four quit or haven't returned, and three new men started this week, two last week. Some of the men who quit ride with Domingo," he added sharply.

Catalina's head came up and her eyes narrowed at the use of Domingo's name instead of Papa, as Emilio had always addressed him before. "We're down to seven men right now," Emilio continued, "but I'm keeping it way until I see what we can do."

"A letter came asking me to go to Santa Fe to bring back two men they've captured," Luke announced.

Instantly Catalina met his level gaze. She wanted to protest, but she knew it was his job, and she had things to accomplish here. She missed him terribly when he was away. Each time they were together again, she thought he looked more handsome than the time before. When she thought about how he had come to her bed in the night, she could feel the heat climb in her cheeks. It had been doubly exciting to awaken and find him in her bed, loving her.

He narrowed his eyes as he studied her, and then a corner of his mouth raised lightly in a mocking smile while he listened to Emilio talk about the new roof of the ranch house. Her pulse drummed, and she couldn't hear a word. Tension sprang between them like heat lightning in summer.

Emilio turned to Catalina. "What have you learned about the freighting company?"

"Friedrich owned seventy percent of the company, Papa owned thirty percent. I found four thousand dollars in the safe, so I took the share that would have been Papa's. There was a note in the safe and Friedrich has a brother who lives in St. Louis.''

''I wrote to him,'' Luke said, ''and I've sent it. You can't liquidate or take over the freighting business until he comes for his claim.'' Luke was appalled there was so little ready cash available for Emilio and Catalina, and he wondered if Domingo had managed to take some with him.

After dinner Luke said he wanted to see Emilio a moment. Luke lit a cheroot, leaning back in his chair while Catalina left them and closed the door behind her. He offered one to Emilio, who took it and lighted it with the ease of one accustomed to smoking. Again Luke marveled how much he had changed. ''Emilio, Domingo may try to come home to the ranch to hide. It's his land.''

''If he does, I think I shall draw and kill him on sight,'' he said with such bitterness it surprised Luke. ''My mother would be alive if it weren't for him and his evil, forceful ways. And it's only a matter of time until people turn on us. It won't hurt me, but it'll hurt Catalina. Ticiano has already changed.'' Anger flashed in his brown eyes, and a muscle worked in his jaw. ''She'll never be able to marry as well as she would have. What he does will hurt her more than she realizes now.''

''I asked her to marry me.''

Surprise and pleasure showed in Emilio's brown eyes and Luke added quickly, ''She refuses now, because she thinks I asked out of pity.''

Emilio shook his head. ''Catalina never has studied people and their subtleties. She is direct with life and she deals with it better than I do, but I know the subtleties. I know you love her, and in time she'll come to see you do.''

Luke kept his features solemn, listening to words that sounded as if they were being spoken by a fifty-year-old man instead of a boy of seventeen. ''No one else knows about it.''

"Your secret is my secret. She will stop and examine her own heart one day. If you aren't killed by Domingo. He's the quickest draw I've ever seen."

"I'll be careful. If he comes to the ranch . . . I'd like to know," he said, aware that the question was pointless because a son would not turn in a father.

"You'll know, and he can't stay. I've already made that clear to my men," Emilio said.

"You're taking to ranch life," Luke observed and was surprised by a flash of contempt in Emilio's eyes.

"I don't like it, but it's something I have to do if Catalina and I are to survive. I hope I can find a good manager someday and turn it over to him." Emilio blushed a deep red. "I want to study law and be a lawyer like you," he said, suddenly sounding more like the seventeen-year-old. "I think I could use my talents better that way than out sloughing through the brush after an old mossy-horn."

"You're probably right. I'll let you read my books if you'd like."

Emilio's eyes gleamed with obvious gratitude. "I'd be grateful forever. Catalina and I owe you much. It'll be repaid."

"If I can just convince your stubborn sister that I don't pity her. How anyone could pity Catalina, I don't know."

Emilio grinned. "I suspect you'll persuade her soon. She's stubborn, but she's in love."

"Then you know more about her heart than she does."

"Perhaps I do. Catalina never stops to consider her heart or soul. She is too busy doing things. If she were a man, we would trade places and get our tasks done more quickly and more efficiently. I should be poring over the books and figures, checking on deeds and contracts. Catalina can ride circles around me and manage the ranch better, but that's a man's task and I can't leave her out there with a bunch of men."

"No, you can't," Luke said, biting back a smile.

"I have a feeling you're both coping with your tasks quite well."

"Yes, but neither of us likes what we do. She would trade in a minute with me if I'd agree."

"Don't you ever agree," Luke said dryly. "Let's go find her. Catalina won't mind our cigars."

Emilio laughed. "She's the one who taught me to smoke."

Luke's head jerked around in surprise. "Catalina smokes?"

"I don't know if she does or not. She told me it's for men, but when I was nine, she gave me a grapevine and I was sick. Then we went to cigarettes."

Luke laughed as they entered the parlor, and Catalina looked up, a frown of concentration on her brow. "I can't get these figures to add up correctly. Every time I get a different amount."

"I'll do it," Emilio said, crossing to take her place.

She stood up and moved away, walking to a chair. Luke watched the slight sway of her hips, the graceful manner of her step. She sat down and caught him watching her. He winked and she smiled in return.

"There's a mail coach coming through tomorrow," Emilio said.

"How'd you know that?" Luke asked in amazement.

"I heard about it at the store. The last one was robbed"—he turned to look at Catalina—"by Domingo."

"You won't call him Papa?"

"Never again," he said flatly. "He turned his back on us. I turn mine on him. I'm sorry he wasn't caught."

"Emilio!"

"You are too, deep down, Catalina."

"Stop it. He's still my father."

"He chose being an outlaw, because that's what he loves best. Not his family or the ranch or his business, but robbing and thievery."

"Emilio, stop it!"

Emilio turned back to pore over the ledgers and she moved to the mantel to stand with her arms folded.

"I'm riding out of here again tomorrow," Luke said casually. She turned to face him while Emilio stopped writing to look up.

"You're going after Papa," she said quietly.

"I'm riding with a stage to Franklin. Right now, I need to get back to the office."

"You think he'll try to rob the mail coach. You're going to guard it," Catalina said flatly.

"It's a big shipment of gold," he replied. "If you two don't need me now, I should get back to the office," he said, leaving to go down the hall to his room, where he took some books out of a bag to give to Emilio. He turned to see Catalina standing in the door. "Your brother wanted to read my books."

"Emilio doesn't like the ranch. If I were a man, I could move out there and take charge."

"Thank the Lord, you're not," he said, setting the handful of books on a table and reaching past her to close the door.

"Is there any way I can talk you out of going with the mail coach?"

"No, because that's my job. That's what I've sworn to do."

"Someone will stay here at the jail."

"Yes, Hans. He's the only one who's married."

"He's not the only one who has a woman who loves him," she said softly, her black eyes seeming to draw him closer. He reached for her and she was in his arms instantly. Pliant and soft, Catalina clung to him, wanting to hold him, to stop what he had to do. His marriage proposal tormented her all the time. She wanted to toss aside worries about the future, responsibility, even the knowledge that Luke might not truly love her, and marry him, but she couldn't. She owed it to Emilio to do what she could to get them independent. She didn't want Luke to marry her so he could care for both of them.

She buried her head against his neck, catching the whiff of leather from his vest, the fresh cottony smell of his clean shirt. Her fingers wound in his thick brown hair while she turned her head, seeking his mouth.

He kissed her hard, squeezing the breath from her lungs. "Someday, Catalina, you'll be mine forever," he said in a husky voice. "How in sweet hell do you think this is pity?" Suddenly bending over her, he molded her body to his and kissed her so passionately her heartbeat roared in her ears. His tongue played in her mouth, thrusting deeply over hers. He pulled up her skirt and slipped his hand along her bare thigh.

Trembling with need, she moaned softly and pushed against his chest. He swung her up, his green eyes stormy with desire.

"If only—" She stepped away. "Emilio is waiting for me," she whispered. "Would it do any good to ask you to stay here tomorrow?"

He shook his head. "I have to go after him, Catalina. If he commits more crimes, people will turn against you and Emilio."

She nodded grimly, knowing he was right. She wouldn't tell him, but each time she went out, she was amazed at the cold, harsh reaction she got from some people. Yet there were others who had been wonderful to her, something she would never forget. "I'd rather bear the brunt of unkindness than have you in danger. My real friends won't be unkind. I better go back to the parlor. I said I needed Emilio's help and then I left."

"Take these books to him."

She accepted the books and hurried to join Emilio while Luke left for the office. She saw him mount and turn down the street, his back straight, shoulders squared, his black hat shading his head, and longing welled up in her. She wanted to marry him! She turned from the window. "Luke sent these books for you to read."

"I'd like to learn the law," Emilio said, blushing hotly.

"I think that's wonderful."

"You do? I thought you'd object to it as foolishness."

"If you're thinking of becoming a lawman, you better improve your shooting," she said mischievously.

"I'm practicing."

"Oh, Emilio, I'm teasing you. You're always so solemn."

"There's not much right now to jest about," he said, running his hand through his thick curls. "Luke Danby loves you."

"I don't know about that. He's being good to both of us, but love goes beyond that."

"If you love him, marry him."

"I love him," she said softly. "But I don't know what he truly feels. There has always been a barrier between us. Suddenly it's gone without a word, but I wonder if it's really gone. Whatever it is, it's something out of his past, and he won't share it with me. And I think he pities us and wants to take care of us."

"I never heard of a man rushing into marriage out of pity," Emilio said dryly.

"No doubt one has. There are probably as many different reasons as there are people. We'll see. When we have a house built, we can be more independent. Then I can see how he feels. I have to have a husband who truly loves me. I don't want what Mama and Papa had."

"No. I like to think she's at peace now. What errands do you want me to do while I'm in town? I have to get the list of supplies I showed you."

"I'm scared Papa will kill him."

Emilio looked up sharply. "I think you have a good reason to be afraid. I think Domingo will try to kill him, but Luke's cool and tough."

"He's honest, though, and there are things he won't do that our iniquitous Papa will."

"Yes, but he knows that. Anything you want to add to this list?"

"No. Emilio, I think Papa may try to return and hide at the ranch."

"I won't let him. We have to separate our lives from his. Have people been unkind to you?"

"Only one or two. Most of them have been unusually kind. The one or two no longer matter."

"Ticiano is one of them, isn't he?"

"Yes. And his family. It's as if we've done something shameful when it's Papa, not us."

"If you have trouble from anyone, promise me you'll tell Luke if I'm at the ranch. Right now, with our losses, people will still be sympathetic, but a few months from now, we may be pariahs. I want to have a ranch house built by then."

She nodded, knowing he was right, not wanting to tell him it had been worse than she had said. One of the men lolling in front of the general store had made a remark about her staying with the marshal, and two men had laughed uproariously. Ticiano barely spoke, and two women had crossed the road to avoid her. She shook her head. She couldn't worry about things like that, there was too much to get done.

An hour later as she hurried along past a cantina on her way to the wagon yard, a hand reached out and caught her around the waist. "Lovely Senorita Piedra. Why the hurry?"

While she looked into a pair of dark eyes and pushed against a broad chest, the man's muscles tightened. "I can take you to your father. Come ride with me."

"Let go of me," she said forcefully.

He laughed and tightened his grip. Several men, strangers to her, drew closer around her as the man edged to the corner of the building.

"I'll scream and the marshal will be here—"

"Sweet young thing with a renegade father. How

much wildcat renegade blood do you have in your veins?''

Catalina yanked a knife from the scabbard at his waist, and held it tightly in her fist. ''You come close and I'll cut you. Any of them touch me and I'll cut you,'' she snapped.

''Now, little lady, don't do something foolish,'' he wheedled, moving closer.

''What the hell?'' came the marshal's deep voice.

The other men scattered, and her tormentor turned to run. Luke's arm shot out, catching him by the shoulder, spinning him around. Luke swung, striking him on the jaw with all his weight behind the punch. The man crashed through the cantina's large window and lay unconscious inside, bits of glass glittering on the floor around him.

Luke took the knife from Catalina's hand and tossed it down. ''One of you boys haul him to the jail and tell them to lock him up.'' He looked through the broken window at the bartender. ''Send him the bill for smashing your window. He'll pay or sit in jail.''

''Yes, sir.''

Luke took her arm and steered her around the corner out of sight of curious bystanders. ''What happened?'' he asked, looking at her pink cheeks, the fire in her flashing eyes.

''He made a remark about Papa and grabbed me. Suddenly there were men all around us. I pulled his knife and threatened to cut him. It happened so fast. I didn't know you were around.''

''I might not have been. Dammit, I don't want you wandering all over town alone.''

''I should have crossed the road sooner and not walked in front of the cantina. I wanted to go to the wagon yard. I told Emilio I'd purchase a new wagon for the ranch.''

''You take someone with you on errands unless it's right in the middle of town where it's safe,'' he commanded.

Her dark eyes flashed and she yanked her arm from his grip. "I'll go where I please. I'll be more careful after this."

"Careful won't cut it," he snapped, wanting to shake her for the scare she had given him. "I don't want you in danger."

"I won't stay shut away in your house, waiting for you or Emilio to help me get things done. I can take care of myself. I was doing fine when you came."

Suddenly he grinned. "That you were. Okay, in the daytime you can go around town on errands, but don't get into obscure places, avoid the cantinas, and don't go out after dark alone. Promise me."

She raised her chin stubbornly, and he felt a mixture of admiration and annoyance. "Catalina, promise me," he said quietly.

She heard the note of steel in his voice and saw the determination in his eyes, and she couldn't argue with him. "I promise."

"Good. Now let's go get that wagon unless you're too nervous."

"I'm not too nervous. I may be too angry. That sonofabitch!"

Luke grinned. "Come on before some woman overhears you and is scandalized."

The next day Emilio left for the ranch, Luke left with the mail coach, and Catalina began the vigil of waiting for Luke's return, praying that he wouldn't be hurt. He had kissed her farewell, swearing under his breath about not getting to be alone with her as much now as before.

She stood at the window, gazing down the dusty street, wondering again about Luke and his proposal. Luke was unfathomable, cool and controlled. His proposal had been sudden, she knew that, and it was so unlike him to act impulsively. She thought about his scars and wondered what had caused them. He had had a fight he wouldn't discuss, and it had scarred him badly, so badly he must have been very near death. Why wouldn't he talk about it?

Luke rode southwest in the mail coach along with two other passengers, two riding to Franklin. Luke chatted pleasantly, knowing they were aware of his badge, and wondered if either of them was there to help Domingo. He expected Domingo to attack the stage. There was too much gold and the shipment was too well known. Luke's revolver was on his hip, and another was tucked into his waistband. It didn't seem like the smart thing for anyone to attack such a heavily protected stage, but he suspected Domingo was as confident as any raider who had ever ridden across the plains.

On the sixth night they stopped at a way station on the Nueces River. The station was little more than a one-room adobe house. A solitary man lived there, keeping fresh horses, earning a livelihood from passengers. The night was hot as Luke went up on the roof to sleep. He took a deep breath, gazing at the myriad twinkling stars dotting the inky sky. A sliver of a white moon shone. The flat land had only cactus and stunted brush, except along the river, where willows and cottonwoods grew. Luke stared at the line of trees on the banks, knowing renegades could easily hide there, but to attack the way station, they would be clearly visible if anyone were watching.

Sleep wouldn't come, and it was easier to sit cross-legged and survey the surroundings.

"Freeze," a voice behind Luke said. "Get your hands in the air, Marshal."

22

RECOGNIZING THE VOICE OF ONE OF THE MEN IN the stage, Luke raised his hands. Suddenly he rolled, the gun almost jumping into his hand as he stretched on his stomach and fired. Something burned across his shoulder, but the man gasped and thudded out of sight on the ground below.

At the sound of the shot, men on horseback broke from the shadows of the trees and pounded toward the house. Luke scooted to the edge of the roof, raising carefully to peer over the edge. It was easy to spot their leader. Domingo's powerful frame would be recognizable anywhere.

Luke fired repeatedly as the men scattered behind wagons and the well and a privy, exchanging fire. He saw Domingo dismount.

In minutes two men ran for the house. One sprawled on the ground from a bullet, another made it to the shelter of the wall of the house. Judging from the men he had counted on horseback, they were outnumbered by four men, which meant Domingo had a bigger gang of followers now.

Suddenly an explosion jarred Luke. The way station shook, windows blasted out. As smoke boiled out the windows, the men charged the station.

Luke fired, watching for Domingo. His pulse jumped when he saw him and he aimed. A shot nicked the adobe, splattering it against Luke's face and he ducked back. When he rose up, Domingo was gone from view. Luke crouched at the edge of the roof, watching men pour out windows and doors, guns blazing. Domingo ran out, a box under his arm, firing behind him. Luke didn't hesitate. In a flash he jumped over the edge, dropping straight down to land on Domingo.

As they rolled, Domingo struck him with a sharp crack on his shoulder that sent a pain shooting across his back. Luke released his pent-up rage and slugged him. He rained blows on him until Domingo managed to kick him off and started to run. Luke yanked his foot and scrambled to his feet as Domingo jumped to his. Luke swung, oblivious of the crack of his knuckles on Domingo's jaw.

Domingo jerked backward, slamming into the wall and fell unconscious. Four men rode away, two of Luke's deputies chasing after them.

"Here's Domingo," Luke said to Ulrich. Luke's chest rose and fell as he caught his breath. "Get some rope and let's tie him up. We're heading back to San Antonio with him now."

"There's one other prisoner, sir, three men dead."

"Load up the bodies on those mules. The others can ride with the stage. Here's one of the money boxes."

"They got away with one. We have one in here."

"Let's go." He stood up and wiped the blood off his jaw, gazing down at Domingo, feeling a deep hatred and burning anger not only for what Domingo had done so long ago, but for what he was doing to his children.

Four days later they rode into San Antonio. Domingo had been surly at first, then boastful, his good spirits returning. He talked to Luke once when they had stopped at a stream. "Someday, Luke Danby, I'll kill you. And this time you'll stay dead, not rise up like some desert ghost to haunt me."

"I'm no ghost. How did you hope to get away with this? And how could you turn your back on your children when they needed you so badly?"

"I wanted to kill Tandy McGuire with my bare hands. I heard you shot Friedrich."

"I did."

"My children are almost grown, and I left them with land, more than my father did for me. All he did was leave me alone on the streets." He spat tobacco in the dirt and glared at Luke. "Respectability is a cloak that hampers freedom. When I didn't have it or know what it really meant, I craved it. Then I learned it's chains to bind a man and take his youth. I'd rather live by the gun and have many women." His eyes came back to Luke and he smiled contemptuously. "Many women like your mother."

Luke smashed his fist into Domingo's jaw, knocking him down, all control vanishing in a flash of fury.

Domingo laughed. "So you'll hit a man with his hands tied behind his back."

"Damn your hide, Domingo. Next time I may put a bullet through your heart and say you were resisting arrest." He jerked his head around the ring of men staring at them. "Do you think my deputies won't protect me if I tell them why?"

Domingo's eyes narrowed and he frowned as he clambered to his feet. "I'll be free before the next full moon. And someday, gringo, I'll kill you. It's going to be slow. That's a promise." He spat another stream of tobacco juice that landed in the dirt in front of Luke's boots.

Luke clenched his fists and walked away, trying to curb his temper. His jaw still ached where Domingo had kicked him, and his temper was frayed by Domingo's taunts. He wanted to be rid of him. "Mount up. Let's go!"

He caught curious glances occasionally from his men, but he wasn't going to talk about Domingo and the past. When they reached town, he put Domingo behind bars, then rode home. He was tired, dusty, and worried about Catalina's reaction to her father's arrest.

Emilio's horse was in back, and as Luke entered the

house, he saw the light spilling from the front parlor. He entered to find them going over books. Emilio looked up, his face bruised and cut. He stood up, extending his hand to shake Luke's while Catalina's breath caught in her throat.

Luke's jaw was bruised and he was covered with dust, but he looked marvelous. She wanted to throw herself into his arms, but she couldn't in front of Emilio. And then she met Luke's eyes, and she knew at once he had either killed or arrested her father.

"Papa?"

"He's in jail. He'll get a trial," he said watching her closely. She drew a deep breath and nodded.

"I know you did what you had to do. He tried to rob the stage, didn't he?"

Luke nodded and glanced at Emilio. "What happened to you?"

"I tangled with a mustang and he won," he said, looking beyond Luke, and Luke realized Emilio was lying. And there could be only one reason why. Someone had probably been unkind to Catalina.

"Shall I summon a servant?" Catalina asked quickly. "Are you hungry?"

"I'm exhausted. My stomach can wait its turn. I want a bath and bed. You two go on with what you're doing. I'll wash off at the pump, and then I'd like to see you, Catalina."

He went to his room and shed his clothes. As he dropped his shirt on the floor, he heard the door. Catalina slipped into the darkened room. "Luke?"

Light momentarily spilled from the hallway, then she closed the door and came across the room to him.

"Honey, I'm dus—"

She wrapped her arms around him tightly, standing on tiptoe to kiss him. His arms closed around her tiny waist, and his hunger for her was overpowering. Her mouth opened on his, her tongue touching his eagerly as he returned her kiss. She thought she would faint from the reaction that buffeted her. His hand combed through her hair, sending the ribbon flying, and dark tresses spilled over her shoulder.

Her heart pounded with relief that he was home safe. She wanted his lovemaking that drove her to rapture. His lean, virile body felt wonderful; his strong arms shut out all problems and fears. His hands moved as swiftly peeling away her bodice as hers did unfastening his pants. He finished undressing, watching her with half-closed eyes. His breathing was ragged while she stepped out of her skirt and stood naked before him. His eyes had adjusted to the darkness and he could see her slender, shapely body with her high, full breasts. He scooped her up and carried her to the bed. "I want to love you until the last shred of doubt is gone in your mind," he whispered gruffly. She trembled, wanting to tell him in moments of passion there were no doubts, no reason, nothing but his strong, hard body and hot kisses, but words wouldn't come and thoughts were a jumble that swiftly escaped her.

He moved between her thighs, poising over her, his manhood throbbing with need. "I can't wait, Catalina. I want you and I want you forever," he said gruffly.

She couldn't answer, because she couldn't refuse him anything. Her body welcomed him as much as her heart, and she reached up to pull him down. He moved slowly, his shaft thrusting into her soft warmth, taking her eagerly. She held him tightly, wanting him to love her truly, not just her body, not offer her his name out of pity, but to want her as his wife forever.

She trembled with eagerness, her softness enveloping him. Her hips rose to meet his, and her eyes closed tightly. She was lost in pleasure that built to a thundering climax that made her cry out and cling to his powerful frame.

His release came and he relaxed, his weight coming down fully as he held her and stroked her. "I've dreamed about you every night. I need you, Catalina."

"I hope so," she said, knowing his words were etched in her memory forever.

He rolled over, pulling her to him tightly. "I'm exhausted to the bone."

"Go to sleep," she said, holding him tightly, wanting to never let go.

His breathing became deep and even while he held her pressed to his length, his hands stroked her back lightly, sliding over her curves and her tantalizing bottom. He would have to deal with her doubts and worries about his motives tomorrow, but tonight she was finally in his arms. Her body was magic, a searing flame, so beautiful, his for now.

When Luke stirred, Catalina had gone. He smiled and ran his hand across the sheets, wanting her back. He gathered some fresh clothing and stepped outside in the first gray light of dawn to wash at the pump. Roosters crowed, breaking the stillness, and as he cranked the pump handle, Ta-ne-haddle sat up from a blanket on the ground.

"So you came in last night, and Domingo's in jail now."

"Just one time," Luke said, bracing himself against the first rush of cold water as he poured a bucket over his head, "I'd like to do something and surprise you. Or hear something before you do."

"He who keeps his mouth shut, hears more."

"Who said that?"

Ta-ne-haddle gave him a rare grin. "I did. Now will she marry you?"

"No. She thinks I asked her because I feel sorry for her." Ta-ne-haddle chuckled, and Luke looked at him sharply. "What's funny about that?"

"I think you two will work it out."

"I hope I'm not gray-headed by the time we do. She wants to get the ranch house built and move out there so they have some independence, and then she'll see if I still feel this way. Women are trouble." He wrapped a towel around his middle. "I'm going to

New Mexico to get two of Tandy's men and bring them back here. Want to come?''

"With Domingo in jail, I think I better keep an eye on the family. People are getting hostile toward them.''

"That's what happened to Emilio, isn't it?'' Luke asked with concern.

"He was trying to protect her. She's beautiful, and now men don't have to fear her father or the Piedra wealth. Her reputation is sullied by staying here with you, and—''

"Well, hells bells! Dammit, I've asked her to marry me. Does she know people are talking?''

"Of course she does. Catalina's a strong woman. She wants to make sure marriage is right. She won't wed just to pacify a bunch of old hens who are cackling over her reputation.

"Dammit to hell.''

"There are a lot of nice people standing by her too,'' Ta-ne-haddle said.

"I'll ride to Franklin, then up the Pecos to Santa Fe.''

"Are you taking a deputy?''

"Nope. I can handle two men.''

"What happens if you meet Comanches?''

"We'll manage.'' Luke went to his room to dress quickly, and then he went down the hall to Catalina's room. He knocked lightly and opened the door to find she was gone. She was in the kitchen, helping a maid to get breakfast while Emilio went over one of his endless lists, and Luke silently cursed the fact that he couldn't be alone with her.

An hour later he left for New Mexico. She kissed him good-bye, looking up at him with her big eyes. "Please be careful,'' she said, standing on tiptoe to kiss him, her full lips parting beneath his. She leaned back finally to study him. "I'll be jealous of all the beautiful senoritas in Santa Fe.''

"I won't be able to see them,'' he said.

She felt something tight constrict her heart. "Yes,

you will. They will make you see them. You're a very sexy man, Marshal Danby.''

He couldn't laugh. ''Catalina. There's something I haven't ever told you.'' There was a pause as Luke considered his words carefully. ''My mother was taken captive on a wagon train. I intend to search for her when I'm in Santa Fe, because I heard there's a man there who might have known her.''

''You've never told me about your family,'' she exclaimed, astounded. ''I thought your mother was still in Boston and your father no longer alive.''

''I've searched for her off and on for years, but to no avail. While I'm in Santa Fe, I'll make inquiries.''

''I'm sorry.'' She ran her finger along his jaw, feeling the stubble of his beard. ''It seems I'm always kissing you farewell.''

''You could change that.''

''If we married, you'll still do your duty and go when you have to.''

''But at least we'd be together more often.'' He swung into the saddle and leaned down to kiss her again.

''I have to be sure about what you feel,'' she said swiftly. ''We had a very unhappy home.''

He stroked her chin. ''When I get home, I'm going to devote some time to showing you how I feel about you.''

With her heart beating swiftly, she stepped back. At the end of the street he turned to wave to her. He hoped they were ready for Domingo's trial by the time he returned and that issue would be settled forever. Domingo would hang for Tandy's death as well as for the others. And he intended to put an end to Catalina's foolish notion that he had asked her to marry him out of pity.

Catalina watched him ride away, and then climbed into the buggy and rode to the jail to see her father.

The next morning the house seemed unusually quiet. She had a list of things to order for the ranch, supplies to get for Luke's household, and she wanted to get some material to make another dress for herself. In the afternoon before siesta she took a golden-brown fried chicken to the jail. Deputy Conners led her to Domingo's cell.

"Ahh, what a smell," Domingo exclaimed enthusiastically, taking the basket of chicken and hot bread from her hands. She gave him a cool keg of water and he pulled the cork out with his teeth, tilting it up to drink.

"Deputy," he said, lowering the bottle. "Here, have a piece of the best chicken this side of the Rio Grande."

Jim Conners looked torn with indecision. Catalina laughed and held the basket to him. "Go ahead."

"Thanks, ma'am. It sure does smell tempting," he said and took a juicy, steaming drumstick. He disappeared around the corner, leaving them alone.

"Very good, Catalina. Bring food every day. Until I escape," he whispered.

"Escape!"

"I'm a man who was meant to roam. Wealth is always ripe for taking. If I stand trial, I'll hang. You're a woman and you can't understand a man's need for freedom. You've never been anywhere, either. You don't know what the world is like, how exciting it can be. How easy it is to get all the gold you want."

"You had all you needed before."

Contempt filled his voice. "Women all want security. Men don't." He looked around at the bars that imprisoned him. "I find it exciting to think I can outwit them and break out of here. I'm ready. And very well fed. *Delicioso!* You look very pretty today, Catalina," he said, eyeing her blue gingham dress as he finished his chicken.

"Thank you. Papa, I worry about this."

"Bah, forget your worries. I welcome the moment. Luke Danby left town, I hear."

"How'd you know that?"

"He's the marshal. I hear them talking. He's after the last two of Tandy's men. Too bad I won't be here to take care of them myself. Will you marry the marshal, Catalina?"

"I might," she said. "Emilio has taken over the ranch."

Domingo laughed. "You would be better suited for it. Even a woman would be better than Emilio. At the first sign of Comanches, he will come running back to town and refuse to leave."

"I think you underestimate him," she said stiffly, loyal to her younger brother. She knew Emilio was trying his utmost.

"Eh? Perhaps. Don't scowl so, *niña.*"

"Papa, where will you go this time?"

"Down into Mexico. We'll get some fat cattle and bring them up and sell them. But better still, there are banks in Mexico, Catalina. Banks with gold. We will be very, very rich."

"It's dangerous," she whispered, appalled by his plans. "We don't know or understand each other, yet all my life we have lived together under the same roof," she said softly.

"That is because you're a woman, actually still a child. You love that cold marshal, Catalina, and for that you'll suffer. Stay away from cold men. They'll disappoint you."

"I'll return tomorrow, Papa," she said, suddenly desperate to get away.

"*Sí. Muchas graciás,* Catalina, for the chicken."

The aspen leaves glistening in the breeze were a shimmering sea of gold on the Sangre de Cristo Mountains when Luke rode into Santa Fe on the seventeenth of October. He learned that the two men he was to take back to Texas had escaped. A group of lawmen were going to ride after them and Luke volunteered to go. Two hours later they rode north and wound into the mountains.

It took three days before they found them with four other men. In the ensuing gun battle, the two men were killed, ending the primary purpose for Luke's trek. Before returning home, he moved into the hotel to spend some time hunting for Hattie.

In the Brown Bear saloon four nights later, he learned that a gambler named Coit Ritter was staying in Taos, several hours north. Luke rode north into the mountains the next morning with a description of Coit and a tight knot of apprehension in his chest. He wanted to know, yet after all this time he didn't think he could bear to hear that Hattie was no longer alive. And he prayed Domingo had lied when he said he had sold her to a brothel in Franklin.

His first night in town, he went to a saloon on the plaza, ordering a drink and sitting in a corner to watch the crowd. A fire crackled in the stove, warming the room, flames as bright as the dancing girls' silk dresses. The only high-stake games of faro in the place were played by men Luke steadily eliminated. They were too short, too fat, too young, too old to be the man he was hunting. The second night he entered the Brass Rail. As he stood at a crowded bar, he realized there was a game of poker underway, something seldom played where he had traveled, but a favorite of Ta-ne-haddle's. It was drawing a crowd of spectators. Luke took his drink and moved to join the throng.

There were eleven men at the wide, round table. A pile of chips stood in the center, a stack of cartwheels in front of one lean man. His hat was pushed low over his forehead, almost hiding his eyes. His fingers were long and tapered, moving with ease as they handled the cards. He had a long thin face and a lean frame. With his hat tilted down and his eyes on the cards, Luke couldn't really see his face. When he had a chance, Luke joined the game, sitting down. He glanced across the table into a pair of silver-gray eyes, and his pulse jumped. It had to be Coit Ritter. The man's ash-colored eyes were a dead giveaway.

For a moment Luke gazed at the pile of Mexican cartwheels in front of Coit and decided he would take every last silver dollar if he possibly could. The thought that Domingo might have handed his mother over to this man like a horse or piece of property made Luke want to draw his revolver on Coit right now. But he had to be certain.

Luke lost the first six hands, and then he began to win. He lost and he won and then he won steadily. Keeping his features impassive, he was being cautious, realizing he was against a man who lived by gambling. Coit held his hand close to his chest so no one could see his cards. If he was cheating, Luke couldn't detect it. Slowly, as Luke's pile of silver dollars began to increase, the men around them grew curious. Both men played in silence, a deadly, earnest game that took all of Luke's concentration and some quick calculations. He lost and he won, but he won enough that finally he was ahead. Coit stood up, throwing in his hand and leaving. As soon as he was away from the table, Luke tossed in his cards, took his winnings, and went after Coit. Yanking on his fleece-lined coat, he stepped outside into the crisp night air. Noise and light spilled from the saloons. Coit stood just beyond the saloon door, gazing down the street, not moving.

"Coit Ritter?" Luke asked.

Coit turned. "Yep, I'm Ritter. I didn't figure you'd quit the game."

"Can we go somewhere private where we can talk?"

Coit's eyes narrowed and he shrugged. "Suits me. Name your place."

"We'll walk over to the hotel. We can talk out in front."

Luke noticed the two guns on Coit's hips, and the way his coat was tucked back behind them so he could draw quickly. They walked in silence to the hotel, stopping in front where light spilled from the windows.

"What did you want with me, mister? I don't believe I caught the name."

"I didn't give it. I'm a U.S. Marshal. My name is Luke Danby."

Coit's eyes narrowed and he sat down on a hitching rail, one foot dangling in the air.

"Glad to make your acquaintance, Marshal Danby."

"I think you know another Danby," Luke said, holding his breath.

23

COIT STARED AT HIM SO LONG THAT LUKE TENSED, ready to draw and fire. At this range he wouldn't have much chance of survival, but he forced himself to wait quietly.

"Danby's not an uncommon name. What's on your mind?"

Luke's heart thudded. Coit had known Hattie! After all these years, he had picked up the threads of the trail. And Domingo had told the truth about Ritter. Hatred flashed like a burst of flame. Coit Ritter had taken his mother like so much property. He had won her in poker.

Trying to control the rage that filled him, Luke shrugged his shoulders. "I'm trying to find a woman named Hattie Danby. I have something that belongs to her. And I'm willing to pay a reward of a hundred dollars for information about her," he added. He knew Ritter wouldn't give him the time of day unless there was a profit in it for him. Luke had known too many professional gamblers. Kindness was not a quality they exhibited.

"What kind of information?"

"I'm trying to find her. Where she was last seen would be helpful. Where she is now would be worth double the reward."

"It was a long time ago that I knew her. Might not be helpful information now."

"I'm willing to pay the hundred dollars for any information about her, no matter how old."

"How'd you find me?"

"I paid a man a hundred dollars for information," Luke said, avoiding telling Coit the truth about Domingo. "Silver jogs people's memories."

Coit shrugged and stood up. "All I can tell you is where I last saw her. That was in Santa Fe and it was years ago."

"How many years?"

"Maybe ten, maybe twelve. It's been so long, I have no good recollection."

"You don't know where she went when she left there?"

Coit smiled. "I don't even know that she left here, mister. She was over at Miss Sadie's Palace of Dreams. One of the girls," he said softly.

Luke was almost blinded by rage. It took all his control to pull out a pouch and shake out the coins. "I owe you for that bit of information," he said evenly.

"Who are you?" Coit asked coldly. "You're too young to be her husband, and her son died."

"I'm a Danby and I have something that belongs to her."

Coit gave him a frosty smile. "Thanks for the hundred."

He turned away and took two steps. Luke started after him.

"Coit!"

Coit turned and Luke hit him, sending him sprawling in the street. "That's for Hattie," he ground out the words, wanting to yank Coit up and hit him again. He stood ready, fists clenched, feet spread apart, but he had a suspicion fists weren't Coit's style.

"What was that for?" Coit asked, rubbing his jaw.

"For whatever you did to her. You better get out of my sight."

"Who the hell are you, anyway?" he asked.

"I'm her son."

Coit rose to his feet and dusted off his hat with elaborate care. Luke had never gazed into such cold, murderous eyes. He knew Coit would try to kill him and he dropped his hand to his hip. Coit glanced down at his hand, gave him another level look, and turned on his heel. Luke watched him, ready to draw, expecting Coit to go for his gun at any moment. He moved over a couple of steps to his right, watching Coit all the time.

When it happened it was so fast, Luke acted without thought, dropping into a crouch and firing the instant Coit turned. Coit's gun blasted along with Luke's, and Luke felt a hot slice across his arm. Coit pitched backward, his gun flying from his hand as the slug caught him in the heart.

Luke waited a moment to see if Coit moved, then he walked forward to gaze down at Coit's inert form. "That's for Hattie," he said quietly. A man came running up, then two more emerged from a saloon.

"I seen the whole thing, mister. I seen him go for his gun. That was some fancy shooting. He's the fastest draw in these parts, I tell you."

"Get the sheriff," someone said.

"You're hit," another man said. "You're bleeding like a stuck pig. Somebody get the doc."

"I'll see the doctor," Luke said. "Tell the sheriff I'm Luke Danby, Marshal from San Antonio. Where can I find a doctor?"

"Doc Johnson is down at La Rosa cantina playing pool. I just saw him," someone in the growing crowd answered.

"That's where I'll be," Luke said, walking away, feeling numb. So far he didn't feel any pain. If Coit had told the truth, Hattie had been in a whorehouse when Coit had last seen her. The thought made Luke sick inside, yet his mother had been a strong woman and an intelligent one. And Coit had left her alive. For the first time, hope grew stronger that he would find her.

He had his wound—merely a graze—cleaned and dressed, and rode back to Santa Fe to search for his mother. From the sheriff he learned that Miss Sadie's had burned years ago and the women had scattered. Luke began a methodical round of bordellos, trying to find someone who had known Hattie, aware she might have started using another name, but four days later he hadn't come any closer to finding a scrap of information. He sat in Miss Jesse Hanks' Parlor House sipping a drink, gazing through the smoke at the stage, where candles were lighted across the front. There were dancing girls and women for pleasure, but all he wanted was to talk to people, to observe. In a week he would have to start back home, and he was going to have to go empty-handed. He shifted in his chair, his long legs stretched in front of him. Hattie's description fit countless women, so that was no aid to him.

A man came out and called for quiet. The piano began to play, and the curtain went up on a chorus line of women. As always, Luke's eyes scanned their faces swiftly, then returned to linger on each one. She could look entirely different by now, and common sense told him that by this time she wouldn't be dancing on a stage, but he studied each woman anyway.

A slender young singer came out and stood to one side of the stage. As her clear, full voice carried above the racket of the men, they grew quiet. Soon they were laughing at the crude lyrics, applauding the high-kicking of the women and the flash of shapely legs and derrieres.

Sitting close to the stage, Luke could see that the girl was heavily made up. He realized she was little more than a child, but she had a strong voice and was able to entertain. With exaggerated gestures she rolled her eyes and wiggled her hips as she sang. He took another sip of his drink and looked at her again, feeling a stir of recognition.

He couldn't think where he could have known her. She was too young, too far removed from San Antonio, and he had no memories of seeing her when he had been in Santa Fe countless times before. He studied her wide, pale eyes. Golden hair was curled in ringlets caught by bands of flowers above each ear, and they bounced with each step. Her cheeks were rouged to a bright red, her eyes painted with black lashes, but memory tugged at him and he sat up to watch her more closely. He knew her from somewhere.

When the performance had finished, the dancers and singer disappeared behind a red velvet curtain. In a few moments Luke heard a woman's voice behind him. "You're new in town, aren't you?"

He turned to face one of the dancers. Her green silk dress was cut low, her black hair piled high on her head. He pushed out a chair with his boot, and she sat down to smile at him.

"Want a drink?" he asked, thinking about Catalina and surprising himself by how strongly he missed her.

"Sure," she answered. "I'm Lace."

"Luke Danby," he answered. "Lace's an unusual name."

"I'm an unusual woman," she answered in a silky voice. At one time she would have intrigued him, but now her charms only made him think more about Catalina. He sat back in his chair, talking to Lace, his mind only half on his conversation. He missed Catalina and decided to take two more days to look for Hattie, then to start back to Texas. He realized Lace was smiling at him, and he shook his head.

"Sorry. What did you say?"

"Who is she?"

"Who?"

"The woman in your life. I'm not accustomed to being ignored."

"Sorry. There's someone in Texas."

She stood up and smiled down at him, leaning down to touch his shoulder. "Lucky woman," she said softly and was gone. He watched the slight sway of her hips as she walked away, then he pushed away his chair and left. Late that night as he lay in bed in his hotel room, his thoughts returned to the young singer. There was something hauntingly familiar about her, and he couldn't decide exactly what it was.

The next night he was back at the same table, watching the same women repeat the performance of the previous night. Lace was in the chorus line, and as she danced to the edge of the stage and looked down at him over the glowing candles, she winked, her full red lips parting in a smile.

It was the singer he was curious about, and he kept studying her, trying to imagine her without the make-up on her face. She had pale golden hair. Her eyes were a light blue, almost gray, the color of the sea. Her face was slightly heart-shaped with prominent cheekbones, a thin, straight nose; the shape of his mother's face.

He knew why she looked familiar. She looked like Hattie. Luke's breath stopped and he sat up straighter, staring at her intently, comparing her with memories of old pictures of Hattie as a young girl with her hair piled on her head. Hattie had had a slightly turned up nose, large blue eyes, prominent cheekbones, and a heart-shaped face with creamy flawless skin. This girl had the same shape face and wide eyes, but her eyes weren't deep blue like Hattie. A sudden revelation struck Luke with the force of a blow.

The girl had a long, thin nose like Coit Ritter. She had pale eyes, almost gray. *She could be the child of Hattie and Coit!*

Stunned, he watched her take a bow, her golden curls bobbing, and he tried to guess her age. She had high, small breasts and she looked about five and a half feet tall. With her painted face, she looked older than she probably was. It had been almost twelve years now since the wagon-train attack. He felt a constriction in his chest as he pondered the possibilities. His half-sister!

Seeing Lace sitting with two men several tables away from him, he motioned to her with a jerk of his head.

She frowned, then said something to them. They turned to stare at Luke and back at her while she rose and came over to Luke.

"Sorry to interrupt you, I won't be long. There's someone here I'd like to meet. Sit down a minute."

She pulled out a chair and sat down, a mocking glint of amusement coming to her eyes. "I'm not your type, huh?"

"He smiled and leaned forward to take her hands in his. "You're a very beautiful woman." He had several cartwheels in his hands and he slipped them into hers without showing any observers. He saw the flicker in her eyes, but she merely closed her hands over the coins and whisked them away into the folds of her skirt. "Which one do you want to meet?"

"Who's the singer?"

Instantly Lace's smile faded and a hardness came to her expression. "You can have your money back, Mr. Danby—"

"Keep the money."

"She's a child. If you want someone young there's Francie. She's only fourteen and she looks ten."

"You don't understand."

"Oh, yes, I do," she said contemptuously. "I understand men."

"You don't this time," he said emphatically, and her brows arched in surprise. "Who is she?"

"April—" She stopped, biting off the word. "Who are you, mister?" she asked in a whisper.

Curiosity was rampant, but Luke forced himself to keep calm. "I'm the Marshal of Bexar County in San Antonio, Texas. I'm up here on a law matter and I go home soon." Excitement coursed in his veins, but he tried to keep his voice calm. He had a hunch he was right about the young singer and he leaned forward. "Lace, I came West with my mother about twelve years ago. We were bushwhacked, I was left for dead, and my mother was taken captive. I haven't seen her since."

"Lord!"

"Who's the child?"

She stared at him so long, he thought she hadn't heard his question. Finally she said, "I'll take you to meet her. You take your money back."

His fist closed over her hand. "Keep the money. What's her name?"

"April Danby."

Luke closed his eyes, his heart constricting. *He'd found his half-sister!* He was another step closer to Hattie. "Where's her mother?" he asked, looking directly at Lace.

"I don't know. April was left here one night. Miss Jesse won't talk about it. April was about two years old, from what I've been told. I wasn't here then. Miss Jesse has raised April. We all have helped."

"April," he said, strange feelings shifting in him as he thought about her. "She's pretty. Does she earn her keep?" he asked, dreading to hear the answer.

"No! We want April to have what none of us have had. She's getting educated. There's a school here and she goes. April has nine mothers. We want a better life for her." Suddenly the hard look returned to her features, and her blue eyes flashed with anger. "We don't want her to have to earn her living on her back. We don't have respectability. Men think we're trash. You know you can't rape a whore. No one would believe lack of consent. Sometimes dogs get better treatment than we do. April is going to go back East to school. We've been saving the money. And we hope she can meet some nice young man and marry him, and he'll take care of her."

"So no one knows anything about her mother?"

"No. We never have. No one has ever tried to claim April."

Luke's hopes of the past few days plummeted. His mother wouldn't have left her own child on someone else's doorstep.

"I think Miss Jesse has always known more than she's said, so you might want to talk to her."

"I'd like that. Is she here?"

"Yes, but I'll tell you now, Miss Jesse and one of the girls, Lottie, those two love April and protect her like mother lionesses. Miss Jesse may throw you out of here, Marshal, and never tell you anything."

"I'd like to try to talk to her. Will you take me to meet her?"

"Come on." She stood up and looked him up and down, as if making an assessment, then she turned to walk away. He followed, besieged by stormy thoughts.

His mother wouldn't abandon her child, and he had a sinking feeling about Hattie. And if April was his mother's child . . . his mind ran over the possibilities. His half-sister. The notion still shocked him. He had never thought about his mother having another child. And he couldn't consider going back to San Antonio and leaving a half-sister behind in a bagnio. As Marshal he collected fees and taxes from them in San Antonio, and he had done so as sheriff in Madrid. He knew the sordid, hard lives most of them led. As far as he was concerned, there was only one course of action to follow.

They left the noisy saloon through a side door, and stepped into a hallway. On the other side was a parlor, and they turned down the hall to a doorway behind the parlor. Lace knocked on a door and he heard a woman's voice.

"It's me, Lace." She turned to Luke. "You wait here."

She disappeared inside and closed the door, but in a few minutes Lace waved him inside. He entered an opulent apartment with red velvet drapes, a flowered rug, gleaming mahogany furniture. A black-haired woman with a streak of silver in her hair was waiting for him with regal disdain. Her ample bosom almost spilled out of the tight green satin dress, and a diamond necklace glittered at her throat.

"Sit down, Marshal Danby. I'm Miss Jesse."

He removed his hat and sat down facing her. "I presume Lace told you about me and my conversation with her. Did she tell you about the wagon train?"

"Yes, but suppose you tell me again."

He leaned forward, going straight through what had happened, and his futile search for Hattie. He didn't mention Coit Ritter, but told how he had recognized April's resemblance to his mother. "I'd like to meet her."

Jesse gazed at him with impassive black eyes. "Why?"

"If she's actually my half-sister, I'd like to take her away from here," he said gently. "Begging your pardon, this isn't where I'd want her to grow up. I'd like to do what I think my mother would have preferred."

Jesse stared at him and nodded slowly. "I love April like my own child, and you're a total stranger."

"I can tell you about myself, give you my record, references in Texas. And I can educate her and give her respectability. I can give her things you can't. Sheriff Lomar will vouch for me. Some of the lawmen around here know me. People in Madrid know me." He leaned forward, his elbows on his knees. "What happened to my mother? How did you get April?"

She looked down at her lap, turning a large opal ring on her fat finger. She looked back at him for long moments, trying to make a judgment. Finally she said, "A man came here and said he wanted to see me. I didn't know him and I'm sure he gave me a false name. He had a two-year-old child with him. He said he had married her mother, and April was a bastard child, born out of wedlock to heaven knows who as the father. He said Hattie Danby was expecting their first child and he would welcome it with all the love in his heart, but he didn't want this child. He didn't know if the father had syphilis, or was a murderer, and he knew he could never be as fair to the child as he would to his own blood kin. And he needed boys, not girls."

Luke swore quietly. "My mother wouldn't give up her child."

"She didn't have to. He told her the child fell in the river and drowned. She didn't know it was alive or he had taken it."

"Damn," Luke whispered, standing up and jamming his fists into his pockets as he moved restlessly across the room. He ended up staring down at the logs glowing on the hearth. "She thought I was killed on the trail. Then this—to lose a husband, then her son, and then this baby . . ."

"Women don't have an easy time of it on the frontier," Miss Jesse said flatly. "I've buried every one of my three babies. Every one of my girls has a sad story. Do you think we prefer this life?"

He turned to face her. "Sorry. But it means my mother may still be alive. I was afraid when I heard April was abandoned that my mother had died, and someone had brought her baby here."

"No. She was alive, but April thinks her mother gave her up too. I didn't see any point in changing that notion. I didn't know the man, and he wouldn't tell me his real name. He said if I didn't want the baby, he knew I could find it a home. He had met me some time years before and he remembered me," she said forthrightly. "He paid me three hundred dollars to take her in."

Luke's hopes had risen and fallen steadily during the night, but once again he felt strongly that his mother was still alive. And hopefully she had married a good man in spite of his taking April away from her. "May I meet April?"

"There's a woman here you'll have to meet. Lottie loves April like her own child. I always thought I would lose April. About a year ago I finally decided I wouldn't. Now here you are, wanting to take her to live with you," she snapped, eyeing him.

"You know it would be better for her," he said gently. "And I hope to marry soon."

"Your woman won't mind a twelve-year-old girl?"

"No." He told her briefly about Catalina, the fires, Emilio, and Catalina's struggle for independence. "I used to think her real father might find her. I should have known better than that. He probably never wanted her in the first place, or he wouldn't have left your mother."

"You don't have any idea who the father was?"

"No. No one has ever claimed April until now."

"My half-sister. That's a shock."

"We plan to send her away to school when she's fifteen."

"I can see to her education and you can keep your funds. Maybe there will be someone else who needs to use them."

"If I don't spend them on April, I'll keep my share and let the girls spend the rest. You can afford to educate April?"

"Yes. I'll pay you one thousand in gold," he said, knowing he was buying another human being, but also knowing he couldn't leave April behind.

Miss Jesse's eyes glittered at the offer of money, and Luke suddenly had a cold feeling. He began to suspect April would never go East for an education, that the fund would stay right in Miss Jesse's hands.

"I'll give it some thought." She stood up and smoothed her skirt, the silk rustling in the silence of the room. "I want Lottie to agree to this. I'll go get her."

As she left the room, Luke folded his arms across his chest, and set his feet apart while he waited. In minutes she returned with a slender, dark-haired woman who walked with a slight limp. The woman was beautiful, with black eyes and honey-colored skin, her silky black hair falling to her waist. Her blue satin dress emphasized lush breasts and a slender waist. She gazed at Luke with anger in her eyes and spots of color in her cheeks.

"I told her that you think you're April's half-brother."

"You don't know this," Lottie snapped, raising her chin defiantly.

"No, I don't," he said quietly, standing to offer his chair to her. "I'm guessing, but when I saw her, she looked familiar. I didn't know her name or her background until I asked. I asked Lace, and she told me her name is Danby. She's the right age."

"There are many pale-eyed twelve-year-old girls in Santa Fe."

"There won't be many named Danby," he said evenly. "Look, I know all of you love her and this is home to her, but if she's my sister, I want to take her home and give her an education."

"Why? Because of your mother whom you haven't seen for twelve years?" Lottie lashed out.

"That's enough reason," he said firmly. "Do you want this kind of life for her?"

"It could be worse."

"She's a young, beautiful—"

"Yes, she is young and beautiful. How do we know what your intentions are where April's concerned? I know men; you can't trust them!" She spat the words at him angrily.

"I told Miss Jesse to check on me."

"And they could so easily lie; you could have paid them. Many men would pay to get April!"

Luke's temper was growing short, but he kept his voice calm. "I'm not paying anyone to tell Miss Jesse lies about me. I'm a U.S. Marshal."

"Do you think that makes you perfect? Or trustworthy?"

"I know it doesn't, but it says something about my character. I'm not a renegade or a gambler."

"You're not at the moment. You could have been one a year ago. You could become one tomorrow."

"You keep her here and what can you promise her? What kind of life is this? What kind of place for her to grow up? And how many men will see her in the next few years, and want her and do something to get her?'' he asked. ''Do you really want to hold her here?''

''I want to make sure she's safe,'' Lottie snapped, jerking her head up.

''She'll be safe. Ask the men about me. I've been around Santa Fe, I was sheriff in Madrid. Get someone to ride over there and ask about me.''

''I can't believe that one minute you don't know her and the next you want to take her in and educate her. You want her!''

His temper was rising, but he forced his voice to stay even and calm. ''I think she's my mother's child, my half-sister. I do this for my mother. I don't know April Danby, but I know Hattie Danby and this is what she would want me to do. This child was taken from her. She thinks two of her children have died. My mother was a fine woman. She was strong and brave and intelligent, and she had some terrible things happen to her. I can't right those things. I can't even find her! But I think April and I had the same mother, and I know my mother would want her daughter educated and given every chance for a decent life and you can't do that here! Look at my face—I'm covered to my toes with scars from that day when my mother and I were ambushed on our wagon train.''

Suddenly tears sparkled in Lottie's eyes. She glared at him, and then she abruptly spun on her heel and left the room.

Luke was breathing heavily. His gaze shifted to Miss Jesse, who stared at the doorway with narrowed eyes before looking at Luke. ''I've never seen her shed a tear. No matter what's happened, Lottie doesn't cry. I don't know if we can let April go.''

''You know it would be better for the child. I won't hurt her. She's only twelve. What kind of monster do you think—'' He swore and broke off, running his fingers through his hair angrily. "I know you've seen monsters that want twelve-year-old girls. Sorry."

"I'll make inquiries about you and let you know tomorrow. This will be a big sacrifice for you, Mr. Danby. Have you really given it thought?"

He faced her squarely, giving her a faint smile. His voice was dry as he answered, "No, I haven't given it thought. I'm just doing what I know my mother would want me to do. I owe this to my mother, to my parents' memory if they're both gone. This is what they would want if they had a choice." As he spoke, Luke suspected that Miss Jesse had already made a decision based on his offer of money.

She nodded. "You come back tomorrow."

"And Lottie?"

"Lottie will do as I say. Marshal, I've got some pretty girls here. You can have a fun night," she said slyly.

"Thanks, but no. I have a woman in San Antonio."

She laughed. "San Antonio's a long way from the Territory. C'mon. You have to go past the parlor anyway." She took his arm and a strong perfume assailed his senses. "You're a strong one," she said, her fingers tightening on his arm. "And I've heard about your shooting. You're a quick man with a gun."

"Word travels fast," he said dryly. The sounds of a piano and laughter came louder, and they paused in front of the door to the parlor where women entertained men. A man played the piano. Some of the women were in satin dresses, others in lacy petticoats that revealed their legs and their lush curves. Luke's pulse quickened at the sight of all the lovely bare skin, but he shook his head. "Not tonight, Miss Jesse."

"She must be some woman, Marshal."

"That she is," he answered thoughtfully. "I'll be back tomorrow night."

"If all my questions and doubts about you aren't answered, you're not going to get near April," she said.

"Your questions will be answered." He placed his hat on his head and left.

He paced his room that night restlessly, missing Catalina, wanting her, thinking of April and Hattie. Some man had married Hattie and was father to another child by her, so perhaps he had been good to Hattie. And he had to have been from somewhere in the West. Luke felt tantalizingly close to his mother's trail, yet he couldn't get any solid lead that wasn't years old and useless.

The next night he sat again at a table by the stage and watched the women: Lace, her shapely legs in long black stockings, and Lottie, who wasn't a performer. He watched April singing with a voice that seemed too strong for someone so young. And then he went back to Miss Jesse's room and knocked on the door.

"Miss Jesse, it's Luke Danby," he said.

She opened the door to face him solemnly. Her dark hair was piled in a pyramid of curls on top of her head, and she wore a bright pink dress trimmed in black lace. Luke guessed her to be in her early forties, though he wasn't sure. But she was still a beautiful woman.

Without greeting she ushered him into the room. "Sit down, Mr. Danby. Would you like some tequila or brandy?"

"Brandy would be fine," he said.

"I talked to Sheriff Lomar today. I've talked to several men about you."

"Yes, ma'am," he said as she handed him a glass. "Thank you."

"You're who you say, and they vouch for your character. Logan Whitmore said he would trust his life to you. That's high praise from a tough old man," she said, taking a drink of brandy.

Luke sipped in silence. He knew Logan Whitmore from the early years when Ta-ne-haddle had bought horses from him. He was a blacksmith and had a barn in town, where he bought and sold horses.

"By the time I was thirty, I thought I never would feel any heartbreak again in my life, but as you grow older you learn about life. Something always finds a way to the heart. I hate to let April go. And frankly, there's a chance she'd refuse to go East to school, that she'd stay right here with me. I can't deny I wouldn't want her. And she could earn a nice sum. She's going to be a beautiful woman. You're a marshal, you should know what taxes and fees I have to pay: thirty dollars each month to the law, one-hundred dollars a month rent for this building; I only charge my girls twenty dollars a month rent for their rooms plus a percentage of their earnings. I have some cribs out behind the building that bring in a better amount, but I'll miss April."

He knew beyond a doubt that she soon intended to put April to work. Thirteen wasn't an unheard-of age for a prostitute. "I'm sorry to take her from you," he answered quietly, swirling his drink in his glass. He decided to increase his offer. "But fifteen hundred dollars in gold is a goodly sum of money."

She licked her lips. "Indeed it is."

"Half now, half when I pick April up Friday morning." He withdrew a bag of money from beneath his coat and placed it solidly on a nearby table.

She eyed it, then reached out and put it out of sight in a desk. "Thanks, Marshal. I'll save that for my old age. I guess you don't think I'm very good to take the money like that. And you probably don't think I really care, but I do. April's good. You won't let people know she was raised here, will you?"

"No, I won't let them know where, but I can let people know some nice ladies took care of her."

She threw back her head and laughed. "Nice ladies? Honey, you know better than that."

"I have an idea you were all nice ladies to April," he said quietly. "I'm damned lucky to have survived what happened to me twelve years ago, and I'll never look down on someone because of bad luck somewhere in her past.''

"Then you're a lot more generous than most people.''

"What about Lottie? Does she approve?''

"What do you care if she doesn't?''

"I'd rather she wasn't so unhappy about it if she loves April, but it won't stop me.''

"Lottie will do what I say.''

"Has Lottie been here as long as April?''

"No. She came about three years ago, and I nursed her back to health. She was married to a man she loved, a farmer, and they were bushwhacked. They killed him and took her. She was pregnant, but she lost the baby. They nearly killed her. That's why she limps. We nursed her back to health and gave her a way to earn a living. She was like someone only half alive until she became interested in April. April is the only person she loves in this whole world, and it's going to hurt her bad, but she wants something good in life for that girl. She gives most all the money she makes to April's fund.''

"Any of you are welcome to come visit.''

Miss Jesse laughed. "Ain't no way you can really mean that, Marshal. Fair cyprians at the marshal's house. Folks would tar and feather you, and run you out of town.''

"No, they wouldn't. I meant what I said.''

"Then you're a fool,'' she said quietly.

"Sometimes it takes a fool to get things done,'' he said. "No one with any sense would give it a try. Let me talk to April.''

"I'll get her. I've already talked to her about you. Marshal, April's an unusual child. She's not really a child. She couldn't be after growing up here. She's a little wild—don't misunderstand. I mean, she just likes to wander off by herself. She's only twelve, but she's all grown up. You'll see.''

Miss Jesse left the room, and suddenly Luke felt nervous. He'd been around few young girls of twelve, much less a brand-new half-sister, and the thought of taking her home to live with him was worrisome. He stood up restlessly, moving to the mantel, resting his elbow on it while he waited. If April had been a boy . . . but then the man probably would have kept her and she would be with Hattie now.

The door opened, interrupting his thoughts. "Mr. Danby, this is April. April, this is Marshal Danby, your relative. I'm going to leave you two alone to get acquainted."

April still had on the makeup from her performance. She wore a blue-and-white checked gingham dress with a white apron, and she stared at him solemnly with wide gray-blue eyes.

Luke crossed the room to her and held out his hand. "Hello, April." She reached up and he shook her slender, cold hand. "Let's sit down," he suggested and she nodded.

"I suppose Miss Jesse has told you all about me."

Again he received a nod of confirmation. "We have the same mother, April," he said gently, wondering if she would be at all like his mother, wondering what was going through her mind. "I was fortunate to spend my first seventeen years with her. I was born when she was very young. You don't remember her, do you?"

Maybe a little," April said, her voice strong and clear. "I remember she smelled sweet and I remember her holding me."

"She would have loved you very much."

"I didn't know her. Lottie, Miss Jesse, they're my mother together."

"I know," he said gently, surprised at her quiet dignity. He felt he was talking with an adult instead of a child. "I asked Miss Jesse if I could take you home with me, April. I know you love Miss Jesse and Lottie and they love you. I know how they planned for you to go East to school in a few more years. You're growing up. I'll see to your education and I'll give you a home and family. We're strangers now, April, but I'll be good to you. I'll try to be a brother to you."

"Why? You don't know me."

"No, but your mother is my mother too, and this is what she would want both of us to do."

"I'd rather stay here. She abandoned me."

"For your own good, Miss Jesse and I agreed you should go."

She was silent. Luke felt at a loss. He didn't know how to put her more at ease or how to win her trust. "How old are you?"

'Twelve. I had a birthday last Wednesday."

"Can you travel day after tomorrow?"

"Yes. Everyone will help me pack." As she spoke, she looked down at her fingers knotted together in her lap.

"I'll come get you Friday morning about dawn, and we'll start back to Texas."

"I don't want to go, but Miss Jesse and Lottie say I have to!"

"I'll try to give you a good home. You can't live here always. I promise, I'll try to be good to you."

"Yes, sir," she said woodenly, and he realized she didn't believe him.

"I'll be going now. I'll be by for you Friday morning."

"Yes, sir."

He left the room feeling strangely disquieted. She was too composed and quiet. He had a suspicion her childhood had been far too brief. He passed through the empty dining room with its carved mahogany table and ornate mirror over a hearth. Lottie stepped into the room from a side door. She looked pale, and anger showed clearly in her dark eyes.

"Miss Jesse said we can trust you with April."

"That's right," he said, certain the exchange of gold would be Miss Jesse's secret. "I've talked to April and we're leaving early Friday morning."

"Mister, you ever harm that child—I'll put a knife through your heart."

"I won't harm her," he said, in an effort to hold on to his patience. "This isn't any place for her to grow up. I'm just trying to do what's right for her."

"Just keep your word."

"Lottie, I'll be happy for you to come visit."

She gave him a scornful sneer and drew herself up taller. "You wouldn't let me in your home, and we both know it."

"Yes, I would. That's a promise I'll keep."

"Are you married?"

"Not yet, but I have a woman."

"You're lying."

"I'm not lying. I'm in love with a woman in Texas, and if we're married, she'll let you come on the property."

"No decent woman would associate with us. Not one."

"I think this one will," he said evenly. "I'll be back Friday morning."

"Marshal, I meant it when I said I'd put a knife through your heart if you ever harm her."

"I won't," he promised.

"You don't look like you had the same mother."

"I look like my father." Luke walked past her, feeling her eyes on him and a burning hatred in the air. He had wrestled with the problem and always he felt that he was doing the right thing, the thing that Hattie would want: take her child out of the brothel before it was too late. And it was painfully clear that Miss Jesse would sell April without a qualm.

On Friday morning, the town was shrouded in mist. Miss Jesse's brown weathered building loomed up through the grayness. April was standing in the front parlor in a brown riding dress and carrying her meager belongings in a small bundle. With her face freshly scrubbed and her golden hair neatly plaited, she looked like the child she was. In the light of day, the fancy parlor, with its piano and overstuffed furniture, showed signs of wear. The rug was worn thin in spots, and there were nicks in the furniture and patches on the satin drapes that appeared so opulent under the glow of lamplight. Luke had collected enough fees from bordellos to know the squalor most of the women lived in, the violence and abuse of whiskey and drugs, and he was thankful to take April out of it, but he was having his own trepidations this morning. Catalina might rebel against a twelve-year-old coming to live with him. She might accept this just as she had accepted responsibility for Emilio, but he didn't know for sure.

Yet he couldn't go back to San Antonio and leave April behind. Shutting his mind to doubts and arguments, he loaded her things on both horses, then went back to get her. Six of the women, in various stages of undress, were talking to her. Most wore fancy nightgowns of cotton batiste, oblivious that the gowns were transparent and clinging, for their only concern was April and her departure. She hugged and kissed each one, as a few eyed Luke with speculation. Miss Jesse stood at one side, waiting, her face as impassive as stone.

Finally April had told everyone good-bye. She turned to Miss Jesse, who hugged her in a crushing embrace.

When she released her, April looked around. "Lottie?"

"April." Lottie stood on the porch. April went outside and Luke followed, going past them down to the horses. He turned to watch them as they hugged and then April mounted up. Mist closed behind them as they rode away in the chilly light of the November dawn. The horse hooves sounded loud with each clop against the earth. They left Santa Fe on the trail southeast, riding down out of the mountains into flat land. There was very little conversation, and Luke kept constant watch for Apaches.

April studied the broad-shouldered man riding in front of her. She was tempted to break and run, but she was so close to town that he would merely come back to get her. She had a derringer Lottie had given her long ago. It was tucked in her boot, where she could get it easily, and Lottie had told her to use it if Marshal Danby bothered her.

She didn't want to leave Santa Fe. She didn't know her real mother; as far as she was concerned Lottie was her mother. No one else mattered. And she didn't want to go live with a strange man in a strange, far-away town. When she reached San Antonio, she planned to run away. She could earn a living singing. She had asked one of Lace's regulars, Mr. Wilkens, who traveled a lot, if there were big towns beyond San Antonio and he had said there were. Nice cities. At Galveston she could get a boat to New Orleans. April had heard the men talk about New Orleans.

Marshal Danby seemed to think he was saving her from whoredom, but she had no intentions of becoming a whore. Lottie had instilled in her a deep hatred of it. And men seemed to be no good. They beat the women at Miss Jesse's or lied to them or cheated them.

She would never be in love, never marry, and never earn a living by selling her body to a man. She eyed the marshal with a touch of fear. She felt the smooth silver butt of her derringer. It wouldn't kill a man, Lottie said, but it would stop him.

"Want to halt, April, and let the horses drink?" Marshal Danby swung down out of the saddle with ease, swinging his long leg over the horse. He dropped the reins and moved off a ways.

"April, if I tell you to do something, do it quickly. We're in Apache territory, and later it'll be Kiowa and Comanche land."

"Yes, sir."

"What's fun for you, April? What do you like to do?" he asked, pushing his hat to the back of his head.

She wondered how he had gotten so scarred up.

She'd seen tough-looking men, but Marshal Danby looked the toughest. "I like to walk and be by myself and play checkers with Lottie and I like to read."

"I have some books you might like when I get home." He squatted down, his long legs doubled and the denim pulling tautly over his lean muscles as he cupped water to drink. She waited, afraid to turn her back on him.

"If you need to relieve yourself, go behind some bushes. Just be careful."

"Yes, sir."

In minutes she was back and he was gone, but when he joined her they mounted up and rode in silence. He didn't try to talk to her, which was a relief. Too many of the men who came to Miss Jesse's were forever trying to engage her in conversations she wasn't interested in having. Too many of them tried to touch her too, and Marshal Danby hadn't done so much as help her mount her horse.

By mid-afternoon she relaxed. The sun was shining brightly, and she was beginning to enjoy her surroundings. They'd passed through a small settlement and she had liked seeing a new place. As dusk approached, though, her wariness returned. They were at the foothills of the mountains, surrounded by scattered cedars and cactus. Luke decided to stop for the night by a stream where there were trees, and he unpacked food he had brought from Santa Fe.

"We'll build a fire and douse it soon, but I think it'll be safe. I haven't seen sign of an Apache all afternoon."

He worked diligently without talking and without asking her help, but she gathered some sticks for a fire, keeping an eye on him all the time. If he had lustful intentions, he was hiding them well.

She ate and was surprised at how good the boiled meat and cornbread tasted. He stretched out bedrolls and sat down on his, his feet pointed toward the dying fire. "What do you like to read?"

She began to list books while she took down her hair and she realized he was watching her.

"April, I know you didn't know your real mother, but you look a lot like her," he said quietly. The forlorn note in his voice sounded strange coming from such a tough-looking man. She hadn't wanted to hear about the mother who had vanished so long ago. But there was something about the marshal's tone of voice that changed when he talked about their mother. For the first time, she wondered about Hattie Danby. "What was she like?"

"She was a fine woman and a good mother. She loved to read and when I was a child, she read to me a lot. And she always saw to it that I had books to read and time to read them."

"She abandoned me."

"No, she didn't, April," he said gently. "Miss Jesse told you that because it was simpler. I'm telling you the truth. Miss Jesse admitted that to me, and I know my mother. She would never abandon her child." He told her what Miss Jesse had told him, watching the dismay in her expression change to bewilderment.

"My real mother thought I died? You think she really cared?"

"I know she cared very, very much."

"I never knew my father, either," April said softly.

"I imagine he was a fine man," Luke said, seeing no reason to disillusion her. "And I'm sure he was smart," he added dryly. "When we get to my house, I have lots of books you can read."

She nodded somberly and he wondered if she had ever laughed and played like a child. "It'll be different now and I hope you come to like it, but you'll be alone more because I have an office I have to go to each day."

She nodded. "I never was alone. There was always someone. The girls and their men were always there. They wouldn't allow me upstairs after lunchtime, but

I went up anyway to stay with Lottie. We used to read, and she liked to sew.''

"Do you sew?"

"Just a little."

"How long have you been singing on stage?"

"Since I was about five years old."

"Five!" he exclaimed, shocked.

"Yes. I drew a crowd and I think the men thought I was cute so they taught me to sing. I used to sing with two ladies, but then I started to sing alone about two years ago."

Luke stretched out on the ground, wondering about her life, how much she was aware of what went on around her, how much it had affected her.

"You ever slept out before?"

"Sure. If it's hot we slept out in back if some of the girls didn't have customers, but I haven't ever left Santa Fe before."

"I'm worn out and I'm going to sleep."

"How do you know we're safe?"

"I've been watching. Apaches don't like to attack in the night anyway." He was bone-weary and closed his eyes. "Are you okay, April?"

"Yes, sir."

He stretched his long legs out, pulled up a blanket, and placed his hat over his forehead. Warily she watched him, but soon she could see his chest rise and fall regularly. She lay down and turned on her side to watch him, pulling the derringer up to hold it beneath her blanket. She dozed and then would wake, but each time the marshal was asleep. Maybe she was going to be able to trust him after all.

During the night Luke raised his head. April was stretched on a blanket nearby, her golden hair spilling over her shoulders. His gaze swept the area and he reached for his gun. Something had awakened him and he wasn't sure what.

He sat up slowly, moving so his back was against a tree trunk, his gaze moving deliberately, searching.

His skin prickled and he felt something was amiss, but he couldn't see a thing that was awry. Cautiously he turned his head and looked around the tree over his shoulder behind him. Brush and trees were thick, too dark to have any visibility in their shadows. But when he heard the leaves rustling, all of his senses snapped to alertness.

24

LUKE MOVED TO THE RIGHT IN A CROUCH. HE
hunkered down beside a thick cottonwood trunk while
he listened. Sleep was no longer possible, because he
couldn't shake the feeling that someone was stalking
them.

He studied the landscape as dawn began to break—
every tree, every bush—but the countryside looked
empty. Moving stealthily, he reached down to shake
April, saw the glint of silver in her hand, and leaned
closer to look. She clutched a derringer. His eyes narrowed in shock, but he shrugged away his surprise.
He couldn't blame her for being cautious. He shook
her, and when her eyes opened, he placed his finger
over his mouth for silence. Her eyes widened when he
motioned to her to mount her horse. To his relief she
did so quickly and silently. As he waved her ahead,
he rode, watching everything around him.

April's skin prickled with fear, but it was reassuring
to know Marshal Danby was right behind her. She was
glad he hadn't noticed the derringer. The first night
had passed without any incident except whatever was
bothering him now. She suspected Apaches and began
to wish she were back in Santa Fe more than ever. Yet
she was enormously relieved that she could trust him.
She hadn't intended to sleep, but she had, and if he
had meant to do her harm, he would have had ample
opportunity last night.

Luke caught up with her and spoke softly. "We'll
stop and wash at that creek," he said, pointing to a

line of trees in the distance. "Water will become more scarce today. Don't get far out of my sight and keep your eyes open for anything strange."

"You think there are Apaches?"

"I don't know," he said somberly. "Just be careful."

All day he had the feeling they were being watched, but he couldn't spot anyone on their trail. When dusk came, he dismounted. They were out of the mountains, but the land was broken with gullies and creeks and low hills, enough to allow someone to stay hidden from sight. He deliberately camped in a grove of trees.

"April, you talk softly, as if I'm here. I'm going to scout the area for a sign of anyone. If you hear two quick shots, mount up and ride. I'll catch up with you, just ride."

She nodded solemnly.

He crept through the brush slowly, doubling back on their trail. He disliked leaving April alone. Even though she hadn't made the slightest complaint, she looked terrified. He was sure someone was tracking them, and he intended to find out who and why. He put down each foot carefully, waiting to shift his weight. A twig snapped and he dropped instantly to a crouch, straining to see and hear who approached. Another rustle, closer this time. He pulled his knife from the sheath, and closed his fist around the hilt.

Another rustle came, still closer and then a shadowy form drifted past cautiously. Luke lunged out, his arm sweeping around the person's throat, knife raised.

Instantly a whiff of flowers assailed him, and he felt the softness of the body pressed against his. An elbow jabbed him in the stomach, and the woman began to fight, but in seconds he held her fast, turning her face.

"Lottie!"

"I had to see if she was all right."

"I could have slit your throat," he exclaimed softly, still jolted by his discovery. "How the hell did you know how to track me like that?"

"I'm half Mescalero Apache, white man," she snapped contemptuously. "Let me go."

He released her and jammed the knife back in its scabbard. "April," he called. When they saw her, he said, "We have company." Luke was annoyed. Now he had two women to escort to San Antonio, because he couldn't send Lottie alone back to Santa Fe. He had seen signs of Apaches twice since they had ridden away from town and he didn't want to take the chance.

April flung her arms around Lottie's neck and they both clung to each other. He stared at Lottie, amazed she could follow him so well. He was surprised to learn of her Indian blood, but it accounted for her raven hair. He would have to take her with him and put her on a stage after they reached San Antonio. April was obviously as delighted as he was annoyed. Disgusted, he busied himself getting out food and blankets.

They ate cold food so he wouldn't have to build a fire and risk Apaches spotting the smoke. Afterward he leaned against a tree while April covered herself with a blanket and went to sleep. Lottie sat facing him. She wore a man's clothing, her slender legs stretched out and crossed at the ankles. In the light of the moon he could see her smile.

"You're angry."

"Yes, I am. I can't let you go back alone. You have to come with us now."

She shrugged. "My occupation can be pursued anywhere. I'll find a wagon train going back to Santa Fe, or I may stay in San Antonio a short time until I'm certain you'll be good to April."

"In the meantime I have to take two women hundreds of miles across Comanche and Apache territory when we may get hit with a winter storm."

"Marshal, if you are half the man Sheriff Lomar said, it'll be no problem at all. I can sleep soundly, knowing I'm in your care," she added dryly and stretched out to pull a blanket over her.

He stared at her in consternation. He was bringing

April home, and now Lottie. What would Catalina think?

Four weeks later, delayed by a storm in the Territory, the question loomed larger as they rode the few blocks home. The sunny warmth of San Antonio was welcome. The city looked beautiful in the December morning: the meandering river looping through town, the air cool and crisp. San Antonio meant Catalina, and Luke's pulse quickened at the thought. He was dusty and tired, but he wanted her badly. As he dismounted, he removed April's small bundle of belongings and carried them inside.

The door was opened by Juan, who broke into a broad smile. "Senor Marshal! *Buenos días!* Ayee, we didn't know you were coming. Senorita Piedra isn't home now, but Senor Ta-ne-haddle is here."

"Come in, come in," Luke said to April and Lottie.

"Did I hear my name?" Ta-ne-haddle asked and emerged from the parlor.

"Juan," Luke said, "get us some glasses of water. Heat water for a bath for the ladies first, and then for me."

"*Sí*, Senor."

Ta-ne-haddle approached and Lottie faced Luke. "I can go now. I wanted to see your house and where April will live."

"Come inside. You don't have to go anywhere. You can stay here."

She shook her head. "It wouldn't be fitting. I won't cause April difficulty."

"Lottie, he said you can stay," April said, her voice a whisper of agony.

Luke took Lottie's arm. She looked down at his hand on her arm, and for an instant he thought she would strike him. "Come inside, Lottie," he said gently, drawing her through the wide front door.

Ta-ne-haddle watched her, wondering who these people were, and if Luke's love for Catalina had changed. If he had taken up with a new woman, Catalina was going to be hurt badly. Ta-ne-haddle couldn't take his eyes from the woman. She entered with a slight limp, but her back was straight. She walked tall and proud, her dark eyes full of fire, her midnight hair a cascade of silk. She met his gaze and he saw a flare of disdain.

"Ta-ne-haddle, I want you to meet my half-sister, April Danby, and her friend, Lottie Parsons."

"Ladies, my good friend, Ta-ne-haddle. I'll show you which rooms you'll have."

"I must go," Lottie said again, and Ta-ne-haddle stared at her with curiosity. Whatever was between them, she wasn't in love with Luke or Luke with her. She looked as if she could happily put a bullet in his heart. And his half-sister. He had never mentioned a half-sister. Ta-ne-haddle's curiosity was rampant, but he kept his features impassive and waited to see what would happen next in the argument between Lottie and Luke.

"You're staying here."

"Please, Lottie," April whispered. "I want you."

"We want you here," Luke repeated gently. "I wouldn't ask you to stay if I didn't mean it."

"You're really a fool, Marshal. Someone in town will know me."

"And they know I'm a damned good shot," he rejoined calmly. "Ta-ne-haddle, show Lottie to the room on the west beside Catalina's. April, you come with me."

As Ta-ne-haddle took the small bundle in the woman's hands, her grip tightened on it, and she gave him a defiant glare that startled him. She was obviously Indian; he wondered what tribe. He motioned her to follow him with a jerk of his head. Luke and April disappeared into a room.

"The child is your friend," Ta-ne-haddle said quietly. "Otherwise, I'd suspect you have none in the world."

"My friends are none of your concern. I want to make sure he doesn't hurt her, and now I find he brings her home where two men live. She's becoming a very beautiful young woman. I have friends, but not in this house."

"This is your room." He followed her into the room and closed the door. "I don't know what happened in Santa Fe or how he found he had a sister, but he'll keep his word."

"If he doesn't, I'll put a knife in his heart," she said emphatically. "I promised him that. And you. How can April live in a home with two men and be safe?"

"She'll be safe. Maybe you've known the wrong kind of men."

She gave him a mocking smile. "I've known every kind of man. Time will tell."

He nodded and opened the door as a servant knocked and appeared carrying a tin tub. "For a bath."

"Come in. Miss Parsons is waiting," Ta-ne-haddle said dryly. He left the room and went to find Luke.

He found Luke in a tub of water, his eyes closed as he scrubbed his head. "Who are they and how did you find the girl?" Ta-ne-haddle demanded.

Luke related the whole story as he rinsed and dried off and dressed in fresh jeans, a white chambray shirt, and boots.

"You're keeping Lottie here with Catalina?" Ta-ne-haddle asked softly.

"Yes. Why not?" Luke asked, and Ta-ne-haddle shook his head.

"I may have spent most of my life in a wilderness, but I know that much about women. My friend, you'll think you stepped between two fighting mountain lions before the week is out."

"That's absurd. Catalina loves me, and Lottie hates me."

"Convince Catalina of that."

Luke paused as he buckled his belt. "That's ridiculous. She'll be convinced thirty seconds after she arrives home. I'm not interested in Lottie."

Ta-ne-haddle shook his head and smiled. "I think you should find another home for Lottie quickly. Send her to the ranch."

"With Emilio? No sir. Talk about trouble. He's young and inexperienced and she's . . . I told you about her."

"My friend, I think you have a problem on your hands," Ta-ne-haddle said with a chuckle and closed the door.

Catalina urged the horses forward, driving the buggy toward Luke's house. Soon she would move back to the ranch. The new house was started and progressing well. She faced the ordeal of her father's trial.

Catalina turned to see Senora Torruella standing in her gateway, waving at Catalina to stop. She pulled on the reins, wishing she could avoid her mother's friend, who didn't approve of anything Catalina and Emilio were doing at present.

"Catalina, I saw you ride past my house this morning. I've been to the market and I must talk to you. Come inside."

"Yes, ma'am," Catalina replied, knowing it would be impolite and useless to argue. She followed Senora Torruella's wide frame through the courtyard into the shady hallway to the parlor, where she sat on a hard wooden chair and faced her hostess.

"Catalina, I feel this is my duty. It's scandalous for a young woman to stay at the marshal's house."

"Yes, ma'am, but he was good enough to take us in when Mama died," Catalina said dutifully. "Emilio and I are very grateful to him, because he's a good man."

"Perhaps. Nonetheless, he's a young man. It's not proper, but that isn't why I stopped you. I offer you my home. You must leave his house now."

"Why?" Catalina asked, trying to hide her amusement.

"I was shopping for fruit this morning. He arrived home this morning after you left."

Luke was home! Catalina's pulse jumped with eagerness. She longed to ride right home to see him.

"He didn't come alone."

It took seconds for Catalina to realize what Senora Torruella implied and to realize beady black eyes were watching her with curious eagerness. "Oh? He brought someone home from Santa Fe?" Instantly she thought of his mother. Perhaps he had found his mother.

"He brought two women from a sporting house," Senora Torruella said smugly. *"Dos putas!* And they're living at his house. You can't stay there with loose women and that Indian and heaven knows what going on."

Catalina barely heard the words. "Two women from a pleasure house? He lost his mother when he was younger. Maybe—"

"Neither of these women are his mother. One is extremely young, and both are beautiful. Now I can send Ramon for your things, and you can just stay right here."

"Thank you," Catalina replied automatically. "Perhaps it wasn't Luke. Did you see—"

"No. I overheard two men talking at the market. The whole town is buzzing with it because he went by the courthouse first before going home. Catalina Piedra, you can't think of returning to that house of sin. Imagine the nerve of the man to bring those women and put them in his own home."

"How would anyone know where they're from?"

"One of the men knew one of the women. It was disgraceful," she said, her black eyes flashing with satisfaction. "I overheard the most shameful things."

"Thank you, Senora, but I'll be moving to the ranch. Emilio has the house completed," Catalina said stiffly. She had to doubt what she had heard. She had to!

"As your mother's friend, I feel responsible. You must move here, Catalina. Your father's in jail, your mother buried, you need someone to look after you."

"Senora, *mil gracias,*" Catalina said, moving toward the door. "I'll go home with my brother. We have the servants and they'll go with us."

"You can't run a ranch. Emilio can stay here too."

"Thank you. We'll remember your generous offer," Catalina said as she climbed into the buggy. She waved and started down the street that was the same as only half an hour before, but now had changed so drastically. Catalina was no longer aware of the warm sunshine, the clear blue sky. All she could think about was the possibility that Luke had fallen in love with another woman.

Senora Torruella was a noisy gossip and troublemaker. She had to be wrong. Luke wouldn't. Yet Catalina knew there were no binding ties between her and Luke. She had refused him when he had proposed . . . yet when he left, she had thought she was the only woman in his heart. A knot came in her throat and she stared stonily ahead as she halted in front of his house. A girl's clear, melodic voice floated in the air and Catalina stopped as if she had been hit. Feeling numb with shock and disbelief, she opened the front door and walked down the hall. The door was open to the first bedroom on the right off the long hall.

A woman stood brushing her hair. She was slender, dressed in a satin robe, and very beautiful. Her eyes went to Catalina's in the mirror, and she turned around.

Catalina fled from the house. She climbed into the buggy and turned in the direction of the ranch without giving thought to what she was doing, with no regard for the fact that the house wasn't completely finished, or the dangers in traveling the distance alone, unaware of the tears that streaked her face!

* * *

April explored the house, happy that Lottie was with her, even though she was in a bad temper and seemed to suspect Luke Danby of evil intentions. April pushed open a door and entered a room lined with shelves of books. Joyously she gazed at row after row. She ran her fingers over the spines of leather-bound volumes and reached up for one. In minutes she was curled on the long black leather settee, her thoughts on the book in her hands, problems forgotten.

"There you are," Lottie said from the doorway. "I looked all over the house for you."

"Look at the books!"

Lottie turned to survey the room. "Perhaps you'll be very happy here," she said quietly. "I'll stay for a time, April, and when I think Mr. Danby is what he says he is, I'll go back. I don't belong here."

"I want you to stay. Luke said you could stay."

"I know, but this isn't my place. I can't let him keep me too. It isn't right, but I'll stay for a time."

"You'll tell me before you go?"

"Of course, I will," Lottie said quietly. "I'm beginning to think you'll be very happy. Look at all these books," she said, moving in front of the shelves. Finally she selected two volumes. "I'll take these to my room," she said lightly and left, closing the door behind her. She entered the courtyard, stopping when she encountered Ta-ne-haddle seated on a bench.

"Sorry. I didn't know anyone was here," she said.

"Sit down. You won't disturb me, and I won't bother you." He bent over bits of metal and she moved closer. She saw he was working on a piece of silver, bending and shaping it into jewelry.

"That's beautiful," she said, watching him work.

"Thanks," he answered quietly, his attention on the silver.

"You're making it for your woman?"

He raised his head to regard her with his one dark eye. "No. Luke asked me to make it for his woman."

She sat down on a stone bench close at hand. "So there really is a woman."

"Yes."

"Perhaps she's the one I just saw. She looked at me and left."

"I think Marshal Danby is about to catch hell."

"Over us? She didn't say who she was."

"He'll work it out. Maybe Catalina needed a little jolt."

"And you?" Lottie asked after a few minutes, feeling at ease with a man who paid so little attention to her. "Where's your woman?"

"There isn't one," he said, pausing to look at her.

"I should have guessed," she answered sharply. "I'm not working while I'm here."

"I didn't ask if you were," he said gently. "What tribe are you?"

"Mescalero Apache, half white. How'd you know?"

"Just a guess. We have something in common. I'm a half-breed too." He went back to work. His strong fingers shaped the thin metal strips, carefully fashioning a chain with tiny links while Lottie sat fascinated, and watched the jewelry take shape. She was surprised. She had expected Luke Danby to use April for one reason only, but she was beginning to change her mind about him. He seemed convinced that April was his sister and he truly intended to help her. Ta-ne-haddle was another matter.

"Do you stay here all the time?"

"No. I was Kiowa too long and it's too strong in me. I have wandering feet."

"How'd you meet Luke Danby?"

"I found him after a wagon-train attack." While he worked, he told Lottie about finding Luke near death, nursing him back to health, and teaching him how to survive. He went through the years, talking quietly, and she relaxed, leaning forward to watch him.

He glanced at her, seeing her so close. Her skin was

smooth and satiny, and she smelled fresh and sweet.
"What happened to you?" he asked.

Lottie glanced sharply at him, but he continued to
work. She never told people about her life. She tried
to blank it out, but with his head bent over, she began
to talk softly, the words coming hesitantly. "I was
married to a good man, Jeb Klause. Parsons isn't my
name, I didn't want to use Jeb's. We were going to
Colorado to farm when we were attacked by renegades. We were only ten miles from town. I was expecting a child. They killed Jeb," she paused,
suddenly struck with self-consciousness, but Ta-ne-
haddle's fingers worked without pause. Defiantly she
said, "They raped me, and I lost the baby. I almost
died. I made it almost to Santa Fe and passed out in
the wagon. A man found me and took me to Miss
Jesse's. She nursed me back to health, as I suppose
you did for Luke Danby. When I was well again, I
went to work for her. I didn't care what I did. I didn't
want to live. My knee never did heal up right again,
so I don't make as much money as some of the
women," she added stiffly. She wondered why she was
telling him things that were so private, but he barely
seemed to be listening.

"How long ago was that?"

"About three years ago. I became friends with
April. She was—she made up for the baby I'd lost."
She felt tears sting her eyes and wished she hadn't
started talking. She stood up swiftly to go, thinking
he wouldn't even know she had gone, but his hand
caught her wrist and he was on his feet in an instant.

"You're safe here, Lottie," he said gently in his
soft, raspy voice. "Luke is a good man. You said you
married a good man, so you know it's possible. Stay
here where you're safe."

"I won't have April's chances spoiled by my presence. There'll be a wagon train or soldiers, someone
going north before too long."

"Isn't there something you can do—seamstress, cook?"

She laughed with contempt. "Seamstress! I could barely eke out a living as a seamstress. Do you know how many seamstresses there are in San Antonio and what they get paid? I'll do this for five more years, then there may be enough money to open a boarding-house. My body isn't important any longer, and my heart was smashed when I lost the man I loved and his baby."

"Your heart wasn't smashed," he said gently, "or you wouldn't care about April." He put his arms around her and pulled her close. For a long time they stood quietly, and then her arms slipped around his waist and she held him. When she moved away, she locked her fingers together.

"Perhaps I misjudged both of you, but if I have, you're both a rare breed of men."

"I think you've seen too much of the wrong segment of humanity." He went back to the bench and sat down at work again and she left. Within the hour, though, she returned to sit nearby.

Early that evening they all sat in the front parlor, Luke pacing restlessly. "I can't understand what's happened to Catalina. No one knows where she is," he said, a frown creasing his brow.

His head came up as they heard a rider. The hoof-beats stopped outside, and in minutes they heard the jingle of spurs and the scrape of boots as someone entered the house.

Dressed in dusty buckskins, Emilio came into the room, his gaze sweeping over everyone until he saw Luke. He crossed the room and swung, putting all his force into the blow.

25

LUKE DUCKED AND STEPPED BACK. "HEY, EMIL-
io!"

Emilio swung again, and again Luke sidestepped
him. The next blow sent him crashing back over a
chair. Emilio followed him, but suddenly his arms
were caught from behind by Ta-ne-haddle, who held
him while Luke scrambled to his feet.

"What the hell brought that on?"

"You! You break her heart!"

"Catalina! Where is she? What the devil are you
talking about?"

"She rode to the ranch today all alone—"

"Alone!"

"Yes! You know how dangerous and foolish that is?
Because of your women!"

"My *what?*"

"Your women, you—"

"Emilio," Tan-ne-haddle said sharply, releasing
him. Emilio turned to face him, a scowl wrinkling his
features, his fists still clenched and raised.

"Son, you ought to learn to get the facts before you
make decisions. And you shouldn't hit a friend without a warning." Emilio stood looking from one to the
other. "What do you mean?" he asked.

"This is April *Danby,* Emilio, Luke's sister. Do you
understand? April, meet Emilio Piedra, the hothead."

April looked at the breathless young man. With his
large black eyes and thick black curls, he was the most
handsome man she had ever seen. And she realized he

was angry because he had jumped to the conclusion that she was Luke's woman along with Lottie. She pursed her lips and tried to keep from laughing at the surprise in his features. "How do you do, Emilio Piedra?" she said.

"You're his sister?" he asked in obvious shock.

She laughed and nodded. "Yes, I am."

Luke watched them, swamped by his own shock. First, he was amazed Emilio had struck him. And now April, who had ridden all the way from Santa Fe without a smile, was laughing and smiling at Emilio as if he had been performing tricks to entertain her.

"And this is April's friend who came along to make sure April would be chaperoned and safe. Miss Parsons, meet our rash young friend, Emilio Piedra," Tane-haddle said. "Now, ladies, if you'll join me, we'll adjourn to the library and leave these two to settle their differences."

They left the room and Emilio's gaze followed April until she disappeared from sight. He turned back to face Luke and his face turned a bright red. "I apologize. Catalina said—she said you brought two women from a broth—from New Mexico to live with you here. I'm truly sorry."

"Emilio, where's Catalina? Is she still at the ranch?"

"No, sir. I told her I was riding into town to see you. I had to come anyway for supplies, but . . . ay, ay, ay! I'm sorry. I don't know what got into Catalina. She said she came home and saw them. Senora Torruella stopped her and told her about the ladies. I didn't know you had a sister."

"I didn't either until I found her in Santa Fe."

Emilio was staring at the empty doorway. "She's very beautiful."

"She is for a fact. You can give the ladies my regrets and stay here with them. Is Catalina staying on the ranch with a bunch of hands?"

"No, sir. She's at the hotel. I wouldn't leave her

behind. You better let me talk to her first, sir. She might not let you live to give her an explanation.''

Luke grinned. ''You stay right here. You can get to know April and Lottie. I'll handle Catalina. Do you have a room key?''

Emilio threw him a long silver key. ''Room 2 on the second floor in the southeast corner. Luke, I'm sorry.''

''Forget it. You have a mean wallop, Emilio.''

Emilio grinned. ''I've had to learn to defend myself at the ranch. Now they know I'm boss, but they didn't at first.''

Luke nodded and left, his denim-clad legs stretching out in long strides. Minutes later he climbed the hotel stairs to the second floor and marched down the hall, unlocking the door without knocking or calling. He threw open the door, stepped inside, and slammed it shut.

Catalina's head snapped up. Looking breathtakingly beautiful in a red gingham dress decorated with black ribbon bows, she stood on one side of the room. Her eyes widened.

''You! You lowlife skunk!'' she snapped, and tossed a glass of water at him. Striding toward her, Luke ducked, and it smashed against the door with a tinkle of glass. She threw a hairbrush and he ducked again, laughter bubbling up in him. He caught her around the waist and scooped her over his shoulder. He chuckled at her name-calling, knowing there wasn't any trouble between them, knowing she must care terribly and have missed him almost as much as he had missed her. He dumped her on the bed and straddled her as he leaned down.

''Bastard!'' she hissed, then met his gaze. He saw her anger melt and desire burn like a hot flame, and his teasing amusement was gone. It felt like years instead of weeks they had been apart. His arousal was swift and hard, his need overpowering. He bent down to kiss her, stretching out on top of her and rolling over with her in his arms. She was soft and voluptuous and exciting.

"I love you and I missed you," he whispered, needing her more than ever. His hands sought her flesh, pushing beneath the neck of her dress.

With a sob she kissed him passionately. His hands tugged at her clothing, until he stood up to pull off his own, wanting to be rid of the barriers between them. Gazing down at her smooth olive skin, the mass of silky midnight hair, he knew no woman on earth would ever be as tempting or as beautiful.

"How I want you," he said huskily, his breathing constricted.

She watched him solemnly, then closed her eyes, catching her lower lip with her white, even teeth as he stroked and kissed her, his hands working magic. Finally he impaled her with his hot shaft, taking her quickly, unable to control his passion. She gasped and cried out, her nails raking his back as he whispered her name and shuddered with release. Finally he sank down on top of her, holding her close and caressing her slowly.

"Catalina, mine. How I missed you! You little fool," he said gently, rolling beside her and raising on his elbow. "How could you possibly think there can ever be another woman?"

"There isn't?" she asked, worry clearly showing in her voice.

He leaned down to kiss between her breasts. "Have I acted like there's another woman in my life?" he asked, his question muffled against her flesh.

She caught him tightly, framing his face so she could look him directly in the eyes. "There's no one?"

"There's only one—*you.*"

"I saw them," she whispered. "Truthfully, there isn't?"

"I should put you across my knee for such ridiculous thoughts, but then you might use the Colt on me, so—'' He shrugged, happy to hold her, knowing all was well between them.

"Then who's at your house?"

"My sister, April Danby, and—''

"Sister!" Catalina shrieked and sat up. "You don't have a sister. And the woman I saw isn't your mother."

"No, she's not," he said, amused by Catalina's violent reaction. "Lottie Parsons was afraid for my sister to travel alone with me. Lottie didn't trust me."

"Luke, why didn't you tell me? Where'd you find her? Did you know you had a sister?"

He grinned and clamped his hand over her mouth. "When can I get in a word and answer your first hundred questions?"

He saw the sparkle in her eyes and removed his hand. As his fingers trailed over her satiny skin, he told her about April and Lottie, their backgrounds, the delay in getting home because of the storms. Listening in amazement, Catalina pulled her bodice up under her chin.

"Luke, why didn't you tell me. Senora Torruella— that woman is all gossip. I should have known better."

"Yes, you should have," he said quietly, looking at the soft white batiste that was such a contrast with her dark skin. Her lips were red from his kisses, her black tresses disheveled, her eyes sparkling with love. Their lovemaking had been scalding and swift, driven by Luke's hungry need, but now he wanted to make love to her in leisure, to watch her as he loved her. He reached out lazily to pull the bodice from her hands.

Her gaze flew to his and she saw their green depths darken with desire. Her gaze drifted down over his lean, virile body, the sinewy muscles and broad shoulders that tapered to narrow hips. Compelled to touch him, she trailed her fingers along his hip and over his marvelous chest.

"The only woman I can think about is you, Catalina. The only one, forever. I want you."

Her heart thudded with joy and she wound her fingers in his hair.

"When are you going to marry me?" he asked gruffly.

"You know I love you," she said solemnly. "But I can't marry until after my father's trial. You understand that, don't you? When the trial is over, then I'll marry you, Luke Danby." The flare of happiness in his eyes made her heart lurch.

"Ah, Catalina, I've waited so long to hear you say that," he said, looking into the midnight-black eyes that always seemed to draw him to her. "You're exciting, love. So happy, so angry, always full of exuberance and passion. Life with you will never be dull." He leaned down to kiss her hard, his mouth opening hers while his hands slid over her satiny skin, cupping one full breast in his rough hand. He loved her without haste, taking his time until they both were quivering with need and their bodies joined in ecstasy.

Later she lay in his arms and she raised herself up to look down at him. "You have a sister. How amazing!"

"There's evidently another child as well," he said, and related the story of how April came to be at Miss Jesse's. "And I think my mother is still alive, but I don't know how to find her. She may be married to a farming man, who could live in the remotest part of the new territory. They could have gone west to California. But I think she's alive and I have to feel in my heart that she's happy. And perhaps this husband and third child will bring her enough joy to make up for the losses she had," he said. He curled a long lock of black hair around his wrist, gazing at her solemnly. "You'll marry me as soon as the trial is over?"

"Yes," she exclaimed eagerly, her eyes sparkling.

"I understand why you need to wait for the wedding, but today when I was at the courthouse, I learned that Judge Roberts is out in the district, and he won't be available for at least another four weeks."

"I have to wait, Luke. I can't marry and go away until the trial is over."

"I understand. As much as I hate to, we need to go home now before we scandalize the town. I'd rather stay right here for the next two weeks. Honey, think about where you'd like to go for a long wedding trip."

She smiled and leaned forward to kiss him, her petal-soft lips opening beneath his, her slender arms wrapping around his neck. Luke forgot his intentions of taking her home.

"Come on," he said, giving her a playful swat. "Get your fanny moving. We should go home."

"Ah, such disrespect. I've known you were a rogue from the first hour you eavesdropped on me."

"I was there first. I couldn't help the eavesdropping. And no red-blooded male could have resisted a peek when you peeled your clothes off to swim."

"Thank goodness you didn't. Otherwise you wouldn't have given me any attention."

"I don't know that I agree, but I'll have to admit, after the sight of you standing out in the river," he said, pulling her to him again, "I couldn't ever forget you."

He turned to hold her, and then as soon as they were ready, they left together, riding double on Luke's horse.

"I should stop and give Senora Torruella a lecture, except I know it would be impertinent. There is enough gossip and scandal now about my staying at your house." She laughed, and he turned to look at her curiously.

"Luke, you have two women from a brothel, an unwed woman, a Kiowa, my brother. Two of us the children of a renegade—we're all misfits, and you have the lot of us living with you."

"I'm glad I do. April is young and I hope somewhat untouched by her past; you two can't help what your father did. Lottie has a heart beneath all her stone exterior, and Ta-ne-haddle is one of the finest men I've ever known. And if people in town don't approve, I don't give a damn."

She leaned against him. "I know you don't. Nor do I. I care what you think and what Emilio thinks, but there's no one else now that Mama is gone. So many changes, so quickly."

"You're changing with them and for the better, Catalina. You and Emilio have done well." He chuckled. "Your bookish brother has learned to fight. He knocked me flat tonight."

"Emilio did that?" she asked. Her eyes developed a sparkle. "Well, good for him. Remember that the next time you start to bring two beautiful women home without explanation."

"Yes, ma'am," he answered, teasing her, and they both laughed. Luke shifted the reins to his other hand, slipped his arm around Catalina, kissed her soundly. "Now come meet my family."

He introduced Lottie and Catalina, amused by the cool assessment each gave the other. "Where's April?"

"In your library with Emilio. They've discovered they both like to read," Lottie answered.

"Before we go find them," Luke said, looking into Ta-ne-haddle's dark eyes, "I'll buy you a new sorrel gelding tomorrow with a glaze and white stockings to settle our long-ago wager. Catalina has agreed to marry me."

"Ah, my friends, congratulations," Ta-ne-haddle said, clapping Luke on the back and turning to kiss Catalina's cheek. She hugged Ta-ne-haddle tenderly. "I'll always be grateful to you, because you saved his life."

Lottie offered congratulations, and then Luke, who couldn't stop grinning, took Catalina's hand and led her down to the library. Emilio and April had books on the table between them and were talking in low voices, both falling silent when Luke and Catalina entered the room. "April, I want you to meet Catalina Piedra, Emilio's sister. Catalina, this is April Danby, my sister."

"How nice to meet you," Catalina said warmly. "Luke told me about you and about your singing."

"You sing?" Emilio asked, and April blushed as she nodded.

"Emilio plays the guitar. Come sing for us," Catalina urged, Emilio joining in.

"Only if all of you will sing along with me."

"Before we do, there's something we want to tell you," Luke said, looking at Emilio. "Catalina's agreed to marry me."

"*Dios!* You had me storming in here to hit him a few hours ago." Emilio snapped, coming to his feet to shake Luke's hand. "I should say congratulations, but I also hope you can put up with my sister's volcanic temperament."

"Emilio!"

He grinned. "Congratulations, Luke. And Catalina, I'm so happy," he added, hugging her. April added her shy congratulations, and they all returned to the parlor. In a few minutes all of them sat together in the warm parlor while Emilio strummed a guitar and April sang softly. She sang a song in Spanish as Emilio's dark eyes watched her. Feelings arose that she had never known before. She felt shy with men, always trying to avoid those who were at Miss Jesse's.

The hour grew late, and it was decided that Emilio and Catalina would stay at Luke's instead of the hotel. The house was large enough to hold all of them comfortably with its bedrooms surrounding the courtyard.

The next few nights Emilio and Catalina stayed in town while they finished business and Emilio made purchases. Sunday night was their last night, and Catalina would move to the ranch because the house was sufficiently finished. It was unusually cold and Luke had a roaring fire in the parlor. He turned the lamps low as they sat around the fire and sang together, Emilio playing the guitar. Luke kept his arm around Catalina, and her dark eyes sparkled with love when she looked at him.

Lottie left to go to bed, then Ta-ne-haddle disappeared. He drifted in and out of the house like a specter, and April accepted his comings and goings without question. Then Catalina and Luke left, and she was alone with Emilio. Sitting close to her, he picked up the guitar and strummed it. She sang softly, gazing into his dark eyes.

Emilio lowered the guitar and reached out to touch a long, golden lock of hair that curled on the sleeve of her pale blue gingham dress. The touch tingled in a way she wouldn't have guessed possible, and she watched him as he moved closer.

"How old are you April?"

"Twelve," she said, wishing she were older.

"Twelve? You're a child," he said, staring at her with his brows arched in surprise.

"No, I'm not," she answered. "I haven't been a child for a long, long time." She knew she had more experience of life than women double her age.

"Have you ever been kissed?" he asked softly.

She blushed hotly, gazing up at him while her heart pounded. "No," she whispered. It was something she had thought she wouldn't ever want to do, but now she did badly. "Have you kissed many girls?"

"A few," he answered, tilting her face up with his finger beneath her chin. He leaned forward and his lips brushed hers with the faintest touch, but it was warm and marvelous and created sensations that rippled through her.

She closed her eyes, lifting her mouth. He brushed his lips over hers again and then settled on her mouth fully, pressing his lips to hers. His mouth parted hers and his tongue touched hers.

Startled, April looked up at him. "You're very beautiful," he whispered, and leaned down slowly, his arm banding her waist and drawing her to him tightly.

He kissed her, making her senses spin in a giddy spiral. When he released her, he gazed down at her. "April," he whispered, drawing out her name in his deep voice. "I'm glad you came to San Antonio."

"So am I," she said shyly, her heart beating wildly as she studied his handsome features.

He frowned and moved away from her. "There's something I doubt if you know."

"What's that?"

He turned to face her. "My father is in jail. Some people won't speak to Catalina or me."

"Emilio," she said, placing her hand against his cheek, "I came from a house of pleasure. Many women in Santa Fe wouldn't speak to me or let their daughters speak to me. And the boys—the things they'd say to me."

"I would like to hit them, each and every one," he said vehemently. "You don't care about my father?"

"Of course not. I'm sorry that you must suffer if you love him and—"

"I don't!" he snapped, startling her. "He was cruel, and we never understood each other. My mother protected me from him some of the time, but I'm not sorry. I think he's done terrible things and now he has to pay for them."

She hated the fierceness in his voice, and she felt emotions racing in her that were newly awakened. She slipped her arms around his neck timidly. "I'm sorry. I used to dream of having a father when I was small, but there have been so many terrible men at the house that I decided it was just as well I didn't know him. Miss Jesse took me in to care for me."

"You had people who loved you, that's what's important. I had my mother and now I have Catalina. We're rebuilding our ranch and I'll manage it, but I don't like it. Luke told me I could study his law books."

"How wonderful!"

He smiled down at her. "I have a book at the ranch

that I think you'll like. It has beautiful drawings of horses in it and the English countryside. I'll bring it the next time I come to town.''

''I'd better go now. It's getting late.'' She stood up and Emilio rose to his feet quickly, setting down the guitar. He walked to the door with her, but before she left the parlor, he caught her wrist lightly, turning her to face him.

''You're a child, April, but I still want to kiss you,'' he said softly.

She raised her face, waiting, her emotions churning. Never once had she thought she would fall in love after knowing the men who frequented Miss Jesse's, but Emilio was a wonder. He was handsome and gentle and loved books. He wasn't coarse or boisterous or abusive. His brown eyes gazed at her warmly, seeming to pull her closer. As he put his arms around her again, he fitted her to his long length, squeezing her tightly. He looked at her mouth and bent his head to kiss her, a feather-light kiss that took her breath away. Her heart thundered and she clung to him, relishing the way he felt, his strong arms around her. When he released her, she whispered, ''Good night, Emilio,'' and turned to hurry away, her pulse pounding with excitement.

In her room she leaned against the door, her eyes closed, reliving in her mind the past hour. She was glad now she had come to San Antonio. Emilio Piedra. Happily she began to get undressed for bed, knowing that her views on men had changed forever tonight.

Emilio and Catalina left late the next afternoon with a promise to be back on the weekend. Emilio had asked April to visit the ranch, and she had promised she would soon. She knew his father's trial was approaching, and he would be in town more at that time.

Monday night Lottie looked for April at bedtime and found her in the library with a book.

''April?'' Lottie called from the doorway. ''It's late. It's almost one in the morning.''

''I'll go to bed soon,'' April answered.

Lottie leaned her hip against the door jamb. "You like it here, don't you?"

"Yes, I do."

"I'm glad. You like Emilio, too."

"Yes. He likes to read just as I do," she said, blushing a little. She cared about Emilio for more reasons than that.

"I think you'll be fine here. I should leave soon."

"Please stay. I heard Luke tell you that you could stay."

"This is the place for you, and you'll have a new life. It isn't the place for me, and I need to go back to Santa Fe. I'll wait another week and then I should go."

"I don't want you to leave," April said, closing her book and throwing her arms around Lottie. "You're like my sister and my mother, Lottie. Please stay."

Lottie hugged her tightly. "We'll talk some more. You get on to bed now."

"Yes, ma'am," April said, and moved away. " 'Night, Lottie."

"Good night, April." She stood in the darkened hallway watching until April went inside her bedroom and closed the door.

"You can stay, you know," came a deep voice, and she turned to see Ta-ne-haddle in the parlor doorway.

"You overheard us."

"I didn't intend to. I was stretched on the sofa in here. Come in," he said softly, holding out his hand.

Resignedly, she placed her hand in his. She had known from the first night she had crossed the threshold that one of the men in the house—perhaps all of them—would want to take her to bed. Finally she had decided Luke would not. She had seen men who were true to one woman, and Luke Danby appeared to be that kind of man. But Ta-ne-haddle had no woman and in spite of his lack of attention, she expected sometime he would want her.

He led her inside the parlor and closed the door.

Moving to the sofa, she sat down in the darkness. "April doesn't want you to go. There are places here you can work and be near her."

She stared at him, her eyes adjusted to the darkness. He sat down on the opposite end of the sofa from her. "You really brought me in here to talk."

"What did you expect?" he asked with amusement.

"What woman is in your life?"

"I told you, there isn't one."

"Do you know the houses here?"

"Yes, and the most pleasant woman to work for would be Dolly's Exchange. From what I've heard she's fair and good to her girls. She keeps her taxes paid, and has testified for the marshal when he's needed her. She's a damn fine woman."

Lottie smiled in the darkness. "You like women, or you wouldn't know the houses and the girls. Here I am obligated to your friend. Ever since that first day I've been expecting to have to make payment."

"I know you have, but you don't understand Luke Danby."

"I don't understand *you*, Kiowa. Is it my scarred legs?"

"With my one eye, do you think I mind your scars?"

"Well, something holds you back."

"I loved a woman once and I lost her. A man has needs, and it's easy to satisfy those needs, but the heart isn't involved when it's purely physical. You should understand that better than anyone."

"Yes, I do. I haven't cared in all these years. It's nothing to me but a way to get money, sometimes a way to get even for what those men did to me."

"You're not someone to use and discard, Lottie. Not to me. I've seen you with April. You're a warm-hearted woman. You're another human being who hurts and feels and cares. I can't love again, and I care too much to use you in any way."

"She must have been wonderful."

"And your Jeb must have been a fine man." He

drew her to him and settled her with her back against his chest. "Stay and talk awhile. Are you sleepy?"

"No. I'm accustomed to having people around all the time. I'm not alone with my thoughts often. I don't like to be alone with memories. As it says in the Good Book, 'It is not good that man should be alone.' "

Ta-ne-haddle chuckled softly. "Do you read or are you religious?"

"I read. That's one of the ties I have with April."

" 'Reading is to the mind what exercise is to the body.' "

"You're quoting either Sir Richard Steele or Samuel Johnson."

"Steele. I haven't seen you in Luke's library."

"I took two books to my room."

"How'd your parents meet?"

"My mother was a captive. We were with the tribe until I was nine, and then we were returned to her people. Later, she married an older man, who was good to all of us. My Apache name was Little Blackbird."

While she talked, she relaxed in the warmth of his arms. He stroked her hair, her arm, talking to her with a deep rumble that vibrated in his chest. She didn't understand him and couldn't recall ever knowing anyone quite like him before, but it comforted her to be with him. And she wondered about the woman he had loved, if she had been very beautiful. She grew sleepy and closed her eyes, listening to him tell her Kiowa legends, winding her arm around his neck.

She awoke the next morning in her room in her bed. She was fully dressed with her shoes removed, the covers over her. She sat up and rubbed her head, thinking about Ta-ne-haddle, knowing he must have been hurt deeply over losing the woman he loved.

A week later they had spent the holidays together at Luke's. They brought Domingo lavish dinners, and to all appearances he seemed reasonably cheerful, but Catalina could tell that jail was a cage that wore on his nerves. They all celebrated Las Posadas, the holiday to commemorate Joseph and Mary's journey to Bethlehem. Then in January they watched the traditional pageant *Los Pastores,* an old Spanish play about the journey shepherds made to worship the infant Jesus in Bethlehem. And as the new year started, a foundation had been laid for a grand new hotel, the Menger, where there had originally stood a boardinghouse and a brewery. San Antonio's population boasted over seven thousand people now. Emilio and Catalina returned to the ranch. Lottie still delayed returning to Santa Fe, and Domingo's trial was set for Wednesday, the tenth of February 1859.

Luke arranged for April to attend school. He hired a housekeeper so there would be a woman there until he and Catalina were married and home from a wedding trip. He wanted April accepted by San Antonio society, and he intended to see to it that she was.

The last weekend of January, all except Lottie and Ta-ne-haddle attended a fandango. It was April's first fandango and she was excited, letting Lottie and Catalina help her at the last few minutes with her hair. Her golden hair was caught high behind her head, rosebuds fastened in it. Her dress was pink gingham trimmed in white lace with short puffed sleeves and a high, demure neckline.

Catalina was a contrast in her deep blue dress made of muslin, something she had bought with a twinge of guilt for spending so much on a dress, but Emilio had insisted. When they went down the hall to the waiting men, Catalina's breath caught at the sight of Luke in his dark suit and white shirt, his shiny black boots. She remembered that first fandango. His green eyes were on her until he seemed to look away reluctantly, turning to April.

"How pretty you look, April," he said sincerely.

"Thank you," she said, blushing. Catalina saw the look of longing in Emilio's eyes and gazed at them both in surprise. Her brother looked more grown up, and his new suit made him appear very handsome. She was proud of Emilio, and wished for a moment her mother could see him, because Sophia would have been proud of him. Then Catalina's thoughts jumped to Luke, conscious of his touch as he took her arm.

Lottie and Ta-ne-haddle told them good-bye cheerily, and Catalina suffered another twinge of guilt over leaving two friends behind, friends who would not be welcomed at the party. She glanced up at Luke's somber look before he left the house, and knew he felt the same about leaving them behind.

They entered a room decorated with fresh flowers. The musicians—a guitar player, a fiddler, and a trumpet player—were tuning their instruments. As they milled about, greeting people, Catalina noticed a coolness from many people, men as well as women. She realized her father had probably made many enemies. Men who were afraid to be unkind to him or his children as long as he was so powerful now no longer had to fear or endure him, and Catalina and Emilio were an extension of Domingo to most people.

Luke noticed too, because his arm tightened around her waist as he turned her to face him on the dance floor. "Would you rather go home?"

"And not get to dance with you after I had this dress made especially for the occasion?"

His white teeth flashed in a smile while he squeezed her waist. "It's beautiful. And as always, you're the most beautiful woman here. The most beautiful in San Antonio."

"Thank you. I hope you always think so. Do you know, I think my brother is attracted to April."

"Do you know that you've been blind if you're just now noticing them? They can't see anyone else when they're together. Why do you think he's started coming to town for supplies constantly?"

"I thought it was because the house is so nearly finished—you mean, Emilio didn't have to run all those errands?"

"Of course not. He could have made one trip instead of five and gotten what he needed. I'll bet he's purchased things he won't need for months."

"No!"

"Now don't get in a huff. You can't stop human nature, Catalina. I intend to talk to Emilio, because I'm responsible for April's welfare, and she's just a child."

"She doesn't act like a child. With her background she's far from childhood, and she's intelligent. She reads as much as Emilio."

"I know that. I want to see her get an education."

"April has read more now than most adults I know. With the exception of you and Emilio, of course. I know my brother. Emilio will love her with all his heart. I doubt if there will ever be another woman for him. He's like that—when he loves something or someone, it's forever."

"He's young too. There'll be other women in his life. There always are."

"Always are?" she asked in mocking speculation.

"You want me to say you're the only woman I've ever loved?" he asked with dancing fires in his green eyes.

"Yes!" she answered.

He spun her around in a quick series of circles, his long legs widening their steps. He leaned closer to whisper in her ear. "You're the only one. There has never been a woman I cared about like you." His breath tickled, and his tongue touched her lobe, making her heart throb. She gazed at him, wanting him, wanting to be his wife and go home with him tonight to his bed.

"Catalina, before our marriage, I'll resign and this time it'll be permanent. Your father's trial will be over; I'll give them enough notice and time to get a good man."

"You're doing this for me. I'm so glad!" She gazed

at him with joy. "Will you like practicing law as well, or will it be a yoke of bondage?"

He pulled her closer. "I like law and I'll like a practice. I've always thought I would do that in a year or two. With you as my wife, the yoke of bondage will be the most exciting tie on earth."

Catalina's pulse jumped again at the look of desire showing clearly in his eyes. She longed for his kisses, wanting him badly, knowing she had to get through the trial before she could think of marriage. Her gaze dropped to his mouth—so well shaped, sensuous, and inviting—and the temperature in the room seemed to soar as she thought about the last time they had been together.

"Perhaps someday Emilio can practice law with you," she said. "Of course, he'd have to get rid of the ranch."

"Not necessarily. He could hire a man to manage it, and I think that's what he hopes to do. If he ever wants to sell it, tell him to let me know first, because I'll buy it."

"You want to be a rancher?"

"Nope. I'd hire someone to run it, but as land becomes more valuable in Texas, ranching will become more important." He glanced beyond her. "Look at all the soldiers here tonight."

"All they do is talk of fighting Indians and slavery. I get tired of hearing about it."

"You may get a lot more tired of hearing about it," he said solemnly, and Catalina felt a chill.

"Surely not more fighting. Texas has had battle after battle."

"Those were with Mexico. If this comes, it'll be family against family."

"I don't think there'll be any war over slavery. And if there is, it's not such a big issue in Texas."

"It's a big issue to Sam Houston, who opposes it. I think he'll run again for governor next election, and slavery will be an issue."

"I don't want to worry about it at a party." she exclaimed, thinking Luke was the most exciting man in the world.

He grinned down at her and held her tighter. As they danced in perfect unison, she loved him with all her being. She was unaware of other people around them, unaware of anything except Luke.

As they danced, Emilio took April's hand and led her outside down the steps to the shadows beneath a mulberry tree. He took off his coat and draped it around her shoulders so she wouldn't be cold in the chilly January night. "I want to talk to you, April, where we can be alone. I brought you something. Hold out your hand."

April gazed up at him, her heart pounding with excitement. In her open palm he placed a tiny present wrapped in paper and tied with a ribbon. Eagerly she untied the ribbon and opened the box. Moonlight glinted on a golden heart on a thin chain.

"How beautiful!" she whispered breathlessly, wonder bubbling in her.

Emilio's fingers brushed hers when he took the chain from her. "Turn around," he ordered, "and I'll fasten it around your neck."

She turned, holding up her curls while he slipped it around her neck. His fingers were warm against her skin, and the magic touches stirred invisible sparks in her. Suddenly his lips brushed the nape of her neck. She closed her eyes, gasping with pleasure. He turned her to face him and she raised her head. "Thank you, Emilio."

"I love you, April," he said in his deep voice. "You're so young, but I love you and I'll wait for you to grow up."

"I am grown up," she whispered, placing her hands on his upper arms, feeling the strong muscles through his shirt sleeves.

"No, you're a child, but you won't always be. I'll wait, because I want you and I always will." His arm slipped around her waist, and he bent his head to kiss her. This time her lips parted eagerly. She thought she would melt with excitement and happiness as she pressed against him, slid her arms around his neck to cling tightly to him. He was a marvel to her, handsome, intelligent, sensitive.

She moved a fraction to look up at him. "Emilio, I love you too. And I'll grow up quickly for you."

"I hope so, April. I didn't know how badly I could want someone until now. That necklace is my heart. It's yours. You'll always have my love."

"I'll wear it always."

He kissed her again, and April thought she would faint with happiness. She clung to him, kissing him back, wanting him to hold her and never stop.

Finally he released her. "We should go inside or Luke will come searching for us. I don't think he approves of this."

"Why?"

"You're too young."

"I love you now and I can't stop. I'll always love you."

He gave her a faint smile and turned to walk back inside, holding her close beside him. After slipping his coat on again, he took her arm. April's gaze searched the crowd and to her relief, Luke was smiling down at Catalina, his attention fully on her. And Catalina's was on Luke.

"Come taste the tamales," Emilio said. "They're the best on earth."

While they were served tamales in brown bowls, they stood in a group of people who were introduced to Emilio by an old friend of his family's. When they met a man and woman named Magallanes, who were new to San Antonio, they studied April with curiosity.

"Have you always lived in San Antonio?" Senora Magallanes asked.

"No, ma'am."

"I knew it," Senor Magallanes said. "You lived in Albuquerque before."

"No, Santa Fe," April answered stiffly, the rosy bubble of happiness bursting when she thought of her past.

"But never Albuquerque?" Senor Magallanes persisted. "You look exactly like someone we know."

"Not exactly," Senora Magallanes corrected her husband. She shook long black hair away from her face. "We met her at a party and saw her again at a wedding. We both had the same friends, but you do resemble her. We thought it might be an aunt."

"What's her name?"

"Hattie Castillo," the man answered, and April's heart missed a beat.

"Does she live in Albuquerque?"

"We don't know her that well. Her husband was the friend of a friend of mine," Senor Magallanes said. "We saw you dancing and remarked how much you reminded us of her."

The conversation shifted to talk about the latest shipment of camels the U.S. Army had imported to send to Camp Verde, and Emilio and April took their tamales to a table near a corner where they could sit and eat.

"Do you think that woman, Hattie Castillo, is your mother?"

"Probably."

"If Luke learns that, he'll leave to search for her."

April stared at him. "It is such a chance—and Catalina loves him so. Emilio, I don't want to tell him yet. He should be here with Catalina. If Hattie Castillo is our mother, she must be happy. I don't want to tell him until I have a chance to think it over." Her eyes clouded with concern. "I used to feel Lottie was my mother, and before her Miss Jesse, but Miss Jesse never was as good to me as Lottie. I didn't care to find my real mother, but as we traveled here, Luke told me about Hattie, and now I'd like to find her my-self."

"Then we will do that someday, I promise," Emilio said, squeezing her hand. The touch sent a shiver of excitement through her. "Catalina needs Luke. You need him. I don't want him to take you away from here. We'll tell him, but wait and give it time."

"I hadn't thought of that!"

"Let the past go, April. And don't be afraid about Santa Fe," he said gently. "You weren't one of the women of the house, and Luke will give you all the respectability you'll need."

She smiled at him, her appetite gone. She would rather listen to Emilio, dance with him, just look at him than eat.

"I want you to come see the ranch," he said. I've worked very hard to get the house built."

"I'd like that," she answered, wanting to be close to him as often as possible.

"Good. I've already talked to Luke about it. All of you are coming to visit, Lottie, Luke, Ta-ne-haddle, and you, next weekend, the sixth. Don't you want your tamale?"

"It's delicious, but I'm not very hungry."

"Neither am I," he said quietly, his wide black eyes gazing at her intently. "Let's dance again," he said and stood up to take her hand and lead her back to the dancers.

Music carried in the air to the jail. A figure scaled the wall and dropped down inside, moving swiftly to the barred window and giving a low whistle.

Domingo moved to the window. "Miguel?"

"*Sí.* The town is at the dance. At least the Mexican part of town, but also Marshal Danby."

"We move a week from Sunday night. He is going to the ranch that weekend, and coming back early that Monday. Sunday night while he is gone, I break out. Have the men ready."

"Sí."

"Take care, amigo," he said. There was no answer and in a few minutes a shadow scaled the wall and disappeared on the other side. Domingo knelt down, picking up a knife and took up work again, scraping out the mortar around a stone.

"This time Luke Danby will be very dead," Domingo said to himself.

On Monday morning, Lottie, dressed in her brown cape and bonnet, left the house to walk the few blocks to a freighting store to learn when a wagon train might be leaving headed north toward Santa Fe. As she moved along the street a man called to her. "Lady, can you help?"

He stood beside a wagon, reaching up as if he were holding something. The wagon was on a narrow alley-way between two buildings, blocked at the end by a wall. "Can you help? Please, ma'am."

She walked down the narrow alley "What's wrong?" she asked.

He smiled and two men stepped into the open end of the alley behind her. She hadn't noticed them before and didn't know where they had come from. The man lowered his hands. He held a rope coiled in one hand. "Well, what I need help with . . . is I need a little loving. Like you gave in Santa Fe," he said, leering at her.

Lottie realized she had walked into a trap. She carried a derringer in her purse, and she clutched it more tightly. The two men behind her moved closer.

"I'll scream," she said. "And I live with the marshal. He'll lock you up if you harm me in any way."

"Harm? Why, ma'am, a beautiful little lady like you? We weren't thinking about harm at all. And the marshal—I don't think the marshal or anyone else in town would get worked up over a whore earning a dollar. Now, do you?"

Lottie knew they wouldn't. The general feeling with

lawmen and townsfolk was a prostitute got what she asked for. She tried to open her purse to get the derringer, but they were on her in a flash. Hands caught her from behind, pinning her arms behind her. Another hand clamped over her mouth while the first man picked up her feet. They carried her farther down the alley, where the wagon would hide her from the view of any passersby.

She struggled uselessly, their hands tightening and holding her roughly until they pushed her down on the ground.

26

A RAG WAS STUFFED IN HER MOUTH AND TIED, making her gag. Hands pinned her down, pulling at her clothing. She gazed up angrily at the men leering at her. There were three men in dirty shirts, tobacco staining the lips of one. They yanked her cape open; one ripped her calico bodice, his hands moving over her roughly.

Suddenly he collapsed on top of her, and then the other two were gone. She heard a groan and a thud as she struggled to get out from beneath the inert body. Prepared to run, she rolled to her feet in time to see Ta-ne-haddle thrust a knife into the stomach of one of the men.

Relief surged in her as Ta-ne-haddle cut the bandanna that held the gag tightly in her mouth. "Let's get out of here," he snapped, climbing onto a barrel and reaching down to lift her over the fence. He dropped down beside her and took her arm, leading her across an empty lot.

"You killed them."

"Only one of them. I don't think they can identify me, and I don't imagine they'll ever try. We have to get home without being seen."

She tried to pull her dress together so it wouldn't show her disarray as she let him guide her. Once he pulled her out of sight behind a building while two men walked past. In minutes they were safely back at Luke's, where Ta-ne-haddle took her around to the back through the courtyard. He led her into her bedroom and closed the door.

"Were you hurt?"

"No," she answered, still astounded that he would murder someone to save her. She was unaccustomed to men treating her with respect or concern.

"I don't think the ones who are alive will talk."

"No," she answered, looking at him intently. She wanted to touch him, she realized, amazed at her reaction. It was the first time in years she had wanted to touch a man.

"All right, change your clothes. As far as everyone else is concerned, we've been home the whole time."

"You killed that man for me. Most people don't think women like me have any feelings."

"I know you have feelings," he said gruffly. "No matter what your past, they shouldn't have hurt you and they're scum."

Experiencing a strange mixture of emotions, she studied him. He cared about her more than anyone had except April. She placed her hands on his shoulders. He watched her impassively, his features set and harsh. She wanted to run her hands across his broad shoulders, knowing he was different from the army of nameless men she had known.

"I can't replace the woman you loved, but you're a very special man," she whispered and stood on tiptoe. Ta-ne-haddle held her around the waist, his head bending as he kissed her. His arms went around her tightly while her mouth moved on his.

On Friday, Catalina strode around the room, organizing the furniture, studying her arrangements. Everything was different from before. It was warm in the adobe house in the winter, it would be cool in the summer with its thick walls and wide shuttered windows that could be opened to let breezes blow through the house. Today was a balmy, unusually warm February day, and Catalina's spirits were as cheerful as the sunshine pouring through the windows. She adjusted another painting, but her thoughts weren't on furniture. They were on Luke. Her father's trial started next Wednesday. And when it was done, whatever the outcome, Luke had promised he would turn in his badge.

She thought about their last time together, and she wanted to be married to him, to bear his children. She had hoped she would conceive, but she remembered running her hands over his scars from that old fight he would never discuss. It was best to work out everything before they were bound irrevocably by a child.

Catalina paused, as she hung a picture on nails she had driven into the thick plaster wall. Her thoughts shifted fully to Luke and the scars he wouldn't discuss. He hated Domingo with an intensity that he could scarcely control. She set the picture down on a chair, all thoughts about decorating the house gone.

"Dios!" She narrowed her eyes and stared into space.

"Are you starting to talk to yourself?" Emilio asked from the doorway.

When she turned to stare at him, he frowned. "Catalina? Are you all right?" he asked as he came into the room.

She focused on him. "I was thinking about Luke. I was thinking about all his scars—he never has told me how he got them."

"He told me he got them in a fight a long time ago."

She ran her tongue across her lips, and her gaze drifted beyond him again. "Emilio, have you ever seen him without a shirt?"

"I've seen him without a stitch of clothes. He's scarred from his head to his toes."

"He hates Papa. I know he does. I think it would have been worse between them if it hadn't been for me. And Papa hates Luke. I've seen them look at each other."

"Catalina, half the men in town hate Domingo. And with reason. I'm his son and I hate him," he snapped.

"There used to always be something between us," she continued, still thinking of Luke and barely hearing Emilio, "some barrier that held Luke back. He didn't tell me he loved me or ask me to marry him until the ranch burned and Papa became an outlaw. From that time on, that barrier has been gone."

"You're not making sense, Catalina. So what made you look as if you had encountered a ghost just now?"

"Suppose Papa was the cause of all of Luke's scars?" she asked softly, staring at Emilio.

"Madre de Dios!" Emilio said, his eyes growing round. "If Domingo did that to him—impossible! Why wouldn't he have come back and killed Domingo when he first found him?"

"I don't know. Luke is so collected and cool. You can't tell what's going on in his mind. And he met me before he met Papa. He barely knew me then, but there was something special between us from the first."

"Luke won't tolerate something that's wrong. He would never live and work near Domingo without doing something to get revenge if Domingo hurt him that badly in the past."

"He said he was in a fight. Later he told me his mother was taken in ambush in a wagon train heading west. But I never asked if he was with her. I always thought they were separated, but suppose they were together? Suppose it was our father who almost killed Luke and took his mother?"

"Luke would have killed him within the hour he had found him. Catalina, you have too much imagination. Ask Luke the name of the man who caused his scars. He'll be here tonight for dinner. I think you're wrong."

After he left, she stared at the empty doorway, her thoughts in a turmoil. If it had been Domingo who had taken Luke's mother, Domingo who had scarred Luke for life, it would be unbearable. Ta-ne-haddle knew who had done it, because he had saved Luke. The man who had done it knew. She sat down, feeling weak in the knees. Her father. If he had taken Luke's mother . . . she thought back to the first times together, to Luke's surprise at the discovery that she thought her father was cruel.

Yet Domingo hadn't acted as if he had known Luke, and Domingo was neither controlled or cool. He let his feelings show. But since Domingo had turned outlaw, he had burned with hatred for Luke, yet that could simply be because Luke was the marshal.

She ran her hand across her forehead, and something deep inside her told her that she was right. How could Luke forgive Domingo enough to love and wed his daughter if he had done those things?

She began to work again. Luke was coming along with Ta-ne-haddle, bringing April and Lottie to stay for several days at the ranch. The men would spend the weekend, then Luke had to go back to town, leaving the others for a few days until he could return and escort them back to San Antonio. She liked April and Lottie both. Lottie was the first woman of ill repute Catalina had known, and she was fascinated by her, trying to fathom how Lottie could live in such a manner.

When Luke arrived in mid-afternoon, Catalina ran forward, hugging him as his arms slipped around her waist and held her tightly. Emilio greeted the others and led them inside while Catalina raised her lips for Luke's kiss.

"I want to be alone with you," he said in a husky voice. "It's been years since we were alone."

"Perhaps tonight," she whispered. "This afternoon we can ride and get away for a time."

He nodded his head. "It should be easy. Emilio and April want to be off to themselves. Now Lottie and Ta-ne-haddle seem to seek each other's company."

"Ta-ne-haddle! He's like a man of stone."

"For the first time since I've known him, in all these

years, he seems truly to care about a woman," Luke
said solemnly. "Love comes in strange ways sometimes."

"Indeed it does. What a rascal I thought you were,
watching me at the river that day."

He laughed. "It's a warm day. Let's ride out there
today," he suggested in a mocking tone, appraising
her blue gingham dress and the way it clung to her
seductive curves.

"We would freeze even though it's a nice day today.
It's still February, and the water's cold."

"We don't have to swim, and I'll keep you from
getting cold," he whispered, his eyes holding a promise that made her heart race. She nodded, her black
eyes sparkling with eagerness as she took his hand and
led him inside.

That afternoon beneath a blue sky at the river, she
lay in Luke's arms between blankets in the sunshine.
Satisfied and happy, she stroked him while he held her
close against his bare side. Her black hair spilled over
their shoulders, and the sun warmed her skin. He
rolled away and began to dress.

"As much as I hate to do so, we should go back. I
feel responsible for April."

"You want to protect her from Emilio," she said,
teasing him.

"Emilio is a man now. And if he's half as hot-
blooded as his sister—" Luke ducked when Catalina
threw her shoe at him. "Hey, cut that out. I'm glad
you're hot-blooded!"

"You make me sound improper."

"You're damned improper, thank heavens," he exclaimed happily.

"Luke Danby! I'll teach you to talk about my being
improper. No more kisses for you," she teased, yanking on her gingham dress.

"No more kisses, huh?" he asked, spinning her
around and looking down at her. Their laughter faded
as longing swamped her and she went into his arms to

raise her mouth to meet his. His kisses were hot and sweet, tantalizing, making her moan softly and cling to him.

"We should get back," she whispered finally. "You wanted to see about April."

"That I did," he said reluctantly, touching Catalina's cheek and throat, wanting to hold her forever.

As she traced her finger along a scar on his cheek, her suspicions about them returned, forgotten earlier in the heat of passion. "Luke, what kind of fight were you in?"

"That was a long time ago, Catalina. Let's forget it," he said, pulling on his leather vest.

She caught him with her hands around his waist. "Was it the same time your mother was on the wagon train?"

"Yes, it was," he answered in a level voice.

Her heart thudded, and she knew what the barrier had been between them when they had first met. "It was my father, wasn't it?" she asked, the words difficult to say and pain making a lump in her throat.

"That was a long time ago. If I can forget the man, you can let it go."

"He did this to you," she exclaimed, horrified, certain yet having to hear it from Luke. "You have to tell me."

"Catalina, you're making a request you're going to regret. I don't want to talk about that time in my life. It can only open old wounds. I won't bring it all up again."

"You have to!"

"No, I don't. The past is gone. And my memories go with it. The important thing is now. The love that we have should be protected and nurtured, not strained with past memories." He took her arm and led her to her horse. "Let's get home," he said quietly.

She gazed up at him, torn between conflicting emotions, but one was clear and all-pervading. Her father had deliberately hurt Luke at a young age, probably taking his mother. The stark, painful reality of it finally struck her. There was no way to excuse her father's actions. Her loyalty to Domingo because he was a father disintegrated like a bit of broken china.

"Luke, I'm so sorry!" she cried suddenly, flinging her arms around him tightly. "He tried to destroy you and he took everything you had. I didn't know he'd ever done anything like that. I swear I didn't."

"I believe you, Catalina. I realized that shortly after we met."

"Luke—"

"I remember standing right here and telling you that you needed to be kissed. I think you still need it," he said in a husky voice and leaned down. His mouth came down hard on hers, stopping all conversation. She clung to him as he bent over her, and dimly she wondered how he could love her if Domingo had been so cruel to him, but then questions spun away into oblivion.

When he released her, she felt dazed, desire fanning to life again, but as she looked into his stormy green eyes, she had to have answers to her questions. "Is that how you found April?" she asked, leaning away. "Did he tell you where to find your mother? Is April his child?" she asked in a whisper. "Emilio loves her."

"No. She doesn't know it, but I'm sure a gambler, a man named Coit Ritter, was April's father. She bears a close resemblance to both my mother and Ritter."

"Does he know what happened to Hattie?"

"Domingo? No."

She squeezed Luke again, hating what had been done to him, horrified that it had been Domingo and realizing how little she had known her father. "How could he be capable of such evil?" she whispered, tears stinging her eyes. "I'm his daughter. Luke. Can you love me and not remember and hate?"

"Yes, I can," he said firmly. "You're not him, Catalina. Just because you have his blood doesn't make you bad. For a long time now, I've been able to see the separation.''

She ran her fingers over his scars. "Luke," she whispered, "we don't have to be back quite yet." Her fingers worked his shirt out of his trousers and pushed it over his head quickly. He looked magnificent with his bronze skin and broad shoulders. The scars were barely noticeable any longer, yet now she suffered in the realization of what he must have gone through.

She traced the scars on his chest, her fingers tangling in the mat of dark curls. He drew a sharp breath, making his broad chest expand, and then he turned to shake the blanket out on the ground again, his muscles rippling as he worked.

"I want to kiss you. I'm so sorry for whatever you went through," she whispered, kissing him as they sank onto the blanket. With a groan he crushed her in his arms and kissed her, his long legs twining with hers.

"Don't cry over me, Catalina. I'm fine now and scars don't matter."

"They did matter long ago. It was my own father."

"Don't let him come between us in any way," Luke said gruffly, framing her face with his calloused hands. "Promise me you won't. You'll have to forget as I've had to forget."

With salty tears coursing unheeded down her cheeks, she nodded. She trailed kisses across his shoulder, wishing she could erase each scar with love, astounded Luke would forget the past and want her in spite of Domingo. Her black eyes gazed at him, seeming to draw him closer. He kissed her hard, his tongue meeting hers in a fiery dance of need that shut out their worry and memories.

In moments he had pulled her dress off her shoulders and tugged away a chemise so he could cup her lush breasts in his hands. He bent his head to take her dusky nipple in his mouth, teasing her, relishing her gasps of pleasure, thinking she was the most exciting woman on earth and he adored her.

He pushed her down, standing up to peel away the rest of his clothes. Instantly Catalina came to her feet to help, her slender fingers moving over him. His blood thundered in his veins as her hands and lips trailed over his body.

Finally he bent over her. Their warm, naked bodies pressed close while his swollen shaft throbbed with readiness. Catalina felt she would melt with desire. Wanting him, letting him pull her down on the blanket, her supple body melded with his. He spread her thighs. His heated gaze was as exciting as his kisses.

She trembled with need, loving him beyond belief, reaching up for him as he came down to possess her. His body was strong and powerful, his lovemaking driving her to abandon. Her soft cries came dimly above the roaring of blood in her ears. Finally release came; she heard him say her name and crush her to him. Their hearts pounded together as he stroked her.

Much later she sat up to look down at him, drawing her hands lightly over his chest. "I want to know what happened to you."

"Catalina—"

"I must know. I can't go through life wondering, imagining all sorts of things."

Luke held her and told her quickly, glossing over some bitter moments, and then Catalina was in his arms, kissing him fiercely, as if her lovemaking could heal the bad memories.

When they finally mounted to ride home, Luke wheeled his horse in front of hers and caught her chin in his hand. "I want you all to myself like the past few hours. And I'm going to make you happy, Catalina. There have been too many heartaches." His voice changed, a teasing note coming. "Of course, I may not have the strength to practice law. I'm not sure I have the strength to ride home now."

"You have enough strength," she answered dryly,

her eyes sparkling with amusement. She reached over to stroke his thigh and he drew a deep breath. She laughed. "You have strength!" She galloped ahead and he raced after her, joy filling him, old hurts diminished even more.

They found Ta-ne-haddle roasting beef outdoors over a fire. Lottie was in the kitchen with the cook and tempting aromas filled the air. For dinner, they sat in the grand new dining room at a long mahogany table. Afterward April sang while Emilio played the guitar, and then they all joined in the singing. Luke sang quietly, holding Catalina's slender hand in his, remembering the afternoon and realizing he could forget that terrible time so long ago.

On Sunday afternoon Luke was standing in the parlor with Catalina when a knock came on the door. Luke moved away, letting Catalina push a stray lock of hair back in place fastened high on her head. "Come in," Luke called and lighted a cheroot as Ta-ne-haddle and Lottie opened the door.

"Are we disturbing you?" Ta-ne-haddle asked.

"No. Come in."

"We have something to tell you," Ta-ne-haddle said, and Luke couldn't hold back a smile. He suspected what they would say and it made him happy.

"Go ahead."

"We're getting married."

Catalina shrieked with elation and threw her arms around Lottie, who had stood solemn and quiet, almost defiant. Luke smiled, looking into the single dark eye of his friend as he reached out to shake his hand. "I'm glad. I'm just damned glad," he said with sincerity.

"We want you both with us for the ceremony. And I want April," Lottie said with concern in her voice."

"She'll be happy for you," Luke said. "Go tell her. She'll be happy about it, I'm sure."

As the ring of the dinner bell interrupted them, and they started out of the room, Lottie caught Luke's arm and pulled lightly. "We'll catch up, you two go ahead. I want to tell Luke something." When they were gone, he looked down at Lottie with curiosity.

"I think I owe you an apology for the first days you left with April. I was too quick to judge you, to think you were like the other men I've known."

"Forget it, Lottie. I'm glad you came. You're good for Ta-ne-haddle. He needs a good woman and now he has one."

"I needed him more, Luke, and I can't ever tell you how grateful I am."

"I hope you two settle here where we can see you."

To his surprise, she shook her head. "I don't think he'll settle anytime soon. We've already talked about that. I was raised as an Apache the first years of my life. I don't mind roaming. We can live off the land, and we both have some savings if we ever do want to settle."

"If that time comes, I hope it's close by so we can see you."

She smiled at him. "Not many people would say that to an ex-fallen woman. You're a good man, Marshal Danby," she said, standing on tiptoe to kiss his cheek. "We better join them."

Luke followed her into the dining room, looking at the shining black hair that fell to her waist. He was glad Ta-ne-haddle had finally found a woman he loved; glad his friend wouldn't travel alone from now on, and Luke hoped for the best for both of them. His gaze shifted to meet Catalina's, and he lost awareness of everyone else in the room. Her dark eyes sparkled with happiness and the seductive invitation he glimpsed so often when she looked at him. For a moment tension arced between them and he saw only her., His heart beat faster, and it was an effort to keep from walking straight to her. He hoped they could marry soon. He seemed to want her more each day, and he hungered to make love to her for hours on end without interruption.

* * *

Before dawn Emilio entered the dining room and found Catalina drinking a glass of fresh orange juice. She glanced up. "Luke will be up in a minute. He and Ta-ne-haddle will leave as soon as the sun is up. Emilio, it was our father who caused Luke's scars and took his mother," she said somberly.

"*Dios!* You're sure?"

"I'm sure. You're right about Domingo. He's done so many evil things."

Emilio sat down, staring beyond her, a string of oaths coming from him. "That was years ago. *Dios!* All those years, robbing and . . . heaven knows what else." He snapped his mouth closed and his eyes flashed in anger. "Think what crimes he must have done. How can Luke keep from putting a revolver to Domingo's head and pulling the trigger?"

There was silence as Catalina stared at Emilio, agony plain in her expression. "It's because of you," Emilio said quietly. "He won't kill Domingo because he loves you."

"I can't feel the same toward Domingo."

"He will hang before the month is up."

An hour later she kissed Luke good-bye. With Ta-ne-haddle he rode to San Antonio, leaving April and Lottie behind. Emilio had work on the far southern part of the ranch and in minutes he was gone, leaving the women with the servants. They had planned to dye material for curtains for the kitchen and they worked over a boiling kettle in the yard, stirring the mixture, talking about wedding plans.

A deep-running current of excitement filled Catalina. The day was brighter than any before, the sky clearer, the air fresher. Nothing could mar her day, she thought as she stirred a curtain in the pale blue dye.

All three women laughed and worked, each happy because of love. Lottie was Ta-ne-haddle's woman now and if he loved Dancing Sun more, at least he had found a place in his heart for her as well.

And April's eyes sparkled with love for Emilio. Lottie knew April's first young love had blossomed, and she thought Emilio would be good to her. She approved because he seemed so like April in many ways. She looked at Catalina bending over the tub, and realized she had been wrong about men. They weren't all rogues and scoundrels. Her Jeb had been a good man, but she didn't think she had known any since. Until now. All three of the men, Luke, Ta-ne-haddle, and Emilio, were fine and good and reliable. She bent over to help Catalina wring out a curtain.

Catalina was the first to hear hoofbeats and stopped work to look toward the road. A cloud of dust showed riders approaching in a hurry, and she wondered if it were Luke and Ta-ne-haddle returning or Emilio and some of the men.

"Someone's coming," Lottie said, hanging a curtain over a line. Catalina watched with curiosity, but not alarm. Comanches were the big threat and she could see the broad-brimmed sombreros and serapes of the men, so the riders weren't Indians. In minutes six riders poured through the gates and Catalina's heart lurched.

"It's Papa," she said, going cold as he rode into the yard and fired his pistol, the blast making a horse rear and whinny. The men with him looked like bandits except for two who had worked for him.

"Catalina, we celebrate! I'm a free man! And I see I have a new house now!"

He climbed down off his horse and came toward her in a swaggering walk, his thick black mustache framing his mouth, his gaze raking over Lottie and then April. Catalina saw him stop, his color draining and his eyes narrowing. He swore as he stared at April. He looked as if he were beholding a ghost. Catalina looked at April as well, and then realized he must be thinking of Hattie. And all the damning things about him were proven beyond a doubt.

"You can't stay here," she said grimly, seeing him in a way she had never seen him before.

"Who is she?"

"I'm April Danby," April replied with a lift of her chin. "I'm Luke Danby's half-sister."

"Dios!" He turned up a bottle of tequila and drink deeply, and a cold stab of fear struck Catalina.

"Papa, you can't stay here. Luke and a posse will look here first."

"Look at this house, like a fortress. We can hold off a posse, perhaps kill a few lawmen."

"No," Catalina cried. "I won't allow it."

He struck her, knocking her to the ground. "Allow? I do what I want at my house. Whatever I want!" He waved his hand at his men. "Dismount and make yourselves at home. We celebrate and wait for the marshal, and then when we're ready, we ride for Mexico."

He moved to April and stroked her cheek. She jerked her head away and he laughed. "A Danby. Perhaps I'll take you with me, little one. You are very much like your mother."

The men went into the house, and Catalina started for the barn to get her horse. "April, you and Lottie, get to town quickly."

The click of a hammer on a pistol was clear, and Catalina spun around to see Domingo and two of his men with pistols pointed at the women. "You won't ride to town and warn the marshal. Come inside, Catalina. We'll celebrate. And bring the lovely ladies. We'll amuse ourselves."

Catalina stared at him, wondering if he would shoot and kill her if she tried to run. Suddenly she turned and ran for her life, determined to warn Luke and Emilio.

"Get her!" Domingo ordered one of his men, and Catalina heard the heavy thud of boots as a man ran after her.

She raced through the gate, panting with effort. When he caught up with her, his arm snaked around her waist, yanking her off her feet. She kicked and clawed at his hand while he laughed. "A little wildcat, eh?"

He carried her back to the house and inside, where Domingo sat at the long wooden dining table. Lottie sat on his knee, smiling at him, looking up when Catalina came in. At first Catalina was shocked that Lottie would cater to Domingo without hesitation. Enraged to see Lottie with her arm around Domingo's neck, Catalina changed her mind when April appeared with a tray of food. April looked terrified, and Catalina realized Lottie was trying to protect her. One of the renegades stood with a maid from the kitchen. She was pressed against the wall, he was inches in front of her, talking to her while she gazed up at him fearfully.

"Luke will come and it'll be soon," Catalina said to Domingo, struggling to break free of the man's grasp.

"Let him come. Emilio built well. We can stand off an army here. It'll be another Alamo. Only we won't all perish. Not with so many beautiful senoritas that could be hurt also."

"How can you do this?" Catalina cried, anger and fear for Luke overwhelming her.

"It is very easy, *muchacha*. With great delight I shall kill Marshal Danby. And this time he'll stay very, very dead. Take her away and tie her where she can't get away," he ordered, dismissing them with a wave of his hand as he turned his attention back to Lottie.

The man hauled Catalina down the hall to the corner bedroom, where there was a large four-poster bed. He gripped her wrists with one hand and lashed them together with a leather thong, then tied her to the bedpost. Catalina ceased struggling, knowing it was useless, hoping he wouldn't tie her feet.

"Getting right docile now, aren't you, little filly?

I'd like to tame you. If you weren't his daughter . . .'' he said, running his hand over her breasts. She closed her eyes and endured his touches. "If he gets killed, I'm taking you with me," he said in a hoarse voice. "Maybe he'll let me take you anyway."

He left the room, and she gazed around for anything to use to get free. The leather was tight, cutting into her flesh, and she leaned against the post, feeling sick. Luke, Emilio, April, all were in danger now. She had seen the way her father had looked at April, and she knew he would take her with him when he left. And he would kill Luke. Aware that every passing moment increased the danger, she jerked uselessly at her bonds.

The minutes were long and the voices down the hall grew more boisterous. Catalina feared for the women and for Emilio, who would ride home at sundown to find the house full of bandits. And if her father made one move toward April in front of Emilio, there would be a battle to the death.

Suddenly a shot rang out and there were screams, then a volley of shots. Catalina's head snapped up and she cursed under her breath that she was tied where she couldn't do anything. In moments the door swung open, and April ran inside. She flung the door closed and raced to Catalina to cut her free.

"The marshal and a posse of men are here. The house is surrounded, and they're fighting."

"Emilio?"

"He hasn't come home yet, but he'll hear the gunfire, he'll come now."

As Catalina broke free of her bonds, the door burst open startling them both. Lottie burst into the room. "Let's get out the window. I think we can make it safely to the marshal and his men. Most of the firing is from the other sides of the house, not here yet. Come on!"

"April, go with Lottie, quickly! I'll follow," Catalina urged, pushing April toward the window. "Try to keep Emilio away from the house."

They climbed through the window and ran. Catalina held her breath, watching them until they disappeared between the rails of the fence and into the barn. Running to the bed, she lifted the heavy horsehair mattress and removed a pistol. She loaded it swiftly and then ran down the hall. The shots were louder now, and a maid screamed. She heard a man yell.

The parlor was empty, but through the window she saw Domingo outside. She raced through the dining room, dashing for the open doors when she heard Emilio's voice. "Drop your pistol, Domingo!" he commanded.

Guns blasted as she raced outside. Emilio pitched forward and she screamed, a sharp pain tearing at her heart as she saw her brother fall.

"Emilio!" she cried, raising her pistol and pointing it at her father's heart.

27

"DROP YOUR PISTOL, PAPA!"

He spun around, his back to the wall, his six-shooter aimed at her. "Catalina!"

"You shot Emilio."

"Put down the Colt. You can't shoot your father."

Tears stung her eyes as she pulled back the hammer on the pistol. "I can and I will if you don't drop your pistol."

The silence lengthened. "You can't shoot me," he said, taking a step closer to her. "I'm your father, your own flesh and blood. Put down the pistol, because you can't use it on me."

"She can't, but I can," Luke snapped, dropping to the ground through the open window behind Domingo.

"Danby!" Domingo crouched and fired at the same time Luke fired. Catalina screamed while Domingo slammed back against the wall and fell to the ground.

Horrified, she tossed aside the pistol and ran to kneel beside Emilio. Luke turned him over, and Emilio gazed up at her with a flutter of his eyelashes. "I love April," he whispered. His eyes closed, and she knew he was gone. Her heart felt as if it were breaking in two. She hugged him, bending over him to sob while she felt Luke's arm go around her shoulder.

"Get a blanket to cover Emilio," he said to a maid who appeared at the window. Luke turned Catalina into his arms while she sobbed. Her pain came in waves, deeper and more catastrophic than any she had known before in her life. She clung to Luke and he held her tightly. When she raised her face, she saw his eyes were red with tears.

"The fighting is over," he said gruffly. "Come inside, Catalina."

"You're hurt," she exclaimed, for the first time noticing Luke's bloody shoulder.

"Ta-ne-haddle knows what to do. He can bind it up for me." He turned her to face him. "I'm sorry," he said gently and held her with his good arm to lead her inside.

"I have to tell April," Catalina whispered.

"Where are Lottie and April?" he asked Catalina.

"They ran for the barn. I have to tell them," she repeated as they entered the kitchen.

"Tell us what?" Lottie asked from the doorway.

More than ever before in her life, Catalina hurt, suffering from her loss, suffering over April's loss. She moved across the room to take April's hands in her own. April's blue eyes widened and pain flashed in them.

"Emilio was killed," Catalina said in agony for April.

"No!" April gasped and Catalina hugged her as both of them cried. April was silent in her weeping, her thin shoulders hunched over, shaking with grief.

They stood in the warm sunshine at a small area of the ranch set aside for a graveyard while the last words were said and Emilio was buried. Sunlight glinted on the thin gold necklace around April's slender neck while she stood straight and shed silent tears. In spite of his bandaged wound in his shoulder, Luke kept an arm around Catalina and one around April until they walked back to the ranch house. Catalina stepped away and he pulled April into his arms to hold her while she shook with sobs.

Luke looked over her head at Catalina, who stood with her head bowed, and he knew she was weeping too. He knew their wedding would have to be postponed again until mourning was over. Time would help Catalina's wounds as well as April's, and he would give her all the time she needed, because he knew how deeply she had loved her brother.

That night they returned to Luke's house in town. For weeks both Catalina and April seemed numb, only half alive. Lottie and Ta-ne-haddle said their vows in front of a justice of the peace and were gone for a few days only, returning to stay with Luke again.

February passed into March, and gradually time began to heal some of the wounds. The month of April came, and Luke watched closely to see when Catalina's grief began to diminish. Daily living with her was stretching his nerves thin. He wanted her badly and dreamed about her, finding he couldn't concentrate at work for thinking about her, trying to resist pushing her about marriage. She assumed the duties of managing his household, and he let her, knowing if she was busy, she would mend sooner.

The last week in April, Luke took her by the hand and led her to his room. "This house is like a hotel," he said cheerfully.

"You asked all of us to stay," she reminded him.

"So I did. I want all of you, particularly all of *you*," he said, smiling and pulling her down on his lap, her black muslin skirt spreading over his knees. "I'm happy to have everyone here, except I don't get a minute alone with you."

"Luke, I worry about April."

"Honey, she's young," he said gently. "There'll be someone again someday. She's a child."

"You know she's no child. She wasn't a child when she came."

"All right, she acts older than her years, but she's still young and she'll mend as time goes by. She's going to be a beautiful woman, and some good man will love her just as Emilio did."

Catalina turned to put her head against his chest while he stroked her hair.

"Catalina," he said, his voice a deep rumble, "I told you I would turn in my badge."

She raised her face to look at him and nodded.

"I did today."

"You're no longer marshal?"

"Nope, absolutely unemployed."

"Oh, Luke, how wonderful," she exclaimed, throwing her arms around him.

"I'll start a law practice, but it may be awhile before I have my first client."

"You have all those stacks of gold, so we'll get along. And now the ranch is mine and I can sell it."

"Nope. Keep it, Catalina, Jasper is doing a good job of running it for you."

"Fine. But if we need the money, we sell it."

"Now, that brings up another reason I wanted to see you."

"Hmmm?" she asked, becoming aware of his arms around her and his mouth only inches away. Desire stirred in her, and she trailed her finger along his bristly jaw, down the strong column of his throat to his collar.

"Are you listening to me?"

"Of course," she murmured, kissing his throat.

He groaned and turned, raising her face with his finger beneath her chin so he could kiss her. His mouth came down on hers hungrily and his tongue touched hers like a flame. She gasped and twisted to hug him, an intoxicating longing making her cares vanish.

Luke leaned over her, shifting her so her head was cradled against his shoulder. While he kissed her, his fingers worked at the ribbons and hooks on her bodice until he parted the material and pushed beneath her clothing to fondle her soft breasts.

She moaned, clinging to him, feeling his manhood press against her. "I love you, Luke Danby. I never knew what love was until I met you."

"I didn't either, Catalina," he said solemnly. "I feel empty without you. That's why I brought you in here. I want to know when we can wed. Emilio would want you to go on with life. It's your decision, Catalina."

"A month from today."

"A month from today," he said quietly, wanting the time to be passed right now. More and more hours of the day she filled his thoughts to distraction. His voice held a tender note she never heard when he talked to others. "I almost forgot. I brought you a present."

"Luke!" she exclaimed, leaning back while he dug in a pocket.

Her eyes sparkled with anticipation, and he had to laugh. "Catalina, nothing is ever simple to you, it's a marvel or it's a catastrophe, or it's something that stirs your anger to a blaze."

"Stop teasing. I'm waiting," she said, taking the package eagerly from him. "You need me with your cool, logical mind. You'll have more fun out of life with me around," she teased, winking at him as she yanked away the wrapping and opened a box.

A diamond caught the light and Luke took her hand while she gasped with delight.

"Luke, it's gorgeous!" She gave a little screech of delight and hugged him. He caught her hand and slipped the ring on her finger. "A month sounds like eternity," he said in a husky voice, pushing open her still unfastened bodice and bending his head to kiss the soft rise of her breasts. She wound her fingers in his hair, her heart beating with joy as she closed her eyes in ecstasy. He groaned and pulled her back in his arms to kiss her hard, wanting to take her to bed now.

Finally she pushed away. "You must stop," she said solemnly. "Someone will come looking for us and if we don't stop soon . . ."

Her voice trailed away, but he answered in a raspy voice full of passion. "We won't be able to stop. I want a long honeymoon. Where would you like to go?''

"I can go anywhere?''

"Anywhere your heart desires. All I want is a bed and to be undisturbed by others.''

"I'd like New Orleans. I've always heard about New Orleans.''

"New Orleans it is, but I'll take you anywhere, Catalina. Europe, Mexico—''

"New Orleans will be wonderful," she said, flashing her ring. "Luke, it's beautiful.''

"It's only a token, my fiery Catalina.''

"We'll be good for each other," she said solemnly. "You're calm and logical, but I'll keep you from being too calm, too logical, eh?''

He kissed her and she clung to him joyously until she stopped him again and stood up, fastening her dress. "Look what you've done to me.''

"I want to do a whole lot more," he drawled, facing her. "I want to take off every stitch of clothing, to kiss you all over—''

"Luke!'' she gasped. His deep, honeyed voice was like a caress, her body heated at the thought of what he said.

The dinner bell rang and Catalina started toward the door. "I told you we—''

He caught her wrist and yanked her back into his arms, catching her and crushing her to his chest, kissing her passionately until she clung to him tightly.

Luke had little interest in dinner, because all he could do was watch Catalina and think about their wedding and honeymoon. He wanted her alone in New Orleans for a month, and he saw no reason they couldn't stay away that long. He had a housekeeper for April if Lottie and Ta-ne-haddle left, and he expected them to leave sometime.

A month with Catalina with no interruptions! The thought eradicated the last shred of his appetite for the beans and rice on his plate, and he set down his fork to lean back in his chair and watch her. She talked with animation, waving her hands, her eyes sparkling with happiness.

His gaze shifted to April, who laughed at something Catalina said. April was young and she would recover from her heartbreak over Emilio, but Catalina was right, she wasn't a child. She knew more about people than many women who were years older. Her unorthodox upbringing had made her independent in a way few women were who had men making their decisions for them and protecting them.

April listened quietly as Catalina talked about wedding plans. April still felt numb, happy for the others, wondering if the pain over Emilio would ever lessen. And she gazed at Luke in speculation. Hattie Danby was alive, probably living in the area around Albuquerque, and it was only a matter of time before the Magallanes would encounter Luke and tell him.

If Luke heard about Hattie, he would leave to find their mother. After all this time, he wouldn't give up. April looked at the sparkle in Catalina's eyes and knew Luke shouldn't leave. He should stay right here and start his law practice. It hurt to stay where memories constantly bombarded her, and the joy of Luke and Catalina, Lottie and Ta-ne-haddle was bittersweet. She was happy for all of them, but it made her miss Emilio even more.

She knew what she wanted to do, and knew if she told anyone they would stop her. Lottie and Luke both would object. For that matter, Catalina would object. April smiled, unaware of what the others were laughing about, making her decision. She would go back to New Mexico Territory, and she would try to find Hattie. It had become more important to her: she understood better how devastated Hattie must have felt to lose two of her children. That old hurt could be righted.

April knew she could sing and earn her keep. Her earnings, together with the meager savings Miss Jesse had given her and the gold Luke had said was hers to use as she saw fit, would take care of her. If things got too bad, she could come back to San Antonio, because Luke and Catalina would always give her a home. Her mind ran over what she would do, and after they finished eating she went to her room to pack.

Early the next morning she rode away from the house, heading back north the way Luke had brought her. She glanced back at the looping curve of the San Antonio River and the town bathed in spring sunshine. All she could see was Emilio's dark eyes and hear him say, "You'll always have my love." She squared her shoulders and turned away, her hand straying to her locket while she scanned the horizon. She had learned a lot about traveling across country with Luke and Lottie, but she planned to stop at the first way station and catch the next stage to the Territory, so she had only a short distance to go alone. In spite of all the women she had grown up around, she had always felt alone, except for the brief time with Emilio, and she wondered if she would feel alone the rest of her life.

Luke was the first one downstairs. The maids usually appeared early, but today he was up before their arrival. Roosters crowed, the sound carrying through the open back door. Luke pumped water and began to make coffee. Turning to light the lamps, he noticed a note on the table and picked it up.

> Dear Luke:
> I'm leaving. Don't try to find me and bring me back. You should stay in San Antonio with Catalina, because she needs you. I've heard our mother, Hattie Danby, is living north of here. Emilio had promised to take me, but now I'm going alone. I'm going to find her. I have my savings and I can earn my way by singing, but I won't come back. I'm sorry to miss the wedding.

I love you all very much. I'll come back someday. If I find Hattie, I'll write.''

Yours with love and gratitude,
April Danby

Luke swore and dropped the paper, glancing at the
open doorway and the expanse outside.

"What's wrong?" Ta-ne-haddle said, coming into
the room.

"April's gone. She's gone to find Hattie, because
someone here told her they've seen our mother.''

"Where?"

"Here, read the letter. She doesn't say where, but
she can't have too many hours head start. I'm going
after her.'' He went striding from the room and when
he returned down the long hall he saw that Ta-ne-
haddle and Lottie were both in the parlor, Lottie was
dressed in simple buckskins like a man. Ta-ne-haddle
motioned to him.

"I've talked to Lottie. We'll go after April and see
that she's safe.''

"You can't do that," Luke protested, thinking it was
his responsibility and not theirs.

"Why not?" Ta-ne-haddle asked with a smile.
"We'll move on anyway. I can't settle down in one
place. We've stayed here this long because Lottie felt
April needed us. I like to roam and Lottie has no ob-
jection. We'll go after April, my friend. We're sorry
to miss the wedding, but this is best. You're needed
here.''

"Yes, you are," Catalina said firmly from the doorway. "What's happened?"

"April has run away," Lottie said. "She said she
has gone north to find Hattie. Someone here in San
Antonio told her Hattie is alive and north of here.''

"North of here could be anywhere," Catalina said
with worry, seeing the hard look in Luke's eyes, and
knowing he would like to find Hattie himself.

"We'll go find April and stay with her," Lottie said. "We're ready to leave now."

"Come tell us good-bye," Ta-ne-haddle said, moving to the door. In minutes they rode away, and Catalina pulled on Luke's arm.

"Come inside."

"Dammit, I think I ought to go look for her. She shouldn't be out there alone, and she can't be too far ahead or too hard to find."

"If anyone can find her, Ta-ne-haddle can, and you know it. And she'll be as safe with him as with anyone else."

"She ought to stay here. That's no life for a woman. She's a baby."

"Ta-ne-haddle and Lottie will find her, I'm sure. She can't be far ahead and both of them are good at tracking. They won't abandon her."

"No, they won't. But they won't bring her back here." He moved restlessly toward the window to gaze outside into the gray morning. Catalina stood at his side, knowing he was having stormy thoughts and well aware he wanted to go too.

"Someone here knows Hattie. She's alive, and they told April where she lives. Damn, I wish she had told me."

"Luke, I won't hold you," Catalina said solemnly. "If you want to go . . . you do what you must."

He looked at her just as somberly, then strode out of the room. She closed her eyes in agony, hating to see him go, knowing he would eventually be back, but it could be months from now. She followed him down the hall.

"Luke."

He turned and she entered his bedroom and closed the door. Her heart thudded with pain and longing as she crossed the room to him and wrapped her arms around his neck. "I won't hold you, but you can catch up with them if you leave a few minutes later than you planned," she said in a throaty voice, her pulse pounding as his green eyes darkened. Instantly he dropped the clothes he was holding in his hands and reached out to pull her to him, crushing her in his arms while he kissed her. In moments he scooped her up to carry her to bed.

She kissed him good-bye within the hour, and after crying violently over his going, she squared her shoulders and decided to move back to the ranch until Luke returned.

The days were long, warm weather coming in May; the earth was green and flowers were in bloom. She worked furiously, getting a wedding dress ready for his return and getting other dresses ready for her wedding trip.

One hot afternoon she went to her private place on the river and swam, missing Luke, remembering their moments together. She lay back, floating in the water, feeling it's refreshing coolness and staring at a bright blue sky with rolling white clouds. She missed him unbearably, suddenly restless. With a twist she rolled over and swam to a shallow part to stand up. Her gaze swept the bank, and she gasped in shock.

28

LUKE SAT ON THE BANK, GRINNING AT HER, HIS black hat pushed to the back of his head. He stood up, brushing off his pants as he ambled down to the water's edge.

"Luke Danby! You scared me—" She broke off her words, coming up out of the water in spite of not having a stitch of clothing.

His gaze swept over her as she waded toward him. In long strides he splashed into the water, getting his boots and pants wet as he caught her in his arms and crushed her to him. His hands slid over her warm, wet body.

"Catalina!" he said in a husky voice before he kissed her. His mouth was hard on hers, his tongue probing deeply, making her want to melt against him.

She paused once, to lean back and look at him. "Thank goodness you're back."

Luke couldn't talk. She was beautiful and he wanted her desperately. His body was hot, scalded with the feeling of her soft, bare warmth pressed against him. He swung her up in his arms and waded out to set her on her feet on a blanket spread on the bank.

"I didn't see you or hear you. How long have you been here?"

"Not long," he said hoarsely, unfastening his collar and yanking off his shirt. In minutes he had stripped off his clothing, and Catalina trembled as she gazed at him, relishing the sight of his lean, muscular body, his hard arousal, the burning look of love in his green eyes.

"I decided I belong here, and I left Ta-ne-haddle and Lottie to find April."

Her heart thudded with joy. "I think that was a wise decision, Mr. Lawyer. Your logic always rules."

"Not this time. It was my heart," he said in a raspy voice, pulling her into his arms to kiss her. After a moment he leaned back, cupping her high, full breasts in his hands, his thumbs flicking over the rigid, dusky nipples. "You're beautiful," he whispered, kissing drops of water still sparkling on her shoulders. He pulled her down on the blanket, kissing her slowly, holding her ankle while he trailed kisses on her slender leg and watched her with his thickly lashed green eyes.

"I missed you more than I believed possible," he said. "I want to hear you cry my name in ecstasy. I want to kiss you all over, Catalina, and touch you until you need me as I need you."

She gasped with pleasure, pulling him closer. His head bent over her thighs as he kissed her and she moaned. Stroking his body, her hands sought his manhood and caressed him until he thought he would burst with need. Watching her as he came down to possess her, he thrust into her softness while her hips rose up to meet him eagerly.

She clung to him, knowing he had come back to her and wouldn't leave again. He gasped and cried out her name as she moaned and held him tightly, feeling one with him in body as well as heart.

Rapture came in a burst of release, and she cried his name, her hands pressing his hips against her. In moments his weight was heavy on her.

"How long before we can have a wedding?" he asked hoarsely, raising his head to gaze down into her eyes.

"Give me until next week, and I'll be ready."

"That's eternity," he said gruffly, turning her to face him.

"How long were you sitting here watching me?"

"Not long. If it had been much longer, I would have come in after you. You're too beautiful, Catalina," he said, kissing her throat.

She saw the love and desire in his eyes that darkened with passion, and she stroked him, filled with love for him. "Your shoulder is all healed from Domingo's bullet," she said, touching the white scar from his wound.

"Only another scar now. Thank heavens you don't mind scars."

"Luke, if you knew how badly I want you, you'd know how marvelous your body is to me. I can look at you forever," she whispered.

He smiled tenderly at her. "You're a lusty woman, Catalina."

With a smile she sat up and looked down at him. He rolled on his back with his hands behind his head as his gaze wandered leisurely over her bare breasts and then up to meet her eyes.

"You looked so pleased," she whispered, feeling desire stir again from his appraisal. He was tanned, all hard muscles and broad shoulders, his body virile and healthy, and she couldn't resist running her fingers down his chest. "I'm glad you came home when you did."

"I'm glad too. I shouldn't have gone, but at the time I thought it was the thing to do. Once I got away from you, I knew I'd made a mistake. My place is with you, love. I belong to you absolutely, Catalina," he said soberly. "I want to make you happy every way I can."

"Good, because I love you with all my soul. And it's good we have the wedding soon." She caught her hair up, twisting it into a long, thick strand, looping and pinning it on top of her head while he watched her with an amused, appreciative gaze. "I would have hated to have to carry our child down the aisle on our wedding day."

His eyes widened and he sat up, and her heart thudded with joy and excitement. *"Our child?"*

"Yes. What did you think would happen with all our lovemaking?" she asked with amusement.

"You're carrying our child now?" he asked with such awe, she was astounded. She nodded, and to her amazement his eyes misted slightly.

"Catalina!" he said, pulling her into his arms. "Our baby. I'm so happy, love! Do you feel all right?"

She laughed. "I feel wonderful! I was afraid you might not be so happy," she said, overjoyed by his reaction. "You said once you didn't want to settle and have a family yet."

"That's before I fell in love with a fiery, lusty wench. Ah, love, how wonderful. I hope it's a little girl with black eyes and black hair." Suddenly he frowned. "Should you be swimming?"

She laughed. "Of course, I can swim. I've already talked to Dr. Ellison. He was about ready to go after you with a shotgun for leaving me."

"He should have. Did you know when I left?"

"Luke, this happened when you left. Remember that day. Even if I had known, I wouldn't have stopped you. You must do what you must do, and I won't hold you."

"Do you know what I would have felt like if I had come home months later or after the birth? Catalina . . . what a time to learn to hold your silence. Were you angry?" he asked after a moment.

"Never," she answered with a smile, wrapping her arms around his neck. "Never, never angry, Luke. I am so filled with love for you, it will take years to show you."

"Then we should have a happy home, Catalina, because I'll do my damnedest to make you happy. I promise. I'll make up for the bad moments, and you'll forget them. Things will be so good."

He began to slip her chemise on, and she laughed

and stopped him. "Since when did you want to *dress* me?"

"I don't want to hurt you or the baby."

She laughed. "You won't hurt us." She trailed her fingers on his jaw and leaned forward to kiss him. He pulled her into his arms, pausing a moment to gaze down at her. "I'm going to love you until you faint from my kisses."

"I hope so. Luke, I hope we're never separated again."

"I'll try, Catalina," he promised, "to stay at your side. I'll always try."

"But you can't promise," she said quietly as he gazed beyond her for a moment and a distant look came into his eyes. "You're worrying if Texas secedes from the Union."

"Our country's future may be caught in a rising storm, but our future isn't," he said gruffly. "I don't want to ever leave you again." He pulled her into his arms to kiss her passionately, and Catalina joyously wound her arms around his neck.

About the Author

Sara Orwig is a native Oklahoman who has had many novels published in more than a dozen languages. She is married to the man she met at Oklahoma State University and is the mother of three children. Except for a few unforgettable years as an English teacher, she has been writing full-time. An avid reader, Sara Orwig loves history, acrylic painting, swimming, and traveling with her husband.